I0601560

Dangerous Thoughts

Archeons, book 1

by James L. Steele

Dangerous Thoughts (Archeons, book 1)
Copyright © 2018 by James L. Steele

Cover art by **ThemeFinland**, themefinland.deviantart.com

Editing by **Renee Carter Hall**, www.reneecarterhall.com

Published by KTM Publishing

Print edition set in Fanwood, Exo, and Playfair Display, all royalty-free typefaces

Print edition ISBN: 978-1-7322824-0-7

Movar

A bubble in spacetime expanded from a single point at eye level. It grew wider and wider until it seemed to rest on the circle of stones off the pathway. The bubble wavered and puckered as it held open against the pressure of the surrounding spacetime trying to collapse it.

The opening caught the attention of several inhabitants of this world, and they approached it. On the other side they saw a planet none of them recognized immediately, of fiery volcanoes and two daytime stars in the sky, one red, the other white. Standing on this alien world were the two sentient beings who had opened this hole. The natives of this world instantly recognized them as Deka and Kylac, two Archeons from the planet Rel.

Several of the people of Movar ran the other way, toward another bubble of similar size hovering less than a claw's reach above the ground. They ran through it one by one and vanished, though outside observers could see an image of them running into the background projected around the surface.

At the first spacetime hole, the crowd had become larger. Two different species of mammal stood side by side, waiting. Half the people stood on four legs and had fur ranging in color from bright green to bright brown. The light from their planet's star made them all glow faintly from the tips of their tails to the crowns of their ears. Their eyes were large, and they had long, tapered snouts that ended with an appendage that resembled a third eye. Even in broad daylight the furred creatures gave off light of their own.

Among them stood furless creatures. Twice as tall as the furred ones, they walked on two legs, but were still hunched over and could function on all fours if necessary. The daylight had the opposite effect on them. The light the furred creatures gave off seemed to fall into their furless bodies, as if they glowed negatively. They were not invisible, but they seemed faded and barely noticeable at a glance.

The Relians visible through the wavering sphere approached it. They grew larger, filled up the opening until finally they emerged from its surface. The first to step through was a theropod covered in blue scales so dark they were nearly black. A red stripe ran up the top of his snout and down his back to the tip of his tail. Immediately after his tail exited the portal, a bipedal canine with digitigrade legs and a slightly hunched posture followed. His belly was white, his forearms were black, and the tip of his tail was white as well. The rest of his body was covered in red fur. They stood side by side and observed the people as the unstable sphere closed behind them.

The furred creatures barked and whined at the newcomers. The furless ones, who stood in shadow even as the daytime star baked this planet in bright light, hissed and clicked at the two. They walked up to the raptor and the fox, touched their scales and fur. The people of Movar only stood as high as the theropod's knees.

Deka and Kylac remained still and received the greeting. They had just come from a world inhabited by people who spoke only one language, and now they had to adjust to two.

They had only been here once, many solar years ago, and under much better circumstances. Quickly they ad-

justed to a new world with new customs and new languages. Words began to emerge from the hisses and whines.

"The portals went out!"

"What happened?!"

"Ricio told us she can't make a way offworld
anymore!"

"She was unconscious for days!"

"We could not reach anyone!"

Deka and Kylac had been among many species who
had evolved in herds, and they never tired of their way of
welcoming newcomers among them.

The crowd became larger. Movars both furred and furless poured out of the portal on the other side. Word had
spread quickly of their arrival, and people from all over the
planet came to greet them. Deka and Kylac knew they did
not make this much of a fuss over every visitor, but the disaster had touched them as well, and they wanted to know
what was happening.

Deka looked around. They had landed on a branch of
a stone path designated for unannounced visitors. The
branch connected with a larger path that reached for a hundred paces in both directions. Other paths split from this
walkway and ended at circles of stone, dozens of them as
far as he could see in both directions. Each would normally
have held a portal to another world, or to another place on
this world. Now he only saw six portals open, and they wavered and rippled, struggling to hold their spherical shape.
Movars rushed out of these portals and joined the group
around Deka and Kylac. Everyone wanted to touch them,
talk to them, hear from them.

The two visitors took in dozens of voices at once, following every word. It was easy to sort them out.

"Yes, it's all true," Deka said, doing his best to speak
the language of the furless species. "Our planet was destroyed."

More questions hit them. More concerned paws and hands touched them.

"That's why we're here," continued Kylac. He spoke the language of the furred creatures, as his mouth and throat were better suited for it.

Soon the path was full of people. Deka and Kylac smelled the concern in the air, and they drew comfort from this. They had scent in common with the mammals of Movar, though these creatures relied more on the eyes than the nose. Finally, every inhabitant of the Movar culture surrounded Deka and Kylac, more than a thousand glowing quadrupeds and non-glowing bipeds.

The herd began moving, and the two strangers among them were carried away in it. Everyone gave the few portals on the stone path a wide berth, roughly following the path. The path ended in a grassy field, and the herd was leading the Relians into it.

The meeting place was not called anything in the Movar language. It was so central to their lives they didn't even have a word for it. Offworlders named it that, and Deka and Kylac stood there now.

Up to their shins in grass, the herd ebbing and flowing around them, they tried to tell their story. Kylac, the red-furred canine, began talking to one of the furred creatures, only for her to wander off and another to take her place. The female that wandered off told the tiny piece of Kylac's story to the others, and it flowed through the herd.

Kylac then told another fragment of his story to the closest male until he wandered off, repeating what Kylac said to others, and they to others, and so on.

Deka, the blue-scaled theropod, also told fragments of the story to individuals who spread those fragments to others. It was not jarring or difficult, merely how the Movars socialized. Everyone had a fragment of the whole, and eventually the herd had taken in the fragments, put them together, and come up with the entire story.

They grieved for the loss of more than twenty thousand people, along with countless animals and plants. The collective grief of an entire culture filled the field. Cries and hisses went up. Kylac and Deka felt nothing. They had witnessed the grief of the last four planets, but none of it reached them. They could not feel anything, not when there was so much to do, so many unanswered questions.

As the planet's rotation took the daytime star to the far side of the world, the glow of the furred creatures became more intense. So did the void the furless ones left in the light. Gradually, everyone went to sleep, leaving Deka and Kylac standing awake in the middle of the field.

They had been exhausted, but a trip to this planet was refreshing. There was something special about being among a people so united in mind and purpose. They sat in the grass and watched.

The land was in total darkness now, but the glow of the furred members of the Movar race created a second star on the ground. The light did not reach the furless members of the herd, who appeared as holes in the light.

The Movars were a sight-based culture. The furred quadrupeds had pigments in their fur that absorbed the ultraviolet light from the planet's star and used it to glow as a means of attracting a mate. The bipedal, furless ones had once hunted them, having evolved to take advantage of this glow, but the furred Movars had excellent eyesight and could spot predators easily, so the furless ones had developed a special pigment in their skin that had the effect of absorbing light. In response, the furred ones developed large eyes to take in an enormous amount of light to better see their predators. Eventually, the predator's anti-pigment became so refined it actually did cancel out light.

As on so many planets, predator and prey remained locked in this conflict for thousands of years. It pushed their minds higher and higher until both species achieved sentience. When they realized they were both intelligent, they merged into a single herd, and the predators found other things to eat. They still retained their strong herd mentality and could not stand to be separated from the group for too long. Few left the planet for more than a day or two unless they brought a dozen others with them.

Something was moving on the far side of the field, at the hub. Deka and Kylac rose to their feet, and carefully moved through the herd of sleeping individuals to meet the glowing quadruped standing on the path. They scented the furless ones out so they would not step on anyone. Deka was especially careful of this, for the claws on his inner toes would slice open flesh without even trying. Kylac had blunt claws for gripping the ground while running, so he wasn't as concerned.

It took them many breaths to cross the field. When they arrived, they cast dim shadows in the green and yellow glow of their fellow Archeon, Ricio. The furred Movar only stood as high as their knees, since she walked on all fours.

"Welcome back to Movar," she said in the Relian language.

"Thank you," Deka said, also in Rel.

"What happened?"

"We'll tell you shortly, but please, from your point of view, tell us what happened here."

She turned and began walking along the path. Deka and Kylac walked at her side, matching her pace.

"I was talking to someone about... I don't remember what. Then I felt incredible pain in my mind. The next thing I remember was waking up in the grass. Everyone told me I had been unconscious for five days. The portals were gone. This was a surprise to me. I wasn't merely asleep. I lost every portal I maintained. Immediately I began reconnecting the different parts of Movar, but it has been difficult."

She looked at one of the portals as they walked by. It flickered and wavered, showing a distorted, unstable view of a region of Movar on the daytime side. She stopped in front of it.

"I... I can't seem to open ways as I once did. It was several days before I could open a new portal at all. I still can't open ways to other worlds. I've been elsewhere on Movar, trying to reopen ways to each region. I returned as soon as I heard you were here."

She turned around and sat facing the raptor and the fox.

"What happened?"

Deka rubbed his hand-claws together. "In sequence or out of sequence?"

Ricio huffed. "I appreciate the attempt, but I'm not in a laughing mood."

Kylac sat down. The reptile sat as well, and Ricio lay on her stomach. While Kylac spoke, Deka looked around the path. The stone circles were so empty without portals resting on them. This entire path once contained hundreds of ways leading to as many worlds. Other planets just a step away. Walk through any of these spheres and instantly one would be a million light years away, talking with a civilization older than one's own planet, and anyone could come and go as they pleased.

Only five portals were open now, all leading to different parts of Movar, all unstable, similar to the portals he and Kylac had opened since the disaster. Like Ricio, neither had been able to concentrate as well as they had before. Whatever happened had hurt them in ways they did not even know they could be hurt.

Deka envied Ricio right now. He missed having a few dozen portals to maintain. He missed musing on them day and night, feeling the connections between different points in the universe and holding them open. Now... His and Kylac's life had been nothing but panic. He doubted either could maintain a portal for more than a few breaths, let alone years. Ricio could at least maintain ways between different parts of the planet now. Not perfect, but lasting.

Normally the spheres were so solid and stable they didn't seem like ways at all, but glass spheres. He hadn't been able to open a stable portal since the disaster, and he missed being able to.

Since their planet was destroyed, he seemed to have lost a good chunk of his ability to concentrate. There had been a time when he and Kylac made perfect spheres and kept them perfect for years at a time, as all seasoned Archeons could.

The story was over. Kylac had told it in sequence.

"I can't imagine..." Ricio said. "The entire planet?"

"It broke apart in front of us," Kylac answered. "We escaped, and then the portals collapsed."

"I kept thirty-one open," said Deka. "Kylac had another thirty-one. Forty linked different parts of our world together. The other twenty-two led offworld. They ended within breaths of each other."

"Left both of us paralyzed for days," Kylac continued. "Everything stopped. Ended. Terminated. There was nothing for us to think about. We happened to end up on the Ya'mah homeworld."

"At least you were cared for," Ricio said.

Deka looked down at the ground. "We scared them. We just fell in, and our way closed behind us. The portals their Archeon held open closed, too, and he fell into the same coma."

"They kept our bodies alive while our minds recovered from the shock," Kylac continued. "Nobody else had come through with us. When we found out how long it had been, we decided to go to Reebe and look for survivors, but nobody made it through that portal before it collapsed. We've been traveling to other worlds, hoping to find someone who survived."

"What of Rive and Friend?" Ricio said.

"We don't know what happened to them," said Deka. "They might be dead. I don't know where Sonjaa and Rupi were, or the hatchlings."

They sat in silence for a while. Ricio lowered her head and rested it between her paws. Deka and Kylac remained silent. Her scent told them she was just beginning to feel the weight of what had happened. She whined, stood up, and walked between the raptor and the fox, comforting them the only way her kind knew how. She tried to huddle with them, but without a herd it was difficult to do so. Deka and Kylac leaned in closer so they could to make their own little herd.

She needed to grieve. Her grief did not reach them. The two Relians felt nothing but raw determination to find survivors and figure out what happened.

"I'm sorry to say," Ricio began, "somebody did come here."

Kylac's ears bloomed. "They did?! Where are they?"

"I think you should see for yourself."

She backed away from them, turned, and trotted up the path. Deka and Kylac ran after her. In a hundred strides, Ricio veered and ran headlong into a portal that just barely held its spherical shape. Deka turned, ducked his head, kept his tail straight behind him, and ran through it as well. Kylac straightened his tail, folded his ears against his head, and followed his raptor. He emerged on a rocky ledge standing next to Deka and Ricio. It was still daylight here, but the star was about to set. Kylac recognized this part of Movar.

Both species had a tradition about death. When a Movar grew old, he left the herd, traveled to the cliffs, and lived there until his body gave out. They had once believed the edges of cliffs were actually the beginning of bridges to the next life, so they made sure to meet their end on a high cliff.

The discovery of portal physics should have made the tradition of traveling thousands of paces to the nearest cliff obsolete, but it only made them more determined than ever to make the journey themselves, without shortcuts. Only in dire emergencies did they use portals to take someone to a cliff upon death.

Kylac, Deka, and Ricio stood facing a line of Relian bodies, some reptile, others canine. Swaths of scales and fur were missing. Huge streaks of flesh and bone gone, exposing organs underneath. Enormous holes had been torn through the bodies. Legs missing. Arms half severed. Faces gouged to the bone. Sometimes part of the bone itself was missing, as if it had melted away, leaving the remainder of the skull smooth and polished.

There were about twenty of them, lain out as neatly as possible, faces turned to the edge of the cliff. Deka and Kylac carefully approached. The scents from the bodies had long decayed, and there was no way to know if any of these people was somebody they knew. Deka grumbled a little; Sonjaa could be among them, and he would never know it.

One of the canine bodies had been sheared in half lengthwise. Deka and Kylac stood over him. Ricio approached a moment later, keeping her head and voice low, as if afraid to wake them.

"I didn't see it myself. The herd told me they poured through the portal just as you see them. I had maintained the way between Rel and Movar, and it collapsed while this one was passing through. These people were still alive. I was unconscious, and nobody had any idea what happened or what they should do, so they carried them here. It was the first way I opened. I'm so sorry."

Kylac dropped to all fours and scented the body, hard, trying to figure out who he was—trying to get something from him—anything! All he could smell was decay. He sniffed harder. He inhaled dirt, snorted it out, and walked on all fours down the line, scenting everyone.

Deka did the same, bent from the waist, trotting up and down the line, trying to identify someone. He smelled nothing but death. No burning, no scent of injury. Flesh and bone were just missing randomly, as if gravity itself had reached into their bodies and taken whatever it wanted.

They walked up and down the line like this several times. They met at the body in the middle, a reptile of the Relian race. One leg was gone, and so was a good swath of the torso. No scent anymore. No way to know who this was, or if this had been male or female.

Deka opened his mouth and screamed. Kylac howled with him. Five planets since the destruction of their world, and these were the first Relians they had found.

Ricio slowly padded up to them. She nudged them together, and they formed a small herd as they grieved. They fell asleep as the star set on this side of the planet.

Deka woke up in the middle of the night. It was cold up here without the star to warm his scales, so he reached out and pulled his fox closer. It woke up the fox, and he tapped noses with his raptor. They met each other's eyes. They had been together long enough to know they were thinking the same thing.

They had only been to five planets. They could not be the last of Rel, and they refused to accept the possibility. They would rest with a herd for a bit, and then they would make a way to a new world. Deka began the calculations.

Ixcy

Deka knelt on the edge of the stone circle. It had been the circle once occupied by the sphere that joined the planets Rel and Movar. He had been pondering the calculations in his mind for four of this planet's days, and he was almost ready to open the way.

He had not been idle this whole time though. He and Kylac socialized with the Movars. Deka helped tend the crops while Kylac helped the herbivores hunt prey.

The furless, predator Movars tended the plants while the furred herbivores hunted. It was a beautiful agreement they had made centuries ago, when they first discovered their glowing prey was intelligent. Both species had demonstrated their commitment to learning about one another by feeding each other. They had become two species, one culture.

The farming and hunting consumed their entire lives at first, but the more they learned about one another, the broader their minds became. They discovered portal physics, and ever since then the portals irrigated the crops and provided shortcuts to the migrating animals the furless ones ate. They had freed the people of Movar to live as they chose. Deka never tired of thinking about it. It was a story repeated on so many different worlds across the contacted universe.

Finding the bodies of twenty-six Relians had been the best thing to happen to them so far. Smelling the victims of the disaster made it real, and facing the reality had allowed the emotion to come out at last.

Kylac had even tried looking for a Movar to have sex with, but since his fur didn't glow, none of the furred creatures on this world were interested in him. He tried enticing the furless ones. Kylac had never been with a creature that absorbed light, and it sounded like a great thrill. They, however, regarded him as rather ugly because he reflected too much light. This frustrated the fox but was a relief for Deka because it had been the first time since the disaster that Kylac showed desire. Deka had been worried about him, as a Relian of the canine species could revert to their old ways in just a couple days if deprived of sex. It had been about thirty days since the disaster, and Kylac hadn't thought about it once until now, so Deka breathed easier watching him try to entice people again.

The fox endured four more days without it. On any other planet, Kylac would have found a partner in just a few breaths. Most everyone in the contacted universe knew about the canine species of Rel, and most took full advantage of them, but not the people of Movar.

The whole time, Deka had been meditating on where they were in the universe, and where he wanted to go from this point. He pondered where the motions of the galaxy would take each planet, where in the orbit each planet would be right now, the rotational speed of each world, and where he would have to aim if he wanted to set them down on the ground. Each planet had a designated area for Archeons to arrive unannounced, and aiming for any specific place took years of practice.

Deka was a good Archeon, and he was determined to make a sphere again. He and Kylac felt so much better after grieving, so he was sure he could do it again.

Kylac stood behind his raptor and watched. Many Movars were watching as well, including Ricio. An Archeon opening a new way was something many would not see in their lifetime, so they were eager to witness this.

Deka came closer and closer. The math flowed like liquid through his mind. He wasn't aware of the numbers calculating orbits, rotations, velocities, spacetime density, gravity distortion, and the numerous other variables. Rather he was aware of the feeling the equations and numbers and changing variables gave him.

Finally, he arrived. His mind had calculated where the next world was. Every equation returned a variable, which fed into the previous equation, which fed into another, forming a cascade of interlocking formulas in his mind. The equations themselves formed a bridge between Movar and another planet several thousand light years away. They opened a hole in spacetime. It wavered, expanded, filled out, and stretched until it became a wobbling sphere large enough to walk through. The Movars who had never seen a new portal open stood in awe.

Deka tried to make it completely spherical and smooth, but it wouldn't lock in place. Something was missing. Some part of the equations he couldn't seem to find. It aggravated him.

On the other side of the portal, feathered people landed in front of the new way and gazed into it.

Deka rose to his feet. Kylac stood at his side, rubbed his raptor's neck with a padded palm and fingers.

"It doesn't have to be perfect."

Deka stabbed the ground with a killing claw and walked into the wavering sphere, Kylac at his tail. As soon as they were through, Deka released the equations. Variables stopped changing at predictable rates, equations disconnected, and the bridge fell away. A feeling of where the planet would have moved since he broke the connection lingered, and it would remain for a few moments before he forgot entirely, then he would have to recalculate everything from the beginning if he wanted to return.

They were now on the planet Ixcy.

Archeons often took great comfort knowing where certain planets were at all times. It made them feel as if they carried an entire culture with them. Deka himself had maintained the portal to this world from Rel, and losing his connection to Ixcy had kept his heart pounding at night even more than seeing his own planet destroyed.

He and Kylac were standing on a wooden surface overlooking a vast ocean, surrounded by massive treetops. The platform was just a few paces above the water, and much like the stone path on Movar, it reached far into the horizon. Concentric growth rings lined the ground, each about a quarter pace apart, polished smooth by generations of people walking here. Certain sections were notably less smooth than the rest of the surface. These spaces had once contained offworld spheres.

This tree stump island had been the site of their civilization's hub, large enough to keep portals to hundreds of planets and still allow visitors room to socialize with the locals. Dozens of other portals would have led to trees around the whole ocean.

Canals had been cut into this dead husk of a tree, creating cracks in the surface and tunnels below where underwater spheres would have been, some linking to oceans on other planets, others leading to numerous parts of the ocean on this world.

Not a single portal was in sight.

Birdlike creatures filled the sky, backlit by a tiny, green-hot star. They leaped from the trees, soared down, and landed on the tree stump, surrounding the Relians. They had bright plumage ranging in the blues and yellows and whites and greens. Especially green. Green on this planet was so vibrant it was painful to look at directly.

These birds stood upright about as tall as the theropod and the canine, wings unfolded and waving around, forming broad gestures accentuating their chirps and warbles. The raptor and the fox took a few moments to shed the Movar languages and recall this one. Deka had the easiest time speaking it, as his vocal chords were better suited to imitating their high-pitched chirps. Gradually the words became clear.

"The portals disappeared!"

"Is everyone all right?!"

"What happened? Where is everyone?"

To Deka's surprise, Kylac spoke first. "Rel has been destroyed. We're looking for survivors. Did anyone from Rel come here?"

The birds continued to chirp and squawk and gesticulate. It was difficult to get a word in with these people. Kylac explained what they knew, which was very little. As the fox did, Deka turned around and peered over the edge of the platform. Just under the surface of the ocean, another group had gathered: the aquatic species of the Ixcian culture.

In moments it swelled from a few dozen fish to a few hundred. They swam up from the bottom of the ocean and from within the tunnels under his feet. The water on this world was so clean one could see to the floor no matter how deep it was. They were probably asking the same questions as their avian companions, but it was impossible to hear above the surface.

Kylac finished telling them what happened, and the crowd erupted with the sound of an entire civilization in collective grief for the loss of a planet. Under the surface came a low-pitched vibration that made Deka and Kylac swoon. Some of the birds still in the surrounding trees had been listening to Kylac, retelling his story to the people below the surface. The fish grieved as well, and it was so loud it crossed the water and into the air.

Hundreds of birds on the stump screaming in grief. Hundreds of fish in the ocean expressing the same emotion in their own way. Gradually the time to grieve ended, and one of the birds approached them.

"Come with us."

Two avians spread their wings and took flight. They lowered on top of Deka and Kylac, spread their talons, and picked them up by the shoulders. Now the Relians knew something bad had happened, as the avians never carried anybody anywhere. There had not been a need before; their Archeon maintained portals to every tree on this world.

"It's Chreeb," said one of the birds as they carried the two Relians over the former hub and toward a tree that towered hundreds of paces in the air.

"What happened to him?" Deka shouted.

"Nobody knows. We were hoping you could help."

The birds surged upward and dropped them on a thick branch. Deka and Kylac ran across it and through an opening carved into the trunk. It was dark inside, but Relians of both species could see in the dark, so their eyes adjusted.

The walkway spiraled downward around the trunk, forming an internal ramp carved out of the tree itself. The interior was wide enough to pace fifty times before turning. Several avians were in here, gnawing and pecking at the wood with their beaks. The birds had to keep these spaces carved or the tree would grow back inward.

The walkway ended in water. Beneath the surface, the fish species of the Ixcian culture had gnawed out an opening of their own. Various fish were chewing the parts of the tree under the surface right now. Maintaining these trees was central to their culture, as they were the only places the two species could communicate.

The Relians approached the water line and halted. Just below them was the lowest section of the ramp, where it flattened and formed a level ring. The water was just high enough to cover the fish, but low enough for someone of Deka and Kylac's stature to stand on a flat surface and interact with the fish and still be able to breathe.

Chreeb lay still on this ring.

Deka and Kylac knew what was about to happen, and they spread their arms and legs.

The birds were obsessed with keeping the water clean. Ever since they became aware their prey had feelings and could think, they had built their culture around never harming them again. They preened themselves extensively, removing all loose feathers, sap, leaves, insects, and other impurities before entering shared waterspace.

Having no beaks, Deka and Kylac could not preen themselves. Since he lacked fur, Deka was exempt from the requirement, but he went through it anyway for their sake. Kylac, however...

Two avians landed on Kylac, flattening the fox on his back as beaks rapidly pulled on clumps of fur all over his body. Five more flew from above and landed on Kylac, and from ear to paw, sheath to snout, they preened him of everything in his fur that might pollute the water. His tail waved wildly in laughter as more and more birds descended on him, flipped him over, and preened his backside.

Deka had but one avian mouthing him with her beak, and she was very gentle about it, as his scales were already clean. Knowing he would be coming here, he had taken the time to bathe on Movar. He also knew Kylac, on the other hand, had not bathed on purpose.

Moments later, the avians flew off Kylac and perched on the spiral ramp above with the other hundred avians waiting eagerly all around the tree. The fox stood, straightened his fur, smoothed his tail with his hands while flicking his ears. He joined Deka at his side, and they stepped into the water together. The intense starlight kept the surface of the sea water warm, so it was pleasant in here. The ramp leveled out, and now they walked on the lower ring in water only up to their hips.

"It is relief to see you again, Deka and Kylac."

The voice came from the tree trunk, an amplified subsonic voice of one of the fish floating between the surface and the platform on which Deka and Kylac stood.

"I am glad to be back," Deka said. He spoke the language of the avians. It did not echo; the tree trunk captured the sound and carried it down through the water.

Unlike so many species in the contacted universe, both sentient races on Ixcy did not take communication for granted. The trees were carefully carved and trimmed, and the water was kept pure. Any change would mean losing their only link to one another, and losing touch with the only other sentient species on the entire planet was too great to risk.

"What happened to Chreeb?" Kylac said.

There were many fish under the surface. It was impossible to tell who was speaking, as the fish did not speak with their mouths.

"Your story fills in some of the gaps in our knowledge," replied the tree trunk. "Now we know what caused it, but not why."

The tree magnified the voice of the fish so much that it transmitted emotion itself. Deka never tired of it.

The Relians waded through the water and stood at Chreeb's side. He wasn't dead; his gills were moving in and out, but slowly.

Kylac rested a hand on the fish. His scales were cool to the touch. Deka also rested his hand on him, careful to keep his claws up so he wouldn't accidentally puncture the skin.

"He still hasn't woken up from the shock," Kylac said.

Deka closed his eyes and cooed quietly.

"We're the first to visit?" Kylac asked. "Nobody else has come?"

"No," replied the voice from the trunk. "You are the first. Has everyone met the same fate?"

Deka felt the fish's smooth scales. "Yes. This is the sixth world we've been to. Everyone felt the shock when Rel's portals collapsed. We were out for days. Every other Archeon was out just as long. Some are awake but still can't think."

"Then he shall wake soon?" asked the voice from the tree.

"Should..." Deka said. "He might just need more time."

"Different species will handle it differently," Kylac said, looking up at Deka. "Chreeb isn't like the other Archeons. We should bring a Selt."

"Why?" Deka answered. "What can they do? The brain must heal itself. Even they can't force that."

Kylac remained silent for a moment. He was sure Deka understood. They rarely had to explain things to one another.

"This isn't just coma from an injury," Deka continued. "This is coma from the shock of multiple portals closing against his will. Think about how it felt when you were under. The bridge tore away, but your mind was still working the calculations. Variables still moving in their predictable cycles, and yet nothing was happening. What does the mind of an Archeon do? Keep trying to reach the destination. His mind is trapped in an equation that has no solution now, but it did have a solution before. There is no medicine for that."

The lack of echo in here felt astounding. Words did not merely hang in the air. They reached their destination and did their work. The silence that followed the raptor's words held weight.

"Can you do anything?" said one of the birds above.

Deka turned his muzzle upwards. He heard exactly who had spoken, but he addressed everyone.

"Chreeb wanted to do everything himself. Whenever there was a portal to another world, he wanted to make it. The more ways he held open, the happier he was. He held onto the equations of Rel's portals harder than most. It will probably take him more time to wake up."

"Deka..." Kylac said. "Ixcian anatomy."

Deka turned and glared at Kylac. The fox was sure Deka knew but didn't want to face the possibility.

Kylac addressed the people in the tree. "The fish have two brains. Involuntary functions in one, the conscious mind in the other. Each part is unable to affect the other. The shock could have damaged his conscious mind but left basic body functions unaffected. Given how many equations he held onto, and how hard he held onto them, the disaster may have killed him."

Deka closed his eyes and snarled inwardly, hands still folded, killing claws down. "He is alive! He'll wake up eventually! He just needs more time than we did!"

"I know you don't want to consider it, Deka, but it is possible. The Selts can feel brain activity. We can't. If they determine he's still alive, then we know we only have to wait."

"I don't need a Selt to tell me if someone is alive or dead! Let me stay with him for a while. Maybe he'll respond to my voice."

"What if he doesn't wake up? We should be ready for that."

Deka huffed and panted a few times, eyes still clenched tight. Gradually, his hands unfolded. "I know you're right. Begin the calculations."

"I already did. I should be ready in a day or two."

Those words filled the tree with hope. Kylac turned and stepped out of the water. He said goodbye to the fish, and ascended the spiral ramp. The birds took flight, swirling up and out the top entrance. They had preened themselves so well not a single feather fell from their bodies.

Kylac reached the top some time later. He stepped out into the green starlight and looked out. Bushy treetops as far as the eye could see. Beneath those, an endless ocean without a fragment of dry land on the entire planet.

Something orange slammed into Kylac and knocked him down, pinning him to the branch. Something white and pink also landed on him. Two avians were on top of him. Kylac's nose confirmed both were female. One of them sat on his sheath, coaxing him out. Kylac liked the feathered Ixcians. They had no rules except to keep it out of the water. It felt good to satisfy himself at last. It had been too long.

2

Chreeb wasn't his real name, but it was his name in the avian language. Deka had long wished he could pronounce his name. It was one thing to hear and understand it, but another to make the sounds himself.

Though the birdlike people on this planet had more in common with him, he gravitated to the alien perspective of the fish. A life he could not understand. An existence he could not share. Relian raptors could not swim, so the water was an endless source of fascination for Deka. Most species evolved their way out of the water long before achieving sentience. Deka was proud to have a personal friendship with one member of one species that had not.

Their perspective on life, and on the lives of those living above the water, was amazing to take in. Being inside a tree that magnified their voices into something an air-breather could hear made the relationship more than just a mere conversation, but an experience.

In years past, when Deka visited this world, he and Chreeb would spend entire days just conversing, each sharing experiences the other could only imagine. The effort to put them into some kind of context the other could understand sharpened both of their minds.

Deka talked about them now, hoping for some kind of reaction. He explained how it felt to stand over a lava flow. He explained the sensations the body experiences while running on dry land. He told stories of when he and Kylac were young. He explained his time with Sonjaa, how they met, how sex felt, watching her lay eggs, the rush of primal emotions he felt while watching them hatch. It was a life Chreeb could only imagine.

Deka reminded Chreeb of the stories about undersea life he had told Deka. Exploring caves deep underwater. Touching the bottom of oceans on other worlds, where the pressure was so great the water congealed into warm ice. He remembered stories about watching trees sprout. The trees on this world began their lives at the bottom of the ocean. The seedlings shot a tiny vine up to the surface to collect light, and the vine grew into a trunk that could support an entire ecosystem. The fish had only heard about the abundant life in the canopies of these trees, so Deka had to explain it in their terms, and doing so had been a delightful exercise.

So many conversations. So much Deka had experienced because of Chreeb. No other water-dweller had ever been able to put into words what life under the water was like as well as he did.

Deka's monologues to the unconscious fish went on for more than two days. He barely slept. He felt if he took his eyes off Chreeb for too long, he would miss something important.

Kylac joined him from time to time, but since having sex inside one of these trees was considered unclean, he did not remain there long. For the first few days, Kylac could barely walk anywhere without finding a partner. He was making up for lost opportunity on many other worlds.

Kylac identified with the avians better than the fish. Flight was something he could not experience, so he spent as much time with them as possible. Kylac was sure the feeling of fur was something of a novelty to them, which is why they liked the canines of Rel so much.

Kylac enjoyed seeing the avian hunting practices. Generations ago, when they discovered the largest fish in the water were as intelligent as they were, the birds abandoned hunting them and began protecting the intelligent life on their planet. It was only when they began to understand what the fish were saying that they realized every action the birds took impacted life in the water. Now the birds did absolutely nothing that affected the water in a negative way, and they made sure offworlders did the same.

The birds hunted the large insects and small mammals that lived in the trees. They kept certain canopies isolated so these animals could thrive and be harvested later. They also maintained ways to spawning regions of non-intelligent fish and eels.

They carried Kylac to the trees of insects and mammals to make ways there. The insects were as large as his head, but harmless, and the mammals were wary of visitors from generations of harvesting, but once they accepted Kylac as one of their own, they came near him. Their hands were permanently formed for gripping branches. They had no fur, but their skin was green, which reflected a lot of light to ward off predators. Some of the avians still had trouble catching them.

There were hundreds of trees reserved just for these creatures. Chreeb had maintained all the portals to these isolated canopies so everyone across the planet had access to them at all times. With Chreeb unconscious, the avians had to fly for days to reach them. The fish also had to migrate to find food, now that the portals linking different parts of the ocean were also gone. With the portals gone, life had once again become little more than a perpetual search for food.

Kylac opened a few ways across the planet. He didn't have a lot of time, and since he was also calculating a way to Selta, it was much more difficult to concentrate. Fortunately, creating a portal linking two parts of the same planet did not take too much effort. He created five of them, but he still could not make a perfect sphere. The way the portals wobbled and pulsed made some birds afraid to use them, and Kylac had no confidence he could maintain them indefinitely. He had maintained dozens of ways between worlds for years at a time without a second thought. Now he could barely keep five open, and several times a day he felt like thrashing and screaming until a few avians approached him and helped him relax.

Kylac deliberately kept the calculations to Selta just short of completion. He was ready by the second day, but every time he climbed down to meet Deka after returning from a hunting tree, Deka did not seem ready. The raptor still spoke to Chreeb, and Kylac noticed more urgency in Deka's voice each day. His scent contained more adrenaline. Then, on the fifth day, Deka smelled of grief.

After a quick preening, Kylac joined his raptor in the water. Deka lay draped over the fish, his mouth very close to where Chreeb's earhole would be if the fish had one.

"Please wake up... I can feel you breathing. Can you even hear me?"

Kylac sloshed through the water. He pressed his hand to the back of Deka's neck.

"Deka. It has been five days."

"I know."

"I'm losing the portals. I can't keep them open for long. We need to find someone who can. We need to know."

Deka slowly rose from the fish's body and stood, never taking his eyes off Chreeb. "I still hope you're wrong."

They walked out of the water, up the ramp, and emerged into the bright green light. Several birds, both male and female, turned and observed Kylac. The fox could smell they wanted to mount him, but noticed he was with his raptor and must have concluded they were doing something important, so they held back.

The birds took to the air, picked up the Relians, and carried them down to the tree trunk where hundreds of portals should have been. They set the two down on the polished surface, and Kylac ran between two canals to the spot where Rel's portal used to be. Deka stood behind Kylac. The fox crouched, staring straight ahead.

Equations, variables, always changing, always moving. Everything was moving, and learning how to move with everything was the most important part. Kylac felt his mind moving with the planets and the galaxies. It became predictable. So predictable there were no light years between anything.

He perceived the universe as it was, not a vast fabric, but a set of points all interconnected. An atom on one side of the universe could affect an atom on the other side. Kylac sensed this, and he made such a connection between two points in the universe. He opened it wider. Wider. It formed a three-dimensional hole in spacetime with everything on the other side projected across the surface. It wavered. Kylac tried to hold it straight, but he still could not focus. He felt like an apprentice again.

Various felines with rippling muscles and saber teeth were visible through the portal. They stood on all fours, tails waving behind them. Several smaller canine-like creatures, also quadrupedal, stood among them.

Kylac didn't try to force perfection. He stood and walked straight through but did not let the calculations go, and the portal remained open.

He emerged on the very spot where the old portal to Rel had been. Its sudden reappearance had drawn a crowd of Selts and Zjr.

"A Relian!" shouted one of the felines.

"Kylac!"

"Sere told us something happened to Rel! Is everyone all right?"

Kylac raised his voice to be heard over them. "The Ixcyians need help! Their Archeon is unconscious! We need to know why!"

There were no fewer than twenty Selt volunteers in earshot. Kylac selected one of the felines, named Rrana, and led him through the portal. They crossed a few million light years in one step and were instantly back on Ixcy's wooden hub.

The birds carried everyone to the tree, and as they descended the ramp, Deka and Kylac explained what happened. Rrana and Kylac received a preening. Deka submitted to it, as it had been a while since he bathed. Then they entered the water. It was too high for Rrana to walk, so he swam to the fish. When he arrived, Kylac and Deka held him up from underneath so he wouldn't have to try staying afloat. He placed a padded paw on Chreeb's head. Everyone waited. He felt multiple places along the fish's head. Then used both paws, which made Deka nervous.

"I feel activity in the first brain, but nothing in the second."

Deka's tail fell. Kylac's ears folded back. Nobody moved.

"I'm sorry," Rrana said. "Chreeb is dead."

The air in the tree was empty. Deka released the feline, forcing Kylac to hold him up by himself.

The canine led Rrana to the ramp, and they ascended together. They left, leaving Deka, the fish, and the birds in attendance to grieve for the loss of their Archeon. The tree trunk captured their cries and carried them into the ocean. Deka's in particular could be heard around the entire planet.

Selta

The way closed behind them, and for the first time since he had begun life as an Archeon, Kylac felt relieved to close a way. It had only been open a few dozen breaths, and the whole time he had felt it pulling away from him. This had not happened since he was an apprentice, and it convinced Kylac that something was wrong with him. If what happened to Rel was enough to kill an Archeon, it must have had a greater effect on him than he thought. He hoped the Selts knew something about it.

He and Deka walked across the hub area side by side. Deka's head was down. Kylac held a hand on the back of the raptor's neck.

"I'm so sorry."

"We could have lost more... What if the disaster killed more Archeons? How many other worlds are isolated? And Chreeb... I wish we didn't have to leave Ixcy like that."

Kylac sighed. "Saali will take care of them until they can find a new Archeon."

"I know she will, but what about everyone else?"

Deka and Kylac walked on a path in the grass worn down by centuries of visitors. It formed a similar path system found on the other worlds, with each branch ending at a small clearing where a portal would have rested. Now these clearings stood empty save for a few ways linking different regions of Selta.

Deka and Kylac had just left one of Selta's Archeons on the ocean world. She was eager to help, but as with every other Archeon they had met since the disaster, she could not connect worlds yet. Saali would keep the ways to the hunting grounds open, both above water and below, and lead the search for an Archeon on Ixcy.

Selta was an oceanless world of grasslands and sparse trees. It orbited a white star, which was itself trapped in an orbit around a red giant. Objects on this world all had a red shadow facing the other direction.

Sabre-toothed felines padded about on all fours. Among them were canines, the Zjr. Deka and Kylac were the two tallest people in sight, easily twice the height. As they walked between the felines and canines, Kylac pondered that if not for his planet's environment, the canine species on Rel might have been remained quadrupeds. Instead, the fox's legs had become elongated but remained digitigrade, which allowed him to function both upright and on all fours.

They approached the place where the crowd had gathered, gently pushing through. The Selts and the Zjr smelled them coming, gave off scents of reverence, and made way for them. They heard voices in one language. Kylac and Deka had already switched from the duel-language culture of Ixcy to the single language shared by both sentient species on Selta.

"Their story matches the lack of adrenaline in the blood."

"It doesn't explain the polish of the bones. I tasted nothing on them. No stress or weakness of the molecules."

"The bones were not broken."

"The pattern of the injuries is not straight, but skewed lines leading up and out. Each person was facing the same way, running toward the portal to Selta. They were ripped apart from behind."

Deka and Kylac reached the center of conversation. Nine bodies were here, all Relians of both species. Bone had been sheared from their bodies, organs and flesh with them. Various felines milled about in here, walking to and from the bodies. The story Kylac and Deka had told gave them new information to work with now.

Saali had told them that the Selts had been occupied since the disaster with trying to revive them. It had been over three hundred years since the death of a sentient creature occurred on Selta, and it had sent the entire world into a panic, with Selts and Zjr migrating to the hub to try to save their lives.

The Selts and Zjr had gathered as much information as possible. By now everyone knew how the victims' blood, bile, lymph, urine, and feces tasted, how much brain activity was present upon arrival, and how it had faded over time.

For the first time in their culture's history, the Selts were dumbfounded as to the cause of death. Massive organ failure and blood loss were obvious, but what caused such injuries? What caused the injuries to be in clean lines through the body? The injuries looked as if straight, square beams had come from the sky at a fifty-degree incline, penetrated the bodies to random depths, and then pulled bones and organs and flesh out with them.

The raptor and the fox walked among the bodies, among the Selts and Zjr still examining them. The bodies had the same injuries, but some of the beams had penetrated in different places. Some Relians were missing pieces of their skulls, leaving the brain exposed, squared off where a piece was missing. Others only penetrated the chest and limbs, leaving the head undamaged.

"No taste of burning, tearing, or fragmenting along the edges," said one Selt.

"Body fluids tasted normal," said another. "Whatever did this left no trace, not even energy."

"It was a planet-wide disaster that killed these people. We should consider what events could do this."

"And now an Archeon is dead," said one of the Zjr. "Living in the body but dead in the mind. What could cause that?"

Hundreds of felines and canines, all gathered around nine bodies. Saali had told Deka and Kylac the people of Selta had been so traumatized by death on their world they were still trying to revive them even as the bodies had begun to decay. Only Kylac's arrival brought them out of their panic, and they switched from saving their lives to determining cause of death. Deka and Kylac sat down and listened.

The two species switched from medical possibility to planetary disasters. Rogue black hole or stellar corpse wandering too close to Rel. Supernova remnants. Dense space-time.

A rogue black hole would not have destroyed a planet so quickly, no matter how large. A stellar corpse, even a large one, would not have chosen parts of people to tear away; the entire body would have been pulled off the world. There had never been a supernova in the vicinity of Rel, and it would not have done this.

They discussed other planetary disasters, such as volcanoes, or a dying star, but nothing matched. Nothing could destroy a world the size of Rel in mere breaths, leaving wounds like these on the victims. It seemed deliberate. Created. Not a disaster.

The deliberation continued into the night. Everyone could see in the dark, so it was no issue. The Selts and Zjr were so involved in the debate nobody paused to eat or drink.

The Selts were not a herd species, but when it came to things like this they acted as one. It was actually the Zjr that had lived together in large groups in more primitive times.

The Zjr were the only ones who could hunt the wildlife, and the Selts, once scavengers of those kills, had gradually inserted themselves as the alphas of each pack in order to benefit from the kills they made.

But disease had ravaged the Zjr and threatened to wipe them out entirely. Evolution favored the Selts who could heal their Zjr so the canines could keep hunting the impossibly fast prey on this world.

This codependence pushed their minds higher and higher until they achieved consciousness. Today, the Selts were the only thing keeping the Zjr from dying, and the Zjr were the only ones who could catch the prey on this planet.

Finally, someone noticed the two living Relians among them. Instantly everyone closed in on them, and Deka and Kylac reclined on their backs in the grass. The Selts placed their paws all over them. Tongues licked Deka's scales and Kylac's fur. A few claws pierced their skin, and felines tasted their blood. Others tasted their urine, still others felt their skulls with both paws. Several felines had their paws on Kylac's skull at the same time, pressing him into the ground.

And then, a sweet smell. The Relians were ready for it.

2

They awoke together and sat up in the grass. Numer-ous Selts and Zjr noticed they were awake and rushed to meet them. More paws on the skull. More light pricks, tasting blood.

Several felines touched Kylac in ten places at once. The canine was instantly out of his sheath and ejaculating. Thirty felines tasted it and announced the analysis to those who could not.

Kylac turned his head to Deka. They had touched Deka in exactly the right places to make him release as well, and they presented the analysis to the others in attendance. Word traveled fast how the Relians had recovered.

Kylac noticed some of his fur was missing, covered instead in a jelly made from some kind of plant mixed with saliva. He knew it well. He had been ready for it, but it still boggled his mind to think that not too long ago, the felines had taken his body apart, examined it, tasted the various fluids, removed anomalies, and then put him back together.

This was the post-recovery exam. They knew Relian anatomy so well they could make Deka and Kylac urinate just by touching them in the right place. They knew the nerves to stimulate in the right sequence and time to make them climax instantly. They even knew the exact sequence of touches and sounds to make for their bodies to secrete more insulin, or growth hormone, or testosterone, or estrogen.

The Selts knew how every species worked. Thanks to their endeavor to keep the Zjr alive, their senses of taste, smell, and touch were so acute they could diagnose any ailment, and if treatment meant taking the body apart, cleaning it out, and reassembling it, it was easy for them.

"You are fit to move again," said one of the Selts.

Kylac sat up. Deka rolled to his stomach and raised his neck. They were sore, but felt better than ever. Deka's scales were uneven in several places around his body. They had opened him up across his abdomen and even opened his skull. Kylac's fur was patchy in the same places, which meant they had been just as thorough with him.

"We cleaned your bodies of impurities," said the feline in front of them, female, likely not the same feline who operated on them. No one Selt would have done it; everyone would have taken part.

Deka found his voice first. "What happened to us? Why can't we make perfect portals?"

"Why are they unstable?" Kylac finished.

"You are only the second and third Archeons we have examined since the disaster. Your bodies held many toxins while prioritizing other systems, suggesting you have been in fight-or-flight this whole time. Other than that, your bodies were healthy. Your brains, however, showed activity similar to Sere's. The entire brain is involved in creating portals, so your entire brain was scarred. Neurons showed slow response time, and your brains are rerouting around the slowest neurons until they heal. That's why you two, and Sere, can't create stable portals or hold them open for very long. But your minds are scarred in a different way compared to Sere. We believe this difference explains why you have managed to make spheres to other worlds, but Sere cannot. We don't know why."

"Will we heal?" Kylac asked. "Will we make stable ways again?"

"Sere is beginning to reach beyond the world again, and he could not even attempt it a few days ago. We believe you will recover eventually, but we can't be sure of anything without knowing what caused this. Unlike the fish on Ixcy, you had more neurons to absorb the shock of Rel's portals closing suddenly. Or rather... We wonder if they really closed."

"What do you mean?" Deka said.

"The bodies of the victims we examined had chunks extracted from them randomly. Think of that happening to the portals. They did not just close. Something reached out and snatched them away, and in doing so tried to take some of your conscious minds as well."

Kylac and Deka faced one another. Then they turned to the Selt before them.

"What could have caused that?" Deka said.

"We don't know, but we have identified the people most at risk from death because of it. Sere is working on making ways to those worlds, but he was traumatized heavily. It may be some time before he can make a stable way to another world again."

Deka rolled to his feet and stood. "Where is Sere?" He held a hand down, and Kylac took it and pulled himself up.

"He's at the hub."

"Thank you. Tell everyone we're grateful for what you've done."

She licked her nose, the gesture for "you're welcome," and rejoined the Selts and Zjr still debating around the bodies.

The disaster had disrupted life here. Normally the felines and canines would be in their groups all over the planet, harvesting plants, creating medicines, and learning as much as they could about the contacted universe. The Selts would regularly examine the Zjr, correcting even the most minor defects of the body.

Now everyone was waiting for the portals to come back, waiting to help anyone who needed it. What they did for Deka and Kylac was rarely done for offworlders, as they were much too busy with the Zjr. The Selts would likely make many exceptions over the coming years, gathering as much information about the disaster's effects on the body as possible so they could be ready for it next time, and hopefully prevent the deaths that had occurred on their world.

Kylac and Deka gently parted the crowd. Selts were examining Zjr, feeling their heads, listening to their hearts and abdomens. The Selts were experts at catching disease at the first symptom, and any sign of disease or weakness was corrected immediately.

One Zjr was asleep on the grass and cut open. Three Selts were licking his insides, tasting for the source of what was threatening to make him sick. They found the infection, pulled it out, and then began sealing the wound with saliva and plant gel.

In the distant past, when the Zjr and Selts had reached intelligence, the Selts stopped merely using them to keep themselves fed. They sought to understand the canines that hunted for them. With understanding came mutual trust, and now the Selts kept the Zjr alive because they cared for the Zjr. The canines no longer hunted prey because they had to, but because they adored the Selts. That was when they discovered portal physics, and they used the portals to eliminate the need to migrate with the herds.

Natural selection had been cruel, but it yielded a population of felines who could taste or smell any ailment in a body through its fluids. They knew how the nerves were networked, and their paws were sensitive enough to detect activity in those nerves. The Selts and the Zjr lived for hundreds of years. Death among them was so rare that their word for death applied only to prey and offworlders.

Deka and Kylac would trust their lives to any Selt. They were all healers by birth, and they knew the anatomy of every contacted species. It was rude to expect medical treatment from them, as their talents were pretty much only for the Zjr, but whenever a new species joined the contacted universe, the Selts were among the first to take their bodies apart and learn everything about them.

Deka and Kylac saw Sere sitting in front of an empty clearing off the path. They knew that posture, that of an apprentice in the last stages of calculating a new portal through spacetime, though Sere was not an apprentice. The raptor and the fox approached quietly and stood behind him, Sere's head only as high as their chests. They waited a few moments.

A point over the clearing spread wider. It became the size of a Selt, and then spacetime pushed back in and closed it. Sere growled at himself and lay down, head between his paws.

Deka lay on his stomach beside him. Kylac sat by Sere's other side. He was tempted to lie right up against him, but he remembered these were not pack creatures.

"I can't make a way," Sere said. "Every time I try to go offworld, the equations pull away from me."

"Did you hear the diagnosis?" Deka said.

"I did. It confirmed their diagnosis of me. The portals didn't close. They were taken somewhere else, and they pulled part of us with them. I will need more time before I can contact other planets." His voice wavered. "So much death... Too much. We can't stop it."

The Selts considered death natural only on other worlds, and for other species. When it touched their world, it was unnatural. Their instinct to save the Zjr sometimes pushed them to extreme panic trying to prevent death from touching anyone. The Selts often had to remind themselves that they could not save everyone. Sere was going through this right now.

Deka and Kylac lay with Sere, facing the empty clearing where a perfect sphere should be. The hub was so quiet. The entire civilization had paused, waiting to know if anyone else needed help. They suspected it was too late, but they were still ready.

"You are so fortunate to be able to make ways offworld," Sere said at last. "You two may be the only ones who can. Please go to Lesa. Make sure their Bellows Archeon is all right."

"Is that one of the species most in danger?" said Deka.

"Yes. Five species are vulnerable, including the fish on Ixcy, but the Bellows are at the most risk."

Deka and Kylac glanced at each other. They agreed. The gas giant would be their next destination.

Sere rolled over to his back, paws in the air. "Kylac..."

The fox caught a whiff of his scent, crawled on top of Sere, and mounted him, happy to help him through the trauma. Deka lay down and calculated where the gas giant would be. He looked forward to seeing the Wings and Bellows again.

Deka fell asleep as Kylac and Sere moaned and panted while the daytime stars set.

Deka dreaded what might have happened to Lesa in the wake of the disaster.

Lesa

"Good thing you got off a few times before we left for Lesa."

Kylac's tail danced around as his ears bloomed. "I know. I'll have to go days without it there."

"We'll have to go days without any contact at all."

Deka was sitting on the worn path in front of the empty clearing where the portal to Rel would have been, in the final moments of calculating a way to the gas giant. He and Kylac had spent the last four days with the Selts and the Zjr as everyone grieved for the lost Relians on their world. The people of Selta dealt with the bodies the only way they knew how: by looking at them. It was symbolic, reminding everyone that though they had made death rare on their world, they must not hide from it when it happens. Deka and Kylac had watched, but did not feel repulsed. They tried to learn the same lesson the people of Selta did.

A few paces in front of Deka, a portal widened to Relian-size and settled on the ground. It was spherical for a few breaths, and then Deka lost the feeling of a few variables, and local spacetime began pushing back chaotically. Deka used to be able to perceive the order underneath, but the feeling was difficult to find again. Deka stood up and walked straight through. Kylac followed his tail and emerged—

The wind sucked Kylac from the portal, lifted him off the ground, and carried him several hundred paces, spinning him around. He tried to scream, but the wind had pulled the air from his lungs, leaving him feeling deflated. He spread his arms out, and his claws screeched across glass.

He was inside a glass tube more than large enough for three creatures of his stature to walk upright. As he tumbled around and around, he caught glimpses of blue and red clouds swirling around at a thousand paces per breath.

The wind slowed, as if it hit a barrier, and it dropped Kylac to the spongy ground. It wasn't dirt. Dirt did not exist on this world.

Kylac rose to his hands and knees, gasping for breath. He couldn't smell a thing, and his exposed skin burned. Everything covered in fur felt all right for the moment, except that his lungs had stretched to the breaking point. He choked, thrashed. His nose was useless here, so he used his eyes to figure out where he was.

Deka lay a few paces away, surrounded by blue-red gas, also gasping for breath. Kylac turned his head in the direction they had come. The glass tube curved around the rim of an island floating in the clouds. The gas giant's atmosphere rushed in through a hole in the tube where Deka's sphere had opened. The wind had set them down at the midpoint, where it slowed enough to let them stand on their feet.

The planet's atmosphere was made of hydrogen and helium with various other trace elements that combined in the clouds to form ammonia, arsenic, and sulfur. Kylac hacked. Deka coughed and gasped. Kylac raised his arms, and the light breeze pushed him closer to his raptor. He grabbed Deka to keep himself from being blown farther away. Deka held him close, and they looked around the tube.

Something flew against the wind and landed inside the hole. Deka and Kylac only saw it in shadow, as it was backlit through the gas. It flashed several colors in rapid succession.

Remain calm I am coming

It turned and climbed through the tube. As it approached it became clearer and clearer. Its body was triangle-shaped. Its arms were actually folded wings, which puckered while it walked. Its head was triangle-shaped as well, blending in with its body so well it was difficult to tell where the head ended and the body began.

A ridge of bone ran along the edges of its body. It produced colors, sometimes glowing, sometimes flashing. Green-white-yellow-black-green-red-brighter-red-fade-to-blue-flash-pink-six-times—

We had no way to warn anybody the Bellows Archeon is dead and the Wing Archeon won't wake up just before the portals went out they doubled in size and took part of the tubes with them the tubes are open now some people were killed we didn't expect anyone to come here—

—white-fade-to-grey-flash-yellow-flash-different-shades-of-orange-brown—

—or we would have repaired the tubes sooner but there has been no time—

The Relians couldn't follow it anymore. Their vision was fading. The Wing stood in touching distance, and it had something on its back. It looked like glass, with many glass pieces inside, all spinning and moving: a machine with six glass pipes connected to a hose made of extremely thin glass that connected to the sides. It shoved two of the pipes into Deka and Kylac's mouths.

Air rushed into Kylac's mouth. He coughed out the poison first and then suckled the pleasant mix of oxygen and nitrogen. Deka was right beside him, still holding onto his fox, sucking down the air from the tube as fast as he could. They had to exhale away from the tube, which allowed more poison into their lungs, but it was better than before.

The Wing let the machine on its back fall to the spongy ground. The ridge along its body lit up: white-pink-orange-flash-blue...

Follow me we have shelters for oxygen breathers

Deka and Kylac helped each other up. The Wing hobbled along the ground past them, following the wind through the tube. The Relians held the machine between them and followed the Wing.

Deka turned his head to the side and scanned the interior of the island on the other side of the glass. Many Wings stood out there in the open. The atmosphere blew against them from one direction, the gas speeding by so fast Deka could barely see it. Among them were creatures floating just above the spongy surface at various heights. Inflated blobs of flesh with a ridge running around their whole body, which flashed and glowed various colors. They were looking at the Relians, chattering amongst each other.

Offworlders here now
How did they get here
Oxygen breathers
Horrible moment to arrive
Maybe they know what happened to the portals

By now they had reached a square cut into the ground covered by a glass hatch. The Wing pulled it open and beckoned them to enter. Deka and Kylac descended a short slope, and the hatch slammed shut above them. The Relians sucked air from the tubes and coughed out the waste along with any poison that made it in. The machine they held weighed them down, so they slumped, waiting in front of a glass door.

The atmosphere cycled. Kylac's fur blew around as the poison air escaped and clean oxygen and nitrogen rushed in. Finally able to breathe the air, they set the machine down and held each other as they coughed and examined each other.

"You're covered... in red scabs," Kylac said.

"Your skin is burned. Some of your fur is falling out."

Kylac gasped several more times. Deka coughed violently, and now he suddenly felt the searing pain on his scales caused by chemical burns from the ammonia in the air. Too much longer out there and they might have melted.

The glass door opened. The Relians stepped through, carrying the now-inert machine with them. When the door closed, they stood in the middle of a menagerie of different people.

Two quadrupedal canines from Emrim.

Five six-legged insects from T'laae, talons folded as close to their bodies as possible.

Three bipedal lizards from Gelleen. Their neck-scales were blood red and throbbing. Kylac's tail waved as he coughed, wondering how three male Gelleens one right after the other would feel.

Deka and Kylac took a few more deep breaths, glanced at each other, and picked a language. Deka chose the Emrim's language first.

"I'm Deka. This is Kylac. We're from Rel. We're Archeons."

Kylac repeated it in the language of the T'laae, which was all clicks and throaty gurgles.

Deka then repeated himself in the Gelleen language.

The inhabitants did not react. Deka and Kylac observed the Gelleens were standing at the end of the room closest to the door, which was lined with a few shelves where small cubes rested. The others huddled by the glass pane at the far end of the room. They smelled terrified, and the odors coming up from the floor told Deka and Kylac nobody had ventured from the wall in some time.

Kylac knew exactly what was happening, but for the moment he was too busy expelling poison from his lungs.

The outside hatch slammed shut again. Deka and Kylac spun around and looked through the glass door. A Wing stood on the other side, surrounded by thin blue and red gas. A Bellows hovered next to it at eye level.

Their body ridges glowed in unison.

Welcome Relians are you hurt

Deka and Kylac could not speak their language. No offworlder could. But the two sentient species that inhabited the floating islands of Lesa learned an alternative language to communicate with offworlders. It was simplistic, but it worked. Deka and Kylac set the machine down, spread their hands, and signed back in unison.

Yes, we are hurt, but we are all right.

The floating blob of flesh deflated and lowered slightly to the ground. It flashed several colors so quickly they blended together into one hue. *Good now I am glad we told someone to keep watch over the tubes in case someone arrived*

The Wing now flashed. *Do you know what happened*

Deka and Kylac gestured their story as quickly as they could, but the sign language was limited in what it could convey. The two Lesans flashed long streaks of white upon the news of Rel's destruction. The Relians signed new details from the Selts of what the disaster did to the Archeons and expressed sorrow at the loss of their Bellows Archeon. That was why they came; the Selts were fearful for his safety. They assured them that their Wing Archeon should wake up once her mind recovered from the shock, but they did not know when.

The Bellows flashed and faded all sorts of colors: *no Relians had been on this world when the portals failed and just before the portals closed they swelled up doubled in size and swallowed parts of the tubes allowing Lesa's atmos-*

phere in many offworlders in the tubes died before we could take them to the shelters all fifty-three islands have shelters for different breathers but we are running out of food for them

Meanwhile the Wing was also flashing and fading: *we are having difficulty keeping them together we can not communicate with any of them and the few who know our language do not know it well enough to understand much*

Soon the colors became synchronized as the two creatures unified their conversation, which indicated it was coming to a close.

The lack of food is becoming a problem the atmosphere generators can run almost indefinitely but we did not expect to hold this many offworlders for so long please take these people back to their worlds

With a synchronized brown-green flash, they finished. Knowing Deka and Kylac were Archeons, they had used the ultraviolet and infrared components of their language as well.

Deka and Kylac signed together in reply. *Yes, we will take these people away.*

Can you be quick, flashed the Wing.

Deka and Kylac thought about how time was measured on this world, and then signed their answer together.

Half a cycle to make a portal for each island. By then we should have a way offworld ready, or it might take another two days.

The Wing and the Bellows did not flash happiness.

Very long but we knew and we will do our best not all are oxygen breathers so take pain not to send them to their death you know the islands' layout

It was a question. Deka signed back for both of them.

Yes, which numbers are what?

Islands one through twenty are oxygen breathers twenty-one through twenty-five breathe only nitrogen twenty-six through fifty-three breathe methane.

Three different types of worlds to portal to. Fifty-three portals to open to other worlds.

Deka signed: *There is no time to take everyone to their home worlds individually. We will send the oxygen-breathers to Selta, the nitrogen-breathers to Kexi, and the methane breathers to Jiniv. They will be cared for there.*

At the same time, Kylac signed: *We will create ways to each world here in this shelter. We will open spheres to each island and bring everyone here to leave from a single place.*

The two Lesans flashed and flickered in unison again. *Thank you and please hurry we cannot keep everyone here forever and we are so sorry about Rel we want to know what caused it please tell us when you learn*

They turned and floated around. The upper hatch opened, they climbed the steep ramp, and the hatch closed again. Deka and Kylac turned in place, observing the people in the shelter.

"I'll work on the ways to the islands and Selta," Deka said. "You work on the other two offworld portals."

Kylac was scenting the Gelleen lizards from a distance, ears flicking. They were huddled together, touching each other, hormones surging. The scents of the others in the room were fearful. Kylac didn't need to be an Archeon to figure out what had happened in here.

"First things first." Kylac approached the Gelleens. "Hello, everyone."

The lizards growled and hissed at him in unison. Kylac sat down among them, close enough for them to catch his scent. Kylac was drinking their scents in, and they smelled gorgeous. The fox slipped out of his sheath, and all three Gelleens noticed at the same time.

Deka rubbed his claws together and turned his head to the wall. He addressed the people pressed up against it. He spoke in the Emrim language first.

"Don't worry. My fox can calm them down."

He repeated himself in the T'laae language, but the people still looked and smelled terrified for Kylac. Deka figured they had tried to reason with the Gelleens before and someone had been hurt, so they had been huddled here this whole time.

Deka decided to let Kylac's actions convince them. He walked across the room to the wall opposite the door. The walls were spongy, made of the same plant matter as the floor and ceiling. A hole had been cut into this wall and filled with a thick plate of glass. Deka peered outside.

The red-blue clouds above were lit by a white star. The island was far enough down in the atmosphere that the star appeared as a blurry disc through the gas.

Deka saw another island in the distance. Huge streamers reached up from it far into the clouds, ending in bulbous, gas-filled balloons that floated on the border between outer space and the planet's atmosphere. They absorbed starlight, processed it into energy, and fed it back down to the body.

A plant rooted to the upper atmosphere.

Thousands of paces below, the gas divided itself into bands of red, blue, white, and yellow. In each band, the wind blew in opposing directions. Further down, the clouds became so dense they behaved like a liquid, and nothing could survive there. The islands themselves were full of gas that suspended them between the dense clouds below and the deadly radiation from space. They were the only habitable regions of Lesa.

Somehow, with the atmosphere constantly roaring, life had formed here. Two species living inside the floating mass of plant life, each developing its own way to move from island to island in search of food.

The Wings had developed bodies so aerodynamic they were barely affected by the wind. The Bellows developed bodies that took in the air and used it to propel themselves around.

Deka turned from the view and glanced at Kylac. The fox was on his back, the dominant Gelleen on top of him. Kylac was moaning and licking the scales up the lizard's arm. The Gelleen was growling and moaning as well while the two lizards behind them fought over who would be second.

The raptor scented the people around the room. They recognized the fox was doing something none of them could, and it was working.

Deka held his hands together, touching the claws in a smile, and gazed out the sheet of glass again. He never tired of seeing this planet. It was so beautiful, and to know that life could thrive here was enough to make him dizzy with awe.

The Bellows and the Wings were neither predator nor prey. They fed off the plants, moving from island to island when they had consumed enough of one so they did not kill it. They helped each other find new islands, and each species grew up together and came to rely on the other for survival. The force of the constant storm was so strong their language did not develop any spoken component. Instead, their bodies became partially fluorescent, and color itself became language.

Fifteen generations ago, they discovered portal physics, and they no longer needed to fly from island to island in search of food. They maintained permanent portals to the islands, and civilization flourished. It was a beautiful culture on an equally beautiful and dangerous world.

They ventured to other worlds and joined the contacted universe. They learned other species wanted to experience where they lived, so they did something very rare and almost impossible on a planet such as this. Using sand from other worlds, they built tubes of glass around each island so offworlders could visit Lesa. Everything that couldn't be made of plant matter was made of it, as glass was the only other material that would not deteriorate in these harsh conditions.

They created machines to cut the soil faster to install the tubes. Machines to create artificial atmosphere for visitors. They were so useful the machines began to take command of other parts of their lives. They began to use machines to process the plant matter into other things. Things to eat. Things to use for other purposes, but all for the purpose of allowing offworlders to visit.

Kylac gasped as the dominant male withdrew, and the next climbed on top. Deka rubbed his claws together and admired the view outside. The others admired the view on the other side of the shelter.

Deka pondered the machines as the second male penetrated his fox. Machines were everywhere on this world now. Deka wished he could see more of it, but they were always surrounded by poison atmosphere. He could never see how the Wings lived their lives. He could never observe the Bellows effortlessly floating through the powerful wind from one island to another. At best, these tubes provided only a fleeting glance at a life Deka would never experience.

The second male finished with Kylac quickly, and now the third nudged the fox over. He rolled to his hands and knees, and the Gelleen climbed on top of him.

Deka looked down through the glass. Just below, partially embedded on the surface, was the machine that kept them alive. It was larger than the portable device they had carried inside, and there were only two hoses connected to it. Deka now wished he'd had the opportunity to learn how these machines worked. It was incredible for a species to go to these lengths to accommodate offworlders at all, and it deserved further study.

The raptor stepped away and turned to the closest inhabitant in the room, the female quadruped from Emrim with yellow fur. She stood about as high as Deka's waist.

"What is your name?"

She did not take her eyes off Kylac and the Gelleens. "I'm Rawoc."

"Nice to meet you. Where is our food supply?"

She gestured with one paw to the wall behind the Gelleens. Deka stepped away from the wall and approached it.

"No, don't go near them!" Rawoc shouted.

Deka walked by the spent Gelleens to the wall they had been guarding. It was lined with small cubes of processed plant matter. Deka picked one up between two claws and sniffed it. It smelled edible, even to a carnivore, made of concentrated nutrients. It wouldn't be filling, but it would keep anyone alive. There were only twenty cubes left on the shelf, and Deka calculated a hundred cubes would fit on it.

"This wall used to be full of them?" Deka asked.

"It was," replied the quadruped. Her mate hadn't spoken a word, and Deka smelled too much fear in his scent. He had folded inward.

Deka turned to her. "Don't worry. You'll be off this world soon."

The last Gelleen had finished with Kylac. The scales on their necks had cooled down, and their scents did not clog the room anymore. The collective scent of the room changed to relief.

"That's right," said the fox, still on his hands and knees. "We'll be on an oxygen and nitrogen planet soon." Kylac repeated himself in the other two languages.

The Gelleen pulled out. Kylac collapsed onto the floor, sinking into it slightly. The two canines and five insects approached Kylac as he lay spent.

"I don't know how you managed to calm them down, but thank you!" clicked several of the insects.

Kylac's tail waved. "I'm a Relian canine."

"I'm sorry, I've never been to your world," said another. "I don't know your species."

Kylac rolled over and stood. "The canines of Rel have universal pheromones."

"Almost universal," Deka said from the shelves.

"Yes, almost, among compatible species. As soon as I stepped inside, I could smell them. I figured it was causing trouble in here."

"It was, definitely!" said the canine.

Kylac could smell she was female, and the other was male. This was a mated pair, and he remembered the Emrim canines were exclusive, so there was no hope of getting any from either of them.

"They were taking all our food, hissing at us for coming near them. This is the first time we've been able to walk around the room!"

"That's not surprising," Kylac said. "Gelleens are territorial during their reproductive cycle. They didn't come here on their cycle, but being shoved into an enclosed space brought it out because they did not think to bring someone of their companion species to Lesa."

Kylac looked over his shoulder and repeated himself in the Gelleen language. The dominant male made a few mumbles and growls. Kylac faced the canines again.

"Exactly as I thought. Don't hold it against them. They didn't expect this either. Being confined stimulates the mating drive, and their higher brains shut down when it happens. Normally their companion species can keep them in line, but they were caught by surprise. They are sorry for what happened."

Deka translated for everyone. Now everyone seemed friendlier to the Gelleens, and distances closed at last.

"We can make our food supply last," Deka said to everyone. "While we're working on the ways to the other islands, I'm curious. What brought everyone here?"

The insects spoke first. They had just recently heard about a gas giant that had built means for offworlders to visit. Their world, T'laae, had no portals to Lesa, so they had taken spheres to six different planets before finally coming to one with a way here. They had walked the glass rings, admiring the views of several different islands. Suddenly the portals expanded and vanished, taking chunks of the tube with them, and poison atmosphere blew into the tube. Fortunately the Wings and Bellows saw what happened, grabbed the portable atmosphere machines, and guided everyone to the shelter.

Deka and Kylac translated their story for the others.

The canines from Emrim went next. They had just mated, and they came to Lesa as part of the celebration. Their Archeon had opened a way to Lesa just for them. Rawoc had learned some of their language, but she did not know enough to understand what the Bellows and Wings had been saying to her since the disaster.

Everyone had only intended to be here for a day or so, just long enough to witness the beauty, to see the Wings and Bellows fly and float effortlessly in wind that would knock any of them down and whittle their skin raw. It wasn't very real, as there could be no scents, but it forced them to use their eyes to take in the experience, just as the Wings and the Bellows did.

The people in the room finally understood one another. For some time, Deka and Kylac wandered the room, standing between groups of people and translating between them. Now that the Gelleens were calm, everyone could finally speak to them.

Kylac was standing by the glass pane translating the Gelleens' story for the quadrupeds when his eyes caught movement outside. A Wing had landed below the view of glass. Kylac walked up to it and looked down. He could barely see the Wing below, crawling around on top of the atmosphere machine.

"What's he doing?" Kylac said, mostly to himself, but loud enough for Deka to hear.

A loud crack filled the shelter. The creature had dislodged the machine from the side of the island.

"You! Stop! Stop!"

Deka ran to the pane. Everyone else followed.

The Wing ripped the machine free, the wind caught it and carried it away. The hoses still connected to the shelter now flapped about.

Deka screeched at it, pounding on the spongy plant matter that made up the wall.

The Wing looked up, spread its arms, and sailed upwards, landing on the glass and glared inside. Its ridges flashed fourteen colors rapidly. Finally it pushed away, let the wind catch it, and glided out of sight.

"What did it say?" said a few people in their own languages.

Kylac stared blankly out the window. "Don't come back."

Deka translated into every language necessary in one breath. Nobody moved for some time.

"What does—" one of the insects began.

"I don't know," Deka said, "but we have maybe half a cycle of air left in here." He paced. "The outside temperature is not too bad, but each of us can only survive in it for a few moments. The real problem is the wind speed."

Kylac was translating as fast as he could. It wasn't easy to keep up. Then he saw the machine they had left by the door.

"Deka, we still have this!"

Kylac leaped away from the wall and ran to the machine that had saved their lives earlier.

"It's small, but it has six hoses, so it should generate enough air for that many people at once." He examined it all around as Deka translated for everyone. "It has intake vents on five of its six sides. It's meant to use the planet's wind as a power source, and it can work from any angle. We need to get this outside."

When Deka translated that, the collective scent of everyone in the room grew agitated.

"How do we do that without letting in the gas?" asked one of the Gelleens.

"We don't." Deka walked to the glass. He tapped it with his hand-claws. "We shouldn't break this. We'll have to go through the wall."

One of the lesser Gelleens spoke up when Kylac had finished translating. They were equals again—no more dominant male pushing them around. "You want to cut through the wall?"

"Won't that let our air out?" said one of the insects.

"Yes, it will," Deka said, "but shortly there won't be any air left in here. Here's what will happen. You." He gestured to one of the insects. "Use your talons to hold onto the far wall as tight as you can. You have good grips. Hold onto each other and make a chain to this wall." He turned to the Gelleens. "You three, hold onto us. Your scales will protect you from the atmosphere for a little longer than the insects. And you two"—the Emrims—"hold on to the insects."

The insects walked to the far wall and formed a chain of linked forelimbs. Their arms were practically long blades that ended in spikes. The last one in the chain held one of the Gelleens in a predatory death grip. That Gelleen held the wrist of another reptile. The last reptile held onto Kylac's wrist. Deka lay on his back, feet aimed at the wall.

Deka raised his feet, flexed the killing claws on his inner toes, and dug into the wall. His claws sank deep into the plant matter, and he sliced down. When he had cut to the floor, he rotated his body, spread his hand-claws, shoved them into the wall, and cut across. He then kicked the wall. The square he had cut puckered inward. Deka kicked again, and the square flew outside and blew out of sight.

Acidic air threw Deka back, but Kylac grabbed him and held him still as poisonous atmosphere rushed in with enough force to rip trees out by the roots. The chain tightened as everyone held each other, anchored to the wall by the insects. The Emrims did their best to hold onto the insects' legs.

Deka picked up the machine, walked against the torrent of air, and shoved it into the hole. Deka had measured it with his eyes to be exactly the right size, and it fit snugly. The poison wind in the shelter died down, and the machine whirled. Oxygen spilled out of the pipes. The chain separated, and everyone gathered around the machine.

Deka and Kylac grabbed all six pipes and held them out. Some took a pipe, and everyone huddled around them. The rest of the shelter was still full of hydrogen and ammonia, but this little pocket by the glass pane was habitable. The air was thin but tolerable, and for a few moments, all they could do was breathe.

"Who was that?!" gasped one of the Gelleens at last.

"I don't know," Kylac wheezed, "but if they did it to us, they probably did it to others."

Deka finished translating for everyone, then he continued. "I still need more time before I can make a way to any of the other shelters."

Kylac translated, and then added, "I'm working on the ways to Kexi and Jiniv. It will be another day or so before I can open one of them."

They stayed still and enjoyed breathing for a while. Their oxygen seemed tentative. One of insects stood up and clicked a few times. The air was breathable up there. Barely.

"Keep watch," Kylac said. "If someone else even goes near the machine, here's what we do."

Deka translated. Everyone agreed.

They huddled around the pipes for a long time, with the insects taking turns keeping watch. Since they were the tallest, they could see the machine the easiest.

A clank came from the door. A Bellows hovered in front of the glass, the same one who had spoken to them earlier. Deka and Kylac got up and ran to the door, choked on the lack of air, and stumbled backwards into the habitable zone.

The Bellows flashed hundreds of colors.

You're alive I almost did not believe what the others were saying you managed to rig a portable machine nobody else had claws able to cut the islandflesh

The two Relians gestured flamboyantly, trying to yell. *What is happening?!*

I do not know but they have killed many of the people in the shelters we only now noticed and managed to bring a few out and hold them in our homes until the portals can take them away but they are miserable

Hold them in your homes, Deka and Kylac signed. *How?*

The same as you did here by rigging atmosphere machines outside and keeping them huddled it is fortunate you could as we would not have reached you in time we did not even know this was happening until someone broke through the door and ran to the surface suffocating

How many are left? Deka signed.

Eighteen shelters about a hundred people they are scattered across multiple homes on the separate islands half are oxygen breathers only twelve breathe methane and thirty are nitrogen

Deka considered that for a moment, then signed. *The plan has not changed. Both Kylac and I can calculate two portals at once, but now I will not open ways to the shelters. I will open a portal on the center of each island. We will help guide everyone to it.*

As Deka signed, Kylac also signed. *We will need a place to hold the nitrogen and methane breathers. Have atmosphere machines ready in your homes on this island and be ready to take them there. Find more oxygen machines and bring them here. We will be bringing more people to this shelter.*

They finished in unison. The Bellows flashed in agreement. *I will inform everyone thank you and I am so relieved you are alive*

The Bellows floated up through the hatch, which closed behind it. Deka and Kylac crouched low, where the air was better. Deka spoke to the insects. Kylac spoke to the Gelleens.

"Here's what we're doing. We are about to leave shortly to pick up the others. We are bringing everyone to this island. Stay here until we return."

They both spoke to the Emrims.

"What about the other shelters?" asked one of the insects.

Deka answered them. "They were all destroyed. Apparently I am the only offworlder with claws that can cut the plant matter."

The canines held their bodies low. They smelled horrified.

"We will be back shortly," Kylac announced.

"Ready," Deka said, in Relian.

In the center of the shelter, a single point expanded to the height of a Relian. The sphere was wavy but stable, and imprinted on its surface was a hilly landscape made entirely of thick plantflesh. Blue and red particles sped by it. Deka had made sure the portal had no spin so the atmosphere bent around the hole in spacetime and nothing leaked into the shelter.

Bellows and Wings on the other side noticed the portal, flashed happy colors, and glided or floated away. Deka and Kylac waited a few moments, and then those same figures returned holding atmosphere machines.

The Relians jumped through the portal and dug their claws into the spongy surface to hold fast. A Wing walked up to them and handed them a machine. Kylac took it, passed one pipe to Deka, and shoved the other into his own muzzle. They ran across the surface, holding the machine between them.

Lightning streaked just above the island, arced around it, below it, and joined up with the lightning above again. Electricity never struck the islands themselves, so everyone on them was safe. The glass tube encircling the island was visible, distant as it was through the dense gas.

The surface platform had dips and hills all along it. Panes of glass had been embedded in some of the hills, some even on the ground itself, and the Relians had to hop over them. Atmosphere machines were perched everywhere, all of them embedded into the soil.

The Wings and Bellows led them through the winding valleys between the hills, where the wind was less violent. It was difficult enough to see with the wind blowing as hard as it was, let alone do much of anything else. Kylac ran with his eyes closed most of the time, holding onto Deka and the glass box that coughed out breathable air. His skin burned, and Deka noticed the wind was tearing fur off his body. Deka's scales were on fire.

Finally they reached a large hole in the ground leading straight down through the entire island. They saw the surface of the planet through it, swirling blue and red clouds appearing like continents against an ocean far below. A band of yellow clouds traveled left on one layer, and a red and brown band flowed to the right. Storms raged within these layers. Wisps of gas sped below, and some curved upwards and coughed out of the hole.

Many openings lined the wall of the shaft. Deka and Kylac looked at their guides. They could not gesture disapproval, but the Bellows and Wings were leading them to a smaller hole in the ground just a little distance away.

They followed. This hole in the ground had been recently carved, as the plant matter was white instead of brown. This was the living component of the island, the part the Wings and Bellows actually ate. The path sloped downward. As soon as their heads were below the surface, the air stopped. The pain stopped. Deka's scales still burned, and so did Kylac's skin. Now the machine stopped, so they held their breath, hoping relief was nearby.

They descended farther and then emerged into a small cavity, one of a network of chambers cut into the island's interior. Only the top two-thirds of the island was habitable though. The bottom third was where the plant stored the concentrated gasses that kept it afloat. Offworlders were never meant to be here; that slope they descended had been hastily carved to save the offworlders stranded here.

Huddled by a wall, sharing five small pipes between twenty people of seventeen different species, were the survivors of this island's shelter. Quadrupeds, bipeds, tripeds, reptiles, insects, mammals—a cross section of the variety of life among oxygen-breathers in the contacted universe. The Relians moved to the pipes and took several breaths until they were able to speak.

"We are Archeons taking you home. Follow us." They repeated it in all fifteen languages. Their voices sounded strange in this atmosphere, weak and high-pitched.

The survivors were reluctant to leave this wall, but at last four broke away. Kylac stopped a fifth; they were full for this trip. Deka and the Wings and Bellows led them outside and to the portal. Kylac stayed with the others, sharing the pipes.

He wished he could smell the bipedal felines from Naahe, and Kylac wondered if there was any way to convince them to let him mount them. He wondered what sex would be like here, surrounded by a poison atmosphere, but he remembered some people needed to be in the right mood and environment to mate, so this was not a good time to try.

Moments later, Deka returned with their guides. Kylac took one last breath and stepped to him, taking the machine from his hand. Four more people joined him, each holding a pipe to their mouth, and Kylac led them out of the tunnel and into the unending storm.

As he walked, he gestured: *I do not need a guide now. Go to the other islands with survivors. Find more atmosphere machines and have them ready.*

The Wing spread its arms, and it sailed up hundreds of paces in a single breath before turning and flying off. The Bellows inflated and propelled itself away.

Kylac walked alone with the survivors. He wished he could talk to them, but sound was useless here. He was glad they trusted him. Finally the portal was in sight. He picked up the pace, forcing the others to keep up. Kylac took the pipes from them as they dove through. Then Kylac poked his head through the portal himself. The exterior wall was now full of atmosphere machines, pipes hanging from them. The Bellows and Wings had been quick to install new machines in here, and Kylac calculated they could provide enough air for twice the number of people that would fit in the shelter.

He withdrew, slipped a pipe into his mouth, and walked as fast as he could through the valleys.

Guiding the remaining survivors was agonizingly slow. Deka and Kylac wanted to ask where the other machines were, but figured they were all in use or destroyed.

Kylac returned from the last group, and now only four survivors remained. Without a need to say it, the Relians agreed to share a pipe.

They emerged on the surface and navigated the twisting valleys. Deka dreaded doing this seventeen more times, but hopefully the other islands would be better prepared for what they had to do.

A Bellows drifted with the wind and kept pace with them. Kylac turned to it. He signed hello but could say little beyond that. The Bellows remained silent. Visual silence was even more noticeable than audible silence.

The Bellows propelled itself straight into them, opened its mouth and grabbed the machine. Kylac gripped it harder, and the two others held it tight and glared at the Bellows. No colors flashed or glowed on its ridge. Deka tried to sign something, but the Bellows propelled itself backwards, yanking the machine from everyone's hands.

The Bellows spun around and flung the machine out. It sailed away and crashed on the soil, shattering to pieces.

The Bellows was still silent. It floated away and dove into the shaft. Deka gathered everyone up and led them to the portal. Everyone was choking and trying to hold their breath, but the wind stole everything from their lungs. Kylac scrambled along the surface to the bipedal canine who collapsed. He helped her to her paws, turned her around, and walked her to the portal.

Deka was guiding the others, and they quickly became dead creatures walking. One collapsed on the ground. Then another, only a few paces from the portal. Deka was starting to lose his mind as well, but he held onto the third person. Kylac held onto the canine and forced her to walk with him.

Lightning streaked overhead, the sound of thunder lost in the constant roar. The portal was just a few paces away —Kylac could see the safety of the other side. He forced his legs to move even though he didn't feel as though he were moving at all.

Deka and one survivor stepped through the sphere. Kylac saw the unconscious reptile and another canine on the soft ground, battered by the poison wind, but had to walk past. His padded feet moved agonizingly slow across the ground. The canine hung from him uselessly.

Kylac swayed with the wind. He wasn't pushing past it anymore, but was being blown around by it. He accidentally inhaled. His breath caught. His mind froze up. He leaned forward and fell through the portal, taking the canine with him. Suddenly his lungs caught air, and he choked.

Deka had caught his breath, and he ran through the portal out into the burning atmosphere. He stopped at the reptile, crouched, nuzzled his head under his body, then wiggled his neck and back under him. He pushed his legs up and lifted the body easily, turned around and leaped through the portal. Deka dropped the reptile on the floor, and then dove back into the sphere.

Others had revived the unconscious survivors. Kylac rose to his paws, gasping for air. Moments later, Deka returned with the last survivor. Instantly he was surrounded by two other canines of the same species, and they began reviving him.

Deka now dropped to his knees, wheezing. He looked at his arms, down his flanks. Blood seeped between nearly every scale. He turned to his fox. Kylac was no better. More of his fur was missing, and he was bleeding from random places on his arms and torso as well. The three Gelleens surrounded Kylac and licked his wounds. Deka rubbed his claws, taking in the caring, parental scent of Gelleens.

Kylac's tail wagged, and his ears bloomed. "One island down! Seventeen more to go!"

Deka scraped his hand-claws together, laughing harder now. The portal closed. "I'm calculating the next island... How are you with yours?"

"Still a couple days away." He collapsed on the ground, sank in. "At this rate, I'll be ready just in time!" His tail waved about between his legs as the Gelleens cleaned him. Kylac scented them and licked their muzzles in thanks.

Deka surveyed the survivors in the shelter. "So how is everyone?" he said in fifteen languages one after another without pausing to breathe.

2

The oxygen-breathers were the easy ones. Everyone shared a machine between them, ran to the portal, and breathed easy once inside the shelter. The previous five islands had been routine, and Deka and Kylac were becoming used to the violent weather even as it eroded their skin.

Forty-seven people now huddled in the shelter. It was cramped, but they were alive. Some knew each other's languages, and Deka and Kylac heard more and more friendly chatter every time they came back with another group.

Deka tried to speed up the calculations, and on any other world he might have been able to open new ways rapidly, but Lesa was no easy world to create a portal. The islands were always moving, sometimes at different altitudes and in different directions around the planet. Creating portals that moved with the islands was tricky, which was why Deka did not even attempt to make a way of his own to this world until he was an experienced Archeon.

He found a predictable pattern and opened a new way into the center of the shelter. The others paused, glanced at it, and took a moment to be thankful they weren't out in that anymore.

Kylac stood and picked up one of the machines they had salvaged from the previous island. Deka picked up another. They had been told this island had been for methane-breathers, and he hoped the Lesans had atmosphere machines for them. They leaped through opposite sides of the sphere together and emerged on the seventh island. Many Wings and Bellows had crowded together on one side. Kylac walked around the sphere and met Deka, and they breathed from the pipes as the air tried to sweep them off their feet.

Just as they were beginning to wonder where the survivors were, the commotion on the other side of the island migrated toward them. The Wings and Bellows floated and glided on one side of a group of eleven survivors. The thick-skinned bipeds had two machines between them. The Lesans had formed a moving wall in the air, blocking most of the wind. Kylac's tail wagged. Deka held his claws together. Word of their plan had finally gotten around, and evacuating the people would be much quicker now.

With the Lesans blocking the force of the stormy atmosphere, the methane-breathers made fast progress across the surface. In moments, they had reached the Relians and were through the portal. The Lesans glowed and flashed many colors at once.

Deka and Kylac signed thanks, and then stepped back through the sphere themselves, relieved not to have to endure multiple treks across another island. The way closed behind them as Deka let the equations go.

The methane breathers smelled surprised to be in a shelter without breathable air. They turned and glared at the Archeons. They were bipeds, standing about as high as Deka at the shoulder. They had no fur or scales, but thick skin meant to protect them from acid rain. Four species from two different worlds. They spoke each other's language, so they wouldn't need translation.

"They have another shelter for you," Kylac said in their language. "Hold on for one moment."

Kylac pushed his way through the people and stood in view of the door. The Bellows floating outside noticed, and floated higher, more alert now.

Methane-breathers! Kylac signed. *Are you ready?*

The Bellows flashed two colors. *We are*

Good, Kylac signed. *Take them. Be ready for more soon.*

The glass door opened. Kylac beckoned the group to go with them, and they followed the Bellows, lungs nearly at breaking point. When the last one was through, the glass door shut, the top hatch opened, and the offworlders followed the Bellows up the walkway. Their machine switched back on, and they took a moment to breathe again as the hatch closed.

The fox turned and scanned the room. He caught many scents, and most everyone here excited him. He was in the mood for a female, and he scented the air for a species that was not monogamous. His nose pointed him toward a Temteh female, a bipedal creature on the other side of the room. They had picked her up from the second island. She smelled nice then, and Kylac wondered if he could convince her to let him mount her. He started to move toward her, but then he smelled something else, halted, and turned to the Gelleens.

The room was too crowded, and their hormones were rising. The scales on their necks were hot—the shelter was moments away from a territorial outburst. Kylac changed course and pushed through straight for the Gelleens. The dominant male had resumed that role, keeping the others down. As soon as Kylac came near, he lunged forward and knocked the fox down to the ground on his back. Kylac enjoyed being face to face with a partner. So few species mated this way. As the Gelleen penetrated Kylac, the fox promised to himself he would visit their planet and meet them under better circumstances.

Meanwhile Deka sat and meditated on the next island. He waited for the Gelleens to finish with Kylac before completing the calculations. He scraped his claws together as he pondered this was what the Gelleens were without their companion species: at the mercy of their territorial nature, easily tossed about by the chemicals in their bodies. They were not unlike a fox without a raptor, and Deka felt a twinge of pride for keeping Kylac from becoming like that for all these years.

Deka smelled Rawoc sitting next to him, her mate beside her. "He is very good with the Gelleens," she said.

Deka rubbed his claws together. "He is good with everybody."

"I admire him."

"Why is that?"

"He can do something about all of this. So can you. I... I can't do anything. I couldn't help you and Kylac move the glass box. I don't even have thumbs. I feel so helpless. I wish I could do something to help."

"So do I," said her mate. It had been the first time he had spoken. "I've... I'm so scared I can't think."

Deka rubbed his claws together gently. "This took everyone by surprise. All we can do is survive."

Rawoc snorted. "I still wish I could help. I hate being useless."

Deka held his claws still. "Both of you survived for days in a room with three territorial Gelleens. You must have done something right."

The Gelleens had not taken long, and now Kylac stood, fur matted, panting. Several people from multiple species thanked Kylac for keeping the Gelleens calm. Kylac navigated through the people, grabbed a cube from the wall, and tossed it into his mouth. He took an extra one and tossed it over nineteen people's heads at Deka. The theropod caught it in his mouth, swallowed it whole. It didn't satisfy Deka's hunting drive, but these things kept him alive for now.

The raptor stood and faced Rawoc again. "Stay calm. Help the others stay calm as well. We're almost ready."

Deka completed the calculations and opened the way. Kylac picked up their machine and hopped through, and Deka followed.

The wind was not easier to tolerate. It only became more and more painful. Bellows and Wings had seen the portal open and were gliding and floating away. The two Relians held still, hoping they wouldn't have to walk across the island again.

Moments later, a small group of nitrogen-breathing survivors emerged from a ditch cut in the ground. Nine survivors carrying two atmosphere machines between them, all running toward the portal, and above them flew a moving cluster of Lesans.

Two Wings and two Bellows dove into the cluster. They caught Deka's eye because their ridges were colorless. Deka took off running, yanking Kylac by the pipe in his hand. Then the fox saw it, too, and he kept pace with Deka, trying to sign a warning, but nobody was watching them.

The silent Bellows and Wings descended on the survivors. The Bellows grabbed one of the atmosphere machines in its jaws and inflated its body. It ascended with four bipeds and two quadrupeds clutching the glass box.

The Wing landed on the other machine and grabbed it with the fingers sticking out the top of its wings. It unfolded its wings and blew upwards, but it wasn't strong enough to carry it up and away.

People let go of the pipes, which flailed around wildly as they struggled to hold onto the machines. Deka and Kylac reached them. The raptor veered left to help the group with the Bellows. The fox veered right to take the Wing.

Deka took one last breath, let go of his pipe, and leaped through the air. He jumped twice his height and landed on the Bellows. His feet came up automatically, killing claws raised, and they slashed downward. The Bellows fell, and so did the machine and the people holding onto it.

Meanwhile Kylac took two of the pipes from his machine, held them up, and rammed the Wing, spraying it with a cloud of oxygen. The Wing flashed colors of pain and let go of the box. The diminished wind caught it and flipped it over and over the surface until it vanished behind a hill.

The large flock of Lesans only just now noticed what was happening, and some glided in closer to help, but it was too late.

Kylac carried the machine over to where Deka had fallen. The survivors huddled around him, sharing their pipes, not sure what to do for the raptor. Kylac shoved a pipe down his muzzle, and Deka came to life instantly. He held the pipe and climbed to his feet. One of his killing claws had yellow blood on it.

The injured Bellows floated up and out of sight. Deka watched it, then turned to the survivors and led them to the portal. The force of the air was less on the lee side of the cluster, but still enough to power the machines. It was much easier and less painful to walk on the surface now.

They reached the portal and sent the survivors through. Once the last person had gone through, Deka looked back at the cluster and signed.

Who were they?

Colors flashed everywhere, and Deka and Kylac took in all the soundless voices. Nobody knew. The Archeons gestured thanks and stepped through the wobbly sphere.

This time Deka ran to the door as the way closed. It was already open, and the nitrogen-breathers were already moving out of the shelter. Moments later, the door closed, and another group of survivors was on the way to safety.

"What's going on? Kylac, we're Archeons! We're supposed to recognize patterns instantly, so why can't I figure out who those people are and—"

"—why they attacked us?!" Kylac finished to fill the silent gap Deka left when he gasped for air. "That's the fourth time we've been attacked! Who are they? Why won't they talk to us?! This should be obvious, but I can't think either!"

Kylac coughed and gasped. Their outburst had quieted everyone in the shelter. Most did not understand, but they knew anger when they heard and smelled it.

The Relians took deep breaths. Their bodies ached from being exposed just that short amount of time, and Kylac was bleeding again. The Gelleens surrounded him and cleaned his wounds. Deka sat down and was prepared to bleed alone as usual, but then he felt a couple tongues on his scales as well. Rawoc and her mate sat to either side of him, licking the blood seeping between his damaged scales.

"Thank you," he said, still panting and wincing at the burns. Their tongues felt so good.

3

Deka opened the way. Kylac picked up the box and hopped through, the raptor following just behind. This was the tenth island. The people on the island had seen the portal and had already started gathering the survivors from the improvised hiding place, twenty of them, all methane-breathers, carrying three machines between them, everyone trading pipes. A cluster formed to shield them from the corrosive wind, and they were moving fast across the landscape.

Another group flew and floated in against the wind, a group as large as the one on the island protecting the survivors. They dove into the survivors and went for the three machines they carried.

The Wings and Bellows shielding the survivors broke formation and dove in to push the attackers out of the way. They flashed all sorts of colors at them, but the attackers remained silent.

The Archeons dashed across the surface. Five Bellows and two Wings were trying to snatch away one machine. The bipeds in the group held onto their glass boxes with their hands and beaks.

Above, Wings and Bellows dove and rammed into each other, with the speaking ones trying to keep the silent ones away from the survivors. Kylac dropped their air machine in the middle of the group, jumped and threw his body into one of the Wings trying to pull the machine away. Painful colors flashed across its ridge, and it let go, but two more rushed in.

Deka slashed with his hands at the creatures trying to take another machine away. He caught one Wing down the back. It fell out of the sky and landed on the ground, still silent but moving.

When Deka landed, he turned around, picked up the pipe, and took a breath. Then he ran a few paces away toward the flock of Wings and Bellows at the third machine. Various winged creatures were holding onto it with their beaks as silent attackers tried to pry it away from them.

Meanwhile two Bellows plowed into Kylac, knocking his only breath from his lungs, and lay on top of him, pushing themselves tight on his chest. Kylac raised a paw and raked his dull claws across their faces. After three swipes he shoved them off, and they rolled into the group of survivors. One of the scaly felines kicked them aside as she fought off two other attackers.

Kylac rolled, found his box, grabbed a pipe, and took a breath. He crouched and leaped into the air, grabbing a Bellows that had its mouth attached to the air machine's handle. He squeezed the gas out of it, and as it deflated, they both fell to the ground. Kylac tossed it aside.

A Wing slammed into his chest, rolling him over, and teeth clamped down on his muzzle. The fox slammed into the legs of another feline, and she clawed and bit the Wing until it let go. The Wing soared up with the wind and then dove back down at the machine resting on the ground—Kylac's machine.

On the other side of the group, Deka leaped at the silent cluster, swiping his hand-claws at the creatures trying to take the third machine. As they let go, other Lesans attacked them, flashing all sorts of colors asking the questions Deka could not. *What are you doing? Who are you? Why are you attacking them? Let them go home!*

Deka landed, vision blurry, mind light and empty. One of the birdlike survivors offered him a pipe. Deka shoved it away, flipped over, and ran to the other side of the group to his box. Kylac was guarding it, swiping at several silent

Wings who were trying to land on it. Deka dashed head-long into the caustic wind, claws out, and ran one of the Wings through. The Wing flashed a single color, went limp, and blew away. Deka picked up a pipe and took a few breaths. Kylac leaped and clamped his jaws around one of the Bellows. When it deflated, Kylac released it and let the wind decide what to do with it.

Meanwhile, above, the flock of friendly Lesans had overwhelmed the attackers. The silent ones were scattering. When the attackers were gone, the Relians grabbed their box, stuck the pipes into their mouths, and ran to the portal, feeling the full force of the planet's violent atmosphere, looking back only once to make sure the others were following.

They reached the portal and dove inside. The others followed, and a Bellows gathered them up and took them to their shelter.

Deka began calculating the new portal. The two Emrims cleaned his wounds. Others also cleaned his wounds. The survivors left Kylac to the Gelleens, who huddled around the fallen canine, grooming his fur and licking the bleeding patches of exposed skin.

4

Island number seventeen. The fighting had started before Deka and Kylac arrived, and it seemed the entire population of the planet had gathered. There were more Wings and Bellows in the air than could safely perch on the surface, and they soared ahead, dodging lightning streaks, crashing into one another, struggling, separating, ramming into someone else again.

Below the battle, the two Relians guided the last three survivors out. These were nitrogen-breathers, quadrupeds covered in both scales and fur. Many silent Lesans tried to attack them, but the flock of friendly Wings and Bellows kept them distracted.

They reached the portal, led everyone inside, and jumped through. Deka closed it behind them.

When the nitrogen-breathers were safely out of the shelter, the Relians lay down, panting and wheezing and aching all over. The Gelleens were all over the fox. Their protective instinct had risen to an extreme without their companion species to keep them in balance. Kylac was sure they really did believe he was carrying their eggs.

"Good news," the canine announced as the three lizards licked the many holes in his skin. "I'm almost done making ways to Jiniv and Kexi."

"It's about time, Kylac." The theropod rubbed his claws together. The Emrims were cleaning him off again, as were several others in the shelter. "I'm ready with Selta."

Deka opened the way just off center in the shelter. The others in the room looked through it at the beautiful world full of breathable air and four-legged felines with saber teeth. Everyone collectively faced the fox.

"We'll meet you there," Kylac said.

Kylac repeated himself in every language in the shelter, but he didn't have to. Once a few jumped in, the others followed. Finally it was down to their original group: the Gelleens, the insects, and the Emrims. The insects gestured thanks and stepped through. The Gelleens were reluctant to leave Kylac. The fox smelled why, and his tail wagged wildly.

Kylac spoke in their language. "I can't lay eggs."

It seemed to remind them to think rationally. They stood, bared their throats, and jumped through. The fox's tail slowed to a gentle twitching. Gelleens never showed their throats to anyone but the dominant male. He hoped their planet had not suffered after the disaster.

The two Emrims backed away from Deka, turned, and hopped through. On the other side, felines overwhelmed the refugees with examinations. They would receive full treatment.

"I'm a few more cycles away from the other two planets," Kylac said.

Deka didn't reply. He sprawled out on his back and just enjoyed breathing for a while. He was bruised, his scales burned, and breathing hurt. Kylac scooted over to him and rubbed Deka's neck up and down with his muzzle.

Deka reached up and felt Kylac's muzzle. A quarter of his fox's fur was missing, and his bare skin, normally a healthy pink, was now raw.

They heard a scraping, tapping sound through the tubes connected to the wall. They leaped to their feet. Deka turned to the pane, wound up, and kicked the glass out. Poisonous air blew in and threw Deka across the room. He smacked against the shelves, sending the few remaining food cubes flying.

Kylac ran up to the hole in the wall, reached down and snatched the Wing as it had been pulling one of the atmosphere boxes out of its cavity. It flapped and struggled in Kylac's grip, but the fox held on with both hands, though he felt himself sliding out of the opening as the wind caught the flailing Wing.

Scaly hands clamped around Kylac's waist and yanked him back inside. Deka fell backwards. Kylac landed on top of him. He tossed the Wing over his head, and it slammed into the wall. The fox rolled off Deka, stumbled over to the Wing, and held it down with one paw. A breath later, Deka's hand pinned the other side of the Wing down.

Deka only had one hand with which to make gestures. So did Kylac. Together they signed complete sentences.

Who are you? Why are you attacking us?

Visual silence.

Answer us!

The Wing now seemed to be giving attention. Finally the first flickers of color appeared on its ridge.

Machines so many machines they are everywhere

Deka and Kylac pressed for more. *Why are you attacking?*

It is the machines they put these people in harm everyone would be fine if these machines had never been there if we did not decide to pander to offworlders ever since the machines came we have done nothing but keep them going all for them

Deka and Kylac glanced at each other.

"Of course..." Deka said. "Why didn't we think of this? Why didn't we notice?"

"A lot of information is slipping past us. Too much."

They turned back to the creature and signed together.

Tell them to stop. Let us take these people home. You can decide later—

The Wing began glowing before they finished. *No the others want offworlders but that is all we do make the machines remake them what about what we want what about us I think the burden is not worth my life and so do many others we want to keep relations with other gas giants and we want to stop living to keep the machines going return to the way things used to be no more machines no more living like this*

The air was getting thin. Deka released the Wing. Kylac released the Wing as well. They gestured separately now.

Leave.

The Wing stood, hobbled over to the opening, and blew away. The Relians turned and faced the Bellows waiting by the door. It began glowing.

They had been complaining about it for years how their lives had become little more than maintaining the devices to keep offworlders safe and to trade with other planets they did not want it anymore and pushed for a return to the old life we never expected them to destroy it by force the disaster made them desperate

The raptor and the fox panted and wheezed as the poison gas blew around the room. They exchanged a glance while the Bellows spoke. They each felt the same thing: regret for not figuring it out sooner. It hadn't been merely an oversight, but a gap in their Archeon perception of reality that correlated to their inability to hold spheres open for long durations. It could be a symptom that the destruction of Rel had harmed them deeper than they realized.

Deka turned fully to the Bellows and signed: *Keep them away from us. They know which island the portals lead to. We only have one more island to visit and everyone will be here.*

Kylac added: *I am close to opening ways to Kexi and Jiniv. Keep everyone safe until I can.*

Deka opened a new way right next to Kylac's. It showed the surface of yet another island. An enormous battle was happening on and over the surface, and perhaps below as well.

The Bellows glowed gently. *I am sorry*

Work this out, Deka signed. *Get everyone together and decide how you want to continue. This happens to every planet that tries to do what you did.*

Kylac picked up where Deka left off. *All cultures who try using machines discover their lives become centered around them. When your Archeon wakes up, find out how they dealt with it. Learn from them.*

The Bellows was silent for a beat, then glowed white around the ridge.

Deka turned and stepped through the sphere. Kylac picked up the atmosphere box and followed.

There were so many Lesans they blocked most of the stormy air without even trying. Below, scattered about in small groups, were the survivors. Large groups of Lesans huddled over them, shielding them from the silent attackers. Word must have gotten around that this was the last island, so everyone had come here.

Wings and Bellows dropped from the sky and dove at the refugees, reaching for their machines. Friendly Lesans collided with them, and they twirled around each other as they fought in midair. The battle was silent—the unceasing wind took all noise away, but it was full of color.

The Lesans noticed the two Archeons at the center of the island, and they began to glow and flash colors. They nudged the methane-breathers toward the unstable sphere in the distance.

Most of them were quadrupeds covered in thick armor plating. Not very mobile, but durable. The corrosive atmosphere probably didn't even tickle them. Kylac envied them right now. He felt as if he had been eaten to the bone.

The crucible of silent and shouting Lesans swarmed closer and closer to the Relians. Deka and Kylac watched, eyes on the refugees. Just standing in the open was painful, and neither Deka nor Kylac wanted to move.

The cloud engulfed the Relians. The refugees reached the portal and jumped through. Deka and Kylac turned and leaped through it as well, gasping into their pipes. There was no air in the shelter they could breathe anymore, so this box was all they had. Deka closed the portal, and they walked to the wall and breathed the precious air coming from hoses attached to the permanent devices outside. Kylac licked Deka's wounds between breaths. Deka licked Kylac's.

They noticed color from the other side of the shelter.

Are you ready, said the Bellows. *The angry ones are almost here*

Kylac winced as Deka's tongue scraped an open sore across his stomach. He gestured with one hand. *Almost. Keep ... safe.*

The Bellows glowed. *Hurry*

It floated up through the hatch, leaving it open this time.

They waited a few breaths, licking each other's wounds. They were bleeding from everywhere, it seemed. Kylac's fur was so mottled he looked diseased. Deka's scales had changed from bluish-black to red. Everything hurt, especially their lungs.

Deka licked Kylac's neck, working some blood out of the fur. Finally Kylac spoke.

"Ready."

They stood, gripped their machine, and walked to the door. Flapping noises came from the opening in the wall, and the Relians stopped and looked back. Two Wings had burst through it, and they dove straight for the Archeons. Some clumsily sailed through and into the wavering portal to Selta.

Deka and Kylac turned around, opened the glass door, and ran out into the tube that ringed the island. When the air touched them, the pain only made them feel more numb.

All around them, silent Bellows and Wings scratched at the glass, breaking pieces off and tossing them away. The Archeons raced with the wind at their tails around the tube until they reached the hole, and they stepped out into the acidic atmosphere.

The island was covered in Lesans, all biting and colliding and breaking off and soaring backwards and colliding with someone else. The friendly ones were trying to keep the silent attackers off the surface.

Kylac stood still in the middle of the island and concentrated as he held a pipe in his mouth. He let the equations return changing values and then fed those answers into more equations. The equations were not math anymore, but the feeling of the universe between his fingers.

Meanwhile Deka jumped around Kylac, swiping at anyone who came near the fox. The wind blew large drops of blood off Deka's body. About fifty paces away, Wings and Bellows led survivors from a hole in the ground. The methane-breathers.

A Bellows landed on the machine. Deka kicked it off. A Wing landed on Deka. He dropped to the ground, rolled over it, and it did not cling to him. He jumped to his feet, then jumped at the air and swatted a Bellows away. He landed, picked up a pipe and took a few deep breaths, then stood guard again.

Kylac felt a connection between two points in the universe form, and the way opened to a view of Kexi's yellow skies. Kylac turned around and concentrated on the other sets of equations he had pondered in the back of his mind. More variables. More changing patterns.

Four Wings landed on Deka. One landed on the machine. Deka kicked the Wing off the box, reached behind his head, and slashed one of the Wings off his neck. Others were chewing on his back.

Friendly Bellows descended on him, and they bit and chomped the attackers. Everyone quickly fell off Deka and became carried up into the battle overhead.

The second way opened, and Jiniv stared back at them through it.

By now all the refugees were on the surface. They shared tubes from glass boxes they carried as they ran underneath the battle.

Five Wings landed on Deka. Five Bellows landed on Kylac. Ten of each landed on their atmosphere machine and carried it away, dropped it off the edge of the island,

and disappeared into the swarm. The Relians swiped and clawed their attackers off themselves.

Refugees knew which portal led to which world, and they poured through. The silent Lesans grabbed their machines, but nobody fought them now. Wings and Bellows defended the raptor and the fox as the refugees poured through.

Kylac closed the ways as the last tails cleared the unstable spheres. He turned and ran. The tube had been shattered all the way around the island, and only a few shards of glass remained poking up from the ground. This was perfect—they didn't have to go around the tube to reach the shelter—it was now a straight run.

Deka could run much faster than Kylac, but he let his canine set the pace. By the time they reached the hatch, Kylac was delirious, his vision hazy around the edges and closing in fast. His lungs seized, but he kept his legs moving.

Deka was right behind him as they descended the ramp to the shelter. His vision was so hazy and he hurt so much he hoped he would die. His eyes would not focus, and his feet stumbled as he reeled from oxygen depletion. The portal before them wobbled and vibrated. Deka strained to hold the equations.

Kylac lost his vision as he stumbled through the sphere.

Deka collapsed just inside the door.

The onlookers through the portal to Selta peered inside, hesitating for several breaths. Then the two Emrims leaped through, fur billowing in the corrosive wind, grabbed Deka's wrists in their jaws, and dragged him closer to the portal. Insect talons reached out of the portal and took their hind legs in a predatory embrace, and together they pulled Deka through the sphere just before it winked shut.

Kylac breathed. Deka breathed. Their vision did not come back right away, but they breathed.

Hithe

Deka and Kylac stepped through the portal and stood on a stone causeway. The portal was not as wavy and unstable as the previous spheres Kylac had opened, which was a good sign the damage the disaster had done to their brains would not be permanent. The way closed behind them.

It was just before dawn, and they observed the black rock on which they stood. The surface of the platform was fifteen paces wide and almost a thousand paces above the ground. The causeway ran, unbroken, over much of the southern continent plus a good deal of the surrounding ocean. It was not natural—it had been deliberately grown over many generations. They scented the air, but the causeways were just as deserted as they appeared.

Kylac walked to the raised lip that ran along the edge. It came up to just below the canine's waist, a barrier of rock meant to keep everyone from falling off the platform. He peered down. Deka joined him at his side a moment later. Below them they could see the reason for the causeways. The hub had been positioned over the ocean. The water beneath was on fire.

Deka turned from the ledge and walked up the road, eyes on the rock. The surface was like glass, just the way the Ven liked it. The road felt just as good as Deka remembered. Smooth but not slippery.

"Deka," Kylac called.

The raptor smelled Kylac farther back, not keeping up with him. Deka kept walking just to feel the stone under his feet.

"Deka, did you notice this?"

"What?"

Instead of walking, the theropod began sliding his feet across the surface, growling and shuddering. He had been here many times before, and he remembered the people were so mellow, so easygoing, barely a care. Deka knew why; he had scales, too, but he didn't crawl on his belly, so he only experienced a taste of it.

Deka snorted, walked down to his belly, and propelled himself across the stone with his feet. Deka growled so quietly he purred. He rolled and twisted his body around on the causeway, rubbing his claws together, trying to give every scale the privilege of touching the stone. He growled louder and louder.

"Deka, come here!"

Deka rolled to his back and faced the clouds. The best feeling was on his back—those scales never felt the ground, so they were especially sensitive to this. He hadn't felt this good since the last time he mounted Sonjaa after a kill.

"Deka, come smell this!" Kylac shouted in the distance.

Deka barely heard him. He kept looking at the clouds. The rising daytime star lit the clouds red on one side, and the smooth stone on his back felt better than sex.

A red canine face slid into his field of vision, ears folded back. "Get up."

Deka rubbed his claws together. "After Lesa, this is exactly what I needed."

Kylac's ears folded tighter against his head. "I told the Selts I should leave you behind."

"I should have made the portal from Lesa to here. Your skin was scaly enough to feel this, too!" Deka clicked his claws together, even his toe-claws.

Kylac grabbed the raptor's hand and dragged him across the avenue. Deka moaned and growled. All he could manage on his own were jerky strides across the stone, but this was one, smooth, long motion. Every scale on his back connected directly to the pleasure center of his brain. This was how the Ven felt all the time.

Suddenly the causeway lost its glassy polish, the slope angled downward, and ragged rock dragged across his back. Deka's breath caught mid-moan, and he rolled over and looked at what happened to the surface. Kylac had dragged him into a bowl depression in the rock.

"This should not be here," said the fox.

Deka looked out across the rest of the avenue. The causeway was covered in depressions like this, all of them where portals were supposed to be. Kylac was on all fours, scenting the unpolished hole they were in.

Deka bent down and scented it as well. "It happened here, too."

Kylac turned his muzzle up to him but did not rise to his hind legs. "Some of the portals expanded before they collapsed. They took huge chunks of rock with them."

"You think there's any danger to those worlds? Those could have been living pieces."

"The portals were nowhere near active rock." Kylac sniffed around in widening circles

"What are you scenting?"

"I'm trying to smell where the portal went."

"Portals don't leave a scent."

"I know, but they interacted with the land. Maybe they left a trace. The way must have doubled in size before closing."

"Maybe Ath lost control," Deka said. "Was it just the Ven species at risk?"

"Both." Kylac climbed out of the bowl. He rose to his hind feet only when he stood on the polished road again.

Deka crouched and leaped out, landing flat on his toes. He rubbed them on the surface, sinking lower and lower, growling in joy.

"Next time I'm leaving you behind," Kylac said.

Deka clicked his claws as he rubbed his feet back and forth on the polished rock.

"Ath is either dead or unconscious," Kylac said. "Barul probably is, too."

He looked around at the hub. Before the disaster, portals would have lined the sides of the causeway. Now it was empty, and in many places were bowls where the portals had intersected the rock and taken it somewhere else.

"Something's wrong," said the fox.

"Isn't that obvious? We should be up to our ankles in Ven by now."

"And what's that?" Kylac pointed with his muzzle at a distant spot on the causeway.

The road was supposed to be smooth and level. Now there were large dips in the surface, and a lump rose from one spot in the distance.

"These people like everything to be smooth," Kylac continued. "They would never let that happen."

"Have a closer scent. I'll be in there." Deka gestured with his muzzle to a smooth, cubic structure off the main avenue.

"I'll meet you there. If you even get that far." Tail wagging, Kylac turned around and trotted along the polished road toward the ragged lump.

Deka walked up the road normally at first. After a few steps, he began to walk by sliding his feet. His body lowered more and more until he lay on his belly. Deka had always wished to know how this felt to them. He knew how it felt for himself, but he had limbs and could not slither, so he had accepted he would never know exactly what the Ven felt.

He pushed himself along the causeway for a few paces, gave up, and rolled to his back. He lay with his stomach to the sky for a moment, wishing every planet had stone sculpted for scales, but that is what made Hithe so special.

The algae on the surface of this world produced a flammable gel that caught fire easily, an evolutionary quirk designed to kill competing species of algae and spread its spores. In time, the algae dominated the entire ocean. A mutation allowed a subspecies to survive on dry land, and it took over the ecosystem within a few generations.

Prior to that, there existed a species of bacteria that secreted solid rock as a waste product. At first the bacteria took years to produce a single pebble, but when the algae began to spread onto the land, the ancestors of the Ven and the Droden began to take refuge atop the growing rocks, where the algae could not reach.

For generations survival favored those Ven that could speed up and control the rock growth to construct platforms high enough to elevate themselves above the flames and noxious fumes. When the Ven became sentient, they had already guided the rock into grand avenues across a quarter of the continent, halfway up to the clouds.

They expertly sculpted the rock to be pleasant to slither upon, and species with scales came from all over the contacted universe to experience this. Nothing was funnier than a Krone rolling around on a causeway, laughing his wings off.

Deka suddenly realized Kylac would never bring him here again if he found him like this. Reluctantly, he rolled over and stood up, facing the hub. Arches reached up to the causeways and then connected with the ground, designed to elevate the people above the toxic, flaming environment but not disrupt the land below.

Deka noticed Kylac had already reached his destination.

The reptile turned and ran to the structure, tucking his arms in to pick up speed. Every step felt so good he wanted to run forever. Deka shook his head and forced himself to forget it for now.

Before him stood a communal building, one of hundreds sprinkled across the network of arches and avenues. Deka remembered from the last time he was here that there was a large pond on the roof with an aquifer leading to it, bringing pure rainwater from the mountains. The Ven and the Droden would sleep and eat in buildings like these. When they traveled, they would sleep and eat in another building, wherever they happened to be.

The entryway was large and inviting. It had stone doors, which were only closed during storms. Deka looked down at his feet. He could see his reflection running beneath himself. He growled, holding his hands together. This was the first time he had been able to run on these roads. Normally they were so clogged with slithering Ven and other reptilian offworlders there was barely any room to walk.

Deka wondered what it would be like with a running start. He realized this chance would never come again, and he would never forgive himself if he didn't take it.

"Just one more!"

He lifted his legs mid-stride, tucked them in, and rolled over. He landed on the floor and slid, spinning halfway around. The scales on the side of his body laughed and sang, and he sang with them straight through the doors.

"Ooooooooooooooooooooaaaaaaaaahhhhh!"

His back slammed into something, and his neck whipped around it. The air flew from his lungs and he gasped and groaned. Deka rolled over and stood before an enormous boulder sticking up from the middle of the floor. It filled two-thirds of the interior from floor to ceiling. His nose involuntarily took in the scent. The rock was alive. The boulder had grown up through the floor.

Deka walked around it, scenting it from all angles. Stone cracked and crumbled under his feet. This made no sense. There shouldn't be any active rock here, not in a communal space.

He walked around the boulder to the second entrance and observed the other side of the avenue. The road dropped off about fifty paces beyond the doors. Deka raced out the door, and then slid to a halt at the ledge.

The avenue ended in a jagged break thirty paces wide. On the other side, the causeway continued normally for another hundred paces and then broke off again. The arch structure supporting the road was still intact, but the rock was coarse and broken.

The causeways were little more than a series of broken islands supported by brittle arches reaching thousands of paces into the distance. Jagged platforms of rock seemed ready to fall in an instant.

A loud rumble crashed behind him. Deka turned around, dashed through the building, and veered around the boulder in the center of the room. He stopped at the open doors. The noise was coming from the distance, just opposite the hub.

2

Kylac doubted Deka would make it halfway to the communal building. He expected to find his raptor sprawled out in the middle of the road when he came back. It was annoying, but his tail waved at the thought. It was good to see Deka laughing again after everything they had been through.

Kylac stopped in front of an enormous lump of rock growing out of the avenue. It smelled alive, even from this distance. The smooth stone was buckled and heaving where the rock grew up through it. Hithe was so quiet Kylac could hear the stone growing.

The canine turned to his left. He saw several more avenues in the distance. He squinted. Some were broken, the edges covered in lumpy masses of rock just like the one blocking this avenue.

The fox felt something shift beneath his paws. He leaped back a few steps as the avenue groaned. The road cracked and shifted a little, and then all was still again except for the active rock. It was growing up to the sky and down to the ground as well.

He turned his muzzle right. More broken streets. More arches missing. More platforms fallen in and shattered. In the distance he saw a structure similar to the one Deka went to investigate. It was supposed to be perfectly cubed, filling up the avenue, but it was now a mass of lumpy, uneven rock. The walls were broken, and the ceiling rested, unsupported, atop a clump of stone. The rock had grown from the inside of the structure and pushed it apart. It was only a matter of time before the entire thing collapsed under the weight of the new rock above.

A loud rumbling came from behind Kylac. It was distant, but the fox felt it through his paws, so strong it felt as if it were coming from directly underneath. He turned to face the vibration.

Just visible through the atmospheric haze in the predawn light, an avenue had begun to buckle. The lump of stone had grown inside one of the arches, and the road above it had heaved upwards. Kylac walked to the raised lip for a better look.

The arch crumbled, and the boulder fell with the arch. The polished surface of the street fell in, smashed against the arch, and crashed through it. A thousand paces worth of street and support structure fell in pieces to the flaming ocean below. They made a splash so large they put out the fire for three hundred paces around them, but only for a few heartbeats; the algae would ignite again soon enough.

Hithe fell silent, with only the distant roar of flames below as background noise. Kylac turned to the lump of rock growing up through the causeway. It was larger than before. He took in his surroundings: the interlocking stone arches supporting causeways, the structures grown from those roads, the flames far, far below. Everything was covered in lumps of growing rock. Huge sections of causeway had fallen, leaving some pieces stranded in midair.

He heard scaly feet padding up the avenue, turned his head, and watched his raptor running up to him. Kylac's tail wagged. He was surprised Deka was able to move at all on rocks sculpted for reptilian pleasure.

Deka slid to a halt in front of his fox. "I think I'm in trouble."

Kylac smelled something wrong with the scales on his back. They looked wrong, as well. Instead of red against dark blue, now the scales on his back were black and raised. Rock was growing on his spine.

Kylac whined and the fur on his back stood on end. "How did *that* happen?!"

Deka backed away, tucking his claws in and curling his head closer to his body, a submissive gesture. Then he clicked his claws together in a bashful laugh as Hithe's parent star peeked over the horizon.

3

The raptor and the fox walked side by side down the causeway.

"All right," Kylac began. "We need to get down to the surface, both for your sake, and to find the people. The fumes inhibit the rock growth, and with the portals gone, everyone else likely went to the surface, too."

Deka already had a line of black rock half a claw's reach high growing down his back and neck. It itched, but he knew better than to touch it.

"Sure... Would they?"

"The portals go out, they wait calmly for a while, then they learn the Archeons are either dead or unconscious. They would migrate to the surface for food."

"How would they get to the surface?" Deka said. "They relied on the portals to make it down there."

"They were doing this long before they had portals to move around the continent. That's where we'll find them, and where we'll find help for you."

"Good." He raised his claw, almost scratching his back. He felt the weight already. "The Ven don't have this problem?"

Kylac glared at Deka, wagged his tail. "You're an Archeon, Deka! You know everything about every world except Hithe! How? How have you never even heard people talking about these things in passing? That's how I learned! Nobody ever told me directly! I just listened to the crowds—you were in those crowds, too!"

Deka rubbed his claws and bumped hips with his fox, knocking Kylac two paces sideways. Kylac teased him about this every time they came here.

"Comprehending these beautiful causeways takes more mental power than it seems. It tests the limits of an Archeon mind."

Kylac righted himself and bumped Deka back. "What, do you memorize the avenues?"

Deka stumbled but didn't miss a step. "Never know when a detailed mental map of the stone will be useful! You will never let me live it down!"

"Nobody else forgets how to be an Archeon on Hithe. Just you."

They laughed as they passed the branch to the structure Deka had investigated. Now they walked between the bowls in the road where the offworld portals had been.

"Enzymes in their scales prevent the bacteria from growing on their bodies," Kylac said. "They can touch it all they want and nothing will happen. Their saliva kills it, and that's how they control the rock growth. All we have to do is find one of them, and they'll kill the bacteria for you."

"What about the rock?"

"We'll have to pull it off. Probably take the top layer of scales with it."

Deka grumbled. "Hope you know a good place on the surface."

"I already started the calculations. Give me..." He turned his muzzle to the yellow star in the sky. Normally he did not have to think about how long a day lasted on a world compared to Rel, or how fast the star moved across the sky, but now the knowledge took time to reach his conscious mind. After a moment, he remembered a day on Hithe was only a quarter of Rel's. "About twenty degrees. I'll make sure to set us down near a farm."

Deka's back itched again. The rock was growing fast.

They stopped at a jagged ledge. The causeway had broken off here and dropped into the sea. The arch support structure that would have held up the next section of causeway was still standing, but the walking surface had fallen into the ocean. The road continued further on, but in isolated, broken fragments. Lumps of active rock grew on these pieces, which meant they, too, would collapse in time.

"So what happened here?"

"It's like this in all directions," said the raptor. "Probably the entire thing is broken and crumbling."

"It doesn't make sense. These people would never let this happen."

They stood on the ledge, taking it in from all directions. They were trapped here on this segment.

"I hope I didn't step in any rock." Kylac's ears folded back, and his tail curled between his legs.

Kylac bent down and scented the ledge. The unpolished rock was not active, and he sat with his legs dangling over the water. Deka could not sit this way, so he rested on his stomach a pace in front of the edge so his scales could be on the polished surface.

Deka whined, taking in the devastation. "This hurts to see."

"Me, too. Hithe's roads were so beautiful, and the way they were built... It's a wonderful story. No other world has this."

"And it's falling into the ocean."

A loud rumble and cracking sound came from the distance behind them. Kylac and Deka looked over their shoulders. Another section of road had given way under the weight of a mass of living rock. The boulder caved in the arch and tumbled to the water below, taking two sections of causeway with it.

Kylac waited until the sound faded before speaking.

"How long since the disaster?"

"No more than fifty Rel days."

"That's eighty-three days on this world. It took just eighty-three days without portals for all this to happen. Deka, this isn't just a disaster. This could be extinction.

They would have gone to the surface only for food, but they can't live there."

"Another planet with a toxic atmosphere."

"We can survive there if we avoid the fires, and I know which plants we can eat."

"What about me?"

"There are plenty of animals to hunt. Just stay away from the flames."

Deka almost scratched his back. Kylac noticed and looked at him. The black rock had only been a thin film running up his back and neck before. Now it had risen to a whole claw's reach high.

"You should see how much it's grown."

"I can feel it. It's scary. Hurry up and open a way."

"Soon." Kylac looked back out over the broken causeways crisscrossing the ocean. Every avenue was cut off either by breakage, or by living rock blocking the way. The breeze was light and warm up this far. The heat from the fire reached this altitude, but fumes stayed close to the planet's surface

"Remember the first time we came here?" Deka said. "Sixteen years ago."

"I should..." Kylac's ears folded back. "It's not there. I can't remember. I'm not used to my mind moving this slowly. I shouldn't have to think about these things consciously. I can't even remember how long it's been since the disaster."

"We were still children. Everyone kept telling me to visit Hithe. It was your idea to go. We had to hop twenty portals before we found a way. I was still a hatchling. I didn't want to go. You had to drag me through every portal. Then we got here, and as soon as we set foot on the causeway, you were bowled over by a couple hundred Ven! They slithered over you as if you were part of the road."

Kylac's tail waved. "Now I remember! Not just over me, but every part of me. Over my eyes, under my tail, everything on me was covered in them."

"They were all over me, too." Deka said. "I knew how they talked, but until then I had no idea what it meant."

"We were pinned under them so long I couldn't breathe."

"Then a couple Droden yanked us out and told us what the Ven were saying. They asked who we were, if we'd been here before."

"And they were covered in Ven as well. Confusing scent. The Ven were all I could smell. I thought they were controlling the Droden or something."

Deka rubbed his claws together. "I used what little I knew of the Droden language. Tried to tell them everyone told me I had to visit. They carried us down the street, around the corner." Deka turned to the structure in the distance, the one with the boulder that had infected him. "It was that place. He took us in there. Much less crowded." Deka paused, remembering, as he had to do when he was younger. Since he had become an Archeon, he hadn't needed to take time to recall a memory; it was always all there on the surface. "It was quiet, but I didn't know the Ven language back then. I missed everything they said. Both of the Droden who picked us up knew the Relian language. He put us down in there, and that's when I felt it at last."

"Your first taste of reptile paradise."

Deka rubbed his claws together. "Rolling around on that floor, Ven crawling all over me, but they weren't crushing that time, and the Droden translated for us."

"Couldn't get you to break away from Rel and have an adventure, but now that you were here you never wanted to leave. Never seen you so happy. Finally you calmed down, and that's when the Ven crawled on us again. Not as a single, writing river of scales, but a few at a time. Enough for us to handle without getting crushed."

"Once we learned how the Ven communicated, that writing river of limbless scales crawling on the road meant a whole lot more. Finally I understood them."

"Offworlders usually can't. It was wonderful to be part of the conversation that time." He looked at Deka, ears folded partially back. "But of course you just wanted to crawl around on the floor."

Deka clawed him lightly on the shoulder. "You get to have sex on every planet we visit. Let me have this one world."

Kylac would have pounced on him, but he noticed the rock on Deka's back had grown by another claw's reach. He looked inward and checked his calculations.

"It was all so beautiful," Deka continued. "People who communicate exclusively by touch. All of them slithering over and under each other. Like nerve cells—ideas move across the entire species, over an entire continent elevated above the ground, and the Droden are there, covered in them all the time, part of the flow, translating for off-worlders, bridging the gaps with voice." He chirped, crying. "Now it's crumbling. Everyone is gone."

Kylac took a few breaths, and then stood and backed a few steps away. Deka rose to his feet as well, bearing uncomfortable weight on his back and resisting the urge to scratch it.

Kylac bridged two points of spacetime and spread the hole wider. It held a spherical shape for a few moments, but then Kylac lost the feeling and it wobbled in place.

"Almost a stable sphere that time," Deka said. "A few more and we'll be recovered enough to make permanent ways again."

"If there's anything left of the contacted universe."

They went through and emerged on solid soil. Black pieces of rock that had broken off the platforms over thousands of years lay scattered about. The air reeked of flammable gas secreted by the algae. That combined with the fumes of the fires in the distance made the air noxious.

One of the old ramps stood before them. In the days before these people discovered portal physics, they had grown the rock into ramps leading up to the causeways. The animals they ate could not survive on the causeways in the sky, so the Droden maintained enormous farms on the surface and harvested animals year-round.

Before portal physics, the Droden were the hunters, and the Ven maintained the platforms and supporting arch structures. The Droden lived one year on the surface, tending their food supply, and then they were free to live on the causeways for one year, and so forth for their entire lives. The Ven had a similar routine with stone maintenance and construction.

Since they had discovered how to open spacetime spheres around their planet, these cycles had been eliminated. They could live on the causeways and return to the surface to eat instantly. With travel time negligible, the farms became self-maintaining. Everyone could come to the farms to eat at any time from anywhere on Hithe, and reaching sections of causeway that required mending did not take entire years. Portal physics had changed their culture, as it had on every world. It had freed the people of Hithe to develop their minds and explore the contacted universe as they pleased.

Being so close to the flames, the ramps needed constant maintenance. Though they were largely obsolete thanks to the portals, the Ven still mended them. Now the one in front of them was shattered and broken, fragments forming a broken incline to the platform high above.

Deka turned around. He wasn't as knowledgeable about this planet as his fox, but even he could tell when something was not as it should be.

"Kylac..."

The fox turned and faced where Deka stared. The farm was empty. No animals inside the chest-high stone enclosure. No Droden or Ven. The entire field was now covered in flaming algae.

4

"The good news," Kylac said, "is down here, the fumes slow the growth of the rock, so your back is safe for now. Instead of one day to complete immobility and crushing death, now you have twenty."

"I like good news."

"The bad news..." Kylac turned and scented around.

"Where is everyone?" Deka finished.

"This is the only place they could have gone. It's the only place they can find food. Why would they let it burn?"

Kylac was out of breath, and on the surface that was very easy to do. He panted. Deka rested a hand on his shoulder, lightly poking him with his claws.

"There were nine thousand people on this world. Someone is still alive. We'll walk around until we find them."

"Walk around? The continent is one eighth the surface area of Rel! Without the portals, we'll be walking for years!"

"Then that's what we'll do."

The raptor let go of the fox's shoulder, picked a direction that was not on fire, and started walking.

"Wait... Wait, Deka!"

He slowed, listened. The fox caught up and kept pace at Deka's side.

"The algae will grow back. We could be caught in the flames."

"Keep a way to the platforms in mind."

"Yes, but—" He ran a few steps to catch up with Deka. "I don't know where they would've gone! We could be out here for days, and there's almost nothing to eat."

"Then we'll have to survive here, just as they did."

"We don't know that anyone did."

"Someone is out there. We will find them."

Deka kept walking. Kylac stopped and stood still for a while, looking back at the flaming farm and the crumbling ramp. The ramp took his eyes upward, at the falling platforms. He turned, caught up to Deka, and walked by his side.

"We never visited the surface, did we?" Deka said.

"No. Never."

"Did they?"

"Just to feed and tend the farms. Sometimes the support arches would need mending, but otherwise never. Nobody wants to live down here."

They walked in silence for a while, taking in the part of Hithe few offworlders visited. Plants grew everywhere, most of them covered in green muck, a testament to how resilient life could be.

Various treelike plants surrounded them, all draped in algae. The trees had been scorched from being on fire repeatedly in their lifetimes, often for years at a time. The fire was out in this region, and the trees were in bloom. Given how thin the foliage was, this was a rare event.

"This must have been a beautiful planet before the algae took over," Kylac said. "That was tens of thousands of years ago."

They walked across the black soil. Very little vegetation blocked their way, but they did have to trudge through the thick slime. Climbing the hills was the most difficult part, as their feet slipped and slid in it, covering them in the stuff. Deka expected it to burn, but it was just slimy.

"How did the Ven survive in this?" Deka said.

"They didn't."

"Then how does anything?"

"That's the incredible thing about life. Somehow it finds a way to endure even the worst conditions."

"Even this? You realize if any of stuff goes up in flames, we'll be on fire! Everything is covered in it! The animals will catch fire, too."

"The animals have developed resistance to it. Chemicals in their bodies prevent it from growing on their skin. If the area lights up, they don't burn with it."

Deka swallowed, croaked. "So what about us?"

"We'll just hope nothing lights up."

"Excellent plan, Kylac."

Kylac's tail waved from side to side. "Actually my plan was to come here, find the Archeons alive and well, the causeways still standing, and then watch you roll around on them for a few days."

Deka clicked his claws. "And have a Droden inside you while a few dozen Ven crawl all over you. Again."

"A Droden female," Kylac said. "I am in the mood for a female. It's been too long."

"Me, too."

The hills leveled out a little, and they were approaching an arch. This one was intact, but to either side, sections of the causeway lay shattered on the ground. The rock had grown since falling, not as much as it would have high above, but enough to notice even from this distance. They did not speak as they neared it.

Deka looked up as they walked under the arch. It was so high he could barely see the underside of the road. Kylac turned his muzzle skyward, too. It had once been so elegant up there. Now it was becoming as ruined and barren as the surface.

Once they were through the arch, Kylac felt able to speak again.

"Deka, I'm sorry we haven't found any survivors yet. Do you remember where Sonjaa was when the disaster hit?"

"No, but I think about it every day. Where would she have been? Where did I leave her? Was she near an off-world portal? Were any of the hatchlings? I have been trying to remember. I should remember that. It was important, I should know where they were, and I don't, and that hurts me."

"Deka, you shouldn't... The odds of her being alive are so slim."

"Either I find her, or I die waiting."

"We may never know either way."

"I'll wait until I do."

Kylac didn't bother arguing. He'd had this conversation with Deka many times since they'd seen what the destruction of Rel had done to the contacted universe, and it always ended this way. He understood how Deka felt about his mate, even if they were emotions he would never experience himself. They walked on for a ways. Deka stepped on some of the slime. He tried to wipe his foot, but there was nothing to wipe it on that wasn't already covered in it.

"Kylac... Is the algae poisonous?"

"No. The fumes are dangerous, but it's not poison."

"Good. When we find something to hunt, it will be covered in it, and I don't want to get sick."

"If we find something... Where are the animals?"

They were climbing a steep hill now, and the trees became thinner. Deka and Kylac slipped and slid on the algae covering the ground, much less pleasant than sliding on the causeways.

The hill leveled out. The trees were gone, and they stood at the top, staring down at a valley. Before them stretched a vast field of gentle hills, all covered in green ooze. The fumes it gave off would make anyone wish they could shut off their sense of smell. One little spark would set it alight, and since the algae was so widespread, the fire would burn for a long time.

Only the legs of the arches that supported the causeways above interrupted the landscape. There were no fallen sections here. Kylac looked up and saw no sections in danger of falling on them.

Deka tried to scent the ground, but all he could smell was fumes.

"No scents," he said. "No signs anything has been this way. Several thousand hungry people could have come down that ramp. We should be able to see something!"

"They're not nearby. We can't walk across the whole planet looking for them."

"All right, so it won't be easy. Think, Kylac, how would a species adapted to living above this survive in it?"

Kylac was silent for a while. He glanced at Deka's back. The rock had grown a little since they touched the ground, giving him a spinal ridge that could have passed for bone in appearance. He collected his thoughts.

"This isn't the only farm. There are a hundred all over the continent. Some are by the ocean, but most are inland. They might have moved to those farms, since there is less algae the further in you go. It can still catch fire, but it's not as thick."

"Can you open a way?"

"I'm already working on it, but I don't know where to aim. It could be dangerous. I could open one on top of someone."

"We'll search every farm until we find them. Pick a spot and we'll go there."

"I don't know the surface very well. I only knew the causeways."

"Most of the causeways are over the land. Just aim lower."

Kylac's ears flicked back. "I'll try..."

Deka thought a moment, remembering the pool above the structure he visited. The aqueducts...

"Kylac. Where would they go for water?"

Kylac's ears flicked back and forth. "Of course! The Ven can swim under the surface and drink the water under the algae. The Droden can't. They would have had to go inland for their sake. There may be lakes mostly free of the algae. And the mountains. They might have gone to one of the farms there, too."

"Take us inland first." He looked down. "And hurry. I want to sit somewhere without getting slimy."

Kylac's tail wagged as his ears perked. "You have rock growing on your back. What's a little algae under the tail?"

5

A sphere opened about half a pace above the ground, and then it started to wobble. Deka's snout peeked out, looked down, and then he jumped out, landing comfortably. A moment later, Kylac landed on all fours beside him. The way closed as he stood upright.

The farm spanned an area as far as the eye could see. The stone enclosure meant to hold in large herds of animals was covered in flaming green slime. Deka and Kylac held their distance. No animals anywhere. No plants. It looked as if it had been neglected for centuries, but on the surface of this world, even a few days of neglect could lead to this.

It was the fourth farm they had found in this state.

Only a large gap in the algae kept them from being set aflame as well. Deka bent down and shoved his nose into the dirt. Kylac followed his lead and sniffed the gap as well. It was a welcome relief—finally a scent, and definitely Ven. Old, but a good sign that they had been here.

Kylac stood up straight. "A few hundred Ven came through here."

Deka stood up straight, looking at the section it isolated. "Someone has to be nearby."

He began walking away from the fire. Kylac observed the blaze for a moment, and then followed.

"Why would they let this happen?" Kylac said. "This was their source of food."

"Someone will be here."

Deka stepped through the slush. His scales were covered in a thin coating of slime. Walking had become necessary to outrun the fumes pouring off his own body. Kylac kicked through it as well. His fur was matted from where algae had splashed on it, and he felt heavy.

They sloshed through it for a few hundred paces, each looking around for signs of habitation.

Then Deka spotted something on the ground, beneath the algae. He leaped backwards when he saw it, sliding to a stop and making two streak marks in the slime. Kylac trudged up beside him and looked down.

The body of a Droden lay under the green slime. The bipedal canine was covered in nine Ven, and all ten bodies had been burned to the bone.

Kylac whimpered. Deka whined, raised his snout, and scanned ahead. Stretching to the horizon were thousands of bodies buried under the algae, all burned. The limbless reptiles were everywhere. They carpeted the ground so thick Deka and Kylac couldn't walk without stepping on someone. Twisted inside these remains were more Droden.

Deka shuddered, dropped to his knees. Kylac whimpered and tried to remain upright.

6

A portal opened up five paces above the ground. Deka leaped through and landed on his feet, bending at the knees to absorb the shock. Kylac leaped out, landing on all fours again.

"Not bad for estimating, but it's still too high."

They were in the mountains, the source of the clean water for the aquifers. It was cold up here, but the algae did not grow this high up. The Relians found the nearest rock and scraped themselves off. They rose in unison, somewhat clean now, and feeling a little safer.

Deka looked down at the algae they had shed, growled and kicked dirt on the rock. The dirt up here was brown, not black. There was still very little vegetation, and little could survive. Deka stood close to Kylac for warmth and scented around.

"Where's the farm?"

Kylac was turning around quickly, taking in the air from all directions. "I thought there was one here."

"Can anything live up this far?"

"I'm sure something can."

Kylac began walking. Deka matched his pace, keeping himself pressed against Kylac's fur. Slick and slimy as it was, it was still warm. They scented the air together but found no life. Only cold dirt.

"Would someone have come up here?"

Kylac didn't answer. He walked them up a steep incline for several hundred paces. Deka was starting to lose hope, and the higher they climbed, the colder he felt.

"I hope you're working on a way out of here."

"I'm almost ready," Kylac said. "I just need to look."

The raptor reached up to scratch his back and then held his hand down. The rock felt twice as heavy as before, and he calculated it must be an entire hand-span high.

Moving was difficult, and the knowledge that soon his back would break under the weight lingered in his mind.

The top of this hill was coming up, but the last few steps were steep. Kylac dropped to all fours to climb it, pulling himself up. Deka tried to jump, but the rock on his back was too heavy. Kylac climbed alone, pulling himself over the crest.

Before him stretched a continental divide. All around were broken pieces of causeway that had fallen from high above. Many of the arch legs were still intact, though, and they curled between the peaks from horizon to horizon. Some of the peaks were higher than the avenues.

"The farm isn't here. I thought they might have come here to escape the algae. They didn't."

Deka looked up at him, wishing he could come down so Deka would have some heat.

7

They were inland again, in the middle of a large clearing that wasn't on fire. Before them stood another enclosure just as empty as the other eight.

They had found some wildlife in their search. Deka had hunted and killed a five-legged something covered in mucus. He and Kylac did not eat the skin; Deka used his claws to cut a large piece off the animal, and Kylac rubbed it all over the rocks on Deka's back. It did not kill the bacteria on Deka's new spinal ridge, but it seemed to have slowed it down further.

Food was scarce, and this made them nervous. The longer they were here, the less they expected to find someone alive. They trudged through the algae with new appreciation for the clean avenues above.

They reached the enclosure at last and climbed over the stone barrier that would have kept the animals inside.

Algae had overrun the place, which meant it had been on fire recently. Every farm had been like this. One after the other abandoned, burned, and empty.

Trees grew everywhere, the only life in this gloomy place, and they were blooming. The wind blew the fumes across the Relians. They coughed and choked on it. In the distance, a storm rumbled.

"They can't be dead..."

"It has not been that long!" Deka shouted at the horizon. "Where are you? Why didn't you leave something behind?"

Algae absorbed his voice. Deka leaped off the wall and landed in slime. Deka snarled at it, stomped his foot, stabbed the ground with a killing claw, and swiped backwards.

"Kylac, something is wrong with the Ven and Droden, and something is wrong with us! We have been to enough farms, we know these people, we know everybody! Why haven't we figured out where they went?!"

Kylac had just climbed down from the wall. "I'm not used to having to think about things either. We can't make portals as easily as we used to. We can't make connections as easily as we used to... They must be related."

"Those people on Lesa... We knew the planet, we knew what they had done, and we knew they would eventually rebel against those machines, but we forgot all of that. How?! We should just know what happened to the Ven and the Droden! What did that disaster do to us?"

Deka kicked a chunk of algae. It flew sixteen paces away and landed in more algae. They felt the rumble of thunder. They turned, finally realizing what it was. In the distance, the clouds rose and rolled. Lightning flashed within them.

Deka poked Kylac with a claw. "Speaking of things we should have noticed sooner..."

"Need a few more breaths," Kylac said.

Deka poked him again. The rumble grew louder. Deka poked Kylac harder. Lightning illuminated the clouds, backlighting causeways and arches inside them. Rain fell.

A bolt of lightning struck the ground, and the horizon burst into flames. The Relians turned and bolted. Deka tucked his arms in, and Kylac dropped to all fours and bounded through the slime, not caring when it splashed in his face. The algae's fumes whooshed as they ignited, and it became louder as the fire sped toward them.

Deka could outrun Kylac, but he slowed down and ran behind the fox. The raptor looked over his shoulder. The fire had spread from horizon to horizon, and it had already engulfed the abandoned farm they fled. The fire line was approaching fast.

Kylac never looked back; he was in the last phase of his calculations.

They ran up hills and slid down the opposite slopes. They jumped over rocks and wound through the trees. The flames engulfed those areas moments later, roaring as they passed.

"Any closer?" Deka shouted.

"Almost there!"

The flames streaked toward them. Deka was surprised they kept their footing.

A wall of trees rolled over the hills, in full bloom. Too thick to walk through, too wide to run around.

"Kylac!"

The canine didn't answer him. He was there, at both ends. He opened a way. It appeared at the tree line, stretched into a wide sphere, and then began to wobble. Kylac held onto it tighter, and it stabilized into a perfect sphere. Kylac bared his teeth and growled with pride and sped up.

The flames kissed Deka's ankles. Kylac sped straight through the sphere, Deka on his heels. The way snapped shut behind them as the flames reached the tree line. The blossoms fells off the trees and withered in the heat. The shrubs closed up and hid within their protective stalks. The reprieve was over. It was time to hibernate again, and they were prepared to wait decades.

The other end of the portal opened far above the surface. The Relians leaped from it, landed on the mountain, and tumbled down the snow-covered hillside. The snow changed to soil, and they tumbled down and down and down until finally they came to a rest at the base, a much higher elevation overlooking the land they had just escaped.

Deka lay on his side and moaned. Kylac raised his head and screamed, half in pain and half in triumph. Then he collapsed on his side and panted.

Deka slowly raised his head. "Kylac..."

"What?" he said without looking back.

"We found them."

The fox raised his upper body, twisted around, and faced the base of the mountain. Stone structures stood just in front of it, rows and rows of them, recently grown, as there were no signs of weathering. The Relians climbed to their feet and stumbled toward them.

A bipedal canine appeared in one of the short openings. The Archeons smelled it was male, and he had twenty Ven clinging to his hairless body, some slithering around, others hanging still, wrapped around an arm, or a leg, or around his neck.

"We're Archeons from Rel!" Deka shouted in the Droden's spoken language. "We've been searching the whole continent for you. What happened?"

The reptiles slithered faster around the Droden and clung to him tighter. The mammal looked forlorn.

"I'm Gruum. Come inside."

They followed him into the structure. A small fire, fueled by algae, roared in the corner. Deka sat in front of it and warmed himself as their host slid a stone slab in front of the opening.

8

"I am... So sorry to hear of Rel," said the Droden. He was sitting on the ground, Ven slithering all over his body.

An arm's reach from him, Deka and Kylac also sat, both covered in slithering reptiles. Their small bodies connected the three larger creatures together as they moved between them.

Now that Gruum had fewer people crawling on him, his bare, green skin showed in places. Droden were born with a thick coat of algae-colored fur, a leftover survival strategy to camouflage them on the land, but quickly lost it due to the Ven crawling over them their whole lives.

Deka and Kylac felt vibrations coming from the limbless reptiles. They were always talking; everything they thought came out in body vibrations which were transmitted across the entire group through touch. This meant the two Archeons were aware of the Ven conversation at all times. Only the Droden needed speech to express himself. The Ven were giving off an overwhelming feeling of grief. They grieved for the loss of their planet, but they grieved even harder for the loss of Rel.

The Droden let the Ven tell the story of what happened to Hithe. They did not communicate with words so much as inducing feelings in others, and right now Deka and Kylac felt moved by a long sequence of vibrations.

The Ven told them that when the portals went out, news had spread quickly across the causeways that both Ath and Barul were dead. The death of both Archeons at once sent a shock through their entire civilization, but there was no way to tell the ones on the farms what had happened.

Everyone on the causeways had remained calm for some time, but eventually hunger won out. Those under the causeways maintaining the arches with living rock had no way to leave, as the work areas were accessible only by portal. Now they were closed, and nobody could reach the people down there. In all of this, there was some hope: Plai.

"Yes, Plai," Gruum interjected. "He was our apprentice Archeon. A Ven. He had only just begun to learn."

The Ven gave the reptile and the canines the feeling that Plai was too inexperienced to open ways to everyone under every causeway, so the people began directing the stone to grow up through the street. It punched through, and the people escaped.

"Didn't they kill the rock before leaving?" Deka said.

The Ven told them they did kill the rock, or at least they tried. By the time they did this, everyone was hungry and thirsty. There were no portals to the farms anymore, and the ramps were often days away, so everyone was in a hurry. Some were bound to miss a few spots.

The Relians whimpered. Gruum whined as well. The Ven slithering on them grieved in their own way.

The feeling from the slithering Ven intensified. Now the Archeons felt everyone migrating to the ramps, too many for the farms. There was plenty of food, but without the portals to the enclosures, the people came in from the outside, and they spread the algae around. When fire erupted, it followed them inside. This happened over and over as they moved further and further inland. Fire consumed everyone in time. With nobody to maintain them, the ramps crumbled, leaving many stranded on the platforms. They had no choice but to leap to the ocean and hope to survive. The Ven did, but the Droden could not survive in the water.

"Nobody was ready for the entire planet to come to the surface," said Gruum. "None of the farms had any warning. There was no time to clear a path. The fires took so many..."

Eventually the fires spread to every farm, the Ven continued. The animals escaped. The people scattered, but they never had a chance, especially the Ven, who were not suited to moving on algae-coated soil. The few that made it to the safety of the mountains were spared the fires but faced starvation.

"We did not witness any of this ourselves," Gruum said. "Except for the farm over there. I saw the people coming down from the ramp, and I saw it catch fire from here. Some managed to make it this far, and we helped them survive."

"You live here?" Kylac said. "In the mountains? Alone?"

"I have lived here with these Ven since I matured. I always preferred their vibrations in particular. We managed to find each other on the causeways every day. Eventually we realized we disliked the noise up there. I did not care for so many different people crawling on me, so we settled for a quieter life eating the cores of the trees that grow here. It is cold and harsh, but I enjoy it. It can sustain a few individuals, but not a population."

Kylac growled at himself. "I knew about those trees. I heard of people like you. It should have been the first place I took us. I forgot. I hate forgetting things."

Deka poked him with a claw, then clicked the claws on his hand together. "It was still a pleasant trip around the surface of a toxic world." He turned to Gruum. "So what about you? What do you do here?"

"We have been learning the written language of S'rin," Gruum answered. "It's a fascinating medium of expression. Entire conversations contained in a single symbol, and the slightest variation changes the meaning. I realized it could be used for more than basic communication. Me and the Ven here have been working on techniques to use the language creatively."

Deka rubbed his claws at the idea. He looked around, noting the numerous clay tablets lying about with different variations of a single glyph. From what Deka could see, Gruum was working on a poem that spanned more than seventy verses.

"A poem written in a language telepathic species only use to communicate with offworlders," Deka said. "I have to read it when it's finished."

The Droden huffed. "I'm not sure when it will be ready. Since the portals went out, I have not been able to concentrate on it. We devoted a lot of time to helping the people recover from the fire at the farm. Even after they left, I have been too disturbed. I enjoyed the isolation when it was willful, but now that it is unwilling... It's not the same."

"The idea verses the reality," Kylac said. "Civilization makes isolation almost appealing."

"And now civilization is gone. There are only a few Droden left on the planet. We stayed behind in case anyone came searching for us. We were the best choice for it, as we were already used to surviving without the causeways and the farms."

"Where is everyone else?" Deka said.

"I don't know. The few who made it this far told me Plai had been working on a portal from the beginning, but because he's still an apprentice, he couldn't do it in a matter of days. It took him all this time to gather as many people as he could to take them offworld."

Kylac's ears stood alert. "He opened a sphere?"

"He would have by now."

"They're just gone?" Deka's killing claws sank into the dirt floor. "Where did they go?"

"I'm not even sure Plai knew where they were going, so long as it was anywhere but here. I did not meet Plai. I only heard of his plan from the others. They left to try to meet up with them."

"Would he have kept the way open?" Deka asked.

"Probably not. He is inexperienced. I heard he had a difficult enough time keeping a portal still."

The Ven crawling on them produced the feeling that Plai was only an apprentice, so it would be remarkable if he opened a suitable way to another world at all.

Deka flinched. The Ven had removed some of the rock from his back at last. As they talked, the Ven remarked that Deka and Kylac had been very innovative trying to kill the bacteria living on Deka's body, but they still missed the ones living in the cracks. It would have started growing fast as soon as they were out of the fumes.

As the Ven peeled the rock from his scales, Deka glanced at some of the pieces that fell off. He had been right. Two hand-spans high and one thick.

"When are they coming back?" Kylac said. "The causeways are falling apart. They have to know it's happening, and soon nobody will be able to live here."

"They know," said Gruum. "Everybody knows, but by the time they realized it, they were cut off from the platforms above."

"The Ven can climb vertical surfaces," Deka said. "Why didn't they climb the arches from the ground and start killing the active rock?"

The Ven reminded Deka how high the arches are, and that they could not climb that high without resting, and there is nowhere to rest.

Deka panted. "I knew that. Why didn't I think of it?"

Kylac waited a few moments and then picked up the thought. "The disaster scarred me and Deka. We can't seem to perceive reality as fully as we used to. Before the disaster, we were normal Archeons. Our minds took in all the information around us: temperature, chemical composition of the air, the size of the planet, how fast it's rotating, the molecules in the ground repelling our feet, chemical makeup of the air—we didn't miss a thing. Now our minds are moving slower, and we can't hold spheres open for long. It's as if our subconscious minds grew back. But for some reason, we seem to be the only Archeons who can open off-world portals at all. The rest of the Archeons can only make ways across their own worlds. Some can't even do that yet."

"I am so sorry," said Gruum. "The disaster scarred everyone. Now that you told me what happened to the portals, everything makes sense. I wish an Archeon had come sooner. We might have prevented this."

They were silent for a while, except for the Ven, who were still pulling the rock from Deka's back, tearing scales off in the process. Deka grumbled and winced.

"So now what?" Kylac said.

The Ven asked what else they could do. The only action they could think of was to wait for the others to return with an experienced Archeon so the Ven could reach the causeways again.

"By then it will be too late," Deka said. "The living rock is spreading. It's consuming the roads with nothing to slow it down."

The Ven seemed to slither faster as they made Deka feel that without portals, there is no way to reach the rock. They wondered if he and Kylac were capable of opening a thousand ways across the continent to reach every piece, but even if they could, it wouldn't help the food situation.

They reminded Deka of the destroyed farms. The foundation of life on Hithe was gone.

Deka growled and drove his killing claws into the ground even deeper. "Get up and do something! Figure it out! Don't..." He panted a few times. Gradually, his killing claws relaxed and rose from the soil. "Don't let this place die..."

The Ven gave off comforting vibrations mixed with grief. The Droden before them felt the same way. They sat quietly for a while in the immense sense of shared loss.

Deka leaped to his feet and screeched. He was still covered in Ven licking and nudging the rock off his back, and they clung to his scales tighter now.

"I will not sit here and whine like a hatchling! We are Archeons, Kylac! We are the people who bind worlds together! We create the contacted universe! We are not helpless! Gruum, are you sure nobody mentioned where they were going?"

"The group Plai had gathered did not come here."

"You people are linked together at all times! Plai was a Ven! You had to be in touch with him!"

The reptiles covering them produced feelings of distance. They had not been connected at the time. They had been scattered all around the continent. Word had gotten around that Plai was going to open a way at one of the mountain communities, and people were migrating there.

Deka growled again, mostly at himself for forgetting something so obvious. "Was there a place Plai wanted to go as soon as he was able? Was there anywhere that fascinated him?"

"Kronia," said Gruum, "Hoorn, Ool'n..."

Deka received feelings of Selta, Jesq, and many others from the Ven.

"Kylac, start thinking about Kronia. I'll make a way to Hoorn. We'll be ready in a couple days."

"Ready for what?" said Gruum.

Kylac's ears folded against his skull. "Deka, we can't just jump to every world they might have gone to. We'll be searching for years."

"It's better than sitting here!"

"There are other worlds that need help."

"I'm not giving up! Do you have any ideas?"

Kylac thought for a moment, ears slowly turning forward again. "Maybe... Do any of you know where Plai's group was?"

"Yes," said Gruum. "It's about six days from here if we walk."

"Has it been on fire?"

"No, it's above the algae line. It's another small community for people like me. Plai was leading them there on purpose so the fires would not consume his portal."

"You said Plai was having trouble keeping portals still. Did his spheres ever intersect the ground?"

Often, said the Ven. Why?

Kylac turned to Deka and stood up. Deka picked up where he was going with this.

"Where is the community? Be specific. We'll make a way there."

9

The site was indeed out of the algae, though traces of it remained where the people had walked and slithered through. Kylac was on all fours, sniffing around a telltale discolored circle in the ground. Deka crouched, also scenting the ground frantically.

The portal intersection had transferred pieces of soil between the two worlds, mixing the two together in the same space. Unlike the bowls at the hub, this one had left an unmistakable scent, and they both recognized it.

Kylac stood. "Ison."

"Ison," Deka repeated. "I will open a way, and I will keep it open. The people of Ison will help you rebuild."

The Ven crawling over Deka's back asked him if he could keep an offworld way open. They reminded Deka of what he had said earlier, about how no Archeon has been able to since the disaster.

Deka growled to himself again. "I refuse to let the disaster scar me! It has been long enough! I will keep a way open!"

Kylac smelled doubtful, but hopeful. Deka showed his teeth to the fox, not in anger, but in determination. Kylac rubbed him across the back and up the neck. Finally, he could touch his raptor again.

Ison was a small world with strong gravity orbiting a blue star. Deka aimed the portal within the hub area to minimize the risk of opening a sphere on top of a person, as all apprentices learned. After two days of pondering the quantum patterns that comprised the universe, Deka opened a sphere. He and Kylac stepped through, caught their balance as the higher gravity tugged them downwards from the inside out. The hub had no portals.

There was a reason Plai would have chosen Ison, besides knowing this world had animals on it they could eat. Ison was very similar to their own in terms of how society worked: a species of mammal paired with a species of reptile, except here the roles were reversed.

The reptiles on this world were the Nahe. They resembled the Ven in that they were serpents, but they stood taller than Deka, slithered on the ground, and they had arms but no legs. Their companion species was the Meva, mammals of similar size to the Ven, but they had no limbs at all, so they slithered on the ground, and they communicated though sound instead of touch.

The people at the hub stopped and looked at the Relians. Members of all four species were here, and everyone was covered in the Ven, who were doing everything possible to avoid touching the ground.

The people began running and slithering toward them. Deka felt the portal behind him slipping away and struggled to hold the way open.

IO

Halfway to the clouds, on top of an isolated segment of platform, a spherical portal opened, and then began to tremble. Ten Droden covered in twenty Ven each poured through the sphere and onto the walking surface. The limbless reptiles slithered off the mammals to a piece of rock sticking out of the road and began licking it. Their saliva bubbled when it contacted the living rock, and soon the entire boulder became frothy.

Just beneath them, where the arch met the causeway, another portal opened. Fifty Ven slithered through and climbed the living rock, which became a wiggling mass of lizards licking the rock dead.

Another portal opened atop a lonely fragment of causeway. Kylac stepped through and stood to the side. He didn't need to create a way to the underside of this section; the rock had broken through the road, providing a path to climb down. More Ven poured through and attacked the rock. Kylac looked across the platform, found another section isolated from the others, and began calculations for another sphere to take them there.

They had been doing this for days. Moving from platform to platform, killing the rock on each section. Kylac hadn't kept this many portals open since the disaster, and it was wearing on him, so he closed the farthest portals to conserve himself once they were done with a section.

Some of the reptiles and mammals of Hithe wanted to begin rebuilding the roads immediately. With everyone doing it, it would not take long at all. The others reminded them of their priorities: first kill the rock, then clean and restore the farms, then remake the causeways.

When the Droden and Ven became tired, Kylac opened a way back to the surface of Hithe, where Deka knelt in front of his sphere to Ison. Deka remained on the Hithe side of the portal. He wanted to be up there, helping Kylac lead the people of Hithe across the platforms, but this portal took everything in him to hold open. The calculations had never felt so fragile before. The corridor through spacetime was tenuous, and he didn't want to risk it breaking and stranding everyone here.

He knelt in place. He hadn't slept since he opened the way. Gruum and the Ven covering him brought Deka food from the other side, and he did eat, but if he so much as looked away from the sphere, it began to slip away from him.

Kylac did not hold the portal open to Deka for very long. When he left with a group of Ven and Droden, he left Deka alone. Deka felt nervous being separated from Kylac, but his fox had not reverted in years, even on Lesa, so he was sure he would be fine without a raptor for a while. So Deka sat or knelt all day, his only company the spacetime trying to crush his portal. When Kylac returned with the group after a day of killing active rock, Droden carrying their weight in Ven walked through and took his way back to Ison to rest and eat. The sight of them returning from successfully killing the rock to someplace safe from the fires inspired Deka to maintain the way. The Ven and Droden did not have good night vision, so Kylac lay next to Deka at night and rested for a while. Deka woke him just before dawn, and Kylac would go to Ison for a new group. Deka would then be alone for the rest of the day again.

Deka watched hundreds of reptiles and mammals through the portal. They wanted to touch him, express their gratitude properly, but no one dared break his concentration. None would ever know how it felt to maintain a portal between worlds, but they knew this could not be easy.

The Archeons of Ison were still unconscious. No other Archeons had made contact with them until now, which seemed to confirm that Deka and Kylac were the only two in the contacted universe who could link worlds. The strain was unlike anything Deka had experienced. Before the disaster, maintaining offworld portals had felt elegant and smooth. Now it felt coarse, unstable, distant. The connection between Ison and Hithe danced at the tip of his claws, and he had to reach further and further out to keep hold of it. Being forced to stare at a portal to hold it open was a sure symptom of a major problem with Deka's mind.

Days went by like this, with Deka reaching, keeping the way open, and Kylac hopping from platform to platform, letting let the Ven do their work on the rocks. Sometimes they killed the rocks faster than Kylac could open a way to the next platform.

On what must have been the fifth day, Gruum walked up beside the raptor.

"Deka, someone would like to meet you. He does not want to wait any longer."

Deka did not want any risk. It aggravated him this was so difficult now. Even the slightest change could break the way. He used to keep a couple dozen ways open between worlds, plus ways between points on Rel, and live a normal life at the same time. He never had to keep a portal in sight to hold it open, even as an apprentice—the patterns he perceived within spacetime radiated in all directions throughout the universe, and he kept track of the variables automatically. He felt wounded in a way he could not describe, but he was determined to conquer this and reclaim his former skill.

Deka held his arm out. Gruum walked closer. A single Ven crawled from Gruum's shoulder, slithered behind Deka's neck, and rested there. The raptor felt vibrations coming from it: My name is Plai.

"The one who saved Hithe from extinction." Deka rubbed his claws together. "Nice to meet you at last."

Plai told him they had lost half their population while he made the way to Ison. The Archeons fell dead, and the portals with them. He didn't know what to do. He only just began learning, and everybody wanted him to fix everything.

Deka rubbed his claws together again. "That will happen more and more. Then when you become an Archeon, everyone will expect you to solve everything. How long were you learning?"

Deka felt a sense of one year.

The raptor shivered. Keeping the portal open and holding a conversation took effort. He loathed feeling like an apprentice again. "No wonder it took you so long to open a way to Ison. No life form should ever pass through the ways you open until you're at least good enough to aim for the right solar system." His voice sounded strained.

Plai told him it was a challenge. So many people died waiting for him. He wanted to open ways to the platforms, but there were too many. He figured he should take everyone somewhere else for help. Ison was in no shape to help, but it was safe from the fires. Plai then produced feelings of gratitude that Deka and Kylac came. Gratitude dissolved into grief at the loss of Rel.

"I'm glad we could help." Deka focused harder, trying to force the portal into a stable sphere. He kept it mostly spherical, even while distracted. He was proud of himself, but he hoped it would not be this difficult forever.

Plai asked if he and Kylac would remain here long.

"No." Deka gasped as he fought the force of spacetime trying to collapse the way. "Other worlds need our help."

A new sphere opened. Kylac emerged from it, and the group of Droden covered in Ven filed through behind him. Each one turned and faced Deka, bent at the knees before him, and filed into the portal to Ison. This gesture of thanks was almost obsolete among their own people.

When the last Droden stepped through, Kylac's way winked closed.

"All the living rock is dead," Kylac said, walking up to Deka and resting a hand on his shoulder. "We're done with the platforms."

Deka now realized there hadn't been a sound of collapsing stone in days. He suddenly became conscious of how long it had been, and he convulsed harder.

"I need to close the way. Gruum, Plai, if you want to leave, go now!"

The bald mammal knelt beside Deka and held his arm out for the Ven. Plai vibrated in thanks across Deka's neck, and then slithered onto Gruum. Deka now noticed Gruum was carrying three clay tablets under the other arm. He turned them up and showed them to the raptor one after the other. Each depicted a single, three-pronged glyph with numerous dashes and dots and marks above, through, and around it. The poem was still a work in progress; Gruum was obviously working on a way to combine the three symbols into one while still maintaining the same aesthetic and meaning. The forms he had chosen were beautiful in a visual sense as well as linguistic—the content carefully chosen to look pleasing written out as well as when comprehended. Deka had never known anyone to take such great pain to pair them together, and they complimented one another so well they made Deka chirp involuntarily, the same reaction he often had to watching his hatchlings at play.

The Droden bowed in thanks and then turned and ran through the sphere.

Deka stopped reaching. The way didn't just slip—it flew away from him. The portal collapsed to a single point and vanished, and Deka fell on his side, asleep.

Kylac curled up beside Deka. A cold wind blew, and the canine draped an arm over Deka's side.

"They will rebuild." Kylac's eyes followed an arch up to the segments of platforms high above the flaming valley. "They will rebuild."

His tail waved. Deka began to snore.

Kattaaka

Kylac took a deep breath as Deka landed beside him. He felt lightheaded. He tipped over, caught himself by widening his stance, and took another breath. He felt even more lightheaded. Beside him, Deka was doing the same thing, deliberately breathing deep and fighting off the rush to the brain.

Kattaaka had extremely high oxygen content in the lower atmosphere. They had gotten so used to the flammable air of Hithe their bodies didn't know what to do with air this pure, so the Archeons forced their bodies to take in the extra oxygen.

This clearing in the forest was supposed to be the hub. The portals were gone, and bowl-shaped depressions were apparent in the ground, meaning the portals had expanded here before they collapsed as well. A few had left discolored spots of soil instead of hollow depressions, which meant the spheres on both sides had expanded, intersected the ground, and exchanged soil.

They were in the middle of a clearing surrounded by enormous trees with leaves the size of Kylac's body and shrubs as large as Deka. The soil here was dead for unknown reasons, so it had been the ideal place to set up a hub for offworld spheres, as nothing grew here, and thus no mindless insects would wander into any of the spheres.

The path out of the hub had become overgrown without so many offworlders walking it, so there was no easy way out now.

Once the dizziness faded and they were confident they would not pass out, they walked to the trees. The Archeons pushed the leaves inward, Kylac with his padded hands, Deka with his snout, each leaf taking as much effort to move out of the way as a sleeping Droden. The plants on this world were not something one could merely walk through or push aside. The branches blocking their way were thick and sturdy. They did not sway. They did not bend. The leaves growing on them were gigantic weights meant to block the wind. It was the strategy the plants had developed to crush competition: block the air to the other plants, allowing the ones that blocked the most air to grow faster.

Kylac clawed a leaf thicker than his arm dangling in front of him. Kattaaka had lower gravity than any of the worlds they had been to yet, which made Kylac feel weak. The leaf was as tough as flesh, and his claws made no marks in it. Deka reached over his fox's shoulder and slashed the leaf with his claws. The leaf bled green blood and remained steadfast. Deka did not want to waste his energy on one leaf, so he turned and searched for a new path through this forest. Several attempts later, they managed to wiggle and crawl their way out of the trees and emerge on a cliff overlooking a river valley.

The star in the sky was yellow and large. Kattaaka was not tilted on its axis, so this world received the full force of its star's rays at all times. The drastic temperature differences between the dayside and nightside of the planet drove the constant wind. The trees blocked most of it, but the Relians could feel it now in the open.

Before them was a view of the dense rainforest that blanketed much of the planet. The air was not only filled with oxygen, it was full of water, and Kylac felt wet just standing here. He looked over at the raptor. The relative coolness of Deka's scales created his own personal dew point, so water droplets formed all over him as well.

Insects flew everywhere. A beetle as large as Kylac buzzed by, stopped in midair, reversed, and flew back to the cliff. Its eyes were large but not compound. Each moved independently of the other, and one eye was pointed at Kylac, the other at Deka.

The language of Kattaaka was nonverbal and nonvisual, entirely scent-based. Communication with these people was difficult, as it required close contact with a scent-based species. The Relians were compatible; their bodies produced similar odors for similar moods and expressions.

The Sixlegs flew off, found a gap in the leaves, and dove through. Deka and Kylac waited. Moments later, rustling and clacking sounds came from behind them. The Relians kept their eyes on the star in the sky.

Two Ninelegs crawled down a tree behind the Archeons. Their bodies were segmented and could function with as few as two legs on the ground. Eight of their nine legs were as articulate as fingers. The ninth leg looked out of place because it was a third digit on the final segment that did not assist in walking. It dangled limply as the insect crawled. They were only up to Kylac's knees in height in this position, but if they raised themselves on their hindmost legs, they would be twice as tall as the fox.

One insect crawled up behind Kylac. It raised its body to its last pair of legs, wrapped the fox's torso in its arms, lifted off the ground, and wrapped the last pair around his waist. Its top two segments towered over Kylac's head, legs clutching his shoulders and skull.

The second insect climbed up the back of Deka's leg, over his hip, along his spine, rose up the curve of his neck, and curled its nimble legs around it. The final segment gripped the back of his leg.

Each Ninelegs had wrapped them in a predatory killing grip. The Relians were used to planets with higher gravity than on this world, and the extra weight only made them feel normal again. What neither wanted to think about was the poison stingers poking between their legs.

The Ninelegs species had a stinger as wide as Kylac's arm on the rear of its abdomen. Its entire lower segment was filled with venom that caused severe swelling to paralyze prey while it consumed it alive.

The insect clinging to Kylac's back held its stinger between his anus and testicles. The one clutching Deka's neck and lying along his curving spine aimed its stinger just above his slit. Evolution had conditioned them over hundreds of generations to aim for this spot on their prey as it was the most vulnerable place on an exoskeleton. Though it was instinctual and the bugs couldn't help themselves, it made the Relians nervous every time they visited this world. After a moment, they calmed down and began to hear with their noses.

You are Archeons from Rel. What happened to the portals?

"Our planet was destroyed," Deka said. "Whatever tore the planet apart also tore the portals away. Every Archeon with a way to Rel is either dead, unconscious, or unable to make a sphere to another world."

The two insects clinging to them did not hear their words. They were taking in their odors. A Relian's scent was much too weak to travel very far and be picked up by anyone else, so the insects digested their signals and parsed them into stronger odors the other insects could detect, and then transmitted those scent signals into the wind.

The powerful wind carried their words over the trees. Flying Sixlegs and treetop-dwelling Ninelegs took in these signals. They rebroadcast the odors to others below the trees. Everyone smelled what they were saying.

Kylac ignored the stinger poking his testicles. The Ninelegs on his back sensed his discomfort and held the stinger a claw's reach lower, but the constant flexing motions made Kylac nervous.

Kylac understood the instinct was too strong to fight, so he ignored the sharp taps between his legs and continued where Deka left off. "The Selts told us your Archeons are vulnerable to brain damage. Are they all right?"

There was a long pause as the Ninelegs picked up the odor of Kylac's words and rebroadcast it to the forest. Then, slowly, answers came from the wind.

They are dead. Dropped suddenly when the portals went out.

"I am so sorry," Kylac said. "I wish we had answers. Were any offworlders here?"

Many researchers. Many lookers. They are safe.

"Relians?" Deka asked.

No. We are very sorry as well.

These were not words. The entire troposphere had changed scent to express grief. The entire civilization cried. The odor broke apart, and now multiple odors hit them at once. Thousands of voices drifting in the wind.

The Ninelegs leaned far over their heads, trying to enclose them so they wouldn't be too overwhelmed by the many voices of this planet, but it wasn't necessary, as the Relians were capable of taking in that many scents and processing what every individual was saying.

The entire population was asking if they would take the offworlders home, for some of them were not well breathing the atmosphere for so long.

"We will take them to Selta," Deka said.

"Is there anything we can do to help here?" Kylac continued.

A long pause. The entire population of Sixlegs and Ninelegs was speaking to them on the wind, but it was not overwhelming for the Archeons.

The portals were useful for fast travel, but we are fine without them. We ask if an Archeon is able not to forget about us.

"We will tell everyone we can not to leave you isolated," Kylac said.

Thank you. Please take the offworlders home.

"Where are they?" Deka said.

We brought all to a place safe from the dangers here, waiting for someone to come. We will take you there.

Two Sixlegs descended from the sky and wrapped all six legs around their bodies, mouths perched on their throats. Deka and Kylac smelled no hostility, but gratitude and eagerness. It was instinctual to hold their mouths to the necks of their prey, so they rested their mouths on those places on Deka and Kylac.

They lifted the Relians off the ground and flew them over the trees. Nothing blocked the scents of this world now. Few worlds tested the limits of how much information their minds could process, but even for Archeons as experienced as Deka and Kylac, this world was incredible. Every scent was a voice. So many scents equaled so many voices hitting them at once.

They opened their eyes at last and witnessed the sky filled with Sixlegs. The treetops were crawling with Ninelegs. Everyone had a unique scent, and it was all up here in the canopy.

Treetops whooshed by below them.

The starlight was bright and hot.

The mood of the planet was hope and thanks. Everyone was relieved to know what happened to the portals, and that the people left behind would be leaving for somewhere safe soon. They still grieved for the loss of their Archeons and so many people across so many other worlds.

Kattaaka was sensory overload. Hot, humid, but beautiful.

2

The Sixlegs took off, leaving the Relian theropod and the Relian canine on the dirt beneath an impossibly high canopy. These were some of the tallest trees in the contacted universe, as well as some of the largest insects. Being so small in a forest this large was always a humbling experience.

Kylac's tail waved around, sardonically pondering that these were noncompatible species, and he would never know how it felt to mount or be mounted by one. His tail abruptly stopped as the Ninelegs on his back shifted, its head and top two segments casting a shadow over Kylac's head.

This way.

Kylac felt a nudge on his side, turned in that direction, and began walking. Deka's Ninelegs nudged him in the same direction.

They followed a tiny path through the forest just barely wide enough for Deka and Kylac to squeeze through single file, probably all the insects could manage to carve out for the survivors. The Ninelegs on their backs remained still, nudging them in the right direction whenever a fork in the path appeared. They tried to keep their stingers away from their bodies, but this only gave the Relians a claw's reach of extra room to move. Gradually Deka and Kylac took it for granted that the stingers were not a threat, and walking became easier.

Various other insects flew and crawled around them. They were almost as large as the Sixlegs and Ninelegs species, but completely unintelligent. Some had wings, while others only crawled on segmented legs, but all of them were lethal in some way. There was no such thing as a harmless insect on Kattaaka.

Even the Ninelegs and Sixlegs were deadly. In more primitive generations, they killed, they survived, and did little else until the day someone discovered there was another intelligent species on the planet. They devoted their lives to learning how to communicate with one another, and this pushed both societies higher. They abandoned their survival mechanisms by choice, not by necessity.

The Ninelegs' stingers were still deadly weapons, but the venom glands had become vestigial among a third of the population. In a few hundred more generations, they estimated, they would not produce venom at all.

As for the Sixlegs, their venom had become unused as well. Their mandibles could still crack open an exoskeleton, as well as an endoskeleton, but they survived just fine without the venom. They used their newly developed minds to solve problems of survival. Now they were in control of their evolution, and they took pride in that.

The thin path ended in a giant hole in the ground. The Ninelegs nudged Deka and Kylac into it, and they descended into the dark. Their night vision revealed the path they took down this gradual slope. It was twisted, uneven, always curving one way or another—designed this way to discourage the mindless insects from wandering inside. This wasn't a colony. The Ninelegs and Sixlegs lived in the trees most of their lives. This burrow had been constructed purely to hide the offworlders.

The Ninelegs clinging to Deka's back gave off a series of odors. Deka sniffed a few times to smell what his translator was saying. *Everyone brought them down here to protect them from the rainforest.*

"You said they were researchers?" Deka asked. "What were they researching?"

Anatomy. Behavior. Venom chemistry. All among the mindless ones.

"Did they say why?"

Yes, but we did not understand.

The one wrapped around Kylac spoke. *You said the Archeons cannot open ways offworld, but you two can. Why?*

"Good question," Kylac said. "I've been thinking it might have something to do with us being on the planet when it was destroyed. Being so close to the disaster could have helped. I'm not sure, and neither are the Selts. Nothing like this has ever happened before, and everyone is still trying to figure it out."

The tunnel straightened out and ended in an oval cavity twice as tall as the Archeons. The cavity was empty save for an improvised workspace covered in pouches full of liquids.

The insects on their backs fidgeted and squirmed, segmented abdomens wiggling and writhing against fur and scale. Their scents became unfocused panic.

Where—where did they—oh, oh, oh—I don't—why would they—no, no—why would they go—

"When did you last see them in here?" the raptor said.

I've never been down here before, said the one clinging to Deka, *but I heard yesterday they were safe.*

"Wasn't someone keeping watch?" Deka said. "What about food? Didn't anyone bring them food?"

Other Ninelegs and Sixlegs.

In unison, Deka and Kylac bent low and scented the ground. Survivors had definitely been here, and their scents were recent. Kylac sniffed the work area. The pouches were internal organs, each filled with venom from various species on Kattaaka. One particular type seemed to be plentiful, but Kylac couldn't identify it.

"Whose venom is this?" Kylac said to his translator.

Fourstalk.

"Who are they?"

A mindless one. They inject their venom into the skulls of their victims. It numbs the entire brain, making their victims eager to let their larvae eat them alive.

The Ninelegs on Deka smelled what Kylac's translator was saying, and continued.

Their venom is only dangerous if their stingers penetrate the brain. We avoid them. They inject our larvae and carry them away to feed theirs.

Deka and Kylac met each other's eyes. The raptor had found a hole in the wall, recently filled in with dirt. The floor of the cavity showed signs of a struggle, though someone had taken great care to cover it up.

They followed the scent out of the cavity and back out the tunnel. There were definitely scents leading out. Now that their translators weren't talking to them, Deka and Kylac smelled them. They both growled at themselves for not perceiving this crucial detail on the way in—before the disaster, they would have noticed it instantly even if an entire civilization were speaking to them.

They ascended the long, twisting incline to the surface and emerged into daylight. Now they could smell a scent trail leading into the forest. A path parallel to the one they took to the burrow led into the forest. It had been recently cut, as some of the leaves were still bleeding, and it was path wide enough for Deka and Kylac to walk side by side.

Deka glared at the torn leaves. "How did they do that?"

"I smell a Yimidrin." Kylac was on all fours, scenting the path everyone took into the forest. "A female. In heat. Several different species. About a hundred footprints."

The flapping of huge, fast wings descended. A Sixlegs dropped before them, approached Kylac, and nearly put its mouth on his head. Kylac kept talking.

"Does anyone have an idea where they might have gone?"

Word had apparently reached the canopy that the survivors were gone. The Sixlegs now gave off an odor of its own.

We rescued them from all over the forest. They could have gone to any one of the places they used to be.

Deka grunted. "Fourstalks found the cavity. Find Fourstalk burrows or nests or wherever they live. The survivors will be there."

The Sixlegs turned to face Deka. His translator had just released the cloud of odor that equaled Deka's words, and the Sixlegs was taking it in.

We never go near the Fourstalks. The burrow could be anywhere.

"So get started," Deka said. "We will follow the path they took and try to catch up."

The Sixlegs opened its back, spread its wings, and took off through the hole in the canopy.

Kylac's tail curled between his legs. "Follow them? Through *that*?" He gestured to the forest with his snout.

"The Yimidrin cut the path for us. Should be easy."

He began walking on the scent path. The Ninelegs clinging to Kylac's back nudged him forward. Kylac stepped slowly.

"Deka, the insects will have the whole planet searching for them soon. They know how to deal with the Fourstalks. We should wait here while they bring them back."

"It's a big rainforest, they're scenting for fifty people on the ground, and the bugs are sight and vibration hunters.

They use scent for communication, not tracking. They'll be lucky to find anything."

"But... everything in there is venomous!"

"So are our translators."

"There's a one in three chance they're not!" Kylac looked up and addressed the insect clinging to him. "Are you?"

Kylac's Ninelegs lowered the stinger a little. *My body produces venom.*

Kylac's sphincter twisted tighter. He trotted after Deka, who was already at the gaping hole in the trees.

3

They had gone from a tunnel through the ground to a tunnel through the underbrush. The leaves were huge and the undergrowth unyielding, and yet a clean hole had been cut through all of it, forming a winding path through the forest around the tree trunks. Claw and tooth marks were visible on all the branches and fallen leaves. Being able to walk so quickly through the forest of Kattaaka was a strange and scary experience. The underbrush normally grew so thick it took the Ninelegs days to eat their way any distance, which was why they stayed in the treetops and walked and flew across the canopy.

In their society, portals had linked many parts of the planet, but most importantly they linked the sentient creatures of Kattaaka to the one place they had never been able to explore: the forest floor. Much of the ground on this world was as mysterious and alien to the natives as the bottom of the ocean was to the Relians. The leaves and branches were so sturdy the insects could not venture to the ground in many places. Portals changed that.

But even with portals, there were no paths to walk through the forest, so for the Ninelegs clinging to their backs, this was exhilarating. A free walk across the forest floor, no effort, no resistance.

A few hundred paces in, the path split in two. Deka and Kylac stopped at the fork and bent to the ground. Deka scented the path to the left. Kylac scented the path to the right.

"The Yimidrin went this way," Kylac said.

"Everyone went this way," said the raptor. "The path continues onward."

"Only the Yimidrin's scent went the other way." Kylac stood. "Why would she carve a second path?"

Deka walked up the path to the right. "Probably found something she couldn't tear through."

Kylac looked from fork to fork and then walked down the path on the left. "I want to know why."

Deka turned around, ran back and peeked around the divide between the two paths. "We'd better keep moving."

The fox didn't listen. Deka snorted, and he trotted after Kylac down the wrong path.

"Why only her scent?" Kylac said. "Why didn't anyone else come with her? Why did they turn back and make a new path? What is down here?"

You can hear where they went and where they did not go as if the ground were speaking to you, said Kylac's translator. *I wish I could hear those things. I always wondered how offworlders did that.*

"Some can't do this either," Kylac said. "We just happen to be a scent-based society. Species who found prey by following their smells on the ground."

We find ours by feeling vibrations in the trees. The Sixlegs find theirs by looking for movement from the sky.

"There's a whole range of odors that are not language you can't sense. It can be overwhelming, but it is always useful."

The path bent sharply to the left. Kylac followed the bend, turned, and stopped. The path ended at a branch from a tree hanging over it. Kylac paused, scented around.

"Kylac! Run!"

The canine heard something and looked up. A green and red insect as long as his arm and three times as wide hovered a few paces overhead. It had three stingers: one on its lower abdomen, one on its head, and one prehensile stinger that formed an extra arm.

It dove, aiming all three at him. Kylac leaped to the side and took off running up the path. Deka pivoted on one foot and bolted back to the fork. Kylac caught up to Deka easily and outran him, skidded to a stop at the fork and waited for his raptor. Deka dashed up to him and stopped at his side. All four looked back. Fifty flying insects hovered at the end of the path now, all of their stingers pointed at them. The swarm closed in.

The Relians took off running down the correct path.

"I told you we should have followed this one!" Deka shouted.

"Now we know why there were two paths! Three-stingers only attack prey that's standing still! They were counting on someone doing exactly what I was about to do, which was stand still and wonder why the path ended! They set a trap!"

"How do you know that? They could've turned back and carved a new path when they saw those insects."

"Only one scent went down that path. If they had to detour, everyone would have gone that way and then turned around, but it was just the Yimidrin."

The trees sped by. The broken underbrush was so dense and heavy it did not wave as they passed.

"Why would the survivors set a trap?" Kylac continued. "How did they know those bugs were there?"

"If the Fourstalks got them with their venom, they probably feel compelled to do some strange things."

"Great! And they have a Yimidrin to do the digging!"

Fifty strides later, they could not hear any flying insects chasing them, and they slowed to a steady walk.

That was—! said the Ninelegs clinging to Kylac.

The one clinging to Deka also gave off a scent of excitement.

"It's a thrill for us, too," Kylac said, panting.

I want to do it again!

"We will. Just let us catch our breath. Hopefully we won't have to run for our lives anymore. Right, Deka?"

"We will. Everything on this planet is trying to kill us. Including the refugees!"

4

"They're setting traps," Kylac said as they jogged down the path. "Does Fourstalk venom make people do that?"

We have never observed it ourselves, said Kylac's translator, its odor tinged with glee at the feeling of running.

"Have offworlders ever been injected with it before?"

Not that I know.

"Why would Fourstalks go after the offworlders?"

"They're mindless insects, Kylac," Deka said, keeping pace with the fox. "They would inject anything that might be prey."

"Even mindless insects know the difference between someone who's affected by their venom and someone who isn't. This doesn't make sense. Ninelegs and Sixlegs make their homes in the tops of the trees, not in burrows underground, so what were the Fourstalks searching for?"

"I don't know, but when we find them I am going to kill that Yimidrin! If not for her, they wouldn't have made it one claw's reach through the trees!"

"Careful, Deka. If she can tear through the forests of Kattaaka, imagine what she can do to your bones."

"That's why you're here." Deka rubbed his claws together. "Your scent will distract her, and that's when I move in."

"Deka, I don't think I can handle a Yimidrin in heat. I'd like to try, but..." He whined.

Deka spoke to the Ninelegs on Kylac's back. "You know right now he wishes you'd shove that stinger under his tail."

Kylac's Ninelegs reared up in surprise. *You do?*

Kylac's tail waved as he jogged. "I can't help it! It keeps poking me, and it's almost in the right place. And if you weren't venomous, it might be fun."

How did you know? asked the Ninelegs lying on Deka's back.

"I can smell it. He's been thinking it since you first climbed up. I taught him to react that way."

The Ninelegs on Kylac's back wiggled and settled. *So... you...?*

"No, don't do it! I don't want to die because we had to stand still for a while!"

"There are insects on this world that will kill you because you stand still, and insects that will kill you for running away. We can't win."

Dozens of brown and pink insects crawled along the path ahead of them. They were about the size of Deka's hand, and they skittered along the ground from one side of the path to the other so fast they seemed to be a single organism. The Archeons halted and watched. They seemed as if they should be making an awful lot of noise, but they were very quiet.

Don't step in there, said Deka's Ninelegs. *Those are Pink Ones. They will carry you with them.*

"Through there?" Deka focused on the tiny gap under the leaves the insects were crawling through.

If you won't fit, they will cut you into pieces that do.

The pink insects made a river twenty paces wide, too far to jump across.

"They won't alter course to take us, will they?" Kylac said.

No, said Kylac's Ninelegs. *They are passive hunters. They walk around the continent, waiting for someone to fall or walk into their path. They consume only whatever is in their way.*

They are constantly moving, said Deka's translator. *Always in a line along the ground, eating only whatever happens to end up in it.*

"What a survival strategy," Kylac said.

"We need a way over them." Deka looked around. "How did they make it across?"

"The Yimidrin again?"

"I don't think even she could break these things up long enough for everyone to make it through."

"Climb a tree?"

Neither could see a sign that the refugees did so; they would have had to cut their way through a lot of leaves and branches. Kylac dropped to all fours and scented the ground again, his nose just a pace away from the edge of the pink insects.

Deka addressed his Ninelegs. "Well, I don't know how they did it, but we'll need a lift from the Sixlegs. Will you climb up and call for help?"

The Ninelegs on Deka released its top three segments from Deka's body and pivoted upwards. *That is a lot of canopy to eat through. I cannot be fast—*

Deka spotted a green and red insect against the leaves diving for him. Deka jumped out of the way, and the insect crashed into the ground, kicking up a puff of dirt, and rolled into the pink river. The Pink Ones flowed over the Threestinger, instantly breaking it into eighteen pieces and carrying them off under the tree line with the rest of the insects. More sounds of exoskeleton breaking apart echoed from within the forest.

Deka and Kylac walked back the way they had come, now looking up. They could barely see the Threestingers through the gaps in the leaves, hovering and darting between the branches, waiting for Deka and Kylac to hold still. Now that all was quiet, they could hear the buzzing.

The Relians walked in a large circle, turning at the stream of Pink Ones, walking back down the path, and then turning up the path, against the river and back around again.

"Another trap..." Kylac said. "It almost worked. It almost worked."

"Kylac, how would they get across? How can *we*?"

I can still climb the trees and call the Sixwings.

"It will take too long. We can't walk like this forever."

"Can you make a path up the tree so we can climb over the river with you?"

Yes, but not quickly.

"Let's get started," Deka said. "We'll keep walking until you're ready."

The Ninelegs clinging to Kylac's back released the fox and crawled down his spine. Deka's insect also climbed down and crawled along the ground toward the edge of the path. They ascended a tree trunk and began chewing on the leaves blocking their way up.

The Relians felt lighter than ever. Kylac jumped as he paced. He was able to jump more than his height without the insects weighing them down.

"Deka!"

The raptor had just taken a casual quick jump himself. "Of course!"

"None of them were weighed down by giant bugs! They would have just jumped across!"

Deka snarled, stabbing the dirt with the killing claws on his inner toes. They turned together, walked toward the Pink Ones.

Kylac's ears folded against his head. "The disaster took portals from the Archeons. What else did it take?" He turned to the river of insects. "Can we make it?"

The jump would be long, but it was possible now. They turned around together, took a running start, and leaped as far as they could. They sailed over the ground far and long, and landed. They held still for only a moment, looking back at where they had jumped.

"It's almost possible," Deka said. "We're just a little short."

They started walking backwards again, glancing up to make sure the Threestingers were still holding position. On their way, Deka and Kylac pounded on the tree their translators were in. The Ninelegs crawled back down and climbed on top of the Relians again. The raptor and the fox kept walking as the Threestingers above watched.

"We forgot about the gravity on this planet," Deka said. "Without you two on our backs, we can jump over them."

Are you sure?

"Definitely. We need to practice a little more, but we can make it. That's how the survivors crossed. Some of them were probably used to gravity even greater than Rel's."

We still must make our way across the trees. We will meet you on the other side.

They climbed back up the tree and resumed taking bites out of the leaves and branches, moving from place to place to keep the Threestingers at a distance.

Deka and Kylac practiced. They figured out how to jump long, but not high. After just three practice jumps, Deka turned around and walked backwards.

"All right, I'm ready."

"Shouldn't we practice a little more first?" Kylac said. "If we didn't remember something so simple, we can't assume we're correct now."

"I'm ready!" Deka took off, tucking his arms in, keeping his tail straight, kicking up the loose soil behind him. Kylac took off running, too. Deka ran far ahead of Kylac, waited until the last reach before his foot hit the pink river, and pushed off. He rose up in a low arc, just a pace above the insects, and tucked his legs in. The insects flowed underneath him, and Deka didn't dare look down or do anything that would make his body less aerodynamic.

He reached the peak of his arc and then started to descend. The other edge was in sight, and Deka tucked his legs in tighter. His heart raced. He knew his calculations were right, and that he would make it, but given the simple details he had missed since the disaster, he doubted himself. It was a feeling he had not experienced since he was an apprentice. He passed over the other edge of the Pink Ones, growling in pride, crashed into the dirt a few paces beyond the river, and rolled. He stood up and turned around, walking backwards as the Threestingers hummed overhead.

Kylac had just jumped. He had been on all fours for more speed, and he tucked all four legs in. He felt as though he were floating across the insects as the air dragged through his fur and billowed his bushy tail. The fox reached the peak of his arc, and he calculated he would land just beyond the river. Deka backed to a spot just in front of where he knew Kylac would land, feeling proud at being able to calculate that so quickly—a reminder that he still was an Archeon, even scarred by a disaster that destroyed a planet.

A tube-shaped body slid from the branches overhead and held its jaws out to catch the fox. Kylac didn't have a chance to scream, and he slammed headlong into the creature. The worm dangled above the pink river, curling up and around the fox, trying to crush him. One of Kylac's arms was free, and he scratched and clawed it, but his claws did nothing to the thick skin.

Deka screeched, took off running, and leaped into the air again, claws splayed, jaw open. He landed on the worm's back and hacked away. His hand-claws did little, but the killing claws on his toes penetrated the skin easily.

The worm wrapped up into itself, still squeezing Kylac. The fox had run out of breath. Deka kept hacking away, clear liquid oozing out of each hole he made and pouring over the Pink Ones skittering by below.

A Threestinger dove down and sank its abdomen into the worm. Then another. And another. More Threestingers dove from between the leaves, attacking the predator where it had perched.

The creature slipped and began to uncurl. Its grip loosened, and Deka smacked the Threestingers into the river with his claws. He climbed around to the worm's front side as it unrolled and released the fox. Deka dropped down and stood on the relaxed portion of the body. He helped Kylac to his feet. Kylac was coughing and leaning on Deka. The worm did not unroll any farther, but it began to slide down. Deka held the gasping fox, looking around and scenting for a safe way to the ground.

Twenty Threestingers had firmly embedded themselves in the worm's upper body, the part that still held onto a branch above. It slipped again, its back now touching the top of the pink river. Its muscles relaxed, and it dropped on top of the Pink Ones. The flow of insects halted and began to dam up against the worm. Deka ran across it, yanking his fox by the arm. He rammed its body, uncurling it across the river as the Pink Ones piled higher and higher.

The raptor and the fox ran across its underside, jumping over Threestingers still embedded in it, and hopped off the end, pausing to look back. More Threestingers dove from the canopy and shoved their abdomens into the worm. The pink river had backed up so much it formed a ramp.

It finally crested the body of the worm, and the Pink Ones spilled over the entire thing. The worm cracked, fractured, and snapped apart. Threestingers vanished underneath the flow. The worm twitched and gyrated violently as the insects devoured it. Everyone took a tiny piece as they crawled by, and the river descended into the body. In just a few dozen breaths, the Pink Ones were at ground level, and all that remained of the worm was the head and the tip of the tail protruding just outside the insects' path.

Still gasping, Kylac turned around and began walking. He stumbled. Deka held him up and helped him walk. Kylac leaned on him until he could support himself.

"That was satisfying," Deka said, growling and rubbing his claws together.

Kylac's tail waved. "Yeah. We almost died, but that was great!"

"I am still a predator!" The raptor screeched upwards.

They walked further down the path. As they did, two Ninelegs crawled down a tree, caught up to them, and climbed up their backs, wrapping their arms around their torsos and holding their stingers between their legs. The Relians began jogging again. Behind them, the Pink Ones flowed as though they had never been interrupted.

5

"I smell only half the group made it over the river," Kylac said, running beside Deka on all fours. "The path had to be there for them to jump over the Pink Ones. How was the path carved? Did the Yimidrin actually get through, carve the path, and then everyone else jumped? How did they cross?"

"Doesn't matter, Kylac. We're here now, and they pressed on. We lost a lot of time, so if we keep running, maybe we can catch up."

"This doesn't make sense. Are there any species that can break up the Pink Ones without being eaten?"

No, said his Ninelegs. *Everyone avoids them. Even the mindless ones.*

"And that river is always there?"

Yes.

"Someone had to carve the path first for them to jump over the insects, but to do that, they would have had to make the path first. How? How did they cross?"

"When we catch up to them, you can ask the Yimidrin all about it."

The trees buzzed by. Deka now set the pace, and the path became narrower and curved in more erratic directions around the large tree trunks, possibly due to the smaller group to lead now. Above them, a small group of Threestingers kept pace.

Various insects walked on the path and moved out of their way when they felt fast vibrations coming toward them. Beetles as big as Kylac crawled under the leaves and out of sight. Flightless, twelve-legged insects with pincers on both the head and the rear stood their ground, pointing both sets of weapons at the Relians as they passed. Deka and Kylac ran single file against the trees on the other side of the path to give the bugs as much room as possible.

Crawling insects were much more common. Kylac figured movement was so restricted within the trees they could not grow any bigger than Kylac's head. Small for Kattaaka, but still lethal.

As night fell, the rainforest became more alive. The Threestingers landed and went to sleep in the trees. The forest screamed with the mating calls of millions. Deka and Kylac's night vision was just as good as their daytime vision as they watched the trees pass by.

Something lay on the path just ahead, and as the Relians approached, they saw insects scavenging a corpse. Deka and Kylac skidded to a stop.

Their translators loosened four of their legs, waved them about, and made clicking and churling noises. The insects surrounding the body held up their numerous stingers, barbs, and toxic mandibles in defense.

The Ninelegs waved around some more and made more noises.

The crawling insects backed away, slid under the leaves at the edge of the path, and vanished from sight. The sound of their footsteps moving away from them became lost in the nocturnal chatter.

The Relians approached the body. It was a mammal, so it had to be one of the refugees.

Kylac remained on all fours and scented the body up and down, inside and out.

What is he doing? asked Deka's Ninelegs.

"Trying to find a scent."

Why? The body cannot speak anymore.

"The scent will tell us who it was, how long it's been dead, and maybe what killed it."

It speaks that much?

"If you know how to understand scent. The body is too chewed up to identify by sight, and his nose is much better than mine. Relian canines have some of the best noses in the contacted universe."

So do we.

"Scents for information, not communication."

I still don't understand the difference.

Deka clicked his claws, always happy to expand someone's mind. "They can smell the presence of other creatures. In primitive times, foxes developed it to find threats in their territory. Their noses are so sensitive they become anxious every time they catch a scent. Relian reptiles raise the canines to channel that impulse into having sex with everyone instead, and Kylac has very strong impulses. For a while, he reverted almost every day. Had to bring him back dozens of times when we were young. Thankfully he took to the lessons better than any other fox I've met. Now they mostly use their noses to tell when they get someone pregnan—"

An insect egg smacked Deka on the side of the snout. "—garh!"

He glared at the fox, who was staring back at him from the body, wagging his tail. "Well you don't have to tell them *that* much!"

Deka rubbed his claws, averted his gaze. He scraped his snout clean. "You're right. Sorry."

Kylac went back to sniffing the body. Deka addressed his translator.

"He gets embarrassed when I tell people all of this, but I can't help it. I'm proud of how far he's come, and how well he's held himself together since the disaster. Especially on Lesa. I was worried being under that much stress might affect him, but he never reverted."

"The Gelleens helped with that," Kylac said from the body.

"Yes, they did. I remember when you would have panicked being in so many fights, around so many scents, but now your first thought is to help them."

"You did raise me well." Kylac wagged his tail as he rose from the body. "I just confirmed I am not the father of these eggs, and I have never had sex with this person."

"I'm surprised. And relieved."

"This was a Griithal, a mammal, used to have fur before the bugs ripped it apart." Kylac did not rise to his hind legs, but he did back away from the body. "Died just before dark. Of what, I can't tell. Too much insect mucus everywhere. Insects have been laying eggs in it."

Deka's translator wiggled. *It's fascinating he can hear what someone is saying after death.*

"If you want to think of it that way," Deka said, rubbing his claws and bobbing his head.

Those are Greenshell eggs, said Kylac's translator. *They lay their eggs in the corpses of others. They hatch quickly and imprint on the first creature they see.*

"Do they kill to lay their eggs?" said the fox.

No, they're too vulnerable when carrying eggs. They only scavenge the dead at that phase in their lives.

Deka huffed. "We're not far behind." He took off running.

"Wait, Deka!" Kylac ran around the corpse and followed. "These insects didn't kill them, so why are they dead?"

They ran fifty paces. The path narrowed even more, and they came to another corpse. Deka did not stop, but ran around it.

The path narrowed more and more as they progressed, and then corpses lay strewn about the path. They could not run anymore, so they walked between them, and only now did Kylac have a chance to stop and scent them. More refugees. Reptiles, mammals, people with scales and skin, people whose bodies absorbed minerals and used them to form plates of protective armor over certain organs.

Kylac examined three corpses, all of them packed full of eggs. "How did these people die in the first place? How so many of them in such a short time?"

"Anything could have killed them," Deka said. "Maybe the Fourstalks venom finally did it."

"There are claw and teeth marks. Insects didn't kill them. The saliva... It smells like." Kylac scented harder. "One of them did it. One of them killed these people."

"We're losing time. Come on, Kylac."

Deka dashed down the path, jumping over several bodies in quick succession.

"Deka, I smell something else!"

Deka stopped instantly, turned around and glared at Kylac, bent at the waist, ready to run. "What?"

Kylac was still on all fours, sniffing. The Ninelegs hugging his chest and stomach and hips wiggled and vibrated.

What else can you hear? What else does the body say? Can you teach me to hear these things, too?

Kylac wagged his tail. "Many of these scents are within your range. You're just used to ignoring them. You can learn to smell some of them."

I am curious about these odors all around me I cannot hear.

The fox reached down with his muzzle, grabbed the first body he could, and pulled the skin off the abdomen and peered inside. Something with a shimmering, green shell stared back at him. It twitched, flicked its mandibles at him, reached out and tried to grab him. Kylac hopped away, rising to his hind legs, ears back, tail between his legs.

The bodies of the refugees started moving. Skin split open, pincers snapping through them, clapping together.

Deka's Ninelegs squirmed on Deka's back: *They've imprinted on you!*

"Canine and reptile saliva on the neck!" Kylac leaped over several bodies, just over the pincers, and caught up to Deka, who had already turned tail and started running. "The refugees killed these people! They set another trap for us!"

"What do you mean imprinted?" Deka said to his translator as more bodies wiggled and insects crawled out.

Greenshell larvae chase the first thing they see after hatching either until they die, or until they eat it.

Kylac stayed on all fours to keep up with Deka, but the raptor still pulled ahead of the fox. Their translators were talking to them, but the Relians were running too fast to catch the scents now. The Greenshells crawled toward them, their collective footsteps growing louder. They were catching up. Deka slowed down.

"Are those things dangerous?" said the raptor.

Not alone, but in groups...

"Of course. Twenty bugs. Think the four of us can take them?"

They have paralyzing toxic venom. Even one cut will be lethal.

Deka turned to Kylac. "Well, what do you think? Want to run forever, or fight them off?"

"Fighting them is exactly what they want! We should keep running. Hope something else comes along that's more appetizing."

"And if nothing does, we'll be too tired to fight!"

"Deka, I know you haven't hunted in a while, but we have a head start. Something will cross the path and distract them soon."

"I'm not waiting!"

Deka slid to a stop, turned around, and spread his claws.

Kylac left skid marks in the dirt, ran back, and stood at Deka's side on his hind legs.

"There has to be a better way, there has to be a better way..." Kylac muttered, spreading his claws and bearing his teeth. "If only those Threestingers were still with us. We could use them right now."

Deka growled down the path.

Kylac swallowed. "I hope these things have thinner skin than the worm."

They do, said his Ninelegs. It crawled off Kylac's back and stood upright beside him.

Deka's translator climbed down, stood with three of its segments off the ground, and they faced the approaching swarm. The bugs were smaller than they expected, only about as large as Deka's head. They were low to the ground, covered in blood and mucus, and their mouths twitched open and closed.

"All right," Kylac said. "Their backs will be armored, so flip them over and stab the underside. It's probably less protected."

"Good thinking."

Deka screeched, charged, and leaped for the nearest one, landing on it with both feet. The insect squished under the raptor's weight, made some noises of desperation, and burst open. Its guts poured out of its underside, and Deka sank into the hollow shell. He rubbed his hand-claws together.

Kylac's Ninelegs charged, rising to its two hindmost segments, and ran on those legs. It towered over one of the Greenshells, dropped on top of it, curled its segments around it, and speared it on its stinger. Its ninth leg sprung to life and pushed the wiggling insect off the stinger as it backed away from six others trying to surround it.

Deka's translator was doing the same thing to another of the Greenshells.

Kylac saw a bug crawling for Deka. He ran up to it, kicked it over, dropped to one knee, and reached into it with his claws. Their exoskeleton was very thin compared to the worm that nearly squeezed the life out of him, and his claws ripped through the shell and into the warm, wet guts within.

He picked up the bug and tossed it. It landed in front of a few Greenshells and bounced through the swarm. They backed away, pointing their mouths up at Kylac, making threatening noises. The fox was about to charge them, but Deka leaped over Kylac's head and landed on the insect in the center, flattening it and spraying its guts everywhere. The raptor jumped on another bug, shoving his killing claws down its back. The claw sank into its exoskeleton easily, and the bug burst under Deka's weight, but this time the guts sprayed out of the slit Deka made.

Deka rubbed his claws together. He leaped onto another Greenshell, cut a slit in it, and flattened it. The guts and fluid sprayed the faces of two insects nearby. They made clapping noises with their mandibles as they backed away.

Kylac leaped, landed on a bug, and tried to reach in with his hand. His claws connected with solid exoskeleton, his fingers crumpled, and he stumbled off the bug, stepping on another. It writhed and squirmed under him and crawled away. Kylac jumped up just as it tried to wrap its mouth around his ankle.

The fox landed on another bug, lowered a foot under its neighbor, and flipped it over. He jumped on that, raked the underbelly with his toe-claws, then ripped the exoskeleton clean open. He jumped off, leaving it bleeding there.

"At least my good thinking works for me!" Kylac shouted as Deka sprayed a group of insects with bug guts.

On the other side of the path, the Ninelegs were grabbing insects and spearing them on their stingers. The Greenshells they impaled swelled up for a few breaths and then burst apart.

Deka leaped from bug to bug, keeping them spread apart for everyone else to attack. He was rubbing his claws together the whole time.

"Are you enjoying this?" Kylac shouted as he reached into another Greenshell's underside, tore its guts out, and threw the bug away while it squirmed.

"I knew this would be fun!" shouted the raptor.

"My fur is soaked!"

"Lick it clean later." Deka jumped straight up as an insect went for his ankle. He landed on it, cut two slices in it with his toe-claws, and sprayed five Greenshells. They backed away, waiving their mouths at him.

"It's your turn!" Kylac kicked one of the bugs at Deka.

Deka held his hand out. His claws speared the bug through its underside, and it hung there. He threw it back at Kylac, who jumped to the side. The Greenshell bounced off another, flipping it over. Kylac landed, swung his tail to change direction, and thrust his arm through that bug's stomach.

Both Ninelegs were still spearing insects. They even speared some of the ones Deka and Kylac disemboweled just to make sure they were dead.

Deka flattened his last Greenshell. Kylac reached into his last one, pulled out its insides, and stood up. The Ninelegs each pushed an insect off their stingers. The path was slick with entrails and broken exoskeletons, some of them still wiggling upside down. Slower. Slower. Then still.

The Relians stood side by side, facing the bodies, panting. The fox was soaked in insect juice. Deka was completely clean, and so were the Ninelegs. Kylac noticed Deka's genital slit was dripping lube.

Their translators lowered themselves to the ground, skittered behind Deka and Kylac, and began climbing their hind legs.

"Aaaaaaaaah!"

"Screeeeeeeeh!"

They both jumped, twisted around, and landed facing the insects, Deka ready to jump and slice, Kylac ready to flip and reach. They panted. The Ninelegs looked up at them, giving off vague scents of confusion.

Finally the Relians remembered who these insects were, and they lowered their fighting stances and turned around again. Both Ninelegs crawled up their legs and over their spines, slower this time.

As soon as Deka's translator was in position, the raptor took off running down the path. Kylac dropped to all fours and caught up to him.

Deka was still rubbing his claws together as he ran. Kylac glanced at him, folding his ears back, and bumped into him, smearing him with Greenshell juice. Deka stumbled, growled, and kept his distance from Kylac. Now the fox waved his tail around as he ran.

6

"It's not important for everyone to get there, but they all agree it's important for some of them to," Kylac said. "They're desperate to reach their goal."

"It's the Fourstalk venom, Kylac. It has to be."

"But not everything matches. The venom affects other insects. Mammals and reptiles and everything else never evolved on this world, so it should not have an effect on them at all."

"Let me know when you figure it out, and if it will help us."

"Understanding what's going on can always help us."

"It helped you a lot back there. Brought you up to your elbows in insect juice." He was rubbing his claws together.

Deka hadn't stopped laughing since the fight, and it was starting to annoy the fox.

The path ended. The Archeons nearly ran into the wall of trees, but they stopped just in time. At the base of one of the trees, between two roots larger than all four of them put together, a hole lead into the ground.

Their translators climbed down their backs and wandered the surface in erratic circles, pausing, walking, pausing again, walking. At last they climbed onto the Archeons' backs again.

This is a Fourstalk burrow, said the one clinging to Kylac.

I can feel them moving below, said Deka's translator. *Hundreds of them.*

"So we were right," Deka said. "They must have burrowed inside the cavity looking for larvae and infected the survivors instead. That's what made them want to come here."

Kylac stared at the hole silently.

"Well, Kylac? Makes sense, doesn't it?"

"I still think we're missing something."

"So let's find it." Deka walked into the hole.

Kylac followed. There wasn't much room down this tunnel, so their translators climbed off and scuttled behind them. Not too far down, they reached a spacious, oval-shaped cavity twice as high as the raptor's head at the center.

Spherical eggs about the size of Deka's foot lined the floor, connected by mucus liberally strung everywhere. Sitting and lying around the wall were the last eight survivors: three furred quadrupeds, three bipedal lizards, one birdlike creature, and one female Yimidrin, her head touching the ceiling in a sitting position. The Yimidrin's claws were as long as her arms, and her scales and fur were covered in plant blood, dirt, and insect mucus. All eight appeared to be dizzy and delirious, but awake and surprisingly calm for being up to their waists in Fourstalk eggs.

Numerous disembodied venom sacs lay about on the far left side of the chamber. The entire place smelled of venom, and these formerly internal organs were the source of that scent.

Kylac's fur stood on end. Deka wasn't laughing anymore.

A strange insect emerged from an opening hidden in the darkness at the back of the chamber. Its body had four segments, six legs total, and four antennae coming out the top of its head. Its lowest segment had a very thin protrusion sticking out of it that was a quarter the length of its body. Even from here and in such poor light, it looked sharp enough to pass straight through bone without resistance.

It raised its head and second segment off the ground, picked up one of the venom sacs, and carried it over to another. The sacs were open at the top, and it poured the contents from one pouch into another, but only partially. It held the pouch up to its mouth, tasting the venom, then walked around the left side, adding drops from various other vessels.

Finally it closed off the bodily organ it was holding, reached down and attached a stinger, and then crawled toward the refugees on the other side of the chamber. Deka and Kylac lay low.

It stopped at one of the furred bipeds. It raised the stinger, aimed, and shoved it into his skull. It held the organ above his head and waited a few beats before removing the stinger. The bipedal mammal twitched and flailed, moaning inarticulate words. The insect crawled up to him, pressed its head to the mammal's, and held it there for a while.

Kylac knew that smell coming off Deka; he was still in a hunting mood, ready to ambush and take them all out. Kylac held his raptor's shoulder, silently telling him to wait and watch.

Another Fourstalk emerged from an entrance in the back of the chamber. The first insect crawled away from the mammal and touched heads with the new arrival. They remained head-locked, intertwining antennae for a few breaths, and then separated. The second insect crawled over the egg sacs to the venom bags and began mixing various liquids together.

While it did that, the first Fourstalk crawled to a female quadruped canine with black fur. It injected her skull with the liquid in the venom pouch. The female had the same reaction as the previous victim, and the Fourstalk pressed its forehead to hers and held it there for some time while the victim writhed and mumbled.

The second Fourstalk attached a stinger to its sac and carried it to a male reptile. It shoved the stinger through his brain, withdrew, and then pressed its forehead to his skull. It waited. The reptile babbled and mumbled and flailed about. The Fourstalk backed away to avoid his thrashing limbs.

The insects moved from individual to individual, injecting them with two different stingers, pressing their heads to each of them after the injection. The refugees moaned, mumbled, and flailed. Both insects kept their distance as soon as they injected the Yimidrin.

While she flailed and shouted nonsense, the Fourstalks set the empty venom bags aside, walked to the rear of the room and picked up another needle and pouch and crawled to each refugee and injected their skulls with this.

One by one each person bled out from every hole in their bodies, even making new holes through the skin. It lasted only a moment, and then the victims slumped over, alive and awake, but still delirious.

Once the people were empty, both Fourstalks crawled to the back of the chamber and disappeared through the passageway on the other side.

"I need to know what's in those pouches," Kylac said. He skulked across the chamber on all fours, hopping over strings of mucus and piles of eggs, and stood on his hind legs on the left side of the room, surrounded by open bags of exoskeleton full of venom and other liquids.

Deka and the two Ninelegs carefully stepped into the chamber, walking around the eggs. The raptor bent down and examined the first victim he came to, a black-furred canine covered in mucus and blood. Deka observed numerous tiny holes in her skull, so this wasn't the first time she had been stabbed through the brain and bled half to death. He walked from victim to victim, scenting and examining them in the poor light. They barely seemed aware of what was happening.

Deka looked over his shoulder at the fox, who was sniffing frantically at the venom bags. He suppressed a grumble and called to Kylac as quietly as he could.

"Let's get these people out of here."

"We can't take them any distance in this condition."

"It's why we came here!"

"Smell this place. This isn't just venom. All of these scents were in the burrow where the survivors were supposed to be. It was all Fourstalk venom, but mixed with other chemicals. The Fourstalks are modifying their own venom."

"Kylac, just help me. Are you close to calculating a way to Selta?"

"I'm still a day away from that."

"Then we hide them somewhere until you can get them there. The cats will figure out what's wrong with them."

Deka picked up one of the reptiles and pulled her, but the mucous lining held her down. Mucus didn't just line the floor, it held the refugees in place. Deka pulled harder, heaving, using his muscular legs. Kylac heard him struggling, turned and ran to him.

"Modified venom is all over her, but it's not inside her anymore. Whatever they did, they purged it from her system. They injected these people with artificial venom. Venom they created. Now, the Ninelegs said their normal venom makes victims complacent. It's how they secure food for their eggs—inject their victims in the brain and they become thoughtless. Still able to move, still able to be led around, but they can't set traps. They can't coordinate to cut a path through the forest. What's going on here? Why are they doing this?"

"Now is not the time to prove you're still an Archeon." Deka pulled harder. "Help me!" He braced his feet against two piles of eggs, grabbed the reptile under the shoulders, flexed his leg muscles, and pulled. The two Ninelegs crawled up either side and began gnawing on the mucus as Deka held it taut.

"Deka, think about this." Kylac paced the room, weaving between the piles of eggs. "I hate that my mind is so slow, but the connections are still there. The Fourstalks went through a lot of trouble to burrow underground and inject these people with an artificial venom that made them come here, and compelled them to make sure nobody followed them. This venom was designed to affect offworlders. Why?"

The mucus broke, and Deka stumbled backwards, holding the quadruped in his hands. Both Ninelegs backed away, rising as high as they could go, making all sorts of clicking warnings. Deka turned. The two Fourstalks were standing silently before them.

Deka dropped the victim and joined the insects at their sides, killing claws raised, snarling.

"Kylac, we'll hold them off."

"There's probably a colony below us. We won't go far, and we can't take all of them out."

"Just do it! We'll figure out the rest on the way!"

Kylac was still pacing around the chamber. "The first venom was meant to draw these people toward them! They're not food for the eggs! They're... They're test subjects. They're purging them of the venom after they're done to restart... With different venom! Oh! Oh, Deka! Deka! I have it! I have it! Finally I understand!"

Deka was flashing his claws and teeth. Five more Fourstalks had appeared behind the first two.

Kylac dashed around the eggs and stood at the venom sacs. A few Fourstalks were walking through a hole in the dirt wall, and Kylac ran past them, sniffing the chemicals, searching for a familiar scent, hopping over heads and stingers.

Fourstalks poured in from the entrance in front of Deka and filled every crack between the eggs, then climbed on top of the egg piles and glared at them. Deka and the two Ninelegs were surrounded.

Kylac hopped from pouch to pouch. His nose took in the pieces and compared them to the odor of the venom that had been injected into a test subject when they first arrived.

"Don't attack them, Deka!" Kylac shouted. "I have to remake the original mix. If I'm right, we'll be able to reason with them!"

Kylac grabbed an empty pouch and scooped some white liquid out of the big vat of unmodified venom. He jumped around, mixing a drop from one vessel, another drop from a different one, and so forth. The Fourstalks looked at him. They periodically touched heads, mingled stalks, and then gazed at the fox running about the room as though insects with mind-altering venom were not there.

The Ninelegs stood with their backs against Deka's flanks, keeping the insects at arm's reach. Deka made hissing and screeching noises, and the Ninelegs made clicking sounds.

To sting, they have to climb on you and angle their abdomens into your head, said one of their translators. *It will be a challenge for someone like you, who stands upright.*

"Good for me. It's you two I'm worried about." Deka hoped his scent was strong enough for them to hear.

Kylac searched for the venom's components and added them to the mix one by one, his nose leading him from one chemical to another. At last he smelled the mixture in the sac, and it matched what he remembered. He set it down in front of the closest insect, backed away, and sat down on all fours.

Cautiously, the Fourstalk approached it. It tasted the mix and touched heads with one insect, mingling antennae. That one touched heads with another, and so forth down the line and all across the chamber and among the insects around Deka and their translators. The Fourstalks dropped their offensive postures. Deka lowered his, too, but more from surprise.

"Kylac, what's happening?"

"If I'm right, I'll be able to talk our way out of this." The Fourstalk with the venom-filled organ closed it up and regarded Kylac. The fox sat still and waited. "They had it figured out. Their problem was finding the right person to use it on. Someone who is mentally capable of learning unfamiliar impulses, and very fast at recognizing patterns. I'm not as fast as I used to be, but I can find them."

The Fourstalks around Kylac touched heads, rubbed antennae together. A spare stinger passed from bug to bug, and then finally to the one with the sac. It rose to its lower two segments, attached the stinger, and approached the fox.

Kylac winced. "This part is going to be tough, though."

The insect shoved the stinger into the side of Kylac's skull. Kylac gasped, but it didn't hurt as much as he expected. Instead, his skull felt cool. His vision flickered, and his hearing cut out every few breaths. Deka was shouting, but Kylac barely heard him. His mind reeled. The Fourstalk that injected him handed the venom pouch to someone else, then touched foreheads with Kylac, antennae twitching around, trying to mingle with something.

Can—can—aaaaaan-caaaaaa

Keep trying, Kylac thought. *Keep trying. Keep trying.*

Yes—yes—ye—I—heeaaaaarrrrr—heaaarrrr—heer-reeeeee

I'm almost there. I'm almost there. Keep trying. Keep trying.

All across the chamber, the insects now touched heads frantically. Deka looked around at all of them, scenting the room but detecting nothing. Even the Ninelegs stood at ease and regarded the Fourstalks with curiosity.

"Kylac?" Deka turned and faced the far side of the chamber. It was full of Fourstalks touching heads, and in the middle of it all stood one insect with its head pressed against his fox.

Kylac's mind had folded in on itself.

Do you—do—you—stand—you—do—do—you—under—stand—you

I am starting to understand you. I am starting...

The Fourstalk pressed its head harder to Kylac's skull.

You do—you—do—understand me.

"I understand," Kylac said aloud for Deka's sake. "You had the mixture correct, but you needed an Archeon to figure out the new impulses fast enough."

Kylac was hit with a thousand thoughts all at the same time, and his mind took them in and processed them all.

Deka looked on, claws folded, neck outstretched. He forgot he was surrounded by insects with stingers designed to penetrate skulls.

"That's better," Kylac continued. "Much better."

The Fourstalk seemed magnetized to Kylac's skull. Then it broke away and touched heads with another insect, then another. They touched heads in a wave all around the chamber. The insects backed away, opening a twisted path between the eggs for Deka to reach Kylac.

"Deka," Kylac said, panting. "The Ninelegs... They need to hear this."

Deka turned to the one he thought of as his translator. "Climb on."

The Ninelegs crawled onto Deka's back. It emitted a bewildered odor. Kylac's Ninelegs crawled between the eggs along the open path. It hesitated when it came to a Fourstalk stinger, and then quickly skittered over it and onto Kylac's back, upper segments looming over his ears. Its stinger now pointed just above Kylac's tail. The Fourstalk held its head up to Kylac's again.

"Tell it again," Kylac said.

A few moments later, Kylac's translator wiggled and twitched. Deka looked around. The Ninelegs looked around at the Fourstalks. They weren't attacking. They weren't aggressive. All of a sudden, these did not seem like mindless insects anymore.

Kylac whined as his vision spun. "Meet the third sentient insect species of Kattaaka."

Deka turned to Kylac. He rubbed his claws together.

7

Deka woke, yawning. He raised his neck and surveyed the chamber. He had stayed awake most of the night, watching Kylac as he locked heads with every Fourstalk in the colony one after the other. It had taken him all night, but the fox pieced together their story and translated it for Deka and their Ninelegs. At some point during the night, Deka's Ninelegs had perched on Kylac's back so it could learn the story as well.

While they conversed, the Fourstalks in the chamber had detached all the refugees from the floor. No one had moved yet, as they were still recovering from the shock of being injected with all sorts of venom mixes and then purged multiple times. Deka had slept when Kylac fell asleep.

One of the quadruped females was awake and scenting the chamber. She caught sight of Deka's raised neck and began to walk toward him.

Deka rolled to his feet and waited for her. She walked by Deka out the entrance. Deka followed her up the slope and into the open air. She stood looking up at the trees, breathing easy. She had a vaguely canine face and stature, black fur, and enlarged ears. Her species had adapted for survival in arid climates. The raptor sat next to the mouth of the opening.

"I am Yeen," she said.

He spoke in her language. "Deka. Archeon from Rel. My fox and I came to rescue you."

"I am relieved you arrived when you did." She sighed. "Relieved is too weak a word."

"What happened?"

"We were here researching the Fourstalks. This time we managed to retrieve some of those venom pouches, and we were trying to figure out what they were using them for.

We had planned to take them offworld, but the portals went out. We were stranded here, so we continued our research in the alcove the Ninelegs dug for us. Something burrowed inside. They injected all of us with the same artificial venom. After that..."

"Kylac already told us what happened from their point of view. The Fourstalks communicate by sharing signals from the brain. They had been trying to communicate with the Ninelegs and Sixlegs for decades, but to do that, they had to inject modified venom into the brain, and the insects always fought back."

Deka rubbed his claws and growled. Now that all the pieces fit together, he felt as satisfied as after a good hunt.

"When you arrived," he continued, "they saw a chance to create ambassadors. Because you couldn't fight back, you were perfect. They broke into the burrow and forced all of you to come here so they could perfect the formula."

"I was listening," Yeen said. "I remember what Kylac said last night. I remember the formulas. I am told the brain of my species cannot sense pain. I disagree now."

She looked up at the trees and across the path she helped carve into the forest.

"We heard you coming, and I felt an overwhelming desire to hold you back. It was my idea to set the traps. When I smelled a insects nearby, I led the group to use them. Threestingers, Greenshells..."

Her scent changed to extreme grief.

"The other day, I never would have forgiven you for that," Deka said, rubbing his claws together, trying to lighten the mood. Then he realized she might not know what that meant. "This is how Relian reptiles laugh."

"I convinced twenty people to sacrifice themselves to the Greenshells. I'm sorry, but I am not in a mood to laugh."

Deka faced forward, keeping his hands apart, and listened to the sounds of the dense forest.

"That venom filled us with overwhelming urge to go somewhere and not let anyone catch us. Every piece of knowledge I had went toward that. We were lucky to have a Yimidrin with us who went into heat after the portals collapsed. She had more strength than all of us combined. Enough to cut a path through the thickest forest in the contacted universe. She even held off the Pink Ones while she cut through that underbrush."

"Is that how you made it across? Make sure you tell Kylac. He racked his brain all day trying to figure that out. He never thought she was so tough the insects wouldn't be able eat her."

She flicked her ears, a weak laugh. "I will. Then we arrived, and the feeling of accomplishment was so great I felt like I had reached my one goal in life. I would have sat there forever, no matter what they did to me."

Deka chirped in empathy for pain. "It sounds worse than death."

"It was, but I am determined to make it worth the deaths of all those people."

"How do you plan to do that?"

"We have made contact with a new sentient species. I will stay here and work with the insects to perfect the formula for the Ninelegs and the Sixlegs."

"You want to stay? Keep getting poked in the brain?"

"I have a feeling it won't be like that anymore. From what Kylac said, it was only a matter of dosage and acclimation. The Fourstalks assumed if the effect was not instant, the formula failed. Now they know it must be a gradual process."

"Did you hear him? About how scent is hidden to them?"

"I did. It's incredible. For centuries the Fourstalks observed the Sixlegs and Ninelegs, bewildered at how they communicate. They found evidence of a sense they don't have, and believed communication was impossible. Then they began using their venom to make prey do other things besides go numb and let their larvae eat them. Odor is completely hidden to the Fourstalks, and they are just learning not everyone perceives the environment the same way they do."

"You should let us take you to the Selts to make sure there's no brain or body damage."

"I plan to go to the Selts when Kylac opens the way, just to be sure. It will be soon."

Deka did not know what to say. He stared up at the canopy. Some of the leaves were still bleeding from where they had been cut. They sat in silence for a time, and then Deka heard movement from the burrow mouth.

The two Ninelegs were crawling out of the hole, followed by Kylac. All three stood between Yeen and Deka. The fox's fur was matted in dried mucus and venom.

"You two need to climb to the top and spread the news," Kylac said to the Ninelegs. "There is a new sentient species on your planet."

When will you be leaving?

"I can open the way any time. I do not think I will be back."

Accompanying you was enjoyable. I think I understand now, how you mixed the venom. How the liquids spoke to you. As soon as the portals open, I want to learn how to hear those things, too.

Kylac wagged his tail. "I would teach both of you myself if we didn't have to leave. Thank you so much for your help."

Deka's Ninelegs was saying goodbye to the raptor as well. Then the two of them climbed up the tree and began chewing their way to the top.

Kylac sat down beside Yeen. He smelled spent. Deka rubbed his claws together.

"I always wondered how it would feel to be with a Yimidrin in heat," said the fox. "Figured since the venom that brought them here wore off, I should help her before she starts tearing the whole colony apart searching for a mate."

Deka was still rubbing his claws.

"I'm glad you're all right," Kylac said to Yeen.

"Thank you. Are the Fourstalks ready to begin helping others learn how to communicate with them?"

"They will be soon. They're mixing more venom. They promise to take it slowly. Give it time, one word at a time if necessary. Try to imagine it from their point of view, if you suddenly gave a Fourstalk a sense of smell, how confused their minds would be at first. They would not know what to do with the signals."

"I wish I could learn like you."

"That tested my limits. I don't envy what you're about to go through. Remember the venom's effects are temporary, and you will have to endure it many times before you become used to it."

Yeen shivered. "I'm not sure I'm ready yet."

They stared at the path. It was already starting to grow back inward. Various insects crawled over it in the distance. Everything was still trying to kill each other, but in its own way, Kattaaka was still a beautiful place.

"It won't be as bad this time," Kylac said, resting an arm across her shoulders. "The Fourstalks know what they did wrong, and they don't have to try dozens of different mixtures. Now they know what works, and they can cooperate with the Ninelegs and Sixlegs, so you won't be iso-

James L. Steele

lated. They also know your minds can't handle these impulses permanently. This is only a first step to understanding one another. I believe a new language will evolve out of this. Something all of us can understand."

She breathed easier. "That's very reassuring, Kylac. Thank you. I will enjoy helping them create one."

The fox turned to his raptor. "Thanks for not attacking, Deka. I had to prove I'm still an Archeon, too. I felt like my old self in there."

Deka held his claws together. "Good thinking, Kylac. Good thinking."

Proxima

The red star in the sky was so weak it barely gave off any light, let alone heat. Its neighbors were much brighter but so distant they did not affect this planet at all. It was so small they could walk around it in three Relian days. It had enough mass to be spherical, but not enough to have much gravity, and yet simple plants had adapted to absorb the infrared and convert it into energy. No animals walked the land. No fish swam in the tiny pools of water that dotted the dim surface. The plants could not sustain any other life forms, as they barely made enough for themselves to survive.

The atmosphere on this planet was just thick enough to support life. The planet had a tiny magnetic field just strong enough to deflect the radiation that destroyed most genetic material, allowing life to cling to the surface.

Deka and Kylac sat on a rock ledge, gazing out over the nearly invisible landscape. Their eyes rested in the infrared light. Their noses had relaxed, only picking up the weak scents of six species of plant life that had taken root on this world. Their ears eased with the lack of wind.

This world had no name. As far as Deka and Kylac could smell, theirs were the only two scents that had ever been here. Every Archeon had a place like this. A place with no distractions or obligations. A place where they could be alone with the universe. This was their world.

Kylac looked up at the nighttime stars. The canine had a clear view of the entire universe. They were inside a nebula right now, but the gas was too thin to see from here. One had to be thousands of light years away to appreciate it. Kylac had seen the planet from that far, and it helped him appreciate where he was.

Deka stared out over the land. In this light, everything was muted and calm. A planet of dim shadows surrounded by dark shadows, and they were the two brightest spots.

There was nothing to eat, and the water here was tainted with too many chemicals to drink, so they never stayed for more than a day. They liked this place because everything was just barely on the edge of survivability. Sentient life would never evolve, but it was proof life could emerge anywhere.

Just barely.

"Thirty worlds..." Deka said.

"Thirty worlds since the disaster," Kylac continued.

"When did they finally start waking up? Oro? Balv?"

"I think while we were on Danaqe. That's when I noticed everyone was awake."

"And we are still the only two who can make ways between worlds."

Sometimes they were the only ones who could make ways on the same world. For some, having portals was the difference between civilization and extinction, and it fell to the Relians to repair the damage.

Stars flickered above. It was not atmospheric distortion. The air here was so clean they were seeing real variations in the stars' light: slight tugs caused by orbiting planets, asteroids passing in front of them, or changes in the star's fusion cycle. All of it was visible here.

"Damage... Why is there damage? Can you think of anything that could destroy Rel?"

"Nothing. I still don't remember where Sonjaa and the hatchlings were. Why can't I remember? I'm an Archeon. I should remember everything about that day."

"And why are we the only ones who can make ways between worlds? Why us? Is it really because we were on Rel at the time? The Selts said the disaster ripped part of every Archeon's mind away. Maybe it didn't affect us as much because it didn't pull us as far."

"That's the best explanation anyone can think of."

Rel was one of the largest hubs of the contacted universe, so the disaster touched every Archeon. Deka and Kylac felt the weight of it. They were the only hope anyone had to make things right, and they needed to reach all of them, fix everything, go everywhere and be everything to everyone. Lately they had taken to calculating the way to the next world as soon as they arrived on another to speed up the process. Doing that for such long stretches of time had taken its toll on them.

"For every planet we help," Kylac said, "five others suffer. The fate of entire civilizations depends on us getting there. When we don't, civilizations fall. Just like Be'ohn."

Deka lowered his head in grief. "If I had known those people were in danger, I would've gone there instead of Hithe."

"Or Lesa, or Tenaka... We can't choose."

"If we happen to be there in time to help them, they survive. If not, they die."

"It's not our fault, Deka. We're only two. We can't help everyone."

"I know that, but it's not how it feels! People are dying because we're not there. Have to help them all... I'm glad for places like Kattaaka. Civilization didn't collapse just because the portals went out."

"Not everyone is like them, and I'm glad. They will rebuild. They will recover."

"Not Be'ohn..."

Kylac fell silent for a while before answering. "No. Not Be'ohn."

"They should have known... Don't grow all your food on your planet's moon. Something could happen, and you'll starve."

"Nothing like this ever happened before. Nobody felt this coming. As far as the Be'ohns knew, there was no risk."

The people of Be'ohn discovered portal physics out of desperation. Climate change was killing their food supply, but one of the moons happened to support that life. They couldn't live there—they had already adapted to the new climate.

Deka and Kylac remembered that now, but they wished they had thought of it sooner. Had they arrived in time, they might have prevented a catastrophe.

"It may not be the end of the species," Kylac continued. "There could've been some offworld."

"Just like ours?"

Kylac's ears folded against his head. Deka faced him and continued.

"There were hundreds of portals on Rel going to almost every planet in the contacted universe. Someone had to make it through. *Someone* has to be alive out there. Why haven't we found them yet?"

"It's not over, Deka."

"So many people are dead because of the disaster, and we can't give them any answers. All we can do is clean up the mess and hope they can take care of themselves when we're gone."

Kylac leaned on him. He didn't say a word for some time.

Everything was quiet here. Scents, sights, sounds. The universe was quiet and distant. Here they did not feel the weight of the contacted universe crushing them. They did not hear the screams of people who died because Deka and Kylac went to one planet instead of another.

The red star in the distance flickered. A wave of plasma peeled off its surface and fanned out in front of the shimmering stars, visible only in the infrared. It wasn't aimed in their direction, so there would be no aurora this time.

"Be grateful we can help at all," Kylac said. "Think what would happen if we had died on Rel."

Deka sighed. "I can't stop thinking about it."

They fell asleep under the stars, the first true rest they had enjoyed since the disaster.

Neben

I

Kylac jumped through the sphere and sank up to his shins in sand. Deka leaped through a moment later. His wide feet kept him on the surface, making him look even taller than the fox. Kylac already felt the equations slipping away from him, and he let the sphere close behind them. They scented the air.

The yellow star appeared as just a sliver of orange on the horizon. Kylac had made sure to bring them here at night, as being out in the daylight was dangerous for off-worlders.

Wilted trees and dead grass covered much of the land. They looked down, surprised to see so much sand, as the planet had been covered in lush gardens with flourishing treelike plants and flowering shrubs. They had been certain this world would not need them right away, and that the people would survive without the portals that maintained their water supply, but now they began to fear what Neben had become without their help.

Scents abounded on the ground and in the air. Birds the size of Kylac glided above, and mammals as large as Deka walked about on the ground. Neither species had a name. They had survived together for so long it never occurred to them to refer to their two species with different names.

When the portal opened, they began to migrate toward the Relians. The Archeons switched to their common language.

"We came as soon as we could," Kylac said to the approaching group of quadrupeds and birds. "Is everyone all right?"

The avians were still dropping in, their feathers shimmering with absorbed radiation. They reminded Kylac so much of the avian species of Ixcy, but for one key difference: these birds made roaring noises through holes in a protrusion at the top of their skulls. They never opened their mouths except to eat and drink, and watching people speak without moving their mouths looked alien even in the context of the entire contacted universe.

The Neben mammals were quadrupeds with plated skin. Their feet and hands were adept at digging through sand. The mammals spoke in the same roars and grunts as the birds, having adapted to their method of speaking centuries ago. Deka and Kylac could speak it well enough, though they were told they had thick Relian accents.

Dozens of voices hit them, and the story was the same. When the portals went out, the water quickly seeped back into the soil, and the entire planet reverted to a desert in just days. They began digging for water. Deka and Kylac understood the significance.

Vast mountain ranges had once covered Neben's surface, but millions of years of weathering had reduced them to flat deserts. Tectonic activity on this world was so slow the weather had plenty of time to eat away at any new uprising in the crust, and thus the land stayed flat and sandy. The sand filled the oceans, trapping all of the water underground.

Digging for water had once been what everyone had to do to survive, and how the two species learned to coexist. The mammals dug for it, and the birds landed on it. Their plumage reflected solar radiation and kept evaporation to a minimum. It was a beautiful relationship, and they lived this way for generations, even after they became self-aware.

When they discovered portal physics, the Archeon opened spheres around the planet, one end above the surface, and the other deep underground, within the water-logged sand. With a spin added to the bottom sphere, these portals continually drew water up to the surface and created wide, winding lakes all across the planet. Neben had been lush with life ever since.

Since the disaster, their lives had returned to digging for water.

By now, word had traveled that Archeons were here. Kylac caught the familiar scent first and turned to it. Qan had just come through one of the portals on the hub. There were only three other spheres on it, all of them wavy and unstable, which meant she had woken up not too long ago and was still struggling to reopen the portals that connected the many regions of the planet.

Qan bounded toward them on four feet. Her body was covered in dozens of circular, scaly plates that protected her from the solar radiation. The mammal's armor absorbed the radiation and released it during the night as heat to keep her from freezing. Her small head stood in contrast to such a large body, which offered little agility, but her kind could stand all day in starlight hot enough to boil water and not flinch.

She rose to her hind legs and embraced Deka in one arm and Kylac in the other, welcoming two fellow Archeons to Neben. She dropped back to four legs and led them to the hub's oasis. Kylac frequently sank up to his knees in sand, but he plodded on after his raptor and the armored quadruped, thankful the sand was cooling off quickly.

A mass of people came through the portals as word spread that contact offworld had been reestablished. Birds flew from all over the planet to meet the arrivals and hear their story.

They arrived at a shallow pool in the center of a field of vegetation. A portal hovered a few paces in the air above the lake. It was full of sand, and water gently poured from it into this enormous pool. The Nebens enjoyed being in places like this. They had once appeared sporadically all over the planet, and Archeons deliberately cultivated and spread them across the globe.

Every community centered around the portal that fed the lake for that area. Here, by the pool, the vegetation was large and bushy and very much alive. Much of it was tree-like, but they only resembled trees in that they were plants and they were large. They had roots that reached thousands of paces into the sand and tapped the water directly. Shrubs and bushes and flowering plants and more trees grew everywhere, and the birds and mammals fed off of them.

Nebens had been growing these gardens for generations, limited in number and size only by the talent of their Archeon. Qan had opened more portals than anyone previous, and prior to the disaster, she had covered an entire hemisphere with a single, winding lake.

Kylac approached the trees, reached up and picked a piece of white, cube-shaped fruit. He took it to the lake and washed it. The plants had developed a gelatinous substance covering their leaves, bark, and fruit to shield them from the radiation. Once clean, the fruit was pure and delicious. Even the Nebens had to wash their fruit and leaves before eating them. The gel contained the radiation, and the gel absorbed the radiation from the water as it sank to the bottom of the lake. Bacteria in the soil fed off the gel and broke it down, leaving only pure, filtered water to circulate back up to the portal and into the lake. The fruit now clean, Kylac munched on it on his way to the pool. Deka and Qan had already slipped into the water.

Normally Deka would simply walk through a sphere to another world at the hub, find whatever prey he was in the mood for, and take it down, but this had not been an option since the disaster, so Deka had eaten on the previous world. He had been in the mood for carnivorous prey that fought back and took a whole group of predators to kill, but had to settle for a small herbivore that hid from him. The meat hadn't tasted very good, but he would be satisfied for a few days.

Qan, Deka, and Kylac relaxed in the pool, the Relians leaning against the side of the lakebed. Qan floated on the surface a little ways out, facing them. The water was warmer than the air and the sand right now, and it felt good to relax. Since the disaster, nearly every civilization on every planet had been in ruins, so Neben was a welcome reminder that the loss of Rel had not destroyed the contacted universe.

The two Relians watched the Nebens commune and eat. Many approached them and heard their story of the disaster. Every Neben had a story of survival of their own to tell. Eventually they dispersed for the evening, and now Qan spoke about how they had managed to survive while she was unconscious.

"Every community around the planet survived by digging and tapping the water," she said. "They have been living this way since the disaster. I only just woke up a few days ago. Reopening the portals has been difficult. I can't concentrate as clearly as I used to."

"Every Archeon who woke up before you says the same thing," said Kylac. "Some are making spherical ways across their own world again."

"I hope I will soon," said Qan. "The birds have been flying around the planet, keeping every community informed on what's happening. They tell me the oceans began retreating into the soil as soon as the portals went out. In just the time I was in a coma, Neben reverted to its desert state. I restored the hub's portal first, but it will take me a long time to restore the lakes."

Deka chirped in grief. "Were there any casualties?"

"A few offworlders across multiple communities. We tried to help them survive the daylight, but we could not dig the pits fast enough."

"I'm sorry."

"I'm told they covered the offworlders in the plantgel," Qan said, "and it helped, but nothing could satisfy their thirst. They tried so hard to help them. As soon as I can, I will visit their planets and tell any family they had what happened."

Deka and Kylac remained silent, enjoying the warm water lapping against them. They grieved with Qan.

"I can't restore the portals fast enough," Qan continued. "I have only reached a few communities. So many people are still living in a desert. I can't seem to calculate multiple ways at once now, so I must reach them one at a time, and every way I open pushes my limit. I feel like an apprentice again. But the birds tell me the people all over Neben knew how to dig and survive. It has given everyone a new appreciation for just how important portals have become in our lives. Without them, life would be little more than digging for water and finding scrub to eat."

"It's been half a Relian year since the disaster," Deka said. "That's a very long time to live this way."

"Opening the water portals was my priority, and it took me quite some time to open what few I have." Qan gently paddled in a small circle in front of the Relians.

"And... I am very sorry to say no Relians were on this world when the portals collapsed."

The Relians were quiet for a moment. Finally Kylac spoke up.

"Every time I hear that, I think it won't hurt. All the places we've been... I thought I would be used to it by now. But whenever we go to a new planet, I let myself feel a little bit of hope for survivors. It still hurts."

"I can imagine," said Qan. "Both of you have done more than anyone could have asked."

Kylac bent at the knees, dipped his whole body below the water for a moment, then came back up. His fur was now completely soaked. It revealed how lanky he was underneath all that fluff.

"You should try opening a way to another world," Deka said.

"I have been afraid."

Kylac shook his head. His fur was now spiky while dripping wet. "Of what?"

Qan stopped paddling, adjusted orientation, and now stood on her hind legs, arms reaching out to keep her still in the water. "I did reach beyond Neben once. I felt as though something would reach back and pull me through to somewhere... Somewhere a portal can't go. That's when I started focusing on the water. I wanted to forget that feeling."

"The Selts told us our minds had been pulled somewhere else," Kylac said. "We're not sure what that means."

"I wish I could forget," Deka said. "Just keeping portals open on the same world is a strain. I miss the years when I kept dozens of them open for years at a time, and I didn't even have to think about it."

Kylac continued where he left off. "It's a scab on the brain. That's why everyone was in a coma. Everyone who didn't die. I'm starting to think things will never be the same again. This generation of Archeons may never recover from the disaster. Deka and I may not. We can open portals between planets, but we can't seem to keep anything open for longer than a few dozen breaths."

"I did it once," Deka continued. "On Hithe. I couldn't do anything else but that. Couldn't let the portal out of my sight. Holding that way open took everything I had. I was determined to be an Archeon again, but I think I hurt myself even worse."

"What do you mean?" Qan said.

"Opening any sphere at all hurts now. It didn't before. I can still open them, but... I thought pushing myself would help me heal. I think it did the opposite."

Around them, the Nebens were washing the fruit and cleaning leaves. The birds ate them as well as the mammals. There were also groups studying mathematics, learning music and offworld languages, hearing about the history of their planet as well as other worlds. Deka and Kylac missed that, pursuing what interested them instead of hopping from planet to planet and cleaning up after the disaster.

"I hope you're wrong," Qan said. "Has no one found Rive or Friend? And what of Sonjaa?"

Deka turned to the water and stared. "No. Nothing yet." He took a few deep breaths. "The hatchlings were almost old enough to have names. By now, they would be old enough to start speaking. And then... Almost time for them to choose foxes."

Qan regarded him for a moment. "Deka, I am so sorry. There were one thousand three hundred and eleven portals on Rel. Many were off the hub. Chances are very good they made it offworld."

"If they're alive... If any of the children are alive, how will this affect the next generation of Relians? If the young raptors can't choose foxes at the right age, will they ever be able to bond with a fox? And what about the young foxes?

Without a raptor to help them tame their instincts, will they ever learn?"

The water lapped the dirt walls of the lake. Deka did not raise his eyes.

"A fox incapable of controlling their instincts," he continued. "A raptor incapable of bonding with a fox. If the disaster forced them to live like that, I hope they didn't survive."

He sighed.

"I have not been there to raise my children... Half a Relian year." He touched his hand-claws together once in a weak laugh. "Friend and I joked that his child would probably end up with one of mine. We had planned to let them meet. Not long until they are old enough for that."

"Sonjaa could still be out there," Qan said. "Friend and Taris would have brought their child, too. Sonjaa's fox was with child as well."

Deka stared blankly at the water. He did not answer. Kylac spoke up.

"Rupi would have given birth by now. She and Sonjaa would have been together. Maybe Sonjaa helped Rupi's child. Maybe all her hatchlings bonded with him or her."

"We were all desperate," Qan said. "The Relians would have adapted."

"Rive and Friend could be out there doing what we're doing," Kylac said. "Trying to find others. Trying to prevent civilization from collapsing."

"They could still be in a coma," Deka said as he looked up and stared off into space. "Between them, they had a hundred and six portals on Rel. If something pulled their minds in that many directions while they were offworld, they could be dead."

"There's still a chance," Qan said. "You've only seen less than a tenth of the contacted universe since the disaster."

Deka turned to Qan. "Sonjaa is out there. I still believe that. She was smart enough to get off the planet as soon as she felt shaking. She would have dragged Rupi with her. Maybe she managed to gather the hatchlings, too. If she did... I hope she chose good names, and I hope they recognize me when we find each other again."

A bird landed in the water, folded his wings, and paddled closer to their group. His feathers glowed bright, which meant he had been out in daylight recently.

"Qan! We found something else!"

"What is it?" she said.

"An opening! It leads down!"

"I'm coming."

Qan swam to the shore, grabbed the edge of the lake, and pulled herself up.

Deka looked after her, not wanting to leave the warm water. "Where are you going?"

"Come with me. You should see this."

Deka and Kylac exchanged a glance. Kylac flicked his ears back and forth, turned, grabbed the ledge, and pulled himself out. He stood on his hind legs and shook the water off. Deka waited until he was done, then climbed out of the water himself, cringing and shivering in the cool air.

Qan had no fur, so she did not shake off. She began padding through the sand, feet not even sinking a claw's reach into it. The Relians followed. The bird in the water who had delivered the news took to the air, soared above them, and flew toward the hub.

"Everyone at each oasis dug their own well," Qan said over her shoulder. "Sometimes they had to dig several of them before they found the water table. One community found something buried in the sand."

"Found what?"

"It is similar to the structures on Kronia."

They left the boundary of the oasis, and sand overtook the dead vegetation. Kylac sank up to his knees and struggled to free himself. Deka backed up a couple steps, held his hand out. Kylac took it, and Deka pulled him out. The fox walked faster to keep up with both of them, sand sticking to his wet fur.

"It's just above the water table. The soil is moist but not saturated. You'll have an easier time walking there. We've been working on removing the rest of the sand since I opened the portals again."

Deka noticed the bird landing by a portal at the hub. The portal was lit and glowing, like the bird's feathers.

"Wait," Deka said. "Is it on the day side of the planet?"

"You will be out of the starlight."

"Really? Where?"

By now they had reached the hub, which only held three portals leading to different parts of Neben. She bounded across the sand to the lit sphere and followed the bird through it. Deka and Kylac jumped through moments later.

Finding water on this world involved a systematic method of digging in wide circles, forming a vertical shaft down to the water table. The walls had to be dug in such a way they would not collapse in on everyone at the bottom, and they had to build a series of steps into the moist sand for the mammals to climb. The higher up, the wider the steps had to be to remain stable. At the deepest parts the steps could be narrow because the moisture held the soil in place.

They had emerged at the bottom of one of these cylindrical pits. It was definitely daylight on this part of the planet, but the angle of the star kept direct light out of the shaft. The portal was situated off to a side nobody was using.

They faced a large tower made of blocks of stone stacked one atop the other that reached halfway up the pit. The surrounding sand turned brown when wet, but this stone was a much darker red.

Deka and Kylac stared up at it.

Around them, dozens of mammals and birds removed more sand from the pit. The mammals had special pouches under their bellies that could hold half their body weight. In primitive times, before the Nebens became sentient, the birds did not dig at all, but today they helped the mammals by gathering what little they could in their beaks and flying it out of the pit. Everyone was dirty, and they smelled exhausted.

Qan was walking toward the structure.

"When they discovered it," she said, "only the top few blocks were visible. That's when they abandoned the well and dug elsewhere. Since I woke up, they have revealed more of it."

Deka and Kylac were walking toward it, gazing upward.

"Sedimentary rock," Kylac said. He stopped at the base, rubbing the stone with his padded fingers. "It's been cut."

"How?" Deka said.

"Did the Nebens ever build anything in the past?"

"Not that I know," Qan said.

She walked around the corner of the tower. Deka and Kylac followed. The blocks were as large as Deka's head and fit so well together that Kylac could not even smell the interior.

Around the corner was an entrance. It appeared recently uncovered, as it still had particles of moist sand sprinkled on it. A few stones had been moved, and the tower was now open.

Qan walked inside, and the Relians followed. Numerous birds and mammals were in here as well, the glow of the feathers keeping the interior lit. The chamber was empty except for a raised circle of stones. Birds and mammals perched on the edge, peering down. Qan, Deka, and Kylac joined them and looked down as well.

The stone circles formed the lip of an enormous shaft reaching into the interior of the planet. Kylac felt no moisture, and the air smelled as if it had not moved for thousands of years.

A bird walked inside, carrying a block of stone in her beak. She hopped onto the lip, lowered herself to the top, and then dropped the stone. Everyone counted.

At the count of ninety-three, they heard the rock hit bottom. All at once, everyone spoke the distance to the bottom was three hundred and seventy-six wingspans. Kylac converted from Neben units to Relian and came up with seven hundred eighty-nine paces.

The stone had disturbed the air for the first time in thousands of years, and Kylac scented the air coming from the shaft. He felt privileged to take in scents this old, even if there was nothing to smell but stone and rock and minerals.

Qan faced the Relians. "Can you make a way down there? I would, but I am concentrating on a way to the next settlement. I will lose it if I try to make this one."

"I'll make it," Deka said.

Kylac drew back from the rim of the well and faced Qan. "That's not just a shaft. There's a cave at the bottom."

2

A sphere opened into shimmering darkness. It held position as a solid sphere for a moment and then started to shiver. Kylac stepped out of it and stood to the side to make room for the other two. Qan stepped through next and stared ahead. A moment later, Deka stood next to her.

They were in a cavern about forty paces wide by one hundred long. Hundreds of crystals covered the floor, ceiling, and walls, each no bigger than Kylac's hand, all arranged in perfectly straight rows with one claw's reach between each of them. The crystals gave off faint blue light, bathing the entire cave in a subtle glow.

The portal was positioned over the spot where their stone had landed. The area directly under the shaft was one of two places where the crystals were not. The other was a winding path down the middle of the corridor. It led into a dark spot within the glow, a passageway further into the cave.

No cut stones here. The walls, floor, and ceiling were solid bedrock. The water had just recently receded, as the cave floor was damp and flecks of moisture still clung to the crystals.

Qan muttered some expressions that had no translation in the Relian language. Deka and Kylac were thinking of a few of their own.

"Do you feel that?" Deka said.

Kylac and Qan paused.

"Flowing electrons," Qan said.

The fox approached the nearest crystal and knelt down to be at eye level with it. "It's coming from the crystals." He sniffed it. "Smells like..." He scented harder. "I'm not sure what mineral this is."

Qan knelt beside Kylac and gazed at the crystal Kylac was scenting. The Nebens were not scent-based creatures, so she did try to smell it.

"Where are the electrons coming from?" Qan said.

Deka bent down near a crystal and scented it up close. A bolt of energy snapped from the crystal to Deka's snout. The raptor yelped and hopped backwards.

Bolts of energy streaked from the two crystals closest to Kylac and Qan and struck them in the face, one bolt on Kylac's muzzle, the other on Qan's shoulder plate. They stumbled backwards a few steps and straightened up.

Kylac glared at the raptor. "Deka!"

"Sorry. Ow."

Kylac turned and walked down the path, surveying the cave top to bottom. It was carpeted with the uniform crystals, floor, walls, and ceiling, all full of energy.

"Crystals don't just hold energy no matter what they're made of. What is this place?"

He looked down at his paws. His red and black fur looked strange in the pale blue light. He kept walking toward the end of the path, looking up and down at the walls and ceiling. The uniformity of the crystals was hypnotic, and the hum of the electricity took his breath away.

Deka and Qan walked abreast down the path a few paces behind the fox. The armored Neben looked so out of place here in the dark cave. The raptor kept his hands tucked in and his tail straight out.

A bolt shot from a tiny crystal and struck Deka's foot. He shrieked again and hopped backwards a few steps. Another bolt leaped up and struck his tail. He jumped forward a few more steps, bumping into Qan, knocking her forward. Several bolts reached out and struck her. They passed through her, through Deka, out Deka's tail, and into another crystal. The shock sent both of them stumbling around, crystal after crystal zapping them from every direction, raptor and Neben yelping. They bounced back and forth from bolt after bolt, and then Deka held still on the center of the path, holding both himself and Qan in place.

Kylac stood at the end of the path, facing them. "Are you two done?!"

His tail wagged wildly. It waved off the path, over a few crystals. A bolt of energy struck it. Kylac's fur coat puffed out, and he stumbled to the side. His arm passed over the crystals on the other side of the floor, and energy struck his middle finger. His fur billowed even more, and he stumbled backwards into the cave opening.

Deka clicked his claws together extra loud so the fox would hear, keeping his hands very close to his chest.

Kylac was staring at something behind them, mouth open, tail between his legs.

"Deka... Qan..."

They carefully turned their heads. Several of the crystals closest to the portal were now as tall as they were, and expanding. Kylac recognized the ones that had first shocked himself and Qan. A separation formed, and the crystal branched out, growing larger, taller, and thinner around the base as it stretched silently, save for the increase in the humming. The base touched the surrounding eight crystals.

Kylac turned to his side. The crystals that had shocked him just now were rising out of the bedrock as well, growing in his direction. A bolt of energy reached out from one of them and struck Kylac on the nose. Kylac yipped and backed further away, and the crystal altered course toward where it had shocked him.

"Qan! Deka! Come on!"

The crystals that had shocked Kylac were growing over the path and the exit. Deka dashed straight for it. As soon as he was near, he dropped to his side and slid under them. They shocked him as he passed by, and new branches of crystal grew underneath the main branch, following the lines of electricity that had connected with Deka's body.

Qan looked back at the portal. Crystals all over the cave were growing, reaching out, touching each other, weaving in and out of each other, joining up, sharing bolts of energy.

She faced the Relians and saw more crystals growing over the path, and even more on the way. Then she dashed down the path, dove under the crystals, and slid into the entrance. As she passed beneath, the crystals shocked her and adjusted their growth, following the bolts and angling their way to the door.

The crystals by the portal were reaching out to it. Deka released the equations, and the portal winked out of existence just before the crystals touched it. They collided with the wall and stopped. By the time they reached it, they were thin enough to be nearly invisible.

From floor to ceiling they grew. Hundreds of them quickly merged into a lattice. Bolts of energy streaked between them. New branches formed from nearly every crystal at once, and these new branches extended toward the three Archeons. They backed up and ran down the tunnel.

Deka stumbled on the uneven floor of the cave. "What was that?!"

"I've never seen anything like that before!" Qan said.

"I've never seen cave crystals do that either!" Deka shouted. "Any ideas, Kylac?"

Kylac's fur was laughably puffy, and it billowed as they ran. "I have no idea."

The tunnel curved to the right, and they emerged inside another chamber covered in tiny, glowing crystals with another thin path on the floor waving through them.

Deka's neck curled backwards at the sight. "What *are* these things?"

"If we could examine one, we might be able to figure out what they're made of," said the fox. "Maybe find out where the electrons are coming from."

"Good thinking."

Deka stepped forward, flexing the killing claws on his toes. He approached one crystal. It launched a bolt of energy at his foot. Deka gritted his teeth and kept walking. He was close enough to the other crystals that they launched energy at him as well. Deka grunted and growled and hooked his killing claw around the base of the crystal. He tugged and pulled as electrons washed over him, but the crystal wouldn't budge from the stone floor.

The crystals nearest him grew into the energy bolts streaking up to Deka like fingers. The crystal Deka was working on wasn't moving, but it was growing up to meet where it had shocked his foot.

Deka dropped to one knee, reached down with both hands, and grabbed it. The energy flowed over him like water. Deka howled and shrieked and cursed in multiple languages. The crystal had stopped growing, but the ones around him were making their way toward him.

Deka twisted and pulled and twisted and pulled. The crystal cracked, and Deka threw his whole body into it, snarling. Finally it broke free from the ground. Deka fell backwards, and Kylac and Qan grabbed him and dragged the raptor away from the branches.

"Deka, that was incredibly stupid!" Kylac said. "Well done!"

Qan sped past them. "Run!"

Half a dozen crystal fingers grew straight for them, humming with electrons. Qan stayed in the center of the path, but it didn't matter how close or how far she was from them. Bolts of energy shot from the ones near the path, and those began reaching for her. A few crystals found each other, exchanged bolts, and merged into a single, thick stalk.

Kylac pulled Deka up to his feet and led him down the path, receiving shocks every step of the way. The crystals adjusted course and followed them, and the Relians kept running until they passed through the exit on the other side. They turned around. The crystals grew and reached in all directions. Some of them met and merged together. Eventually no crystal in the room was asleep in its bed; all were growing, touching each other, sharing snaps of electricity.

Then, all at once, they seemed to decide where to go, and new branches formed, reaching straight at the exit from the cave. Qan led the way into the tunnel, Relians on her heels, and they ran until they could no longer feel the hum of electricity.

They sat down on the cave rock. Deka still held the broken crystal in one hand. It was large, heavy, and solid as rock. It wasn't glowing anymore. A dark piece of cave crystal. Nothing more. Shaking from the voltage he absorbed, Deka handed it to the fox.

"There. Examine all you want."

Kylac took it from him, scented it, tasted it, listened to it.

"It's a mineral. Perhaps many minerals. I can't tell what it is." His tail wagged and his ears perked. "But it has all the properties of a Relian reptile: durable, nearly unbreakable, full of energy, occasionally destructive, and prone to sudden changes in mood. With your permission, Qan, I want to name this stuff Dekanite."

"I like it," she said, shaking her head from side to side in laughter.

Deka was still shivering and twitching, but he did manage to rub his claws together.

3

The next chamber they found was twice the size of any of the previous cave rooms and also covered in glowing minerals. They walked down the middle of the thin path, trying to avoid the bolts of energy.

"I'm starting to think these paths were meant to make sure whoever was in here would be shocked and trapped in the chamber," Qan said.

"I don't know how," Kylac said. "The voltage isn't that high, and if you wanted to trap someone, why give them a path to the other side? Why not make them walk on top of these things?"

"Heeek!" Deka screamed as a bolt struck him on the head. The glowing mineral grew along the path the electrons took through the air, straight for where Deka stood.

Kylac was still holding the crystal fragment, rubbing it up and down, idly wondering how it would feel under his tail, when a bolt from one of the crystals on the path reached out and struck it. The crystal glowed for a moment, and then went out again.

"Deka..." Kylac slowly turned around. "Think you can grab us two more of these things?"

"You grab one! I've been shocked enough today!"

"I'll give it a try..."

Kylac opened his mouth and clamped his teeth around the fragment. He knelt close to the tiny crystals neatly arranged along the ground and leaned forward. Electrical current jumped from them into Kylac's mouth. The crystal absorbed all of it. Kylac reached down and cupped the nearest crystal between both hands. Current flowed through his paws, but it flowed directly to the mineral in his mouth, so it did not shock him. He twisted it as it grew toward the piece between his teeth. The thing was too thick to manipulate at first, but as it grew, it became thinner. Kylac predicted exactly when it would be thin enough to break, waited for that moment, then twisted his hands. It cracked and snapped free, leaving a stump of broken crystal on the floor. Now the current jumped to the new crystal in his hand. Current stopped flowing through him, and both pieces absorbed it.

By now Qan and Deka had caught up to the fox. Mineral fingers behind them were still reaching out to them.

Kylac handed the new crystal to Qan, who took it in her mouth. Then he looked down, found another crystal that had grown thin enough to break, and twisted it free. The fox rose and tossed it to Deka as current from three crystals snapped him across the back. Now the current jumped into the fragment, sparing Deka more pain.

The fox stood up, took the crystal from his mouth, held it out in front of him, and ran across the path to the exit. It absorbed every shock. Deka and Qan followed him to the end of the path, around the corner, and down the tunnel. The crystals kept growing into each other, sharing current and merging.

They passed through two more chambers as large as the one above. Try as they may, they could not walk through any of the rooms without being shocked, but this time the pieces of Dekanite absorbed the stray electrons for them.

Deka, Kylac, and Qan stepped out of this chamber. Behind them was a cave full of expanding crystals forming a lattice that eventually tightened into a cube of humming blue matter.

They turned and bolted down the sloped tunnel.

Kylac stumbled, then sat down on the damp floor. Deka and Qan joined him a moment later. All three gasped for breath. The air was getting thinner and thinner the further down they went. Behind them they could hear minerals scraping up against each other, electricity arcing from one crystal to another.

"I'll bring a portal down here," Kylac said.

"Give it a spin so we can breathe," Deka said.

"And an exit."

"We can't leave now!" said Qan from the side of her mouth. "Not until we reach the end."

"How do we know it ends?" Kylac said.

She spat out the piece of Dekanite. "Those crystals. Every room. Notice how they're arranged. They didn't just grow there. Someone planted them in that way. Arranged them so anyone walking through would be shocked. Why? There must be an end to this. Hopefully we'll find the answer there."

"Just in case," said Kylac. "I'll make it an exit, too."

Deka stood up and walked on to the other end of the cave. He peeked around the corner.

"We're here."

Kylac rose to his hind legs, gasping and panting, and walked to Deka's side. Qan left her piece on the floor of the tunnel and ran to catch up. She turned the corner and stopped, eyes widening.

The tunnel opened into a cave so vast they could not see the other side. All three Archeons calculated it was twenty-one times as large as the small cavities they had just passed through. Dekanite covered the walls and ceiling, forming a hypnotically uniform pattern of glowing crystals all around them. The floor was free of crystals, and tiny pools of water still rested on the rock in places.

They stepped inside, taking in all the sights and smells. A few paces into the chamber lay a hunk of Dekanite about a quarter of the size of Deka himself. It drew their attention, and they met in front of it.

The Dekanite appeared to have limbs, but it wasn't glowing. The raptor reached down and picked up a piece, and sure enough it was all attached. He lifted it off the floor, let it dangle limply. It had a head, a torso, and six limbs, forming a vague shape of an insect that could function on six legs, four, or two.

Deka set it down and surveyed the cave again. The floor was much lower than the cave entrance, comprised of solid rock, still damp in many places. An occasional drip from the ceiling made tiny sounds across the cave. The vast cavern glowed softly in the Dekanite above and from the walls.

Other six-limbed bodies lay sprinkled about. Qan approached one and examined it. The heavy Dekanite was the same as the other: clear crystal arranged to resemble six-limbed bodies, dark and lying alone, as if discarded.

Kylac approached another and picked it up. It hung from his grip, each limb dangling. He moved the limbs, but he could not see how they were jointed. The body appeared to be a single, solid piece of crystal, and yet somehow it was flexible at certain points.

"Stay together," Deka said. "It seems safe in here, but I don't like the scent."

His voice did not echo.

From wall to wall, the cave floor was bare rock. The air was thin but comfortable so long as they did not try to run. Stalagmites dotted the floor here and there, meaning the cave had flooded in the past, and the moist floor attested to a recent flooding.

Paths had been worn into the rock, perfectly straight and angular, wide enough for just one person of their stature. The Archeons walked on one of them, scenting all around. Stone towers and smaller buildings were all over the cave, their red rocks standing out against the blue glow of the cave walls. They approached one right now, a large rectangular structure made of stacked stone blocks. The path led to an open entrance, and they stepped inside one at a time.

Deka entered first. Twenty Dekanite bodies lay on the floor in various positions around a stone table set up lengthwise in the center of the structure. The table was made of the same stone used to form the ceiling, walls, and floor, and it was at the height of someone who only stood half as tall as the raptor.

At each Dekanite's station were devices that looked out of place among all the stone: metal tubes, syringes, cylinders made of glass, and glass cubes twice as large as Kylac's head. The cylinders were filled with water, and within them floated pieces of crystal of various sizes.

Deka was drawn to one tiny crystal on the table. It was glowing. He approached it, holding his Dekanite shard in front of him. It was even tinier than the ones in the cave tunnel, its glow faint. The top third of it was missing.

Deka leaned over the table and examined it closer. Though it glowed, he felt no electromagnetic field around it. He held the crystal right up to the glass. Nothing. He reached inside the canister and touched the crystal. Still nothing. He wrapped his hand around the crystal itself and lifted it out.

Kylac was busy examining the metal syringes and tubes on the table. Each position seemed to be a workstation, with the tools at each hand position, the crystal just left of center, and the large cube just right of center. He picked up two of the tools, crouched to be at the correct height, and held them as they felt they should be used.

The glass cube lined up with his right eye, and Kylac peered into it. He scented it, but it gave off no odor. Though the glass was smooth and perfect, it had been etched with some kind of pattern too fine for even his eyes to make out. It wasn't merely scratched on the outside; the interior of the cube had been etched with lines so fine they blended into a single mesh of crosshatches. The only way Kylac could tell they were there was by how they distorted the background through the cube.

His left eye focused on the cylinder and the piece of Dekanite within. He held the tools in his hands above the piece of Dekanite. He felt he should be looking at both of them at the same time while he worked, as everything had been positioned to make this easier. He moved the tools over the crystal while gazing into the cube.

Qan, meanwhile, examined one of the walls. A hundred crystals—even tinier than the ones in the cylinders—lined stone shelves built into the wall, each contained in glass, and each cylinder filled with water. All the crystals glowed faintly.

She picked up one of the glass vessels and peered at the nub of mineral inside. She turned and carried it to where the Relians were. The fox was standing with the tools in his hands.

"What are you doing?" she asked.

"Putting myself in their place."

"What do you think all this is? What was going on here?"

"Well... That little thing you're holding appears to be a seed. I'd say they were growing the crystal. They started the seeds here, then planted them in the caves."

"Any ideas how they could have planted them on the ceiling?" Deka said, walking up to them with a new shard of Dekanite.

Kylac held the tools in his hand, bent down, and touched them to the crystal. "I don't know."

"What about the stone?" Qan said. "And the glass? And the metal? How could they have worked any of it? Sculpting metal and glass takes much effort, especially for objects this precise."

"Let's keep searching." Deka walked back through the building and out the exit. Kylac set the tools back where he found them and followed. Qan set the crystal on the shelf and walked outside.

Deka paused in front of the door, scenting the area. Kylac smelled it, too.

"What's wrong?" Qan said.

"Something's changed," Deka said, turning around.

Kylac turned around, scenting the air from every direction. Gradually their noses led them upwards, and then Qan looked up.

An enormous, pointed column of Dekanite loomed far overhead, extending forward, growing thinner as it stretched. The electromagnetic field it generated hummed in the otherwise quiet chamber. They followed it with their eyes back to the cave entrance.

Qan muttered something else that did not translate.

Deka took off toward the largest structure in the area, the tower. The other two ran after him. The closer he came to it, the more it resembled the stone tower they had found on the surface, but much larger, over fifty paces on each side. He walked around it but found no entrance. By now Kylac and Qan had caught up.

"Qan, how did they get into the tower on the surface?" said the raptor.

"Several of the stones should be breakable."

Qan walked up to the stone, pounded it with her hand, and listened. She moved around the tower base, pounding the stone block by block.

Kylac looked up as he followed her around. The giant crystal was further along, slightly thinner now as it moved. Its growth was visible, and it was headed straight for the opposite wall, where thousands of tiny pieces of Dekanite glowed. Current flowed through the column. The pattern reminded Kylac of the patterns he glimpsed through the glass cube at the workstation.

"Here it is."

She outlined the stone with her paws. Deka handed his shard to Kylac, backed up a few paces, charged, leaped into the air, aimed both his feet, and landed flat on it. The block moved inward a little, making a scraping sound and leaving a mark on the rock where it had been. Deka pushed off, landed on his feet, backed up, and charged again. He pushed the block another claw's reach in.

Kylac looked up. The column of Dekanite had moved even more, visibly thinner, but still as big around as the tunnels they had descended. Kylac calculated that the combined mass of every crystal in each of the caves they passed through was in this column.

"Those crystals back there," said the fox. "They found each other and merged into one. How did they follow us? What is this stuff?"

Deka landed on the stones again, his killing claws stabbing them. He pushed off, backed up, and charged again. Each landing pushed the stone in a little bit more.

"Deka, you know what happens when that thing reaches the wall," Kylac said.

"I know!" Deka was gasping for air. He charged again, weaker this time, and pushed the stone a tiny bit inward. He backed up, panting and gasping. He wanted to run again, but he dropped to his hands and knees instead, still wheezing. "Qan...?"

The Neben examined the stones. "We're almost in. Maybe I can..." She rose to her hind legs, braced both paws on the edge, and pushed. The stone slid sideways now.

Water roared through the crack in a torrent. Deka, Kylac, and Qan stood out of the way as it passed by. They waited for several breaths, all the while the humming column overhead stretched closer and closer to the wall.

Deka snarled, stepped into the water, and kicked the block further inward. The flow increased. He kicked again. The stone moved a little more, and the flow increased again. He kicked several more times, moving the stone completely out of the way. The water filled the opening as it rushed out, catching Deka in the flood and sweeping him away. Kylac caught Deka's foot and pulled him out of the water and onto dry rock. The raptor stood up, dripping wet.

"That water smells as though it hasn't moved in generations," Kylac said.

"What's it doing in there?" Deka asked. "Why is there a tower full of water in the middle of a dry cave?"

They stood and waited for the water to drain. They waited a long time, watching the column move closer and closer to the wall. Finally, the water flow slowed to a trickle.

Qan walked up to the opening and squeezed through.

Kylac followed, still holding onto both broken crystals. Exhausted and short of breath, Deka stumbled behind his fox into the structure.

Dozens of Dekanite bodies lay inside. The floor was made of red stone, as were the walls and ceiling. A spiral staircase built into the wall led up the tower to another level. They walked over the bodies and to the steps. Deka ascended first.

Kylac waited for the Neben. She rose to her hind feet and walked upright. Kylac followed Deka, and Qan followed Kylac's tail up.

This second level of the tower was full of Dekanite bodies as well, all twisted around and dark. A few dozen glass cubes had been stacked neatly to one side of the room.

"Why did they seal themselves in?" Qan said.

Stone tables rose out of the floor. More glass cylinders with Dekanite seeds lined the tables, all dark.

They fanned out and examined everything. The two Relians scented everything they could find. Qan examined more of the tables. They met up again at the stairs, and then they ascended to the next level. There were so many Dekanite bodies they could not explore the room without walking on top of them. They continued up the stairs.

Floor after floor. Bodies twisted and bent and piled on top of each other, all as dead as the stone which entombed them. Stacks of cubes around the walls. Tables with empty glass cylinders, all filled with water.

Deka emerged at the top level of the tower and gazed upwards. Kylac and Qan followed a few breaths later. The topmost floor was completely open and had a clear view of the cave's ceiling. They were only fifty paces down from it. The Dekanite seedlings were visible now, thousands of them arranged in perfectly spaced rows, all glowing blue.

The three of them turned around in place, gazing up at the Dekanite and the menacing blue column protruding from the cave entrance, gradually growing to the far wall, energy coursing through its interior and occasionally flowing across its surface. In moments it would contact the opposite wall.

"I wish we had more time," Qan said.

"So do I," Kylac replied.

Deka's head tilted to the side. "I feel a little guilty. Did we destroy something just by being here?"

"These crystals were definitely planted," said the fox. "I think we just met the ones who planted them."

A spark as thick as the column itself erupted from the tip and connected with a hundred tiny minerals in front of it. The shock cascaded across the walls and ceiling, running over every piece of Dekanite. The walls became a horde of fingers reaching up to it. The ceiling reached down toward the point of contact, pieces stretching out, touching, merging together and continuing, silent except for the hum of energy and the occasional crack of electric discharge. A few of them became so thin they vanished from sight.

Every shard covering the walls and ceiling touched the column and became part of a single structure. The hum intensified as current flowed through and over everything. Fingers sprouted from the underside of the column, sending lightning down and striking random spots all along the cave floor.

The portal opened behind them. Kylac turned away from the cave and ran through. Deka and Qan stepped through to the hub. They watched through the sphere as the humming minerals streaked to the floor.

The crystals followed the lightning all the way to the bedrock and halted, forming a forest of solidified lightning bolts. The trunks of these branchless trees pulsed and hummed with energy. The column above had thinned to half its original size.

Streaks of lighting shot out horizontally from each stalk. Fingers of crystal followed the paths the electricity made, weaving a three-dimensional lattice and filling every cubic pace between the glowing trunks. They were not finished exploring.

Kylac closed the sphere before anything touched it.

4

They rested in the lake by the hub. Above them, a portal gushed out water. Hundreds of Nebens surrounded them. The story had circulated around the planet thanks to the birds, and thousands had come from all across the planet to hear about what they had found.

Deka and Kylac relaxed by the shore again, leaning against the ledge. Kylac was hungry, but he would not eat until Deka could eat. He had been working on the new portal calculations since they emerged from the cave. Qan paddled around the pool in front of the Relians, mind racing. She hadn't stopped talking since they left the cave.

"An entire civilization under our feet! Who were they? What language did they speak? How did they manage to survive down there without starlight, and where did the electricity come from? Why did they live down there? They needed to live on the surface at least some of the time —where else could they make the glass and metal? And why did they build that tower underground? It was too far from the cave ceiling to plant the crystals, so why would it be there?"

The canine imagined himself back at the workstation. He held imaginary tools in his padded hands, looked at an imaginary crystal with one eye, and the cube of glass with the other. He imagined the tips of the tools, trying to discern how they were used and the significance of the crosshatching patterns inside the cube.

"And why build that tower underground? Why make a shaft leading down to the cave and then seal it up, but leave the tower for others to find? And how is it possible for them to be alive at all? Crystals can't metabolize, they can't adapt or function..."

Kylac blinked the imaginary tools from his mind, lifted his legs, and floated on the surface. He hoped someone would swim or fly over who smelled interested in a Relin canine. After all that, he needed some kind of release.

Deka turned to face his fox. He rubbed his claws, envying the fox and the Neben mammal. Deka's body was not made for swimming or floating, so all he could do was lean against the wall and enjoy the warm water lapping his neck.

"How do we find other caves?" Qan said. "Perhaps... Yes, yes, the Jilit! Their voices have enough energy to penetrate the sand! They'll hear if anything is down there! As soon as I can open a way offworld, I'll bring some of them here. All this time we never thought anything was under the sand, but there could be a whole civilization down there!"

Deka and Kylac caught a new scent and turned. An extra portal rested in the distance. Other people, bipedal, with no armor or glowing feathers. Amphibians.

Deka leaped out of the waver and over the ledge. Kylac swam to the shore, grabbed the ledge, and hoisted himself out. Without bothering to shake off, he bolted across the thin vegetation to the hub. Deka and Kylac recognized the world and the Archeons.

Another sphere opened nearby, and a bipedal creature walked through. She walked much like a bird but had no arms. She met the amphibians, and sounds of elation came from the group.

Neben birds landed near them. Neben mammals also ran up to them.

Deka and Kylac were almost there. Seeing them wasn't enough; they wanted to smell they were alive.

Towe

I

Kylac ran through the sphere. The portal took him to a rainy world covered in marshes, full of amphibians and armless theropods. Deka leaped through immediately after, grabbing his fox around the shoulders and screeching in joy.

This was Xce, and they were standing on this planet's hub. It was set up on muddy ground on a path lined with twigs and branches. The semicircles off to the side of the path were full of spheres.

Deka and Kylac walked up the path of sticks and branches. They recognized every world. One sphere showed a view of a planet with volcanoes and intense heat. Another showed the oceans and trees of Ixcy. Another showed Selta.

Deka began running up the path, relishing the feeling of warm rain against his face. His heart skipped at the sight of restored hub.

Deka stopped at a particular sphere resting just above the semicircle of sticks and branches. Kylac halted beside him. They saw a view of a planet they never thought they'd see again.

Deka jumped through, and Kylac followed. The sphere carried them a couple million light years across spacetime, and they landed on Inti, a small planet with gravity so weak none of the people had arms or legs. For generations they had drifted with the wind until some of them evolved means to control their drifting. Both sentient species resembled the Bellows of Lesa, but they breathed a heavy oxygen and nitrogen atmosphere.

Their hub was not built on the ground, but spread out across the sky, and it was full of spheres. The Relians grabbed handfuls of air and swam upwards. Portals to various planets sped by, none of them spinning, so the atmosphere stayed perfectly still, moving around the portals instead of falling into them.

Kylac swam ahead of Deka, flicked his tail, changed direction, and plunged through another sphere. Deka swung his tail, twisted his body around, and followed his fox.

They emerged on a world with very high gravity and crashed to the hard ground. Kylac lay on his stomach, and Deka plopped on top of him. It was cold here. Deka didn't like it, but Kylac relished it.

Umrae was tilted so far away from its star there was no temperate zone. The entire planet was frozen, but the plants had evolved a means to generate their own heat. Snow fell in the upper atmosphere but melted as soon as it touched the canopy of the trees, changing to rain. Outside the tree line, the temperature was far below water's freezing point.

The hub had been built into an area with trees, and the icy wind blew between them and chilled Deka's scales to the bone, contrasting with the soothing warmth radiating from the plants.

Many short quadrupeds covered in thin fur were here. The plants they ate filled them with more heat, so they were never cold. Kylac wished the plants were not poisonous to offworlders, as he always wanted to know how it felt to eat fruit that generated its own heat.

Deka rose from the fox and stumbled through the high gravity around the hub. The trees were low, just barely over Deka's head, so the habitable zone on this world was tiny. If he jumped, he would leap into frozen air, and then land in tropical temperatures again.

The hub was full of portals, two rows on either side of them extending down a line of tree trunks for hundreds of paces in both directions. Deka shrieked in joy again and took off running through the trees, looking from side to side at each sphere he passed.

Kylac ran to catch up. As he ran, he heard people talking to him, expressing grief at the loss of Rel, but Kylac couldn't stop now. He had a reptile to catch.

Deka turned sharp and dove through a sphere. Kylac followed, and the way took him thousands of light years away from this cold world with warm plants and set his feet on a world of solid, warm metal.

Kylac stood next to his raptor as they observed the hub of Towe. It had been another major hub of the contacted universe. Hundreds of spheres glowed on the path. Deka and Kylac had been to every one of those worlds, knew their languages, customs, and how to survive on each planet. The raptor and the fox leaned on each other as they caught their breath. Weight lifted from them.

Moments later, an amphibian and an armless theropod stepped through the sphere and waited behind them. A couple thick-furred quadrupeds from Umrae followed. Then a limbless creature from Inti floated out of the portal, instantly dropped to the ground, and waited, looking up at the Relians. They never left their planet for one with stronger gravity, as getting around on other worlds was difficult and humiliating for them, so this was special.

Qan jumped from another portal and began walking toward them.

Then Sere.

Then Saali.

Then a few birds from Ixcy.

More people poured out of the portals and began converging on Deka and Kylac. Word had gotten around the planets quickly that they had found two of the Relian Archeons, and everyone wanted to meet them.

The Relians took in their scents. Among compatible species, scent signals were generally understood, and everyone smelled concerned and worried about them.

They collected around the Relians, and Deka and Kylac embraced everyone, licked some people up the snout, rubbed necks with others, touched chests, rubbed groins, touched thighs, licked ears—just a sampling of every form of greeting possible across the contacted universe.

For a while, it felt as though the disaster had never happened. No distance between the planets. No waiting to travel from one world to the other. No culture isolated.

People came from all over the contacted universe. They consoled them, delivering the unhappy news that no refugees from Rel had made it to their worlds. None.

The raptor and the fox weren't concerned with that now. They were just relieved to breathe everyone's scents again.

2

Towe was a world covered in metal. Volcanic activity, wind, and water patterns had separated the crust of the planet into a layer of iron, a layer of aluminum, a layer of copper, and many more. It was one of the most curious places in the universe, and so many people came to experience it that it had become a hub world. Rel had once been like this, containing portals to every planet in the contacted universe, which made the hub so large it needed portals of its own to navigate it.

The sky was always black and always showed night-time stars, even in daylight. It had no radiation shield in the form of an atmosphere, or a magnetic field. Rather, Towe had nineteen moons orbiting it at high velocity, which had magnetic fields that deflected and absorbed radiation emitted by the parent star.

The closest star was low on the horizon and rising. It obscured the portion of the sky in its glare, and the refraction of the atmosphere was visible around it, but otherwise the sky was perfectly black and starry. Eight of the planet's moons hung in the sky, aglow in radiation that did not reach Towe.

The ground was smooth and polished, and the life forms that called Towe home were as unique as the planet they inhabited. They were quadrupeds made of flesh infused with iron and copper. Their companion species were bipeds also made of flesh with aluminum and other trace elements mixed in, forming plates that protected the critical organs. Both species had no internal skeleton, rather the metal infused into their skin and all throughout their bodies was enough to support their structure. They had no central nervous system, so they had never been in danger of death because of the disaster.

The Relians stood in the middle of a crowd of people from all over the contacted universe, touching them, shouting at them, grieving for the loss of Rel, thanking them for all they had done.

"I'm sorry we didn't come," Deka said to one furred quadruped that towered over his head. "We had to go to the worlds that needed help most."

She leaned down and touched snouts with him.

"I'm so relieved to breathe your air again," Kylac was saying, embracing two thickly-furred bipeds, feeling their groins as they felt his in turn, which was how they became acquainted. "I'm sorry we didn't come. We had to—"

"Don't apologize," she said, in the Relian language. "We were fine."

Archeons they had not smelled in over half a Relian year stood around them, and Deka and Kylac greeted each of them by name. Deka was scratching the scales of one reptile, not enough to draw blood, but enough to pull her scent out of her skin. She was running her claws over Deka's snout, doing the same thing, even though it didn't work well with him. They then switched to the Relian greeting, wrapping necks.

Everyone was relieved to smell, see, taste, touch, or detect the electromagnetic field of Deka and Kylac again. Deka scented everyone, and even now he knew this only represented a fraction of the entire contacted universe. There were many other races not present—those that did not breathe oxygen, those that required low gravity, or higher radiation from the star. They could not be here, but this was still an enormous crowd, and from the number of portals at the hub, they had only reconnected with under half of the planets in the contacted universe.

Finally they relaxed, and then everyone listened to the story from the Relians' point of view. Most had heard about Deka and Kylac and what happened to Rel, but now they wanted to hear about what they had done since.

Deka wanted to let Kylac begin, but Kylac was busy having sex with the Archeons from Umrae, so Deka started with what little he knew of Rel's destruction.

Finally the Umrae were finished with Kylac, and the fox continued where Deka left off. They were eager to hear more about the disaster that had separated them for so long. Nobody had imagined such a thing could ever happen. They smelled disappointed that the Relians had no answers. All Deka and Kylac had were stories of other planets they helped recover from the disaster.

Several Archeons had tried to go to Lesa, but there was no atmosphere, and now they knew why and were glad Deka and Kylac had been there first. The survivors of that world had only been able to tell them what happened, not why.

With the stories came questions. When those passed, the people began to part. A few of the Archeons opened new ways on unoccupied portions of the hub, and a few more planets reconnected with the contacted universe.

Lost in the crowd had been the Towe themselves. Their Archeons walked up to Deka and Kylac now. One, Kelm, was made of iron and flesh, walking on four legs. The other, Ee, walked on two legs and was made of aluminum-fused skin.

"Deka," said Kelm. "Kylac. I am relieved to know you are still alive. I gave up hope a long time ago."

Deka and Kylac rubbed wrists with the two metallic creatures. Then they touched their necks to Deka. Then they gave Kylac's sheath a squeeze. It was not the usual way to greet someone in their culture, even a Relian canine. Kylac's tail wagged at the thought of going again so soon.

"I figured Towe would be fine," Deka said. "Everyone else though... Oh, there were so many places that needed help."

"They found you on Neben," Ee said. "Followed the portals all the way here. I hoped you would go to a contacted planet eventually."

"How long have you been able to make ways to other worlds?" Kylac said.

"Only a ninth."

Eighteen days on Rel.

"Every Archeon must have recovered at the same time," said Deka.

Ee sat down. "I think so."

They all sat down, and Deka lay on his stomach. The ground was warm from the light of the daytime star, which was a comfort.

Kylac looked around at the plant life. Instead of burrowing into the ground, the roots spread out on the surface, clinging to tiny imperfections in the metal. When it rained, the plants absorbed the water right away, keeping the land from flooding, and they survived off the atmospheric nutrients dissolved in the rain.

"We were unconscious until half a year ago," said Kelm. "When we woke up, making portals at all was a struggle."

"We did it," said Kylac, "but the portals would not stay spherical. It was difficult enough for us to make ways across the same world, let alone reconnect with other worlds."

"How did you do it?" said Ee.

Kylac's ears flicked. "I don't know. We can guess, but we really don't know how."

"And it takes effort!" Deka continued. "I kept a way to Ison open for days. Took everything I had, and I could not do anything but that. Didn't eat, didn't sleep, barely drank. Doing any of those things made me lose the way. I haven't tried it since. It hurts too much."

"You should," Ee said. "The portals are stable again; we're reconnecting with other worlds. People are pooling together to help them recover."

Deka sighed as he rolled over and sprawled out on the hard metal. It was no polished causeway, but it still felt pleasant.

Kylac rolled over, lay his head on Deka's thigh, and sprawled out. "I want to sleep. Right here. Forever. Every planet was a strain to find, and we could only make ways just long enough to jump through."

"And the only Relians we found were dead."

"We saw them," said Kelm. "On Movar. I know of nothing that can tear people apart like that."

Kylac and Deka realized at the same time it would have been especially horrible for the people of Towe to witness. Their skin was nearly unbreakable, so seeing bodies maimed and disfigured like that would have been profoundly disturbing to them.

"I'm sure there are survivors," said Ee. "The community is still rebuilding the portals. Both of you can go with anyone and help them make new ways to Towe. Permanent ways now."

Kylac and Deka thought about it for a moment. Their thoughts were separate, but as usual their minds were one.

"Not yet," they said.

They slept without the weight of the contacted universe on their shoulders.

3

Deka knelt on the metal ground, facing a spherical, perfect, beautiful portal. Beside him, Kylac stood, a portal in front of him, also spherical, also perfect and stable.

As soon as it opened, Deka felt it—the pulling—the reaching—the loss of grip and the need to keep reaching or it would fly away. The equations locked in place at first, but they did not become automated in the back of his mind. The variables wandered out of Deka's reach, and he had only held the portal open for less than twenty breaths.

Kylac held his portal open for about the same amount of time as well. They intended to keep them open forever, but something felt wrong.

The equations pulled away from Deka. He growled and forced his mind to hold them, to keep up with the motion of the universe. He had kept a way open to Ison for far longer. It had been incredibly painful, but he could do it, and now he held on again.

It didn't feel the same this time. He growled louder, and then the equations slipped away, and the portal winked closed. He hadn't been conscious of his mind losing the sphere.

Kylac strained to hold onto his portal, but it also slipped away from him and collapsed. Kylac whined and held his head as pain shot down his ears and throbbed at the top of his spine. Opening portals had never hurt before, let alone keeping one open.

The other Archeons around them approached, offered words and scents and touches of comfort. Deka growled internally. Kylac whimpered and whined as his mind burned.

This was their fourth attempt. Even with practice and exercise and conquering the strain, they could not keep the portal open for more than a tenth of a day without incredible pain, and despite pushing through the pain over and over, they did not seem to be improving.

"Deka..." Kylac straightened up and faced his raptor.

Deka growled louder.

"I think the disaster hurt us worse than we thought."

Deka jumped to his feet, killing claws raised, teeth bared. "The disaster did not cripple us! Try again!"

"Deka, I'm tired. It hurts too much."

"We both did it once. We can do it again."

"Yes, to the exclusion of everything else, fighting constant pain, unable to move or speak or eat. Now we can't do it at all."

"Keep trying!"

Deka knelt and meditated. Only apprentices needed to do this. Kylac sat on the hard metal and concentrated on what the universe really was, not how their senses perceived it. He feared how easy it was to keep a portal open initially, and then how difficult it was to hold open. The disaster had taken something from him and from Deka, he was sure. Deka didn't want to admit it. Kylac could not force him.

4

Deka had held the portal open for almost a tenth of a day. Some of the other Archeons were standing by. Kylac had given up long ago, but Deka was on his ninth attempt, and he had to stay in this position, kneeling, facing the portal, focusing all his senses on it.

He had tried to speak, but excruciating pain had been the result, and he had to reach and struggle to keep a grip on the way at the other side. Every waking breath was full of urgent dread that this would be the last moment he could keep the way open.

Kylac approached the lone raptor, knelt, placed a hand on his neck.

The portal in front of them flickered and wavered. Deka growled.

"Deka, I think we both have to accept it."

Deka growled louder.

"The disaster took something away from us," Kylac continued. "We kept the ability to keep ways open short term, but it took our long-term skill."

Deka screeched and shot to his feet, facing his unstable sphere with his killing claws raised, hands spread, mouth open.

Kylac whimpered, tail between his legs. "I don't want to admit it either."

"We will recover!" Deka said through clenched teeth. "I won't let it hurt me!"

Kylac waited.

The portal snapped shut.

Deka's attack stance dropped. His whole body sagged. "I didn't even feel it slip away."

Kylac leaned against the raptor. Kelm and Ee stood close as well.

"Did the Selts examine you?" Ee said.

"Yes. They determined we were hurt, and that the scarring was different from Sere's, but they couldn't say how."

"They've examined more Archeons. You should go back. Maybe they can tell you how your minds are different."

"That's a good idea," said Kylac. "Come on, Deka, let's return to Selta."

"What can they tell us?" Deka said, voice cracking in frustration. "More of what we already know. We're not Archeons anymore, Kylac. Not if we can't keep the ways open."

Kylac led him away from the open field and back toward the hub in the distance. Deka walked, leaning on his fox.

Life had returned somewhat to normal in the last twenty days or so. People came and went. The portals were active again. The hubs bustled with activity, and Kylac and Deka missed feeling part of it, knowing their spheres bridged the light years between these distant cultures. It was something unique to Archeons, and without it, they felt useless. Deka and Kylac were the only two so far affected in this way, and neither liked being the exception.

Deka walked on his own now, without the fox's support.

"Kylac..." Deka's growling turned from anger to sadness. "I can't do it. It feels worse when I try it again. It's not getting better."

"I know. The way to Selta from Ixcy. I kept it open longer than I felt comfortable. Now I can't hold them open for even that long. I hoped we could work our way back up to it, but what if we did more damage pushing ourselves?"

"Maybe the Selts can tell us how we can recover."

"Brain damage is beyond them. Not even they can re-build neurons."

Deka stumbled, and his pace slowed. Deka had tried much longer than Kylac had, so he felt even more drained.

"And still no survivors," Deka said. "Over two hun-dred worlds we've heard from now. Didn't anyone make it out alive? They haven't even caught scent of Rive or Friend. Or Sonjaa. Or our hatchlings..."

Deka stared at the ground as he walked. Kylac walked closer to him, pushing right up against him.

"They're all dead," Deka continued at last. "All of them. And we don't even know why!"

They were some distance from the sphere to Selta, but it felt good to walk to a planet whenever they wanted with-out having to wait days to calculate a new way. Many peo-ple were mingling on the hub. Many different species, adapted to survive in as many environments. Some flew. Some walked on two legs, some on four, some on six, or eight, or ten.

Deka passed a Ninelegs. It didn't smell familiar, but he wished he could ask how things were on that deadly world now. Deka faced forward and kept walking. The scents varied as much as the languages. It was just like old times, before the disaster.

A few Zjr passed. Kylac scented them but didn't have a chance to say hello. He didn't know them personally, and he wondered what brought them here.

Portals hovered around them, all perfectly spherical, people stepping into and out of them. Bright worlds, dark worlds, rainy worlds. The contacted universe was coming together again, and the two Relians were not part of it. They felt just as isolated as before.

Someone in the distance screamed. Then another.

The portals beside them wavered, wobbled, and winked away. Other portals expanded, eating the ground and several people nearby. More screaming, and those portals vanished, taking pieces of bodies with them.

More spheres collapsed. Deka and Kylac shoved and pushed through the terrified offworlders to where they heard Ee and Kelm screaming. The crowd was moving in that direction as well.

Some portals whipped to the side, shearing off arms, legs, antennae. Other portals wobbled and flickered before disappearing.

Finally every portal was gone. The people on the hub held their breath. Some of the people who had lost limbs cried and screamed.

Deka and Kylac pushed through and found Ee and Kelm lying unconscious on the metal ground. Kylac listened to Ee and heard shallow breathing. Deka listened to Kelm, who was not breathing.

The Relians stood and looked around at the hub and all these people stranded here, many of them writhing on the ground, bleeding.

Xce

The portal closed behind Deka, and he and Kylac scanned the horizon. A shallow sea, only ankle deep, extended in all directions. It covered an entire hemisphere of Xce, broken up in multiple places by land that rose just barely above the water.

The portal hub was set up on muddy land, covered in sticks and branches so offworlders wouldn't have to walk in the mud. The hub was empty, not a single portal open, not a single person around.

They ran off the path into the shallow water. A light rain was falling. It was almost always raining on this region of the planet, and Kylac's fur became soaked in mere moments. It clung to his bare frame, weighing him down.

Land was in the distance, and Deka chased it. Kylac tried dropping to all fours to keep up with his raptor, but after just a few strides he concluded his face was too low to the ground to be comfortable, and the water was just high enough to splash in his face every time he landed.

People had gathered on the landmass. Deka approached, climbed up the soggy soil, and merged with the amphibians and theropods. The amphibians could walk on two legs or four. The featherless, raptor-like creatures looked and moved similar to Deka's own species, but taller and lacking arms.

Deka's nose caught the scent of their Archeons in their midst. Everyone turned and gazed at him absently.

Deka waited a moment for someone to show him where their Archeons were, or to tell him what had happened since the portals went out again, and then he remembered the creatures of Xce were neither scent-based nor sight-based. On this planet, sound was the primary sense, and nobody recognized him because he had not spoken. That knowledge still came to him after a delay, and Deka growled inwardly at the disaster for taking some of his mind away.

"Where are your Archeons?" he called out.

At the sound of his voice, everyone rushed toward him.

By now Kylac had climbed out of the water and onto the muddy ground. The amphibians and featherless, armless birds had gathered around Deka and didn't even notice the fox.

"Did we lose another planet?" someone said.

"I don't know!" Deka shouted back. "I don't know what's wrong. I'm sorry we didn't come sooner, but we had to send as many of the people on Towe back to their home worlds as possible. What happened to your Archeons?"

They had not noticed Kylac. The fox remained still, observing, marveling that they did not even know he was here. Being a scent-based creature, watching a society such as this always fascinated him. To Kylac, nothing existed unless it had a scent, but to the salamanders and armless theropods of Xce, something only became real when they heard it. Kylac would not exist to these people until he made a noise.

They led the raptor further inland, moving away from Kylac, and the fox took in the rest of the landscape. The people here thrived in the rain. They were always wet, and every plant on this region of the world was either half submerged or completely underwater. The ground around the fox was permanently saturated, meaning no matter where Kylac stepped, he was in mud. He walked quietly inland, stepping in everyone else's footprints, hundreds of them, all aimed in the same direction.

The salamanders and featherless birds of Xce led Deka far inland and then made way for him to reach the center of the group. Four bodies lay on their backs, partially submerged in clear water, two of each species. The Archeons. The amphibians had green skin. One had yellow spots, and the other had brown and red spots. The featherless theropods were both covered in white skin, but one had pink spots up and down his body.

Deka stepped between two of the salamander bodies, knelt down, and listened for breath. Then he realized the people of Xce could tell who was breathing and who was not.

"Are they still alive?" Deka asked.

"In the body," said one of the birds. "This is the second time they've fallen…"

"They survived the first," Deka said. "I hope this doesn't kill them."

He reached into the water and weaved his fingers between the salamander's. The water here felt so warm. After a moment, Deka remembered that the microbes living in the water were warming his scales. They ate impurities and released heat as a byproduct. They were on his scales right now, eating whatever was on it, which warmed his hand and feet.

"Is everyone all right?" Deka asked, still looking into the salamander's eyes. They were closed, but the eyelids were so thin they appeared to be open. "Can you live long without the grove?"

One of the amphibians answered. "We did for a while, but they woke up just a few days after the first disaster and restored the colonies. Now those ways are out again. Everyone is hungry, and if we don't eat soon, we'll have to migrate again."

"Just like our ancestors..." The bird splashed her tail in the shallow water. The others laughed, too.

Deka looked around at the theropods and amphibians gathered here. They didn't smell hungry and desperate yet, but that could change in an instant. He saw his fox standing in the distance—in plain sight but hidden from their auditory world. Kylac wagged his tail, laughing with them.

Deka remembered the shoreline. There had been no colony. He scented the air and confirmed the colony of bacteria they kept here was gone, which meant the other colonies around the ocean must also be gone by now.

Kylac's ears folded back, and Deka lowered his neck. He and Kylac had reached the same conclusion. They could open ways anywhere on the world, but there was no way to know where the next colony would be, or for how long. They would either have to go to the trees and restore the portals, or open ways across the whole ocean and hope they found a colony by chance. Either would be faster than migrating, but the people needed to eat now.

Fortunately, Deka had a sense of smell, and he could lead them to food faster than they could on their own.

Kylac stood tall and waved a hand to Deka, very slowly. When he had the raptor's attention, he used the sign language of Lesa.

You lead them to food. I will reopen the ways at the grove.

Deka bobbed his neck

Kylac began moving away, stepping in everyone else's footprints so he would make little noise across the watery soil. Deka watched him, rubbing his claws, wondering how long the fox could remain hidden.

2

The grove lay a thousand paces away from the portal hub. The trees stood only neck high, arranged in rows and columns, their roots almost completely exposed. This far inland, he stood on solid ground that was wet but not muddy. It was still raining, and the trees liked the temperature lower than the surrounding land, so they created their own pocket of atmosphere, and a dense fog covered the grove.

Generations ago, the salamanders and armless birds cleared away the soil in this area to make room for the plants and their extensive root systems. Each tree had its own cavity in the soil filled with water. With the trees' roots exposed, the waste they generated floated to the surface of each pool. The rain overflowed the pits, and the waste ran off into dozens of channels that led to eight endpoints surrounding the grove.

Those eight places were where the portals should be. They carried the runoff from the trees directly into the soil at various points around the planet. The runoff fed the microbes in the soil, which produced waste products that fed the bacteria in the water above, which created a reproductive frenzy among them and sustained the colonies of bacteria at each settlement.

Before the discovery of portal physics, the bacteria in the water periodically flared into wild colonies hundreds of paces wide around various parts of the ocean. These colonies grew up, died off, and then reemerged elsewhere. The salamander species migrated around the shallow sea searching for these colonies. It was the only thing they could eat. The armless theropods once followed the amphibians as they migrated, hunting the slowest and the deafest.

Then one day, several thousand years ago, each species realized the other was intelligent and began devising ways to understand one another. With understanding came co-operation, and the theropods began hunting the other animals that migrated with the bacteria.

Learning about another intelligent species led to the discovery of portal physics, which in turn led to discovering what caused the bacteria colonies to grow. It turned out the microbes under the soil fed off the acidic runoff of certain trees that grew inland. It took time for the plant's waste to work its way up through the wet soil and run off into the ocean, which was why the flare-ups of bacteria were sporadic and could occur thousands of paces away from land.

The people of Xce now cultivated these plants and used the portals to divert the runoff to several particular areas of the planet, forming permanent colonies just offshore of every settlement on Xce.

Now the portals were gone again, the colonies had dissipated, and the people were desperate.

Kylac approached one hole in the soil where a tree was rooted and peered inside. A grey mass floated just beneath the surface and extended a few claw's reaches down. The colony smelled pungent, and Kylac tried hard to imagine life without being able to smell this.

Kylac had the better nose, but Deka had an easier time moving around on this world. Fur was a liability here, and Deka's large feet didn't sink as far into the saturated soil.

Kylac had a rough idea for where to place the portals, and he began calculating. He didn't bother shaking off; he was used to being soaked and heavy already, but the water was so warm he didn't lose any heat. With nowhere dry to sit, he crouched next to one of the trees, up to his waist in water.

The bacteria found many impurities around his sheath and under his tail and began releasing heat as they fed off them. Kylac's tail wagged, his ears folded back, and he panted. He started rubbing himself, working the bacteria deeper into his fur. More heat was his reward, and he panted harder. He was happy to indulge while he calculated, as he hadn't found a willing partner on Towe. He didn't expect to find a partner on this planet either, as few on Xce liked fur, and they were too hungry to be aroused.

A few salamanders and armless theropods walked through the fog. Kylac closed his mouth and held still. He liked being hidden to these people. Something about being hidden in plain sight was fascinating, and it spoke volumes about how the senses shaped perception of one's reality, the study of which formed the foundation of portal physics and his own development as an Archeon.

A couple dozen people wandered into the grove, an even mix of both species. The salamanders fanned out. They bent over at each tree, dipped their snouts into the water, and mouthed around. A few found the tiny colonies growing near the trees, but those weren't even enough to sustain a hatchling.

Kylac wondered why the birds were here. There were no animals to hunt in the grove, and they could not eat the sour fruit that grew on these trees.

The fox sat waist-deep in the water, watching the group scavenge. The birds were hunting, too. There were no animals around, and yet they were walking around as if stalking the animals that ate the bacteria. They crouched low, like Relian raptors, taking high steps above the water. As Kylac watched, the birds walked slower and slower, making less and less noise. The salamanders didn't notice.

Kylac slowly rose from the water. The armless birds had grouped together, stepping high and light. They were now to the point where they made no noise at all, and they had surrounded the salamanders in the grove. One of them was eyeing a nearby male with black and orange skin, shiny and smooth as the rain washed over him. Kylac quietly scented the bird from a distance. The scent reminded him of Deka just before a hunt.

The theropod shot forward, baring rows of sharp teeth, feet now making noise in the water but too close for the salamander to react. Kylac leaped out of the water. The theropod didn't know Kylac was there until the fox was on top of him, pulling him to the ground. The fox held his head to the ground for a few moments and then released him. The young male rolled to his feet and dashed away, fast and noisy. The other birds surrounding the grove ran after him, vanishing into the mist.

Kylac turned around. The salamanders were glaring at him. The one with black and orange skin spoke first.

"Who are you?"

"I'm Kylac."

They recognized his voice and rushed to him.

"Why weren't you with Deka?" someone said.

"I was wondering where Deka's fox was," said someone else.

"Why did you hide?"

The salamanders had gathered in a tight group around him. Kylac scented the birds in the distance. Their scents had become strangely alike. No individual minds. Just instinct.

"I wanted to know how long I could stay hidden. Listen, everyone. I'm here to reopen the portals to feed the colonies. I should be able to hold them open long enough to get them started. Deka is gathering everyone up to find a wild colony. Why aren't you with him?"

"I didn't want to wait," someone said.

The others smacked their tails down. They weren't laughing; they were agreeing. They used the same gesture for both.

Kylac kept breathing the scents of the birds. They were still out there, hiding in the fog. The other salamanders seemed to notice, and all of them were looking around through the mist.

"Kylac," said the black and orange salamander. "What's happening?"

Kylac swallowed. The scents of the theropods in the distance sank to the bottom of his gut and rotted. "Hunger."

3

Deka scented the air. The wind was always light but warm on this ocean. Even when cold air moved through, it felt warm. The air was warm, the water was warm, the people were warm. This was definitely an amphibian's planet. The only theropod on the entire planet with arms stood at the front of more than a hundred people, salamander and armless bird alike. More people had heard of his arrival and came to join him.

He smelled no colonies anywhere nearby, and this worried him. These people had been hungry for days. He was surprised they had not started migrating by now, but some of the people had told him the last time the Archeons had woken up just before they reached that point, so they still held out hope.

Deka doubted it would work out so well this time. Even as he calculated a new way around Xce, he wondered how many people on other planets were dying because he and Kylac went here and not there.

The portals hadn't been open that long, so most people gathered on one of the main hub worlds, like Towe. No off-worlders had been on Xce, which was good for them, as there would be little for anyone to eat here. The fruit tasted terrible, the ground was wet, it was always rainy, and there was no shelter of any kind anywhere.

Deka hoped to gather as much of the population as possible and take them to food. Plenty of wild colonies grew all over the ocean, so it should be easy for a scent-based creature to find one.

The raptor began walking, stepping high so he wouldn't splash, his wide feet keeping him from sinking into the soil. The birds and salamanders walked on either side of the blue-scaled Relian through the shallow sea.

One particular bird walked beside him, and Deka took in her scent from a distance. The birds of Xce had nice scents. Very Relian-like. They were the most similar species to the theropods of Rel in the contacted universe, save for one detail.

Their lack of arms was rather disturbing. They always appeared injured, and every time Deka saw one he couldn't help but feel anxious. It was a leftover instinct from his own species' primitive time. Any deviation from the normal physical form must be an injury, and families would protect the sick one. This reaction gave all Relians a feeling of intense compassion for these birds. Though they could do almost anything with their snouts that Deka could do with his hands, Deka still felt he had to help them.

The Selts had long ago tasted the DNA of the reptiles of Xce and determined them to be halfway between reptile and avian. People referred to them interchangeably as both. Their DNA was identical to a Relian's apart from just nineteen gene sequences, and Deka marveled at how much of a difference that made, as Relians were much closer to reptile species.

The star set on the horizon. Deka walked them onward, and then he was ready to open the portal. He stopped. Held still. A sphere opened before them. Deka made it larger than normal so more people could fit through at once.

Deka stepped through the large sphere and emerged on the other side of the planet, where the star still shined high in the sky over the settlement farthest from the hub. The people heard him splash in the water and ran toward him. More poured out of the portal and reunited. They had been cut off from each other since the second disaster.

The raptor scented the air. No scent of bacteria here either. Deka huffed and began working on a new way.

One bird approached him. "Is there any bacteria left?"

Deka snorted, and his killing claws rose. He turned to face her, taking in her scent. She had spoken in the Relian language.

"There is," Deka said in Rel. "Finding it... is... It is the difficult part."

"How long will we have to wait?" She had excellent pronunciation.

Deka couldn't concentrate. "I don't know. As... As long as it..."

Her scent. Deka couldn't get enough of it. He stepped closer to her. Scented her neck harder. Deeper. Scented her whole body. He stopped just short of scenting under her tail, and then he realized what he was doing and hopped away. She stared at him, neck held high and curled backwards in bewilderment.

"I'm sorry," he said. "Your scent... It reminds me of Sonjaa. My mate."

Her neck uncurled and relaxed. "I have a scent?"

Deka rubbed his claws together. She wouldn't know what that meant, so he smacked the water with his tail. "Everyone does. And yours... It's so similar. For a moment I thought... What is your name?"

"Cheh."

"I'm Deka. There is food out there. I'll find it."

She bobbed from the base of her neck, keeping the rest of her body still. Then she turned around and joined the others. Everyone had been reunited with someone, and they were eager to hear each other again. Deka opened his mouth, about to call her back, but stopped. In his head he knew this was not Sonjaa, but the scent compelled him to follow her.

Deka snorted, cleared his nose, and let the calculations run through his mind instead. Moments later, he formed a connection between two points in spacetime and opened the point at both ends into a sphere to another settlement. The star was rising on this part of the world. He stepped through, and another five hundred people were on the other side, shin deep in the shallow sea.

"I'm here to lead you to food," Deka announced as he moved away from a sphere four times larger than he was.

People began pouring through behind him. They quickly found relatives and friends, all separated when the portals went out. It was the second time they had been cut off like this, and now everyone was scared.

Deka walked through the crowd, sniffing the air. No bacteria here, and the air smelled equally devoid of it in every direction. Deka began meditating on a portal to their next settlement. He sat down in the water, and the bacteria warmed his slit. Deka lightly rubbed his claws together, idly thinking Kylac had probably done this ten times by now.

A familiar scent approached him. Cheh stood just a few paces away, and Deka breathed the air coming off her. It was as though Rel had never been destroyed and he had not spent the last half year traveling from planet to planet cleaning up after the disaster—like waking up from a bad dream and finding your fox and your mate and hatchlings by your side, and everything is all right.

"I haven't eaten since the colonies vanished," she said in Relian.

Her voice reminded him of Sonjaa now. It hadn't before. Deka walked closer to her. "Are the hatchlings safe? Is Rupi all right?"

She stared at him, neck curling backwards.

Deka realized what he had said. He turned away and cleared his nose. It didn't help. "I'm sorry. You... You remind me so much of my mate."

"You had eggs with her?"

"Yes." Deka preferred not to look at her. The voice. The scent. They were perfect. Everything except the lack of arms. "Six eggs. Three hatched. They were still young when the disaster happened."

"Were they on Rel when it was lost?"

"They were. So was I, but not nearby."

Deka hoped she would respond. He wanted her to speak again; every word took him back to his mate and hatchlings, and he could keep dozens of portals open for years at a time.

She did not reply. Deka slowly turned and faced her. Even acknowledging her lack of arms, the trick her scent played on his mind did not subside.

"How long has it been since you ate?" he asked.

"Sixteen days. How long can Relians go without eating?"

"I can survive up to fifty of your days before starving. Comfortably, I can live for nine. I prefer to eat once every four days. The canine species on Rel can only live for half that time, and they prefer to eat more often."

"The joke is the canines need sex more than food."

Deka rubbed his claws and then smacked his tail in the water. "That may as well be true, thanks to the reptile species of Rel."

She stepped closer to Deka. She stood a whole head taller, with longer legs, but she walked so much like a raptor.

"Where is your canine? I thought raptors and foxes were inseparable."

She was right in front of him. So close if he stuck his tongue out he would hit her. Deka tried not to breathe.

"He's on Xce."

"He is? Where?"

"He's in the grove, restoring the portals from the trees. Probably trying to convince one of the salamanders to mount him."

She smacked her tail a few times. "Does he favor creatures without fur?"

"He doesn't care. He's tried it with noncompatible species. Didn't work, but he had to try."

"When did he arrive? I did not notice him."

"He can be very quiet when he wants to be."

"Did he have a mate on Rel?"

"It doesn't work that way with foxes. They don't take permanent partners."

"But raptors do?"

Deka was almost finished with the calculations. Normally he would just continue talking and let the equations fall into place, but it hurt to do that now.

"Just a moment."

He backed away from her, turned, and walked a few paces. He stood still, mentally reached into the universe and pulled a piece from the other side through. A sphere expanded in what had been empty space. The people on the other side noticed, and they gathered around the portal.

Deka looked back at Cheh and then leaped through. She followed immediately after. Another settlement. The bacteria colony was gone, and the people were isolated and hungry.

"I am an Archeon," he announced. "I'm here to help you find food."

Birds and amphibians shouted and rushed to meet Deka. Deka returned their greetings and answered their questions as best he could. Now that the portals had gone out a second time, everyone wanted to know how their Archeons were.

When the people had calmed down, Deka scented the air. A faint odor drifted on the wind. He turned his snout to the water he was standing in. He bent low, sniffed it, tasted it. Millions of bacteria flowed over his tongue, and yet they would not feed anyone. The colony had to grow large enough to form a soupy muck floating between the surface and the floor. He swallowed the water. The bacteria couldn't live in Deka's gut, so they would not harm him.

He began walking to the horizon, toward the scent. The people followed the sound his feet made. He had gathered about two thousand people in total, some still pouring out of the portal. His group now included most of the planet's population. He couldn't reach everyone, and he hoped the rest would find food on their own.

Cheh walked beside him. Having her in his line of sight gave him a moment to notice how she was not a raptor. Her lack of arms, her high steps, her taller gait. His eyes told him this was not Sonjaa.

"The scent for the bacteria is this way," Deka said.

"I still don't understand what you're doing," she said, "but I admire it."

Deka held his claws together as he walked. Hearing her voice made him feel so warm. "You speak Relian very well."

"I have always had a talent for languages."

Deka's heart stopped for a moment, and he stumbled. "Sonjaa did, too."

She switched to the avian language of Ixcy. "I speak other languages. I've been told I should be an Archeon, as quick as I have learned them."

Deka was still trying to wrap his mind around it. He fell silent for a few steps. Cheh turned her head and looked at him. She smelled eager for him to reply.

"That is how it starts," Deka said at last, in Ixcy's language. "If you have a talent for something like that, the Archeons will try to snatch you up as an apprentice."

"Sraal told me much about it. I think I understand the ideas behind it and how it works. I wanted to ask him if I could begin learning."

Deka growled in concern. "That's a huge thing to ask, Cheh. Not everybody can do what an Archeon does."

"But everyone is capable, yes?"

"Not everyone, no. Archeons learn how to break down the barrier between the conscious and the subconscious, and it takes a special kind of person to take in that much information and hold all of it in your mind at once. It can be overwhelming."

"How did you begin?"

Deka turned away from her and faced the shallow ocean that reached from horizon to horizon in all directions. "I actually began as a hatchling."

"That young?"

"I was very young. Someone told Kylac he had a talent and should find out if he could be an Archeon. He started learning. Then I started learning, and I was capable as well. I didn't want to do it at first, but Kylac was eager, so Rel's Archeons began teaching us."

"I learned it's common for Relian Archeons to be in pairs."

"Yes, that's true. I would not have tried it if not for my fox."

"I don't understand," Cheh said. "You have a mate, but you also have a fox?"

"Every fox needs a raptor," Deka said. "Every raptor needs a fox."

Deka raised his snout. He just realized it had been a while since he had scented for the bacteria.

"What do you smell?" she said.

"The bacteria is stronger. We're going in the right direction. I can't judge exactly how far away it is. Kylac could. His nose is much better than mine. I miss him already."

"There is a whole universe of scent hidden to me. It makes me wonder how I could possibly learn to open portals when I can't even smell."

"There are people who have no eyes, and they navigate between worlds perfectly. Every species has different ways of sensing reality. None of that matters because being an Archeon means perceiving the universe as it is, not as your senses filter it to your mind. Everyone is aware of what the universe really is, but not everyone can learn to take down the barrier between the conscious and the subconscious. Not everyone can commit to the life."

"I've heard of the life. It is intimidating, but I think I might like to learn."

Deka rubbed his claws together, slowly. He wasn't laughing at her. Meeting someone who was interested in what he did always made him happy.

The wind shifted. Deka smelled something different coming from the people of Xce, and he turned around, scenting rapidly. His eyes confirmed his suspicions.

Cheh hopped back and followed his gaze. "What's wrong?"

The population of Xce was many paces behind them. Two thousand people, bipedal salamander and featherless bird. Something seemed wrong with their collective scent, and the way the birds walked also seemed wrong. Deka watched them as they caught up to him.

"Deka?" Cheh said.

"Look at them. Do you see anything wrong?"

She scanned them. "Nothing looks wrong."

"Then listen. Does anything sound wrong to you?"

She held still and listened. She leaned forward. "Actually... Yes."

"What do you hear?"

"The birds. They're not splashing as they walk."

"Notice where the birds are."

She looked again. "On the outside."

"They're walking on the outside while the salamanders are on the inside, and since you don't have a sense of smell, I'll tell you the scents the birds are giving off are wrong. I can't put it in words, but something is out of place, and one of the things you will learn when you become an apprentice is to trust your subconscious. Your own mind is aware of more than you know, and every species experiences it—a feeling of something not right, a hunch. That is subconscious knowledge trying to come to the surface. As an Archeon, you will learn how to have access to both at all times, and when you learn how to do this, you will discover what your mind is capable of—memory will expand, language capacity will broaden, pattern recognition will come quickly to you—you will start to perceive the universe and everything in it as a series of interlocking patterns, and you will learn incredibly fast—which you'll need to do when on other worlds—all of these things await you when you become an apprentice, but right now I need you to help me."

Cheh blinked and shook her head. "Sure—"

"Follow me and protect the salamanders, but don't kill anybody!"

Deka tore through the water, splashing loudly. He flexed his claws and followed the scent. It drifted and wavered, but he could tell where it was coming from: a male bird with red skin. He wasn't walking with the others; he was herding the salamanders. Every bird was doing it, and the scent coming from them was dangerous. Hungry.

The red theropod saw Deka running toward him and veered away with a screech, charging into the salamanders. About a dozen other birds followed him. The salamanders heard the splashing, turned and saw the birds coming for them. At first they did not know what to do, but then instinct older than their civilization moved them, and they dropped to all fours, slipped under the water, and squiggled away fast.

Deka reached them just as the lead male plunged his snout beneath the water trying to find a neck or a tail. Deka jumped onto his flank but held his killing claws up. He knocked the red male to the ground and then stood on top of him and looked around.

The other theropods were dipping their snouts into the water, but so far they hadn't found anything. Cheh dashed in and charged one of the females, stopping just short of ramming her. The other female jumped away, hissing at Cheh.

Every bird stepped back, hissing at both her and Deka. The salamanders around them moved away. The entire group had stopped.

"Everyone!" Deka shouted. "Food is not far away! Wait until we reach it! Do not give in to the hunger!"

All was silent.

"All the birds, walk with the salamanders. Do not surround them. Do not herd them. Salamanders, do not let yourselves be herded! Walk on the outside of the group. We do not have far to go before we find food for everyone. My fox is at the grove restoring the portals. We will stay until your Archeons wake up."

Silence. Then birds and salamanders passed Deka's words down, and they moved noisily amongst each other. Deka began to smell less separation between the birds and amphibians.

Deka turned and followed the scent of bacteria again, and this time he did not walk too far ahead. Cheh walked at his side. Deka scented her, glanced at her, and then kept his eyes on the horizon. He wanted to ask why she was here with him and not back there with the rest of them, but he did not speak. He liked having her close.

4

A sphere opened at one of the channels in the foggy grove. It was small, not meant for any person to pass through, and dark, opening directly into the soil. Kylac spun this one at the grove but left the other side stationary. The water would enter the portal, but the soil would not exit on this side. The seeding had started. The salamanders stood back and watched. They were making sounds of awe and hope, seeing a portal here again.

"But it will take days to feed the bacteria," one of the males said.

"The point is to start the process," Kylac said. "All of you should be with Deka. He'll find the wild colonies. I'm here to restart the permanent colonies." Kylac's tail waved. It was waterlogged and merely flopped about just above the water. "Makes me wonder how you people found food at all. If you can't smell it, how did you find it?"

"We migrated," said the black and orange salamander next to him.

"I know, but did you just wander around this ocean and happen to stumble across it?"

"That's why our population was only about three hundred for thousands of years."

"Right. I should know things like this, but I'm not as sharp as I used to be. I'm going to try to speed things up. I'm calculating two portals at once. One for the trees. One for the rest of you."

"For us? Why?"

Kylac scented the air. "They're still out there."

The salamanders looked around. Kylac knew they were listening more than looking.

"You can't hear them," Kylac said, "but I can smell them. They're hunting you. Walking very quietly, just as they used to."

"They would do that?"

"Hunger does this to everyone. The higher mind closes, and base instincts come forward. Theirs is to hunt you. Yours will be to run and hide and find bacteria in the water, just as you were doing earlier."

Kylac turned. He smelled them everywhere through the fog. It was unnerving, and he felt absolutely immobile with his fur soaked.

"It's not safe for you here. I know how they move and how they think, and I have claws and teeth. You do not. Deka is out there finding food. I know how he thinks as well. He'll have set up portals linking the different settlements together. He can hold all of them open for a while. All you have to do is go through them until you find everyone. That will be where he picked up the scent."

"What scent?"

"Bacteria colonies. I'm sure he hasn't gone far. You'll hear them."

"But even if we do, there won't be enough food for everyone."

"If you stay here, I guarantee you will be attacked. There is no food here, but you are food for someone else."

A few of the salamanders wandered away, staying close together as a group. The others began to wander, searching the water.

The salamander with black and orange skin stayed next to Kylac. Kylac's tail wagged.

"What's your name?"

"Doma."

"You seem to be in the best state of mind out of everyone here. How long since you ate?"

"Days."

"Hunger hasn't taken you yet. You'll probably have to convince the others to leave. I have a feeling if you don't, they'll wander around here until they die."

The salamander looked back at the group as they roamed the grove, dipping snouts into the various pools. They had already probed those pools, but they were doing it again and again.

"It scares me, Kylac. What's happening to us. It's like I don't know anyone anymore. The birds... My people..."

"Hunger does that to everyone, Doma."

"It won't happen to me."

Feet pounded the ground through the mist. The salamanders heard it before Kylac did, and Kylac smelled them approaching. He spread his legs and fanned his claws.

A featherless, armless theropod burst through the fog. The salamanders stumbled backwards, condensing into a tiny group, then one by one they dropped to all fours. Had they been out in open water, they would be submerged, but in the grove they were still exposed.

More birds came through the fog, circling their group, winding between the trees. Kylac stayed on the outside of the salamanders, running back and forth in a small arc, holding the theropods at a distance.

Doma imitated Kylac, raising his bald hands up and keeping his tail straight behind him. He tried to match Kylac's defensive stance, but his legs were plantigrade, so he could not hunch over properly. Kylac's teeth were bared. The salamander tried to bare his, but since he had no teeth he looked ridiculous. Kylac glanced at him, trying not to laugh because Doma was guarding the other side of the group of salamanders and keeping the birds away from them.

Ten theropods ran around them in opposing directions, feet hitting the ground as hard as possible. Kylac recognized this as an instinctual behavior from generations of hunting the salamanders in the shallow sea. They would splash up so much water they drowned out all other sounds, keeping the salamanders from communicating with each other. The prey would only hear the sounds of the predator's footsteps, and it would send them into a panic. It was working.

Kylac snarled and growled, trying to raise his voice above their noise. Doma was trying to make sounds like that, too. The amphibian sounded so ridiculous, but it was helping. They were breaking the sound barrier the birds were trying to erect around them.

The group of salamanders stayed huddled together on all fours. As far as Kylac was concerned, they were mindless animals right now.

One of the birds shifted direction and charged. Kylac dropped to all fours, jumped and landed on it, raking his claws across the bird's back and flank. His claws were dull, but he still drew blood, and Kylac resisted the urge to clamp his jaws around the bird's neck.

The bird went down, sliding across the soil, kicking it up and exposing the mud underneath. Kylac stood and jumped off. He smelled another one running close. Kylac ran on all fours to her, but she saw him coming and veered away just as he came within striking range. Kylac backed away and stood guard as the birds circled in opposing directions.

He looked over at his helper. Doma was doing exactly as Kylac did, charging an attacking bird. The salamander leaped onto the bird's side, but instead of trying to claw and bite, he hung from the theropod's neck and forced him to crash to the ground. Doma wiggled away, rose up to his hind legs, and stood between the hungry salamanders and the predator. Kylac noticed skid marks all over the ground on Doma's side and deduced that this was the third bird Doma had taken down.

The bird rolled to his feet and scrambled away. The others circled for a few more breaths, but nobody else dared to rush the salamanders huddled in the middle. Finally, they broke formation and vanished into the fog. Kylac and Doma held still for a while, and then the salamander turned to Kylac. Kylac waited until the scent of the birds changed from high alert to anxious waiting, and then he dropped his defensive posture.

The salamanders remained huddled, still hungry and scared. Kylac jogged around them and joined Doma at his side, wagging his tail. "That was good for a prey species."

Doma's tail smacked the ground a couple times. "I've studied predators my whole life. Visited many worlds before the disasters, lived among predators."

Kylac's ears bloomed. "Really?"

"I want to help you."

Kylac's tail wagged wildly. "So I don't need to say you have no defenses and can't do any real damage to the birds?"

"No."

"And I also don't need to warn you that if you don't go through the portal, you might be ripped apart and eaten by hungry predators?"

"No."

"Good. I hate stating the obvious."

Doma's tail smacked the ground. "The birds won't go away just because the salamanders leave. They'll hunt you, too. Let me help."

"Do what you can to keep them off me. I'll protect you as best as I can. But remember, as soon as the birds figure out you have no claws or teeth, they will not be afraid of you."

"I know."

Kylac's waterlogged tail wagged faster. "I don't think you realize what you're doing, but I'm glad for the help."

He turned away then and focused on the group of salamanders. A sphere appeared between him and them. The shallow sea of some other location on Xce was visible on it, and another portal was on the other side.

Doma moved around the group, stomping, shouting, and pushing the other salamanders into the portal. They rose to their hind legs and stepped through one by one. Even in their state of hunger, they knew what a portal was.

Kylac scented the air. "Deka hasn't closed the portals yet. Last chance to change your mind."

The salamander stood tall, carrying himself as a predator would. Kylac let the portal close, leaving himself and Doma alone in the grove.

"You admire predators?" Kylac said.

"They have fascinated me since I started breathing air. I wondered what it was like not to be afraid of anything or anyone. To hold someone else's life in my mouth."

Kylac walked over to one of the channels and held still for a moment. The equations in his mind connected two points in spacetime, and another tiny way opened. The runoff from the trees began flowing into the soil on another part of the planet.

"I hope you're ready to be one for a while."

Kylac heard footsteps through the grove. So did Doma, and he stood alert. Kylac turned and watched him. He wondered if Doma liked fur, and how it would feel with a salamander, and with predatory theropods all around them.

5

Deka felt the portals he had left across the settlements straining his mind. Reluctantly, he closed them, yearning once again for the days when he seemed to have no limit to how many he could keep open at once.

The raptor walked beside Cheh. She had been asking him all sorts of questions, wanting to know what the equations in Deka's head sounded like. She imagined they must be incredibly loud, all the portals he kept open on this world between the settlements, and she wanted him to describe the sounds they made.

When Deka told her they made no sound at all, she could not believe him. Everything made a sound, no matter how small or how quiet.

Deka tried to explain that the equations produced no sounds, scents, or vision. It was a sense Deka could not even explain, a sense every species was missing and had no way to mimic but could still manipulate. A sense of the universe. A sense of reality.

"Well, when I learn, I'll tell you what the equations sound like to me," Cheh said.

Deka rubbed his claws together as he splashed across the water. He admired how easily she walked, how her body was built for walking in shallow water. The differences between their bodies were so subtle, and the longer he breathed her air the less he noticed them.

"Please do. I want to know."

"I should have asked sooner," Cheh said. "I could have been an apprentice by now. I could do something to help. I'm worried it's too late. Are the Archeons still alive?"

"I think they are, but I can't say. This disaster didn't affect me. It could mean another planet was destroyed."

"One of the other hub worlds?"

"Possibly, but there's no way to know without trying to go there. Kylac and I might find it."

"Rel was a big enough loss. I can't imagine losing another. Do you think anyone will rebuild the portals again?"

"After this? Until someone figures out what's causing it, I'll be surprised if any Archeon wants to take the risk again. The contacted universe may never be the same."

"It's... It's just..." She trailed off.

"What?"

"Sorry. I haven't eaten in so long... How far are we?"

"The scent is stronger, but I can't tell exactly where the colony is. Otherwise I'd open a portal right now and take everyone to it. Kylac could, but I'm not a fox."

"I wish you could. It hurts."

Deka turned and looked back. The group was downwind, making it difficult to catch their scents, but they were starting to separate again. Deka stopped, turned around, and walked straight down the middle of the congregation. The salamanders were in the middle, and the birds were walking on the outside again.

"Intermix, everyone!"

The birds and salamanders were sullen, slow to move, and they smelled delirious.

"Do not walk separately!" Deka called out. "Stay together! Food is somewhere ahead of us! Hold yourselves together until we find it!"

Deka did not like the scent coming from the group. The salamanders smelled alike. Most of the birds smelled alike as well. When the salamanders stepped, the birds turned and noticed. Whenever the birds took an audible step, the salamanders backed away. They had backed away as far as they could into a single cluster.

They did not hear each other as fellow citizens of Xce, but predator and prey. They did not hear him as a Relian raptor. The salamanders heard him as a predator. That meant—

Deka jumped to the side just as a large male with pink skin splashed up behind him, teeth snapping where Deka's neck would have been. Deka screeched at him, fanning his claws and swiping the air between them. The large male backed away, showing his teeth, kicking the air.

Cheh stood beside him, snarling at the male and kicking the empty air as well.

The salamanders backed away. The birds were starting to run around them, converging around Deka, Cheh, and the large male.

"What's he doing?" Cheh asked.

"He thinks I'm the dominant bird among them. He's trying to take me down. Right now I'm the only thing keeping them from attacking the salamanders."

Deka lunged, swiping his hand at the male's snout. The challenger backed away, screeched as loud as he could.

Deka screamed louder.

The armless bird screamed even louder.

Deka snapped his teeth at him and screamed louder still.

The challenger charged, kicking up water. Deka leaped onto him, and the pink-skinned bird toppled over, with Deka landing on top of him. Deka tried to clamp his teeth on the bird's neck, but he squirmed out of it, stood and faced off with Deka again. Deka stared him down, screaming as loud as he could.

Finally the challenger submitted and backed away, and the other birds slinked away as well. The salamanders were wandering.

"This is not working," Deka said.

Cheh turned from Deka to the cowering theropods. "What do you mean?"

"Come with me!"

Deka called out as he ran around the group. The birds followed him.

"Everyone, get behind the salamanders. We're going to herd them from behind."

Cheh blinked a few times. "What? Why?"

"They're too hungry to think. We have to use their instincts to our advantage."

"Deka... I don't know how to say this, but those salamanders... They're just mindless at this point. Wouldn't it be better—?"

Deka growled at her. She shrank back.

"Don't think like that," Deka said. "Notice what you just did? You yielded to me. You hear me as the dominant one of the group. You're suffering from hunger, too, Cheh. These salamanders aren't mindless. They're fellow people of Xce. No matter how hungry you are, never forget that."

"Deka... I'm so..."

Deka called out to the birds. "Everyone, form up around them! Push them forward."

Even in their famished state, the birds understood and obeyed. Following Deka's lead, they formed a U around the salamanders, and Deka ran to the front, caught the scent of the bacteria, and led on.

Cheh walked at Deka's side. Her gait was less sure, and she spoke less, yet her scent was still strongly reminiscent of Sonjaa. Her skin was so unlike a Relian's, and yet it still reminded Deka of Sonjaa. His senses told him this was his mate. It took an act of will to convince himself otherwise.

6

Kylac and Doma stood back to back. The birds were visible only as shadows through the fog, circling them, some running left, others running right, stomping loudly.

Kylac had opened four portals. Four more to go and the grove would be complete again. So far they had not killed anyone, but the birds were hungry, and they were getting braver.

"I admire you," Doma said. "You're not afraid of them. Your first instinct isn't to hide and hope they go for someone else. You stand and fight."

"I'm terrified," Kylac said. "You just can't smell it."

"But you're not a prey species. This is easy for you."

The birds were keeping formation. Nobody dared to break it again, and yet they were not fleeing.

"Doma... Having predator instinct is not a wonderful thing. Just look at them. They've gone mindless with hunger, and what is their first thought? To take someone else's life."

"They're not like this!" Doma said. "I've lived with these people all my life. A few days without food..."

"It's horrible how fragile civilization is."

"Everything in me wants to drop to the ground and hide!" Doma shouted over the footsteps. "Wait for them to be satisfied and leave me alone. I envy you, Kylac. I wish I had your instincts."

Kylac was silent. The rhythmic sound of footsteps around them made concentrating on portal calculations difficult.

"Do you know anything about the canines of Rel?" he asked.

Doma's tail hit the ground. "I've met two Relians before. Pair of females. I had just matured, and she didn't even have to entice me. She was just so eager and fun to be around. I felt weird with her raptor watching us. Someone told me you're the most promiscuous species in the contacted universe."

"Did that someone tell you what my kind was before we met the raptors?"

"No. I was more interested in watching the raptor hunt with the birds."

"Relian canines were the most bloodthirsty, violent people you ever met."

"They were?"

"Yes. Before we discovered portal physics, before we met the raptors, we were fiercely territorial. We killed everything that came in scenting distance. We even killed raptors."

The salamander was silent. Kylac continued, shouting to be heard over the stampede that ringed them through the fog.

"For thousands of years, that's all we did. Our instinct was to keep every scent away from us because everything could be a threat to our survival. We call it scent anxiety. The raptors teach us to channel that impulse into sexual aggression. If not for them, we would still be seeking out and destroying every scent that comes close. Think what would happen if we ever left our planet with that kind of instinct. I've heard people say that without the raptor, the fox would become a cancer consuming the entire universe. So when you talk about predator instinct, don't be so sure it's a good thing. Predatory nature can consume you."

The birds still circled. Doma was even more intimidated by it than Kylac, and yet he stood firm.

"Being prey consumes us, too," Doma said. "All I want to do is hide."

"Civilization emerges because people choose conscious thought over primitive impulses."

"So what about them?" Doma said. "Are they animals?"

"No. Just hungry. You're more prepared to deal with it than they were. Deka and I are here so this doesn't happen to the entire civilization. I am not supposed to be fighting. Deka is here so I don't have to fight. If I keep doing this—"

Suddenly one of the birds charged them. Kylac met her head on and scratched her across the neck. The bird reeled and stumbled away.

Another bird charged Doma. The salamander leaped on him, hung from his neck, and brought him down. As he fell, the bird raised his foot and scraped his claws down Doma's back. The salamander fell from the bird's neck and screamed. The bird hit the ground and tumbled, bowling into another, mud splashing around them.

The birds' formation broke, and they dispersed into the fog. Kylac rose from attack stance and walked to the moaning salamander, who was sprawled out on his stomach, bleeding. Kylac clamped his hand around Doma's snout.

"Don't make a sound. They'll know you're wounded."

The salamander screamed with his eyes instead. Kylac let go of him and scented him from head to tail. Doma was bleeding from three large gashes that ran from the shoulder down to just above the base of the tail.

"Get up."

"I—I—I don't—I don't think—"

"I know it hurts, but get up."

Doma knew it as well as Kylac: the bacteria in the water would clean the wounds. It was how the salamanders survived horrible injuries in more primitive times. Still, he didn't move.

Kylac bent at the knees and hoisted Doma's body upright. The salamander clung to Kylac as the fox walked him to the nearest tree. Doma was cursing. The words did not translate.

"Be glad that bird didn't get your slit," said the fox. "You want pain? Try that. Deka screamed for days one time that happened to him." Kylac's waterlogged tail flopped around. "He never teased me about exposed genitals again."

Doma was trying to laugh, but walking was too painful. Finally they reached a tree, and Kylac lowered Doma's hindquarters under the surface. The salamander lowered himself the rest of the way. The bacteria began eating the infection inside the claw marks, but he would be in a great deal of pain for a long time.

Kylac sat next to him, dangling his paws in the tree water. "So how's the instinct now?"

Doma didn't meet his eyes. "I want to sink here and hide forever."

"That's normal. You're wounded."

"What was I thinking, going against teeth and claws? I have nothing! All I can do is make them angry. What am I *doing*?"

"Calm down, calm down. You're wounded, so your first thought is to go back to what was safe. What would a predator do in this situation?"

Doma thought about it for a while. The tree pond filled with his blood. "Keep hunting."

"The predator still has to risk his life to hunt for food. Even when wounded, he still has to hunt."

"I can barely move!"

"If you don't move, you will die. Now you have to function even while wounded."

"I don't—I don't think I can!"

Kylac stood and walked across the grove. He crouched, closed his eyes, and opened another portal. The rainwater flowed into it, and Kylac suddenly became conscious of the rain soaking his fur again. He looked over his shoulder at the salamander's head poking up from the water.

"When this is over, would you like to try another fox?"

Doma glared at him. The tip of his tail rose out of the water and splashed back down. "How can you think about that now?"

"My raptor raised me well."

Doma panted through his nose a few times, looked around at the fog, and then back to Kylac again. "It would be my first time... With any male. I've been curious."

Kylac licked his lips. "I'll make sure it's your best."

7

Deka tried to see through the rain, but everywhere he looked the water was all the same.

He turned to Cheh. She hadn't spoken in a long time. Deka had been talking to her all the while, trying to encourage her to speak. He wanted to hear her voice again, and keep her mind active, but he wasn't sure it was working.

"Being an Archeon is so demanding there is usually just one or two per planet. The hub worlds have more. Rel had four. Rive and Friend, me and Kylac. You're probably wondering what we give up. I keep saying we have to give up a lot to be an Archeon, but I have a mate and hatchlings. Kylac has sex with everyone he can. Rive didn't have a mate. I think he avoided relationships. Friend was raising a child with Taris. He would have been with her exclusively until the child was old enough to bond with a young raptor. We live normal lives, but we give up the freedom to live quietly. Everyone depends on us to keep the portals open. We are so keenly aware of our environment and how the universe works we can lose track of the people in our lives. That happened to me many times. Some Archeons are content folding into this feeling of being united with the universe, but I fear it. I'm glad for a fox and a mate and hatchlings and all the other people I know to pull me out of that. Chreeb... He was one of those people who kept me from becoming trapped inside my own head. We lost him to the disaster. I still cry for him. He was a one of a kind person. People like them remind me there's more to life than pondering the nature of reality and learning how to manipulate it..."

Cheh walked in silence. Deka felt nervous being so close to her, but he did not want to let her scent stray too far from him. Something told him he had to keep her close.

He turned back. The birds were still in formation, the salamanders moving with them. It was a delicate balance, and Deka decided it was time to reassert himself in case anyone back there was thinking about lunging for an easy meal. He turned and walked around the inside, between the birds and the salamanders, scenting them, listening to them. He made enough noise to assert himself to the birds but not enough to scare the salamanders.

Deka rounded the rear of the group and then began running up the other side. Cheh was still at the lead, and the group was following her. Deka did not like the silence.

One of the males splashed toward the salamanders. Deka spread his claws and charged him. They met halfway and squared off. This male was not cautious, and he lunged forward, striking Deka's shoulder with one foot. Deka ignored the pain, grabbed the male's leg in his jaws, and yanked it out from under him. The male flipped, splashed in the water, and lay still. Deka jumped on top of him, raking his killing claw across his stomach just enough to leave a mark but not enough to draw blood.

Deka hopped off. The challenger rolled up and scurried back into the crowd. Nobody was watching, but everyone was listening. Their scents were so much alike. They walked the same. Sounded the same. They were all hungry.

He kept walking up the group, splashing and calling. Everyone was still in formation, even the salamanders. He had made a complete circle, and now he walked on ahead of them and joined his mate at her side.

Deka nuzzled her neck, making cooing noises. She did not reply. Deka was about to do it again when he caught himself. He walked at her side but kept his distance.

8

Theropods were everywhere, attacking Kylac and Doma from all directions. They were not circling anymore. Now they came from behind, from in front, from the sides. Kylac smelled them just before they landed on top of him, and the air they gave off would have been enough to terrify a Krone. Desperation. Hunger. Need. Kylac sympathized with them and wished he could reason with them, but all he could do was keep them away.

In the back of Kylac's mind, something rose. Knowledge that all he had to do was clamp down on their necks, and their problem would be solved. It would be so easy.

The urge became stronger by the breath. Kylac hadn't felt this way in a long time, and it only ever happened when Deka wasn't here to keep him from reverting to the old ways.

He leaped away from one of the birds charging straight for him, swiping his claws across his flank as the bird sped by. The bird shrieked and stumbled but kept running into the fog. Kylac heard him turn around and rear up to make another pass.

Kylac looked at his hand. His claws had blood on them. Kylac licked the blood up. It was starting to taste good. Kylac tried to stay calm—tried not to let scent anxiety take him.

A few paces away, Doma was hopping around, dodging the predators charging him. The birds were making so much noise, but Doma managed to weave between the stampeding theropods, grabbing necks and legs and forcing them to the ground. The injuries he inflicted rarely drew blood, but they created confusion.

Kylac held the equations in the back of his mind. He wasn't far from opening the last portal, but this one seemed to take forever.

Doma leaped and grabbed a bird's leg, sending both of them to the ground. The bird flipped over, pulling Doma underneath and dragging him along the ground. The scabs running down Doma's back reopened. Moving was difficult for him, but he rose to his feet and kept moving. The bird rolled upright and stomped into the mist with the rest of them.

Kylac limped over to Doma and rested a hand on his shoulder. He leaned on the salamander as he caught his breath. Doma panted as well.

"Doma..."

The scent of his blood caught Kylac's nose. Instantly Kylac's nose found the wound, and he started tasting the blood. Doma held still, confused but trusting.

Kylac growled suddenly and shoved him away. He snarled at the fog, trying to make everyone stay away.

"Kylac?"

The fox snarled at him. He licked the blood from his claws. It hadn't tasted this good in a long time, and Kylac missed it. He ate meat, and the meat always had blood in it, but his mind tended to leave the taste of blood void in his mind. Now he remembered what he had been missing for so many years.

Kylac dropped to all fours and charged the salamander, teeth bared. Doma turned and ran. Kylac easily caught up to him, jumped on his back, and clamped his teeth on Doma's neck. A single drop of blood touched his tongue, and it tasted so good.

Suddenly the birds returned through the fog, and Kylac realized where he was. The blood taste vanished, and he heard Doma's cries of pain underneath him. Kylac stepped off the salamander just as one of the birds rammed into him. Kylac sailed backwards and rolled on the ground, stopping on his stomach. He lifted his head and saw what his nose already told him. The birds were charging through the fog straight for them.

"Doma! Get up!"

The salamander had curled up on the ground and held as still as possible.

"Doma!"

Doma crawled on all four feet, almost slithering, toward the closest tree, and slipped under the water. The birds ran past the pool, straight for Kylac. The fox stood up, splayed his claws, and charged them.

The birds weren't expecting it. The two in front of Kylac stumbled to a halt. Kylac slammed into them, raking his claws across whatever he could reach. He drew more blood. Kylac landed on all fours, faced three more trying to attack them.

Blood tasted good. It smelled good. The scents made him anxious, not aroused, and he liked feeling this way. Kylac let himself go.

He snarled and launched himself at them. He went for the legs this time, clamping his mouth around anything. He tore legs open, raked abdomens, ripped ragged lines in their skin. One of the birds retreated, and Kylac chased her, caught up, and clamped down on her tail. She lashed it about, tossing the fox off. He crashed to the ground, rolled upright and faced six more armless theropods.

His fur was raised, even though it was wet, and it made him look huge. Kylac howled at them. They screeched back. He charged and clashed with the theropods in a mass of claws and teeth. Claws and teeth raked his fur. Kylac's mouth closed around something and struck bone.

Suddenly the birds were retreating, and Kylac stood alone on all fours, skin torn in multiple places, blood all over his muzzle, paws in a small puddle of blood. Kylac bent low and scented it. It smelled so good. He dropped and rolled around in it, but his saturated fur absorbed none of the scent.

The birds had scattered to search for easier prey. The grove fell quiet and peaceful.

Kylac's nose found the only remaining scent in the area, and he rose to his feet, bloody teeth bared. Doma had poked his head above the water. Kylac snarled at him, and the head sank down. Kylac charged, determined to extinguish that scent before it could harm him, or at least make it bleed so it would be no threat. Doma submerged completely.

Kylac skidded to a stop at the edge of the pool and peered in. He could see the salamander below the surface, curled up on one of the tree's roots.

Kylac reached in with his jaws, grabbed Doma's arm, and yanked him up and out of the water. He dragged him away from the pool, stood on his chest, and snarled at his face. Kylac wanted more of his blood. Blood was good. It meant whoever owned it would not harm him. He wanted more good taste.

"Kylac! Stop!"

The fox snarled.

The salamander reached under Kylac and squeezed his sheath.

The blood taste evaporated. Kylac suddenly remembered where he was. He remembered Doma. New desire took over—a linkage between two impulses Deka had conditioned within Kylac many years ago. He instantly slipped out of his sheath.

The impulse changed back into scent anxiety, and Kylac gritted his teeth and snarled again, every muscle in his body tensing up to help extinguish a threat in his territory.

A breath later, Doma's scent became arousing. Kylac gasped and fell to his side. Doma wriggled away and propped himself up on his elbows, looking at Kylac.

Kylac curled into himself, alternating between snarling and convulsing. After a few breaths of going back and forth, he opened his eyes. The salamander's scent went straight to his muscles, and Kylac bared his teeth and snapped his jaws at him. Doma's scent then went straight to his loins, and Kylac whimpered.

"Help me! Please!"

Doma raised a hand. Kylac could tell he was about to flip over and crawl back to the safety of the pool by the tree, but Doma stopped himself. Instead he reached out to Kylac and rested a shaky hand on his cheek.

"I can do that."

Kylac uncurled and leaped on top of the salamander, shoving him to his back. Doma raised his legs. Before Kylac became anxious again, he lay on top of Doma and penetrated him. Doma's scent remained arousing.

"Understand what I mean now?" Kylac said as he frantically bonded with the salamander. It reaffirmed that he needed to keep him close—to keep everyone close—everyone was friendly, especially Doma.

"Being a predator wasn't as easy as I thought it would be," Doma gasped.

"You chose thought over instinct. That's what matters. Thank you."

Kylac opened the last portal. The strain of maintaining all these ways tugged at his mind, but he endured. Doma held him as Kylac thrust.

9

The scent of bacteria was stronger than ever, and finally Deka saw dark water in the distance. The colony stretched from horizon to horizon, and plenty of animals were in it—four-legged animals, two-legged animals, all gathered to feed.

"There it is!" Deka nuzzled Cheh's neck. "Smell that! Beautiful! Keep walking!"

Deka began calculating and looked back over his shoulder. Several of the males in the distance had broken formation and were attacking the salamanders. Deka ran down the gap that separated the two species. Most of the birds backed away as he approached, but two more of them stepped into the gap and croaked at Deka. Deka screamed back.

More screams, more splashes. It spread across the whole group. The salamanders dropped to all fours and hid under the water, leaving Deka the only thing standing in front of the armless birds.

Deka cut the air with his claws. They kicked the air with theirs.

Someone struck Deka's flank. Deka turned and charged that female, slashing her across the snout, and she stumbled away submissively. Then he heard splashing from behind, spun around, and smacked his attacker with his tail. Before the bird could recover, Deka jumped in and slashed him down the shoulder.

He glanced at the rest of the group. Birds were trying to charge the salamanders, but Cheh was running up and down the gap, holding them back with nothing more than her voice.

One bird rushed past Deka. Deka leaped and slashed her thigh. She stumbled and fell into the water. Deka scrambled to his feet and ran up the gap, screeching to everyone, holding most of them back.

Deka turned around again. Sonjaa was still running up and down the gap on the other side, keeping them away.

It was Sonjaa. Her brown and green scales with white spots. Her scent. Her voice. The female who had chosen to have his eggs. Deka called to her, but his voice drowned in the air with so many others.

He ran back down the gap, keeping them in line. Several clawed his snout or his flank, but he always hit them back. Deka was dripping with blood by now. Any other opponent would be intimidated by either the sight or the scent, but not the people of Xce. They kept coming. They kept screaming. Deka screamed back, since it was the only thing they seemed to respect.

Deka turned to his mate. Sonjaa was fending off a group of males and females, all trying to get around her at the salamanders. They clawed her face. They clawed her arms. They knocked her down and stepped on her beneath the water.

Deka heard a faint voice in his mind: *"Deka, help me!"*

As they raked their claws through the water, they kicked up blood. Deka screamed at them and tried to charge, but the salamanders were in the way, and it was so far to her.

"Deka, what's happening?!"

So far. Deka tried to push through, but the salamanders would not move. The theropods continued slashing and kicking up bloody water.

"Friend! Rive! Help me, please! Someone! Help!"

Deka screeched.

The equations returned. The portal opened exactly where Deka wanted it. He spread his arms and kicked the water behind the salamanders. They moved under the water, crawling through it and over each other in a frenzy of movement. The birds saw the salamanders moving and gave chase, rushing past Deka.

The salamanders headed for the portal. Deka could just barely see them slipping through. Deka looked beyond it, at the other sphere at the horizon, inside the wild colony that smelled hundreds of paces wide. The salamanders poured out of it, fanned out, and gorged themselves. The animals bounded away from the incoming salamanders, straight for Deka and the shrieking birds.. Deka rubbed his claws together in anticipation of a hunting frenzy.

The armless reptiles heard the animals coming, turned away from the salamanders, and charged the approaching flock.

Deka stood still and breathed easier A moment later, a cloud of bloody water engulfed his feet. Deka ran toward where he saw her fall. There was so much blood he could not see anything, so he reached in with a hand, but found nothing. No body. No source of the blood. Deka ran in circles, searching for Cheh, but she was not here. He shivered so hard he fell to his stomach. The bacteria in the water began cleaning his wounds.

On the other side of the portal, the amphibians stood in a cloud of bacteria, pulling up mouthfuls and swallowing it whole. The theropods hunted the other animals that had gathered around the colony and ate their fill. So many animals slaughtered. So much death. Blood filled the ocean as far as anyone could see.

A bird with green scales watched the amphibian just a few paces away. The red-skinned salamander stood still and regarded her. They stared at one another for some time, neither wanting to move from that spot.

I O

Deka sat in the grove. It felt good to be out of the water, even though it was still raining. Kylac sat next to him. He had just released the portals he had held open.

The Relians had been here for nine days, taking turns holding the ways to the grove open, keeping the people fed. The colonies had been stable, the animals had returned, and the settlements had been restored. The Archeons of Xce had been awake for a while, and now they were well enough to keep spheres open across their own world again. They were too scared to try making offworld spheres.

Deka and Kylac had spoken to all four of them. They told them it felt the same as before: a portal had been pulled from them, and it tried to take part of their minds with it. They never thought it would happen again, and they didn't know if they'd feel comfortable opening an offworld sphere again.

The scars from seeing their civilization revert to animalistic times would take longer to heal. The salamanders had never thought of the theropods as predators before. The reptilian birds had never thought of the salamanders as prey. Each side had seen itself in a way it had only heard stories about. Both species were still coming back together, adjusting to the reality of what had happened, of how close they came to setting civilization back thousands of years.

"I'm ready, Deka."

"So am I."

Kylac leaned against him. Deka was glad to feel fur again, even if it was drenched.

"We arrived just in time, and we stopped a civilization from collapsing."

"And only one death."

Kylac's scent spoke for him. The silence was welcome.

Kronia

The portal closed behind them, and the two Relians stood side by side in a valley between two snowy mountain ranges, a powerful river cutting straight through the middle.

This world's hub was minimal, with simple dirt paths indicating where walkways had held the portals leading to other planets. Kronia was unique in that it had a large area specifically for portals that were not permanent.

The planet had a diverse biosphere, with different climates depending on latitude and elevation. Mountain climates, desert climates, rainforest climates, cold weather, hot weather, rainy seasons, dry seasons—and the Krone lived in every region. People came from all over the contacted universe to experience it, and to witness how the elements did not touch the Krone.

Deka walked to the river. The water was muddy, full of silt from upstream. He turned to the mountains and shivered thinking about what lay ahead.

"It's not even cold yet," Kylac said, walking up to his side.

"I know. I wish he would come down to us for a change."

"He might still be unconscious."

"Norh? He probably felt the disaster pulling his mind away and yanked it right back."

"Under those scales, they're just as vulnerable as any-one else."

"Not the Krone. Underneath that hard exterior is a hard interior."

"Oh, you just need to have sex with one. Then you'll get to know who they really are."

Deka clicked his claws together. "I still don't know how you did it."

"Neither do I!"

Kylac leaned against his raptor. The warmth coming from his fur helped Deka feel better. They might have to wait a while before the Krone returned to his cave, and Deka would have to rely on Kylac for heat.

"I remember when we first visited," Kylac said. "One of Rel's permanent ways. Norh himself maintained it. We arrived in winter."

"I remember the winter." He growled. "I remember."

"Not even apprentices. Here we were, two children, just running off to Kronia, and I'm freezing! It was my idea!" Kylac bumped Deka's snout with his nose.

Deka nudged him back. "I remember you wanted to catch a Krone's scent. We heard so many stories about them all our lives. You dragged me to the portal, and then..."

"It was blowing snow, and I'm keeping you close to me just for some heat. I figured we came all this way, I had to meet one, so I started walking. The portal would always be here and we could leave anytime, warm up, come back. Great idea! If we reach the point of freezing to death, all we have to do is turn around and go home!" Kylac's tail waved around. "So what's the first direction I want us to go? Up the mountains because that's where the Krone live! No-body mentioned there would be no spheres connecting the various places on the planet. Nobody ever said that! So we climb. You're shivering the whole time, I'm up against you, trying to block the wind and the snow, and I say keep going! We're not leaving until we meet a Krone!"

"I didn't know how close to freezing to death I was. I was so young I had no idea."

Kylac huffed, flicked his ears. "That's why you keep me around."

"Up the mountain. Not a sign of any life. By then I was so cold and tired I fell over, wishing I could sleep."

"I didn't know what to do. Couldn't get you to move. Couldn't convince you to do anything. So I lay on top of you."

"He landed in front of us, kicked up all the snow, and he was blocking the wind. Norh. Kronia's Archeon. Bigger than I ever imagined. The Krone never land to meet anybody, but he landed for us. He bent down close and told us to turn back now. The storm is about to get worse. His breath was hot, and the scent coming from it..."

"It seems to contain everything in the universe. It's full of life, experience, happiness. Sorrow."

Deka shook his head and held his snout with one hand. "It made me want to move again."

"Never smelled a scent like that before. Just something about breathing it in... It makes any scent-based species want to get up and conquer something!"

Deka ran his claws lightly down Kylac's arm. "Nothing touches them, nothing affects them, nothing scares them. It's in their scent, and it's contagious, and all of a sudden I was hot, and I had to move!"

"You led *me* down the mountain! I didn't have to warm you until we were halfway to the hub."

"Then I looked up again. There he was. Sitting at the top of a cliff, looking down on us. He stood in the snow and the wind, and the cold never touched him. He was watching us, making sure we made it back to the portal. His wings were slightly unfolded. I didn't know what that meant until later."

Deka rubbed his claws.

Kylac's tail waved. "What do you think he would've done if we hadn't made it?"

Deka clicked louder. "Probably carried our lifeless bodies back to Rel and told our parents to try again, and this time make smarter children."

"Hard to imagine he'd have his penis in me a few years later."

"And somehow you survived."

"You think his scent made you feel powerful? Try Krone semen! I had that feeling for days!"

"I thought you reverted permanently! You were trying to pick fights with everyone."

"Not the first time that ever happened."

"No…" Deka's hands separated. No laughing now. "Kylac, are you sure you're all right?"

"I'm fine now."

"Doma was lucky you weren't too far gone." Deka lowered his neck and rubbed it against Kylac's. "I'm sorry I wasn't there."

Kylac reached up and rested a hand on Deka's snout. "You don't have to keep apologizing."

"I should have thought of what might happen if I left you. You've been stable for so long I forgot you can still revert."

Kylac whined. "Do you think…? Could the disaster have taken that from me, too?"

"Probably not."

"If I hurt myself worse on Ixcy and Towe, what if I…?" He shivered and whimpered. "Did I lose some of the stability you taught me?"

Deka ran his neck down Kylac's back and nudged him until Kylac stopped. "If you made yourself less stable, I don't think we'd be talking now. I'm just proud you brought yourself back."

He raised his head and look up at the mountains again. Kylac reached out and held Deka around the neck as he stared at the peaks.

Deka had finished calculating. They were Archeons now, so they could make their own ways to the different parts of Kronia. No more hiking up mountainsides. The Krone themselves had no use for such portals, so they did not make them.

The sphere opened before them. It led to a dark cave, free of snow and ice but not from cold. Deka shivered and then stepped through. Kylac followed him.

The rocks in here were jagged and frozen except for the one in the center. Its surface had been polished smooth from Norh lying on it over the centuries. Just being here, catching his residual scent, made Deka and Kylac feel larger than they were.

Norh was not here. Kylac scented the cave. He circled the entire thing, scenting the entrance as well, and then came back to Deka.

"The scent is recent."

The raptor stood against the fox, absorbing his heat. "Hopefully that means he is awake and out hunting."

Kylac leaned against Deka and led him to the smooth bed of rock. Deka lay on it and growled, rubbing his claws together.

"Almost as good as Hithe."

The sphere leading back to the hub wobbled a few times and then returned to a perfectly spherical shape.

Kylac lay blocking the wind coming through the entrance. It was snowing outside, but none of it entered the cave. Deka closed his eyes, breathing in the Krone's scent. It seemed to warm him up from the inside, and he believed he could wait here forever.

2

Deka crouched low in the snow. He was freezing and miserable, but he was also hungry, and the three-legged mammal in front of him barely noticed him. As far as this animal was concerned, all threats came from the air, so Deka did not exist.

He charged, kicking up the snow. The furry animal stared at him. Deka landed on top of it. His killing claws came down and sliced open the creature's neck and abdomen at the same time. The animal lay dead three breaths later. Deka picked it up with both hands, slung it behind his neck, and carried it up the mountainside.

He stepped into the cave and scented the room. Kylac had not returned yet. The fox could handle himself, but Deka still worried. The disasters had brought out the worst in everyone, including the two of them.

The portal down to the valley was still open, spherical, only wobbling a few times when the equations seemed to touch a tender place in his mind. It glowed daylight against the darkness of the cavern, the warm, lush river valley just a few steps away. Deka maintained it in case they needed to warm up, and so they would have a second place to hunt. Kylac was out there, picking fruit from the bushes and trees. Deka was thrilled he could maintain a way for this long at all, but it only led a few thousand paces down a mountain range. Even a sphere this close strained him, so his mind had not healed at all.

They had been waiting for three days. It took a Krone about five days to fly around the planet, so they had not anticipated waiting even this long. Whatever Norh was doing must be quite involved.

Deka set his prey down on the cave floor and spread the body open with a single claw. He shoved his muzzle inside, pulled the internal organs out, and swallowed them whole. He enjoyed the heat they filled him with more than the fullness in his stomach.

He regarded his prey's lifeless eyes. He wondered if he could be eating an intelligent creature and not even know it. He had spent days of his life imagining what the Krone had felt when they realized they had done exactly that. Deka ate his fill and then sat facing the corpse.

Moments later, his fox jumped through the portal.

"You finally caught something." Kylac's tail wagged. He stepped over to the animal, reached in with his muzzle, and started pulling things out and swallowing them. "Oh, this is good! I've been trying to eat the fruit around here, but it's awful."

"You wouldn't survive here long," Deka said, rubbing his claws. "You're a disgrace to the Krone homeworld."

"The entire Relian culture is!" Kylac said with a full mouth. "Two species, one can't live without the other. It's everything the Krone are not."

"Everything they wish they were."

"You should say it to Norh's face."

"You first."

Kylac swallowed, still waving his tail, and took another bite. "Is that why you keep hunting in the snow? Trying to prove you're worth Norh's respect?"

Deka sighed. "Every time I meet a Krone, they're looking down on me. I always wondered what it would be like to be on equal terms with them."

Kylac looked up from the mammal and licked his lips. "I feel the same way. One whiff of that scent..." Kylac growled. "I feel as big as they are, but they still gaze down on us and laugh. So you're forcing yourself to deal with the cold."

"What are you doing to be more Kronelike?"

"Trying to hunt! The animals evolved to run away from the Krone! They're fast!"

"Don't hunt anything, Kylac. I don't want you reverting again."

"I don't think I'll ever catch anything."

"I'm glad."

Kylac lapped up the blood from the floor. There was now nothing left of the body but bones and fur. Kylac sat beside Deka, blocking the wind coming from the mouth of the cave. Deka was glad for the fox's heat. On this world, he didn't want to need it.

3

A portal opened on the ground in one of the warm valleys, and a dark blue theropod and a red canine stepped out of it. Deka chirped and shivered from the sudden heat. Kylac was already warm and did not notice.

Flowers grew everywhere in this valley. Yellow, white, ultraviolet, pink, orange. Growing waist-high, they filled the entire valley from end to end.

A stone structure rose out of the flowers just ahead of them, and the Relians walked through the field up to it. The structure was rectangular, made of blocks of black stone larger than Deka and Kylac combined. It was about a thousand paces long and almost a hundred high. They were walking straight for an entrance large enough to accommodate a fully-grown Krone plus give them flying room.

They stepped through and stood still for a moment. Inside the unlit building were other stone structures arranged in no particular pattern or order. Each was made of red and grey rocks, and they formed buildings large enough to hold two or three people Kylac's size. Some were larger, like the tower rising out of the ground that reached all the way up to the top of the black stone covering it.

The Krone themselves had erected the stone enclosing all of these buildings thousands of years ago. It was the only thing they ever built, and possibly the last thing the Krone did together before punishing themselves.

The Relians entered one of these stone buildings. Inside were various pieces of furniture—chairs, tables, raised platforms for sleeping. Grooves had been dug into the ground and led outside. It was believed the people who lived here ate their prey raw, and the channels took the blood out of this dwelling.

There were symbols and markings up and down the walls. Kylac ran his hand over some of them. The Krone wanted everyone to be able to read them, and Norh himself had taught Deka and Kylac the written language of the Lost. The Krone themselves spoke it now—not a trace of their original language was left in their speech.

Only fifty of us remain. They've taken thousands this year. We're not safe even underground. Our prayers for them to move on have not been answered. They fly overhead all day. All night. These last few years sometimes there are so many of them they block the daylight. They wait for us.

Another read: *My name is Tge'd. I am the fifth daughter of G'nath. We were musicians. All of us. I played the Zreed. If I am to die here, I want someone to remember my happiest moment...*

The raptor and the fox walked from building to building. Each was a dwelling house meant for a small family unit. They looked as though they had been occupied only a few short years ago, but this community had been abandoned for thousands of years. The words on the wall were some of the last additions to the stonework.

Mother father and sisters are gone. I am alone.

No food. Few of us remain. Very tired. I remember when it wasn't like this...

Other villages gone. Prayers do not work. They are not listening. My name is...

Stone was the only thing they had to write on. They wanted something permanent. Something others would find someday so they would not be forgotten.

Deka and Kylac stepped out of the last building and walked to the large structure in the center of the small city. The entrance was also wide enough for a Krone to pass through. This building was large enough to contain the entire community. Inside, an altar lay at the far end, and a life-size sculpture of a Krone loomed above it.

Deka and Kylac sat in one of the long, stone pews facing the statue. They tried to imagine living at the mercy of the elements, barely able to move about the planet, living with a race of flying reptiles who could go anywhere they pleased, seemingly unaffected by snow, wind, rain, hail, lightning, or any of the elements.

Being sky dwellers for the most part, the Krone had never once taken a close look at the animals on the ground. The giant reptiles soared through the air, swooped down, and captured prey without a moment's thought about who they were killing.

This particular species had been the Krone's favorite, and they had hunted these furred mammals to the point of extinction. It was only when none could be found that some of the Krone came down to the ground and investigated the animals they had been hunting.

For the first time, the Krone saw that their prey constructed things out of stone. They had written language, history, art, and culture. They were no animals. By the time they realized this, it was too late. Their companion species was dead.

The last generation of Krone society preserved these buildings as relics of the people they had destroyed. Whenever Deka and his fox visited Kronia, they always visited a few of these preserved communities. They took in the atmosphere, and they imagined life as these people knew it.

Though their species name was unknown, they left behind more than enough to understand what happened to them.

Kylac walked up to the statue. It stood three times taller than Kylac and was easily ten times longer, a vaguely Kronelike form. They had the proportions correct, but the statue had no facial features. The head was smooth stone all the way around.

"They never were able to get a close look at the Krone. Who would want to?"

Deka joined Kylac at his side. "Then they took refuge underground, but they still had to come out and find food."

"I would worship the Krone, too, if I thought it would help."

"And their last words captured the moment they realized it wasn't working. I wish we knew what kind of people they were before they had to live in fear."

Kylac turned around and faced the rows and rows of stone seats facing this statue. Writing covered the walls and many of the chairs. Everything except the Krone statue had something etched on it. More messages of despair from a dying people. The structure was completely silent, but the words still screamed agony and hopelessness.

Deka walked toward the entrance, and Kylac followed him out the door, under the black stone sky, and to the main entrance. They exited to beautiful daylight and flowers.

The Krone themselves had scattered the flower seeds. While the Krone themselves did not hold the idea of the flower as a metaphor for renewal, they knew their companion species had. The two Relians walked through the flowers.

"When I'm around the Krone," Kylac began, "I feel as though I can do anything. Then I come here..."

"The Krone feel the same way. They need it as much as we do. A reminder that not everyone is like them. Most people live at the mercy of forces they cannot control."

"Well, it hasn't made the Krone any friendlier, but they did take the time to make sure their companion species was never forgotten."

They reached their portal and stepped through. They were now back in Norh's freezing cave, and Deka shivered again. Kylac barely flinched, but Deka forced his metabolism to compensate.

It was the fourth day since they arrived, and still no sign of the Krone Archeon. Kylac had already been working on their next destination, and he opened the way now. It stood next to the other two portals in here.

Kylac stepped through, with Deka just behind his tail. This way took them to one of the desert regions. Another black stone structure had been erected, but it was buried in sand, so only the entrance was exposed. Norh had told them the Krone cleared the sand away once in a while.

Kylac panted profusely as they approached the artificial cave. His body had ways of getting rid of excess heat, but he still preferred the cold. This was Deka's kind of weather, not his.

As they entered, the temperature dropped. Inside were structures made of animal skin. No stone here. The Krone had carried the black stone thousands of paces over the planet just to preserve this place.

Hundreds of little cloth dwellings, the animal skins still intact for the most part, as there was so little water here things decayed slowly. Deka and Kylac didn't touch anything, and they tried not to breathe on anything either.

From what the Krone had learned, the people in this region moved with the seasonal rains, and this village had been mobile. Same species, but a completely different way of life, adapted to the climate. They had built nothing permanent, but the Krone had made it so. These cloth dwellings had been here for hundreds of years, preserved with the writing still visible on them.

More farewell messages as the people slowly died off. Names. Summaries of their life, their children's, their family's. Some contained pleas for help, cries for mercy, written prayers to the flying reptiles to spare them. The last of the people were so afraid, and yet they still tried to appeal to the creatures that hunted them.

In the center of this community stood a sandstone sculpture of a Krone, the tallest object here, though it was much less than life size. Deka and Kylac walked up to it and held its gaze. It stood just slightly above their heads, featureless, faceless, but unmistakably Krone.

They wandered around the tents and huts for a while, reading the silent screams and tearful personal histories recorded on the skins.

For centuries after the Krone understood what they had done, the entire species went into a kind of collective mourning. Instead of hunting, taking their prey back to their nests to feed their hatchlings, they landed and learned everything they could about the life they had extinguished. They realized the sounds their prey made had not been mere screams of pain, but language, and they inferred their written language from that. They learned their music, their poetry, their building techniques. The Krone had learned how to perceive the planet as these furred bipeds did.

The Krone punished themselves for what they had done. Their society had killed their companion species, so they disbanded and lived in personal exile. Krone females laid eggs in these preserved communities and then abandoned them. As they had denied an entire species existence, so they planned to deny existence to their own.

The Archeons returned to the entrance, passing hundreds of tents and thousands of silent screams. They took the portal back to the cave, sat down, and waited for the residual Krone scent to charge them up again. Deka still shivered even as he stole heat from his fox.

4

Deka and Kylac walked through another cave high in the desert mountains. The cave was cold, but the wind coming in through the mouth was warm.

This cave was the only place where any remnant of ancient Krone society remained. The Krone never intended to preserve their old way of life, but it was still here.

The cave was empty, and the rock floor was smooth from the bodies of thousands of Krone lying on it over the centuries. Embedded in the rocks were old scents that should have vanished long ago. Deka and Kylac came here to remember what the Krone were before they knew about their companion species.

The Relians walked around, noses to the floor, scenting everything. They smelled females lying on the stone. They smelled clutches of eggs resting on the cave floor. They smelled footsteps of males walking around.

Before they knew of their companion species, the Krone had gathered in caves like this, or in clearings in the forest, or in calderas of active volcanoes. They lived communal lives, hunted in groups, gathered food in groups, raised the hatchlings together. As many as a hundred Krone lived in a community. Once they realized what they had done, they abandoned their old society.

The Relians' heads filled with old scents, distinctly Krone. Deka and Kylac stood in the center of the cave. They could imagine it packed full of giant reptiles socializing, sharing thoughts on mathematics, theory, and astronomy. All of that ended in an instant.

The eggs they had abandoned hatched in the settlements of their dead companion species, alone. Almost all of them died without a community to care for them, but a handful of hatchlings did survive. Their numbers dwindled from a few million to under one hundred. The Krone now lived apart from one another. They rarely spoke to one another. They rarely gathered in groups. Gone was the society of old that lived communally in mountain caves and forests, sharing ideas, regarding the animals below as mere prey.

The new generation that emerged had grown up in the ruins of the civilization their kind had destroyed. They learned on their own, survived on their own. They lived with the Lost as their imaginary companion species. They deciphered the language of the Lost, made it their own. Each individual discovered music, language, art, mathematics, and science by living with the mystery all around them, and each Krone discovered the truth individually.

A Krone's life became an unguided journey of discovering the achievements of an extinct species. Their prey's advances in physics became the Krone's. Their knowledge of mathematics became the Krone's. The Krone learned how to see, touch, taste, and sense the universe as one of these mammals would. This was when the Krone discovered portal physics. Now every Krone was a capable Archeon, though few wanted the responsibility of maintaining the offworld ways for the planet. Norh was this generation's volunteer.

5

Kylac had become no better at catching the fast mammals, so he gave up trying for fear of reverting again. He noticed Deka tolerated the cold better than when they first arrived. All he could do was wave his tail. There was something about the residual scent in the cave that made them want to prove themselves, and Kylac wished it could be permanent.

While they waited, they had plenty of time to remember what brought them here, but while surrounded by Krone scent, they did not brood on the thought of the collapsed civilizations, death, and destruction because of the disasters. Instead they felt a powerful urge to go out there and save the entire universe from the devastation—to find out what was happening and stop it, no matter what it was. It could be a rogue black hole eating planets, and they felt strong enough to catch it and throw it back where it came from.

Finally they heard something outside the cave mouth, and the empowering scent of Krone strengthened. They both felt hot with determination and resolve. They stood up to meet the Krone as he walked down the passageway into his cave.

A head poked around the corner. The front legs came through next, and the rest of his stocky torso followed, wings folded to either side of his back. The quadruped loomed over them. He was three times taller than Deka and five times longer, not including the tail. His yellow scales clung tight to his body, not a loose flap or a weak muscle anywhere. They had once been as vibrant as a star, but age had dulled them to the color of sand. Though a reptile, he had the mannerisms of a mammalian species.

He took in their scents. His own scent was unmoved, which disappointed the Relians. Earning a Krone's respect was an impossible goal, yet everyone strived for it.

Norh spoke in perfect Relian. "How long have you been here?"

"Six days," Kylac said. The Krone's scent had a secondary effect on him. He was halfway out of his sheath. Norh glanced down at it, but his wings did not move.

"There's been another disaster," Deka said. "Did you know?"

Norh stepped the rest of the way inside. Deka closed the other portals in the room as the Krone walked to his rock bed. He scented it, reading their scents all over it, and then climbed on it and sprawled out. It looked as though the rock had formed there just to hold him.

"I did." Norh was silent for some time. His scent wavered in strength. Finally he spoke again. "After the first, I was unconscious for a third of a Relian year."

Kylac's ears bloomed. "That long?"

"I had just woken up and started contacting other planets when it happened again."

"We were on Rel when it was torn apart," Deka said. "We've been traveling from planet to planet, trying to fix everything."

"I know the world we lost this time," Norh said.

Deka and Kylac held their breath as they waited for Norh to elaborate.

"Genzin," the Krone finished.

"How do you know?" Kylac asked.

The giant reptile lowered his head to their eye level. "It tried to take my mind away again. I felt where it was coming from. It tried to pull my mind outside of the universe. I closed my spheres before it could."

"Outside?" Deka said. "What do you mean?"

The Krone was silent. Krone were not accustomed to explaining things more than once. Deka grumbled at himself, thinking he had just lost another chance to earn Norh's respect. Deka looked at his fox.

Kylac was trying to breathe normally. "Eight thousand people..."

Deka turned to Norh again. "Was anything nearby that could have caused it? A rogue black hole? A brown dwarf?"

"It did not come from inside this universe," Norh said. "Something from the outside tried to pull the portals through, and it destroyed Genzin in the process."

"Out... side," Kylac stammered. "Archeons are still speculating about what could exist outside the universe."

Deka shook his head. "Portal physics has no variables or equations for anything beyond the universe, let alone something outside affecting it."

Norh shifted on his bed. "That is where I felt my mind going. A place portal physics does not describe."

The Relians stared at the cave floor, lost in thought for a while.

"And..." Kylac hesitated as he faced Norh. "Have you found anyone from Rel? Any raptors or foxes?"

Norh's wings sank slightly. "I have not."

"Where *are* they?" Deka chirped in grief, folding his hands to his chest. He stared at the ground. "Somebody must have been offworld. They can't all be dead. And now Genzin."

"It troubles me as well," Norh said. "I grieve for the loss of both worlds. If I find any Relians, I will keep them at the hub until you return."

"Are there any offworlders here now?" Kylac said.

"I just finished sending them home." Norh turned to Deka. "Have you learned anything about what is happening?"

"No, nobody has. You seem to know more about it than anyone."

"What happened to Rel was not an isolated event," Norh said. "I do not want to open ways to other planets now. I will not keep permanent ways until the cause is found."

"You're not alone," Kylac said. "We're hearing that from every planet we visit. It has me worried. Everyone in the contacted universe is isolating themselves. None of the Archeons want to go through that again."

"It hurt us as well," Deka continued. "Kylac and I can't seem to keep a way open longer than a few breaths."

"The disaster took something from you," Norh said. "It tried to take me as well."

"How did you stop it?" Deka said.

"I felt my ways on Genzin being pulled into another portal. One that engulfed Genzin and took it out of the universe. I simply followed my ways back to Kronia and closed them."

Norh was silent for a while. Then he yawned and spoke again.

"Stay as long as you want. I need rest. I wish you well finding survivors, and I congratulate you on helping people recover."

He rolled over to his side and lay on the smooth rocks, instantly asleep. Krone stayed awake for as many as twenty days at a time and then slept five days straight. The conversation was over.

Deka sat down with a sigh. Kylac pressed against him. The wind from the cave blew Kylac's fur around. It was the only sound in the cave.

A portal opened next to Kylac to a desert region, just in front of the preserved ruins.

"Come on," said the fox. "Let's go someplace warm while I make a way offworld."

"I'd rather wait here."

"Deka..." Kylac's tail waved. "It won't help you earn his respect."

Deka faced the sleeping reptile before them and sighed. "I wish I could."

"Even after all these years, he still barely acknowledges us."

"At least you had sex with him," Deka said, rubbing his claws gently.

"Only once, and then never again. Still, whenever I hear his voice..." He wagged his tail harder and peeked from his sheath, just a little.

"I'll never be equal to a Krone," Deka said, "but I have to try."

"Me, too."

A huge gust blew in through the cave. It waved around Kylac and enveloped Deka. The raptor shivered, stood up, clinging to his fox, and they walked through the portal together. It closed behind them moments later.

Earth

The portal slipped away from Deka's mind and shut behind them. The Relians stood on something unfamiliar. Kylac looked down at his feet. The ground was soft but rough, and an artificial odor came from it.

The raptor, meanwhile, was looking all around him. They were inside a structure that smelled like dead plant matter covered in concentrated chemicals. The whole place had a chemical smell.

"Deka... Where are we?"

"It's supposed to be Bynadium."

"This..." Kylac was still scenting the floor. He dropped to all fours, scenting it harder, burying his nose in it. The fibers tickled. "Deka, what is this stuff?"

"You have the nose. You tell me."

"I don't recognize it! It smells like... Like... I can't tell!" Kylac stood and looked around at the walls for the first time. "I can't tell what anything is made of!"

"There's some plant matter here," Deka said. "Aluminum, iron... Other than that... Kylac, where are we?"

"*You* opened the portal!"

"I made a way to Bynadium!"

"Well, it's a good thing we didn't land on a world where it rains iron!"

"I don't know how we got here! I don't know where *here* is!"

They searched the modest interior space in silence. The floor was covered in this artificial fiber. The walls smelled of some substance Kylac and Deka couldn't identify. A vague plant-odor came from a structure against one of the walls. Kylac walked up to it, scenting it the whole way. It was not fixed to anything, just resting in place. On it were various objects, some made of stone, and others of a substance Kylac had no name for. Still others were made of wood or metal or glass.

One object in the center of the shelves had a curved glass face. Kylac gazed into it, and his reflection stared back at him. The rest of the object was made of more of that substance he could not identify.

Deka was examining the various things hanging on the walls. Mostly images. Some were pigments spread onto a plantlike fiber behind glass. Some of the pigment was thin, revealing lines and symbols visible behind it. The more realistic images depicted waterfalls. Eleven different images of what appeared to be the same four waterfalls hung around the room.

"Kylac..." Deka said.

The fox looked away from his reflection. "What?"

"Come see this."

Kylac walked over to him and stood in front of one particular image hanging on the wall.

"Does this look familiar?" Deka asked.

It depicted some sort of life form, furless save for the patch on its head, with pale skin and small eyes with round pupils. The rest of the skin was covered by something that appeared as artificial as the floor. Two such life forms stood in front of a waterfall, mouths open to show the teeth.

"Are those the inhabitants of this planet?" Kylac said.

"If they are, then I really don't know how we got here. I've never met these people."

"And I've never smelled things like this before," Kylac said, turning around, facing the shelves against the far wall.

Between them and the pictures on the wall was a piece of furniture. Kylac walked to it, examined it lengthwise. He turned around and sat down in it, looking into the dark piece of curved at eye level. The seat was plush, and it kicked up a tremendous amount of dust under Kylac's weight. It filled his nose with noise. He sneezed.

Deka studied the furniture. "They're bipedal. Kylac, this is probably someone's home."

"We don't even know where we are, and somehow you brought us into somebody's home?"

Deka clicked his hand-claws together. "Maybe I'm just that good."

He tried to sit on the plush seat next to Kylac. It was wide enough for three Relian-sized people to sit, maybe more, depending on how wide they were. Deka wasn't made to sit in this manner, but he plopped down in it anyway, tail curling back around and taking up the third space. The structure groaned under his weight, another puff of dust flew into the air, and Kylac sneezed again.

"Hey!" shouted the fox. "I think I smelled something!"

Kylac rose and flopped into the seat again. The cushion kicked up another cloud of dust, and this time Deka sneezed.

Kylac was scenting the air around himself. "Yes! There is something! A living scent. It's not just noise." He scented. He growled. "It's gone."

He lifted up and threw himself back into the cushion. Dust enveloped him. Deka tried to wave it away as he sneezed four times in a row.

"Stop that!"

"I'm investigating!" Kylac vigorously scented the air. "There it is! It smells... male. Male scent! Unmistakable! It could be a compatible species."

Deka sneezed three more times. Kylac wagged his tail, stood up, then threw himself into the cushions beside Deka. The puff of dust hugged both of them. Deka sneezed violently six times and stood up, facing his fox, rubbing his claws and growling. Kylac was waving his tail. Then he sneezed.

Light flooded the room. The raptor froze in place and stared over Kylac's head. Kylac's nose caught the air coming from behind him, which matched the faint, dusty scent from the couch. The fox stood up and moved next to Deka.

A creature stood in a doorway, male, just taller than Kylac at eye level, but fourteen claw's reaches below Deka's. He wore lenses over his eyes, and his skin was partially covered in plant matter drenched in artificial chemicals.

His mouth opened. His words made no sense.

"Where did you bring us, Deka?"

"I wish I knew."

The creature stood at the door, still speaking. Assuming the scent signals were the same as the majority of compatible species, this male was in fight or flight mode, scared but also fascinated.

"Uncontacted species, definitely," Deka said.

Kylac took a single step toward the man, keeping his arms to his sides. The male was still talking. They listened closely.

"Deka, he has no claws, and he's plantigrade."

"Flat-footed?" Deka rubbed his claws. "What did he evolve from?"

The creature at the door stopped speaking and stared at the raptor.

"Deka, don't do that again."

"What?"

"Don't laugh. His scent changed from excitement to fear."

Deka sniffed the creature from a distance, confirming. "I'll try..."

"My name is Kylac," said the fox as he climbed on the seats and knelt behind the back, holding onto it. "What's your name?"

The creature in the door said something.

"His language reminds me of the Wiovin," said Deka.

"You're right, everything spoken on the tip of the tongue, barely anything at the back of the throat."

The person at the door was silent again, eyes darting back and forth between them and something against the far wall. Kylac figured the creature wanted to go there, so he climbed off the plush seats and joined Deka at his side. The unfamiliar person cautiously stepped around the seats and walked to the opposite wall, to one of the shelves. He took one thing from the shelf and another from the rack next to it, and then carefully approached them, holding the things out, one in each hand.

He spoke again, and Deka and Kylac began to hear patterns. It sounded similar to several languages on other worlds, but they had not listened long enough yet to attempt it.

Kylac looked at what the creature was holding. It was rectangular, about two claw's reaches thick, and it did not smell familiar. Kylac dared not touch it.

On the rectangle he could make out a blurry image made of tiny dots of pigment, and it caught Kylac's eyes. The dots formed a canine walking on four legs, with red, black, and white fur similar to his own. The head was wrong, but the basic shape was correct. If a Relian canine walked on four legs all the time, it would look like this. Kylac leaned closer, involuntarily scenting the package. His nose would not rest until it could identify that scent.

"Kylac..." Deka said. The canine turned to him.

Deka was holding something that reeked of that unfamiliar scent.

"Deka, we don't know what this stuff is! Don't touch it!"

"Look."

Kylac now looked at what Deka was holding. It was a tiny statue of a theropod, and it had a snout, two arms, and stood hunched over. The shape resembled Deka, but without the colorful scale pattern.

This whole time the creature was talking. Deka and Kylac were taking in his words, minds parsing them for patterns.

"You sure they're uncontacted?" Deka said.

"Aren't you?"

"Yes... but..."

Deka turned the theropod figure around. His fingers squeezed the legs together, the neck lunged, and the jaw opened. It caught Deka off guard, and he dropped it. It landed on the plush floor with a muffled *thunk*. Deka's heart stopped, fearing it would break, but it did not. Deka exhaled, bent from the waist, and picked it up again.

Kylac still did not want to touch the stuff. He merely looked at the depiction on the rectangle in the creature's hand. He wasn't sure what the other creature was, but the one that had his fur color and markings was striking.

By now Deka and Kylac had heard enough of the strange person's words. They drew from their knowledge of other languages and constructed words of their own based on the patterns they had observed. They waited until the creature finished speaking.

Kylac looked at him. "My name is Kylac," he said, making the sounds he deduced must be correct.

"I am Deka," imitating the tip-of-the-tongue sounds the man was using.

The creature stared at them for a few breaths. He was out of breath when he spoke. "Holy shit, you speak English."

"Still learning," Deka said. "Keep talking. Use many words. We will learn faster."

"My God, a talking dinosaur... Who the hell are you?"

"What is your name?" Kylac said.

"I'm... My name is Stephen. How did you get in my house?"

"We will explain, but we need more words," Deka said. "Continue speaking. Where are we?"

"This is Earth."

"And what is this?" Kylac pointed to the rectangle Stephen still held in his hand.

"It's a movie. *The Fox and the Hound.*"

"From what is it made?"

"It's... It's made of plastic."

"What is plastic?" Kylac turned to the shelves. "And what is all of that?"

"Plastic is... uh... it comes from oil. Do you know what oil is?"

"No."

"Petroleum?"

"I do not know the word."

"Well, that's what it is. And that's my entertainment center. I keep all the knickknacks I've collected over the years on it. That action figure in your hand." He pointed to Deka. "Alex gave me that. He's my nephew. Loves *Jurassic Park.* And that thing there is the TV. VCR on top of that, then cable box. And those things next to it are my tapes. That's what this is."

Stephen waved the plastic rectangle in his hand, opened it, took something else out, also made of plastic, and held it out to Kylac. The fox cautiously took it in both hands. He tried to hold it in his claws to keep it from touching the pads on his fingers and palms.

"Do you understand anything I'm saying?" Stephen said.

"No," Kylac said, "but we are learning your language. Please continue."

"All right... Uh... I'm Stephen. My full name is Stephen Roger Penarrow. The date is September seventh, nineteen ninety-four. I gave you that movie because that's what you look like. A fox. But walking on two legs. And naked. And you..." He faced Deka. "Uh... holy shit you're a fucking dinosaur. Bu—please, I can't think of what else to say. Who are you? Where do you come from? And how are you speaking English?"

"We're from a planet called Rel," Kylac said. "I'm not sure what our species names would be in your language. But..." Kylac looked at the plastic box Stephen held at his side. "It seems we resemble something you already know. That makes this process easier. You may call me that. A fox. What would you call him?" Kylac turned his muzzle to Deka.

"Velociraptor."

"That's a mouthful," Deka said.

"I can't believe you're talking to me. From another planet? No shit? What are you doing in my house?"

"We are Archeons," said Deka.

"What is an Archeon?"

"We make ways."

"Ways? What do you mean?"

"You don't know what a portal is?" Kylac said.

"No."

"What species live on this planet?" Deka said.

Stephen tried to speak several times before finally forming an answer. "Ummm... Lots?"

"Who is your companion?" Deka said.

"My companion? Brenda. My wife. She died years ago. We didn't have kids. We wanted to, but she wasn't ready."

Everyone was silent for a moment. Finally, Kylac spoke. "I think we miss each other's meaning. What we are trying to ask is, what is the other intelligent species on this planet?"

"Dolphins are pretty smart. Some dogs are. But nothing like us. Human. That's what we call ourselves."

"What is dogs?" said Deka.

"They're... Well, they're like you, Kylac, but they walk on four legs and can't talk."

"So you are the only intelligent beings on this planet?" said Deka.

"Yeah. Why?"

Deka and Kylac glanced at one another. They just now realized what kind of world this was.

"You're aliens?" Stephen said. "Real goddamn aliens?"

"Correct," said Deka.

"Real fucking aliens," Kylac said.

Stephen glared at him.

"Did I use those words correctly?" said the fox.

The human's stare softened. "Yeah..."

"Good. I do not want to offend. What is that covering your body?"

"This?" Stephen looked down. "I always wear a shirt and boxers to bed. Habit from the Army."

"You wear garments?" Kylac said. "Why?"

"I was just going to ask why you're naked. You got dog junk and I'm trying not to laugh."

"Naked?" Kylac's tail waved a little.

"How large is this planet?" Deka said.

"Uh... I don't know off the top of my head."

"Where on this planet are we?"

"This is the north country. Near Watertown, New York, and Fort Drum. United States. Got out of the Army, married, and I decided to settle here with Brenda. We were going to start a family."

Deka turned and walked to the cloth hanging from the wall. He lifted it up. There was glass behind it, and a view of the outside greeted him. It was nighttime here.

"Don't!" Stephen dropped the plastic rectangle, lunged forward, and pushed the fabric over the glass again. "Someone could see you!"

"Are there more people around?" Deka said. "When can we meet them?"

"That's, uh, probably not a good idea," said Stephen. "Nobody's ever met an alien."

"Would they not want to?"

"Maybe... Well, sure, but—no! No, it would scare the hell outta them! And everyone on this street owns a gun! They see you, you'll probably get shot!"

"I don't understand those words," Deka said, "but your scent and voice seem urgent, so I conclude that would be bad."

"Yes, very."

"Are you glad to meet an alien?" Kylac asked.

"Hell yeah."

"And you have not shot us, so why should they?"

"Because... Look, just trust me on this, as individuals we're very smart, but you get us in groups and we become paranoid and trigger-happy."

Deka and Kylac were silent for a moment. They glanced at each other, each thinking the same thing. Deka turned away from the fabric and faced Stephen directly.

"You're lucky you came here and not one of my neighbors. Some of them would shoot first and ask questions later."

"I would answer any questions they had even if I were shot," Deka said.

"Not if you're dead."

Deka's hands separated. "I understand now."

"Look, guys... Who are you? What are you doing here —and holy shit those claws are huge."

Stephen was staring at Deka's hands and feet, as if for the first time. Now that he was less than a pace away from the raptor, perhaps he really had just now noticed. Deka held up his hand, and Stephen backed away. It appeared to be an involuntary movement.

"Do not be afraid," Deka said. "I ate yesterday, and you do not smell like prey." He rubbed his claws together.

Stephen took another step back, bumping into the plush cushions, and fell into the seat. It was definitely designed for his anatomy. Kylac sat next to Stephen. The fox sneezed once.

"Bless you," Stephen said.

"Kylac... Is it not a little too soon to..." Deka did not know how to finish the sentence in this new language.

"Never too early to try," Kylac replied.

"What do you mean?" Stephen said.

"How do I smell to you?"

"How do you smell? Uh... Like a dog? Why?"

"What is a dog?"

"Um... Look, why are you two in my house? How did you even get inside?"

"We did not intend to come here," Deka said, walking to the cushions. He could not sit on them, so he lay on the floor. His head was almost to their eye level. "I'm still not sure how we arrived. This planet has not been contacted. Somehow the way I made took us here instead of where I wanted to go."

"The way you made," Stephen echoed. "Is that a spaceship?"

"What is a spaceship?" said Deka.

"Something aliens are supposed to have."

"I do not understand."

"Neither do I," Kylac said, holding Stephen's arm, rubbing against him. Kylac was giving off quite a scent. Stephen did not seem to react to it.

"Would it help if I showed you?"

"Probably," Deka said. "Since we're here, I would like to learn more about this world. And if we can't leave this building... What do you have in mind?"

Stephen looked around the cushions. He leaned forward, looked around the floor. He felt under the seats. Grumbling, he stood up and lifted his cushion.

"Ah hah!"

He pulled something from under the cushion, replaced the padded seat, and plopped down again. Kylac leaned against him again, trying not to sneeze from all the dust Stephen had kicked up.

"Uh... why are you doing that?" Stephen said.

"I'm trying to learn about your species."

Stephen turned to Kylac. "Are the foxes the touchy feely type?"

"One might say that."

Stephen looked at the raptor on the floor. "Then the raptors are cold and distant, right?"

"No."

"Oh. Uh..." He pressed a button.

Electricity hummed from the dark mirror on the other side of the room. Deka and Kylac had flashbacks to the crystal caverns on Neben—they leaped to their feet, alert and ready to run. Several breaths passed. The electromagnetic hum continued. Stephen had frozen in place on the seat.

"Sorry...? I just turned on the TV."

The box was alight with flickering colors, and tinny sounds came from it as well. Deka and Kylac recognized the words, but they were difficult to hear because they sounded metallic and distorted. The blurry image on the screen flickered constantly.

Kylac slowly realized he was not about to be electrocuted by a growing crystal. He sat back down, close to Stephen again, and Deka turned to face the TV and lay back down on the carpet.

"I'm sorry," Stephen said. "I didn't think it would be that big a deal." He made a few sounds, short exhales. Neither Deka nor Kylac was sure what they meant. "Now I'm glad I kept cable. X-Files doesn't start until the sixteenth. *Deep Space Nine* doesn't start until the twenty-sixth. Of all times for there to be nothing on."

Stephen pressed buttons on the plastic thing he was holding. The screen flickered. New images appeared. Deka and Kylac watched. It was unpleasant to watch the images on the screen and listen to the mechanical voices coming from it, but they did not interfere.

"This is the Prevue Channel," Stephen said. "It shows me everything that's on. Maybe we'll get lucky."

Images came from the corner of the screen. Voices came from it constantly. Symbols slowly scrolled from bottom to top. Deka and Kylac figured they were part of a written language, but they did not know how to interpret the symbols yet.

Many breaths passed, and then Stephen spoke. "Damn, nobody's showing it right now. Well, that's all right."

Stephen pushed off the couch and walked to the second set of shelves. The tapes. He pulled one out, held it in his fingers, and let a piece of plastic slip out of the sleeve. He inserted it into the box on top of the TV. The VCR.

Stephen then sat down, clicked a few more buttons, and the screen went dark. Then it changed to a bright blue.

FBI WARNING

"My sister gave this to me for my birthday. It's not the best episode, but it's decent. *Encounter at Farpoint*, series premiere of the new *Star Trek*. Wish you'd come just a couple weeks later. I coulda shown you *Deep Space Nine*, or *X-Files*. I don't have any tapes of those. I knew I shouldn't have taped over them. Damn me, just when I need them."

He started making more of those sharp exhales combined with a higher-pitched voice.

"In a minute, you'll see spaceships. I'm gonna show you what humans think aliens are like. Will you tell me if we're even close?"

"We will, won't we, Kylac?"

The fox had practically climbed into Stephen's lap. The human just now noticed where the fox was. He smelled agitated but did not interfere, probably for the same reason Deka and Kylac did not complain about how difficult it was to watch the TV.

"That's a spaceship!" Stephen said. "The *Enterprise*. Most famous spaceship on TV."

"Space. The final frontier."

It was a strain on the eyes to see anything on the flickering screen, and the mechanical sounds coming from it were abhorrent to the ears, but Deka and Kylac understood what it represented. Kylac's tail waved. Deka rubbed his claws.

Kylac slipped his hand down Stephen's boxers.

"...where no one has gone before."

2

Stephen jerked awake and stared at the fox on top of the covers. Kylac rolled over and met his eyes. The fox licked his lips, and then he leaned over and licked Stephen's. The human sat bolt upright and stared at the far wall.

Many breaths passed. Humans called them seconds. The seconds added up to more than a minute. Then Stephen turned to Kylac and whispered.

"What the hell...?"

Kylac reached behind Stephen's neck. He had found several places on the skin that stimulated the human, and he exploited one of them now. Stephen panted. The blanket above his crotch tented slightly. The human leaned into Kylac's hand, held it, rubbed it. Then he leaned over and pressed his lips to Kylac's. It had a stimulating effect on Stephen, though it didn't do much for Kylac. After a moment, Stephen released Kylac and sat upright again as the canine dropped his hand.

"Oh my God. I wasn't even drunk. What happened?

A little bit of dried semen was still on the fur around Kylac's muzzle, and he licked his lips again. The taste made him peek out of his sheath. Stephen's eyes darted to it, and then he turned to the wall again.

"Relian canines have universal pheromones," Kylac said. "They're appealing to almost every compatible species. I wanted to know if you were compatible. Would you like to know what I learned?"

Stephen stared absently. He did not answer.

Kylac sat up, scooted up against the human and leaned against him. "When we first arrived, I thought you might not respond to scent at all, but I could tell I was having an affect on you. You just weren't aware of it. Also I wanted you to get rid of those clothes so I could see what you really are. You are definitely a compatible species, which is a relief. It means we can learn from each other, and we have more in common than you might think."

"Holy shit..."

Kylac expected to smell sweet afterglow, but instead Stephen's scent was becoming more and more agitated and confused. Kylac held him around the waist.

"What's wrong?"

Stephen had become a statue. "How did you make me do that?"

"I didn't make you do anything. My scent just... advertises. Yes, that's the word in this language. It only advertises I'm available and interested. I always am."

"I wanted to tell you about *Star Trek*. I wasn't thinking about... *that*."

"You sure seemed to be last night."

Stephen hung his head.

Kylac rubbed his cheek against the back of Stephen's neck. "Why are you so anxious about it? Are you all right?"

"It's... uh... I haven't done anything like that since I was a teenager."

Kylac curled up against him. Stephen still smelled aroused, but anxious. "Tell me."

The human collected his thoughts for a moment.

"Sophomore year in high school. Used to hang around this guy. Peter was his name. We were best friends. Got into his father's liquor one night. Neither of us got that drunk—the shit was disgusting—but it was just enough. I guess I decided I really liked him. He was drunk enough to let me. We did stuff. We were still doing it weeks later, without alcohol. I didn't think anything of it. Then he moved away, and I started seeing people in school getting bullied for being homos. Never felt like that again for another guy. Shit... I thought I grew out of that. I started getting involved with women—I thought I was over it."

He started to shiver. Kylac sat upright all the way and held him around the shoulders. "Over a thousand different species respond to this scent, but they don't feel confused afterward."

"You do this all the time?"

"Every day if I can. Lately I've been lucky to get it once every few days. Nobody else thinks twice about it. Why do you feel this way?"

"I never told Brenda about him. I never told anyone in the Army—I'd be thrown out of the service. Everything I felt for him I felt for Brenda, so I thought I grew out of it. I was glad I grew out of it. And now..."

"Grew out?" Kylac nuzzled his neck. "Why did you hope for that?"

Stephen was shaking less. "Lots of boys in school got beat up for being girly. I saw it happen. If they saw you just being around a guy a lot, they'd shove you into the wall. I was afraid it was happening to me. Was such a relief when I found out I liked women. I never looked back. Until now."

"Why? Why would they attack someone for that?"

"Because it's... It's just wrong."

"Nobody thinks it's wrong where I come from. Everyone has things that stimulate them, and they act on them. There's no reason not to, especially among scent-based creatures. Everyone can smell who's interested, and if they're with someone who isn't scent-based, they know their signals. Nobody feels bad about it."

"It's different here."

"What kind of people are you to attack someone for not being like the others?"

"I don't know. Maybe you can tell me?"

"I'll need more information about your kind before I can say. Be honest, Stephen. Did you like it?"

Stephen shivered again.

"I can tell you want to go again," Kylac continued.

Stephen faced him. He raised his arms and embraced Kylac, pressing his lips to the fox's mouth again. A moment later, he released Kylac's muzzle and held his gaze.

"That *was* amazing," he whispered.

Kylac reached up and felt that spot behind Stephen's neck. "I can go twenty times in one day. Still haven't hit my limit."

Stephen sighed, shivering a little. "I better get dressed."

He swung his legs off the side of the bed and slipped out of the covers.

Kylac slid off the bed and stood up, stretching. "Where I come from, if someone isn't interested, they don't respond to my scent."

Stephen groped around on the floor and found the frames with the lenses that went over his eyes. "It's just wrong." He slipped them on as he walked to a door at the foot of the bed.

"That's a strong word."

Stephen pulled the door open and started rummaging through drawers. Kylac kept talking.

"I haven't learned everything I need to know about you yet, but so far I know that scent affects you more than you realize. One of the determining factors for whether or not two species can understand each other is if they are sexually compatible. Not in the sense of whether or not the two can bear young, but if reproduction works the same.

"It forms the core mentality of the entire species. Everything a person does and thinks is based on how reproduction works. It is one of the first things to evolve, so it forms the bottom layer of the mind, and everything that comes after builds on top of it. If two races have similar reproductive methods, their core mindsets will be basically similar. If two races have two completely different methods of reproduction, then they won't have a core perception of the universe in common and will probably not be able to understand each other. Language may be translated, but concepts, ideas, the very way they understand reality will be too different. They'll know of each other, but they won't be able to comprehend much about each other."

By now Stephen had dressed in a shirt and longer pieces of cloth that covered the legs. He turned and faced Kylac with no scent of nervousness now.

"So you got me to sleep with you to find out if we can understand each other?"

"Well, first, it's my nature, thanks to Deka. It keeps my instincts under control. Second, I needed to know if we can understand each other at all."

"Wasn't *Star Trek* enough?"

"That was only pictures on glass, which confirmed you are a visual species. It was not reality or exploration. This was." Kylac patted the bed with one hand.

The human shivered.

Kylac waved his tail. "Stephen, I forbid you to feel bad about it. My scent told you I was available, and you responded to it normally. So far I deduce that social pressure forces you to be one thing or another. It could be a leftover from primitive times meant to enforce conformity to ensure the group survives. Something your culture has yet to move beyond. Where I come from, you can be all things. Deka should be awake by now. I wonder what he's been doing."

The fox walked past Stephen, out of the bedroom, and into the living room. Behind him he heard Stephen muttering to himself.

"He touched me and my clothes came off. He has magic hands. That's gotta be what happened."

Deka lay in front of the couch, holding the remote control in his hand, working the buttons with one carefully placed claw.

"What else did you learn?" Deka said, in Relian.

Kylac sat on the couch behind him and faced the screen. "It's just as we thought. His species is suffering because of it."

"Is there hope?"

"Probably not. We'll know for sure when we leave this house."

Stephen walked into the room and stood to the side of the couch. He smelled stunned when he saw Deka facing the TV.

"Morning, Deka," he said. "Why are you on the floor?"

"The couch groans under my weight. I do not want to break it."

"Oh, right. Thanks. Anything good on?"

"TV is painful to watch. How do you endure it for so long?"

"Painful? What do you mean?"

"The screen flickers constantly, and the sounds it generates are difficult to hear. Is this really what your range of hearing and sight is?"

"Flickers...? Is it like bars going up the screen?"

"Yes, I see those, too."

"That's the refresh rate you're seeing," Stephen said. "TVs work with an electron gun shooting the screen, lighting up different pixels. I think it only goes at sixty times a second or something."

"Ah, that is why."

"You can see that? Your eyes must be a hundred times better than mine."

"Ears, too," said Deka.

"Damn... Um, okay. It's breakfast for me. What do you two eat? And... do you know how to use the bathroom?"

"I smelled you use it last night after you and Kylac were finished," said Deka.

"Oh... Sorry... So you know how a toilet works?"

"I figured it out."

"I did, too," Kylac said. "You passed out after you climaxed for the third time."

"Well! Good! That's out of the way! What about food?"

"I don't need to eat for another two days," said Deka. "Kylac is an omnivore, and I am exclusively carnivorous."

"You only eat meat? Well, I got some hamburger in the 'fridge if you wanna try any."

"I am satisfied."

"Okay. What about you, Magic Hands?"

"I will try it," said the fox. "Is it meat?"

"Yes. I'll cook it up right now."

"Cook?" said Kylac. "Heat it over a fire, you mean?"

"Yes."

"That won't be necessary."

"Uncooked? Of course. Let's go!"

Stephen walked to the kitchen and opened the refrigerator. The sound caught both Kylac's and Deka's ears, and they stood at the same time and followed it. They halted where the plastic tile floor of the kitchen met the carpet. Kylac sniffed the floor to make sure it was made of plastic. He still didn't like touching it.

Cold air fell on their feet. Deka looked inside the door Stephen had opened. It was much cooler in there. Stephen reached in, pulled out some sort of plastic package, and then bumped the door closed with his elbow.

"Why is it cold?" Deka said, sniffing it through the plastic.

"It's wrapped in plastic," Kylac said. "The floor is plastic, the TV is plastic, the remote control is plastic. You even wrap your food in it? What *is* this stuff?"

"I wish I could explain it better."

He opened a drawer, took out something, and used it to cut the film covering the food. The room exploded in delicious scent. It pulled Kylac onto the plastic floor, and both he and Deka huddled over it, scenting it vigorously.

"Hold on, hold on." Stephen peeled the plastic back, leaving a tube of meat on a plate. He picked up the tool from the counter and cut it in half. "There. I was saving this for tacos, but..."

Deka opened his mouth and took the first half in one bite. Kylac was a little more cautious. He scented it, tasted it with his tongue once. Twice. Three times. Then he bit off half the remaining piece, chewed it up and swallowed.

Stephen watched. He did not blink.

"That's..." Deka began. He chewed it a few times and then swallowed. "That is filling. Unsatisfying, but filling. What do you think, Kylac?"

"I taste a hint of the plastic on the surface. Next time I will cut off the outside before eating it. Other than that and the cold, it is very good. You don't taste the plastic in the meat, Stephen?"

"No. You can?"

"My sense of taste and smell is much stronger than Deka's, but his is still very good."

"What creature is this?" said the theropod. "Are they good to hunt?"

"Uh..."

"Is it predator or prey? How many predators does it take to bring one down? What defenses does it have, and does it evade attackers or fight back?"

"Uh, not really. They just stand there and graze all day. They're dumb and slow."

"That is disappointing." Deka's hands sagged. Stephen noticed, then looked at the raptor's face again.

"So it doesn't taste all that good to you?"

"He's a carnivore," said Kylac. "His tongue doesn't work the same as yours and mine. My tongue tells me you have good food on this planet. Is that all there is?"

"Yeah, I only bought enough for me. A meal or two. It's okay. I can buy more after—holy shit I work today! Shit!"

Stephen looked up at something hanging on the wall that was making regular knocking sounds.

"It's too late for me to call off. Do you think you'll be fine for a..." Stephen rubbed the back of his neck, clenched his fist. "Shit. No. I'm not going to work! Not when I have aliens in my house!"

He stepped over to the wall, lifted something made of plastic off something else made of plastic, raised it to his ear, and pressed some things on the plastic thing that were also made of plastic. Deka and Kylac listened as it made noises in Stephen's ear.

"Hey, yeah, Barb, it's Stephen."

Kylac's ears bloomed. Deka turned his head so one of his earholes was closer to Stephen. They heard a mechanical, weak voice coming from the earpiece.

"My car won't start," Stephen said. "I can't make it to work today."

Voice sounds, so narrow and weak the Relians barely heard anything.

"I'm sorry. My car won't start." He paused. "I know, I know, I'm sorry. If I can't drive, I can't get to work. I'll be in tomorrow, I hope, if I can get it fixed." Another pause. "Yeah, I know, bye."

He replaced receiver and turned to Deka and Kylac. "Well, that's done. I have today off, so we can do anything you want."

"Can we go outside now?" Deka said.

"Except that."

"Why not?"

"It's broad daylight. Everyone will see you."

"I want to know this world. I cannot do that through the TV. There is no scent, no feeling, barely any sound or image. Is there anyplace we can go safely during the day?"

"Well..." Stephen said. "I have an idea. I can take you on a trip around town. Watertown isn't exactly a metropolis, but there's still lots to see. Just hop in the back seat, throw a blanket over you, and you can look and smell all you want."

"Back seat?" Deka said.

"Of my car."

"What is a car? And you said it will not start."

"The car's fine. I lied to my boss to get a day off."

"You did what?" Kylac said.

"I lied, but otherwise I'da had to go to work today and leave you alone for ten hours with nothing to do. So what do you say? How 'bout a car trip?"

The raptor and the fox shared glances.

3

It was cramped in the back of Stephen's car. Deka had to fold his tail in on itself to fit, and the blanket covering his body was cumbersome. Pleasantly warm, but it smelled artificial and made his scales itch.

Kylac sat in the front seat, wearing a large coat with a hood over his head, which covered him completely except for the snout. Unlike the blanket, this did not smell too artificial and was thus more tolerable.

Stephen sat in the other front seat. He was reaching across Kylac, rotating a handle, and the glass covering the window descended into the door.

"Sorry I don't have power windows. I bought this car because it was cheap, not because it's comfortable."

"I think I agree," said Deka.

Stephen turned around in his seat and twisted the handle in the back, behind his seat. The glass descended most of the way down and then stopped.

"And sorry, Deka, I can't roll your windows all the way down, but now you can hang your head out and catch all the smells you want. Just please don't take the blanket off. You will freak people out."

He sat up, twisted his hand forward. Noise came from the front of the car, it rumbled, and the distinct smell of burning carbon hit their noses. Stephen twisted his body around, looked out the rear window, and backed up. The sudden lurch of movement turned the Relians' stomachs.

"How does this work?" Kylac said.

"Internal combustion engine. It burns gas, the gas moves pistons up and down, turns a crankshaft, and that turns the wheels. I've had this thing up to a hundred and ten miles an hour."

"Is this how your kind gets around?"

"For moderate distances. I'd take you on a plane ride if I could get away with it."

The car stopped. Stephen got out, closed the garage door, then climbed back in. He backed out the rest of the way, and the car stopped, lurched, and then drove forward. The acceleration made their stomachs turn again.

"Let me know if you get motion sick," Stephen said. "I'll try not to take sudden turns. Never rode in a car before? Anybody else in the universe have these?"

Deka was resting his snout on the window, peering out from under the blanket. The smells that reached him were astonishing. "Actually no."

"Really? No cars? So how do aliens get around?"

"They have their own means of doing so," said Deka. "What they can't do, portals take care of the rest."

"Okay..." Stephen stopped at a red hexagon. He looked both ways, then pulled out and turned left. "So...

We kinda got distracted last night. I was going to try to help you understand the episode."

Kylac's tail wagged. He was panting hard with his mouth open and tongue hanging out. "Penis is very distracting to you." It wagged harder, and Kylac kept panting.

Stephen glanced at him, and the distinct smell of discomfort came from him. "I didn't expect that at all. I'm still a little..." He gritted his teeth. "I guess we need to watch that episode again."

"I was watching the TV."

"You were? When?"

"The whole time we were having sex."

"While...?"

"I listened to the sound when I could not see, and watched when I could."

"And... you, Deka? You were watching us the whole time."

"I was watching both of you and the TV, yes. We are Archeons. We are aware of all information in our surroundings. It may not seem so to you, but we were paying attention."

"You can do that? Even while having sex? Oh, man, I've heard of people who can do that. Can all aliens do it?"

"No," said Deka. "We happened to have the trait, so we became Archeons. We watched the entire tape."

"Well. Good. So we didn't get distracted. You guys promised to tell me some things. I know it wasn't easy to watch, but please tell me if we got anything right."

Kylac faced the window, taking in the air. Now *this* was real. This was exploration. This was Earth. It smelled very much the same as the temperate areas of Kronia. Similar flora, similar pollen in the air, similar artificial structures everywhere.

"Your mindset is unique," Kylac said, tongue out, body pushing as much hot air out of him as possible. This coat was unbearably stifling, but he endured it. "Every species we make contact with does not try to explore space with physical vessels. Your view of the future is thinking of ways to make shuttles and space vehicles so they can carry you to other planets."

Deka continued where Kylac had left off. "This is not the way civilizations begin to explore outside their planet. All species begin by stargazing, but after that, once a culture discovers portal physics, they abandon these ideas."

Kylac resumed. "Space is too vast for anyone to conceive crossing physically. Everyone discovers portals long before they think to make vehicles. The difficulties portal physics presents are far easier to overcome than the difficulties in surviving in space and sailing from one planet to the next."

"Damn, Kylac, how do you talk like that?"

"Like what?"

"You're panting up a storm over there. You okay?"

"It is how my body expels heat. I am not suffering."

"Oh, good. So no spaceships then? None?"

"None," Deka said. "There are no spaceships. No vessels. No cars."

"Huh... I saw a UFO when I was sixteen. I was hoping you could explain that. It wasn't you? It wasn't anyone you know?"

"What's a UFO?" asked Deka.

"An alien spaceship. Or something you can't explain in the sky."

"I don't know what you saw, but no species in the contacted universe uses ships to travel through space."

"Oh. So that means we got everything wrong."

"Not everything," said Kylac. "There are bipedal species, but most are quadrupeds, or can function as both when necessary, as I can."

"You can walk on all fours?"

The houses were becoming more numerous and closer together. The scents of plant and stone became more concentrated, more domesticated and less natural. A major settlement was approaching.

"Also, no alien species speaks English," said Deka.

"That's the universal translator. It wasn't mentioned in that episode. That reminds me, how did you learn English so fast?"

Deka watched the houses go by, taking in the scents. "It is something Archeons can do. We perceive spacetime as a series of patterns. Language develops along patterns as well. They are easy to figure out once you know this."

"And what is a portal?"

"We will show you soon," said Deka, "but your vehicle is effective for now. A little sickening, but there are so many scents here. It reminds me of Kronia."

Stephen drove up and down numerous streets. Many buildings stood here, and the hum of electricity was everywhere, coming from wires hanging by the side of the road, sometimes passing overhead. Half the land was covered in pungent-smelling artificial material.

"What is this path made of?" said Kylac.

"Asphalt. It's made of oil and I think old tires."

"I hate the smell. Can we leave the asphalt?"

"In a few places. I could take you to a park, but there will be people around. Plenty of forest away from the cities."

"That would be nice, but I want to know where you live as well," Deka said.

"Well, this is it. Downtown Watertown. Snows eight months out of the year here. You shoulda been here last winter. Worst snow I've ever been through. Even the locals tell me it was bad."

Suddenly the structures smelled old, and their appearance changed as well, but it quickly ended as they drove through it. There were many other cars on the road, but the drivers gave Stephen no looks. They were anonymous. It was similar to Xce, being among so many people and yet completely hidden, but in a visual sense.

"Why does nobody greet us?" Kylac said.

"Because we're driving. Can't talk to anybody in another car."

"Don't they recognize you?"

"I don't know them."

"You do not know the people in your settlement?"

"Watertown ain't no big city, but it's not small either."

Kylac and Deka thought about that for a while as they took in the scents of the city.

"So how many planets have you contacted?" Stephen said.

"There are six hundred and fourteen worlds in the contacted universe," said Kylac.

"Including this one?"

"We've only contacted you. Not the whole world."

"Oh. Of course." Stephen made quick exhales from the diaphragm. The Relians deduced it was how the human species laughed.

They stopped at a red light. Kylac looked out the front window. "What is that? And why do you stop at them?"

"Stoplights. They regulate traffic. Red is stop. Yellow is caution. Green is go."

They continued very slowly through the city, stopping every few dozen paces it seemed. The constant start-and-stop motion made both Relians dizzy, but as with the television, they did not complain. It was how Stephen lived, so they would live it, too.

"Can this thing take us outside the city?" Deka said.

"Of course. Gets about five hundred miles per tank."

"How far can we go?"

"Well, New York City is about five hundred miles away. I could take you there, but that city is dense, and you won't smell anything but asphalt and concrete. Been there once. Never again. The people move like robots."

"Where else on the planet can we go?"

"In one day?" Stephen said. "Around town, maybe a couple hundred miles out. Not much to see, but most of the country is like that, so I guess it's a good taste of what it's like. I could take you to the Thousand Islands, but it's always packed."

"Do you not have a means to travel long distance?" said Deka.

"We do, but it's expensive, and it involves other people."

They were silent for a moment. Then Kylac spoke.

"We can make a way. Are there any maps of this world with elevation and some kind of reference system to where we are in the universe?"

"Ummm... I'm sure there are in the library."

"We also want an idea of the planet's broader history," Deka said. "Where should we go to do that?"

Stephen thought about that as they sat at a red light. Drivers in other vehicles looked at them but did not seem to notice anything unusual inside Stephen's car.

"The Smithsonian," Stephen said. "It's a museum. They have a natural history exhibit. Problem is there are people there. Unless... You said you can go to other planets by making portals to them? Think you can get us into a museum after hours?"

4

Deka and Kylac were studying the globe Stephen had bought. It showed the entire planet, all the continents, the oceans, some of the major cities, and borders of all the countries.

Photocopies of a topographic map of the area of a place called Washington DC were strewn about the floor. Also lying on the floor was a book on dinosaurs, a book about the red fox, other books on various wildlife, and one on astronomy, all borrowed from the library. The globe had come from a store.

Deka and Kylac spoke to each other in Relian while Stephen leaned against the wall and watched. The globe was immensely useful—finally they saw the world as a whole, and they could figure out where they were on it and where they needed to be. Calculating coordinates on a new planet to someplace they had never been was tricky and would take a while, but it could be done.

The star maps helped them find their location relative to known stars. Now Deka knew this planet was very close to their personal world orbiting the red star, and he must have been trying to go to Bynadium and that place at the same time and ended up here. Somehow. It still made no sense, but now they knew how to leave and return.

It had taken all day to reach this point, which was good, because they could not go there until dark anyway. Now it was just after nine o'clock at night, and the Relians had figured out the measurement system here. One breath was close to one second. One minute was equal to sixty-five breaths. Two feet equaled one pace. A claw's reach was about half an inch.

Knowing all of this was vital to reading the maps, as the units had to be converted into something the Archeons could use. Once they knew how the right angle was represented in this system, the rest became easy to deduce. Now they knew exactly where they were and how to go anywhere they wanted on this world, plus or minus one pace in elevation.

Finally, around ten o'clock at night, long after the yellow star had descended, the Archeons stood and cleared the area around the wall of living room.

"Watch," Kylac said.

He stared off into space for about twenty seconds. Then a sphere opened, silently, filling a good section of the living room. The main entrance of the Smithsonian, just inside the front door, was visible through it.

Kylac looked back at Stephen. His mouth was open, and he smelled of fight or flight again.

"That is a portal. A way."

"And it takes us to the museum?"

"It can take us anywhere we want to go once we know our location in the universe."

"I can't believe you just said that. How did you open it?"

Deka walked by them and stepped into the sphere. Stephen jumped backwards, holding onto Kylac. Deka was visible on the other side, scenting around.

"I'm sure there's a night watchman there. Maybe several. Maybe—I dunno. Is it safe?"

"Walk through it."

"But what is it?!"

"The best way to explain it is to live it. Walk, Stephen, and make sure no part of you misses the portal. Keep your arms and legs close."

Stephen stared for a few seconds and then steeled himself, let go of Kylac, and marched straight into the dark sphere. Kylac followed immediately after and stood beside the human, who was looking around them in awe. It was dark in here, but just enough light came in from outside to see the shadows of the museum.

"Holy shit... We're here. But—" He turned around and saw the portal still there, showing a dim view of Stephen's living room around its surface.

"We can return any time," Kylac said.

Deka had already walked far ahead of them, claws lightly tapping the floor. Kylac followed.

"Wait!" Stephen said, shouting but trying to keep his voice down. "I can't see a damn thing!"

"You can't?" Kylac said. Then he remembered Stephen had turned on a light the other night. His tail waved around, and he walked back to the human, took him by the arm, and led him.

"How well can you see?" Stephen said.

"Everything is as clear to me as it probably would be to you in daylight."

"Wow... And oh my God I haven't been here since I was a kid."

They caught up to Deka at last.

"So... Please tell me how we got here," Stephen said. "And keep your voices down."

"You said nobody would be here," Deka said.

"Well, no, nobody's here, but there's always security."

"If we meet anybody, we have a way home."

"But we'll be seen."

"To catch prey, you have to leap," said Deka.

"Right," Stephen said. "So that thing we just went through. What's it made of?"

"The universe," answered the raptor. "Peel back your perception of reality, that's what you find."

"But...?"

Deka led them into the museum, and Kylac led Stephen. The human was clearly trying to figure out what he wanted to ask.

"You said you have not been here since you were a kid?" Kylac said. "Why?"

"Too far, parking in DC is impossible, and my job is eating my life. Hard to have a life when you gotta pull fifty-plus hours a week just to keep up with the mortgage and bills. And in the north country, your heating bill can be more than the mortgage in winter."

Kylac said nothing to that. They walked through the dark museum and finally emerged in one of the exhibit halls.

"Here we are," Stephen said. "There are the bones I was talking about."

They were visible even in the darkness. Bones of creatures that stood five times higher than any of them.

"T-rex is there," Stephen said. "Diplodocus is over there. Triceratops is... somewhere. I think they have an allosaur, too."

"What is a T-Rex?" Deka said.

"Looks kinda like you, but ten times bigger."

They walked toward it and stopped at the barrier. The sight reminded the Relians of the statues on Kronia, except these were not stone or sand. These were bones, forming the interior structure of a creature that once lived. They scented them from a distance.

"These are not bones," said Deka.

"Well, no. They're plaster casts of the bones. The originals are somewhere else."

Deka growled. "Is nothing on this planet real?"

Stephen winced. He stood frozen for a moment and then laughed. "You're right. Everything here is fake. But look at them. Don't they remind you of anything?"

"Yes," Deka said. "They resemble multiple avian and theropod species on many worlds."

"And you looked at the book on foxes I gave you, Kylac. Why do you look like a fox? Deka, why do you look like a dinosaur?"

Deka was still staring up at the T-Rex skeleton facsimile. "I believe the term in your language is convergent evolution."

"What's that?"

Both Deka and Kylac turned to Stephen.

"All right," Kylac said. "You have two planets. Same environment. Same ingredients for life. Same weather, same temperature, same everything. It makes sense that similar life forms will adapt to survive on both worlds. What works on one planet tends to work on another if the conditions are similar. That's why we resemble things that live here. A lot of creatures on other worlds would remind you of things here."

Deka gazed at the fake skeletons. "And it seems reptiles once dominated this planet."

"Giant mammals, too," Stephen said. "I think there's a mammoth skeleton around here somewhere. Maybe saber toothed tigers. Or that might be another museum. I can't remember."

They wandered the exhibits, Kylac leading the human by the arm. Stephen was walking nearly blind through most of the exhibits. Kylac leaned his muzzle close to Stephen's ear and spoke low as they moved around the museum.

"Your senses tell you the floor is solid, the air resists your movement, and that you are walking on a stationary surface. This is the information you are aware of because the needs of survival forced your evolutionary ancestors to focus only on the information that helped them survive in their environment. Their brains learned to accept only what was most immediately useful, and ignored the rest. In this manner, your own mind limited your perception of the universe to whatever helped it survive in the distant past.

"But the senses still take in a lot more than is needed for basic survival, so the mind sets up a barrier between what it needs and what it doesn't. The conscious and the subconscious. For most species, this mental structure persists long after they achieve sentience as a leftover from those primitive times.

"There is a way to know the real universe again. Archeons learn how to put the conscious and the subconscious back together, become aware of everything their senses once ignored, and perceive all of reality. This allows us to control it. Portal physics is the result.

"Every point in spacetime is connected. Atoms on one side of the universe can affect atoms on the other side, and Archeons can control these connections. The universe is made of connections. Connections are patterns, and patterns are mathematics. It is possible to navigate the entire universe with nothing but conscious thought recognizing these patterns."

"That's..." Stephen began. "Damn. So how are you keeping that one open?" Stephen gestured over his shoulder with his head.

"Archeons can establish permanent ways at two ends, but we must be physically present at one of the ends when we open the way, and then we are bound to meditate on the calculations to keep it open. We can maintain dozens or even hundreds of portals at once all across the universe and still live normal lives. We are the bridges between cultures."

"Why don't they just build machines to do that? Why do you have to do it?"

Deka spoke from a distance ahead. "An unconscious mind cannot perceive reality, Stephen. Have you ever had an idea that made perfect sense but was so simple you wondered why no one ever thought of it before? An idea so profound you actually felt proud of yourself for thinking of it?"

"Yeah. Couple times."

"What happened to it?"

"I tried to write it down, and nothing happened. I forgot it."

They passed the natural history museum and entered the gift shop. Deka and Kylac browsed the selection of stuffed animals, pieces of amber inside plastic containers, books, magazines, and other souvenirs and trinkets.

"The idea was perfect in your head," Deka said, "but when you tried to solidify it in the real world, it could not hold together. The math that comprises the universe is like that. It can only exist in the mind of a self-aware creature. It must be contemplated, not recorded or expressed."

"You're doing all of it in your head? I can't even do my taxes without a calculator. So you can go anywhere you want, at any time?"

"Not quite. It takes days to calculate ways to other planets. It's incredibly complex math."

Stephen followed the Archeons as they moved from exhibit to exhibit.

"And somehow you're able to do all this and have a conversation at the same time?"

"Yes," Kylac said. "The mind is aware of much more than you realize. Deka and I are aware of all of it. Well, almost all. It doesn't make us perfect—there are still things we miss, especially since the disaster. Everything you don't realize your mind is taking in, such as air temperature, distance to the horizon inferring the size of the planet, the area measurements of these rooms—we have learned to take in all of this information and hold it consciously. The calculations happen automatically for an experienced Archeon. Deka and I can calculate up to two portals at the same time, and it wasn't difficult even before we were injured. We can't keep ways to other worlds open for very long anymore. Even ways between different points on the same world are a strain. There was a time we both maintained dozens of them at the same time."

"This is how real aliens explore the universe, Stephen," Deka continued. "No ships. No machines. Very few species use machines, and those that try come to realize they'd rather live to expand their own potential instead of maintaining artificial devices."

Stephen held still for a moment. Deka and Kylac moved further on, examining everything they could. They ignored their sense of smell for the most part, as it gave little information on the content of the exhibits. Finally Stephen started walking and caught up.

"So if you can travel anywhere in the universe, does that mean you can travel through time, too?"

"No," Kylac answered. "Time travel is impossible."

"Really? Even the idea?"

"The idea has always been around," Kylac said. "Rive and Friend theorized on it."

"Who are they?"

"Rive and Friend are the other two Relian Archeons," Deka said.

"Friend? His name is Friend?"

Deka clicked his claws together. "His name happens to correspond to a word in your language. The sound is a coincidence. They are a strange pair. Rive doesn't enjoy hunting. He is capable, but he prefers not to, so he lets his fox hunt for himself. He doesn't have a mate either. Prefers to spend all his time thinking about the nature of reality."

"Sounds like a bookworm," Stephen said.

"I enjoy your language," Deka said. "It's so figurative and visual. Yes, a bookworm, though no actual books are involved. Just ideas."

"Friend has good genes he needs to pass on," Kylac said. "He has a very stable mind. Sometimes I'm jealous of it. Rive insisted Friend needed to have children. He has a mate now. Taris is her name, and they were raising a child together. Friend is also like Rive. Spends a lot of time having big thoughts about the universe. Some Archeons become so wrapped up in this perspective they forget to live normal lives."

"Rive speculated a lot on the nature of time," continued Deka. "So did Friend, but Archeons agree that time is more of a perception than a reality. The only record of the past is your own memory of it. It's not a physical place you can go."

"I guess that makes sense," said the human, chuckling. "Good to know some things are science fiction even to aliens."

He walked with Kylac through most of the museum. Deka and Kylac looked at various displays, but Stephen didn't see anything. Kylac could tell he was lost in thought. They had just given him a taste of reality outside his planet, and he was trying to take it all in.

"You said you were injured. How?"

"Our planet was destroyed," Deka said.

"The whole planet?"

"Yes," said Kylac. "We were there when it happened."

"Oh my God... Just... Destroyed? By who? What?"

"That is a good question," Deka said. "We're still not sure what happened. People were talking about how the animals at the hunting grounds had been behaving. They were lying down, and they smelled terrified of something. They weren't running from the predators as they hunted them. Even I felt it. Everybody had a difficult time concentrating on anything. I promised to go and observe it myself as soon as I adjusted a sphere."

"We were standing near a portal," Kylac said. "We heard this loud rumble coming from the distance. We turned back, and there was this something pulling the planet up and away. It was taking parts of the world in long pieces. Huge beams of soil came up from the ground. Pieces of people were mixed in there as well. It was as if spacetime itself were reaching out and pulling the ground up. If people got in the way, they were pulled apart, too."

Deka continued. "The ground disappeared right in front of us. We tried to keep the ways open, but they were collapsing all around us. That's when we dove for the closest sphere. We lost consciousness for days. The portals we kept open to other planets ripped away from us, too. We were told whatever tore our planet apart also tried to tear our minds away with it. The Archeons fell unconscious for days or weeks. Some died from the shock."

"Months later they had just begun to rebuild the contacted universe," Kylac resumed, "and then we lost another planet. We have been the only two who can make ways between worlds. That's how we've spent the last year of our lives, hopping from world to world, trying to repair the damage the disasters caused."

"Your entire planet? Just... gone?"

"It is unprecedented," Deka said. "Another Archeon we know thinks something outside the universe caused it, but beyond that, we have no idea what happened."

They had made a giant loop around the entire museum and had come back to the skeletons. Stephen leaned on the railing in front of the T-Rex exhibit.

Deka leaned against the rail as well. "So what about you, Stephen?"

"What about me?"

"Why are you here? How have you lived?"

"My story? It's not nearly as impressive as yours. What the hell can I say to compete with all of that?"

"Competition is not necessary," said the raptor. "We are here to learn, and static exhibits made of artificial material will only teach us so much."

"Well... okay. I was born in California. My mother was American. My father was from the Philippines. He emigrated as a young man, decided to stay. When I was a kid, I wanted to be a scientist. Told my mom I wanted to find a cure for pollution. Then I failed every science class in high school, and I kinda never had a plan after that. Joined the Army when I was nineteen. Got stationed in Fort Drum for a good chunk of it. Decided not to reenlist when I hit thirty, settled down here and married my girlfriend. She died three years ago. Left me alone in that house... Thought about moving, but where else should I go? Wanted to go back to school, but it's hard to do that when you gotta keep a full-time job just to scrape by. Mom and dad passed away while I was in the military. Melissa, my sister, she visits me once in a while. I don't hear from any of my buddies in the Army anymore. Nothing to talk about. Really, ever since Brenda died, all I've done is go to work and come home. Even thought about joining the Army again, but they wouldn't take me. I'm too old. It's how it goes, isn't it? You spend so much time wanting to get out, then you're out and all you want to do is go back."

The Archeons remained silent.

"Sounds pathetic, doesn't it?" Stephen continued. "After hearing what you two can do. You can make doors to any planet you want, any time you want. You've been saving civilization after your planet was destroyed. What the hell am I doing? Joined the Army? Became a paper pusher. Dabbled in PASCAL after getting out, failed at that, settled in the north country, been going to work fifty, sixty hours a week just to keep up."

He paused again for a few breaths. Deka and Kylac waited.

"I need to know something," said the human, turning to face them. "I think everyone in the world just has this feeling that something is wrong. Like, I've been following the shit that's going on in South Africa. Riots, mass murder, shootings... Over what? People with one skin color trying to keep people with another color down. How did we let this happen? And how can you spend all your life looking for the right person, then just when you think you're happy, she gets cancer? Then you're stuck the rest of your life paying her medical bills, even though none of the shit they did worked, even though she had insurance. This place doesn't even scratch the surface of our history. Two world wars, the Cold War, the Civil War, the Crusades, revolutions, Red Scare, Protestants verses Catholics, monarchies, slavery. Everyone wants to know. Why can't we seem to do better than this? Why isn't the world a better place? Does stuff like this happen on other planets, or is it just us?"

The Relians remained quiet for a minute. The fox leaned against the human, letting his pheromones do their work, and Stephen calmed down. He still didn't realize how Kylac affected him.

"I'm not sure how to answer," Deka said at last.

"I was hoping... It's what we really need. Someone to point out what we're doing wrong so we can start doing it right. I'm surprised a guard hasn't see us yet. I think we should leave now."

Stephen turned and headed back toward the entrance, and the Archeons followed. The human must have gotten used to the poor light, for now he walked without guidance. The portal at the main entrance was still open, and they passed through it together. Stephen turned around and looked back at the sphere. Kylac closed it.

"That is amazing," Stephen said. "Five hundred miles. Just like that."

"Five hundred miles," Deka said. "Five million light years. It's all the same in portal physics."

"I'm sorry, but I still don't understand. Well, that's it. Listen, guys, today was a good day, but I can't call off work again tomorrow. They'll fire me for sure. How long do you plan to stay?"

"I've been working on a way offworld since Kylac started on the way to the museum," Deka said. "Our destination is not too far from here, so I should be ready to go by morning."

"That soon? I was kinda hoping you'd stick around longer. There are places all over the world I'd love to see. I can get you more maps."

"We need to leave," Kylac said. "Remember we told you we were fixing the damage the disasters caused? We're still fixing it. We came here by accident. Other places need us."

"Yeah, I know... I just..." Stephen rubbed the back of his neck. "I'm glad you came. If you ever want to come back, I'll keep that side of the room clear for you, and meat in the freezer. Just heat it up."

Stephen's scent became anxious again. Deka and Kylac waited for him to say what he was really thinking. It took the human a moment to gather the courage.

"I don't know how to say this, so I'm just gonna blurt it out. Can I come with you guys? I want to see what you guys do out there. How real aliens live. Can I?"

The Relians did not have to exchange glances to agree.

"I'm sorry, Stephen," Deka said, "but the places we go are dangerous. We cannot take you with us."

"Just one world? A walk around the park, meet some people? It's a day trip for you, but to me it's impossible."

"If you knew some of the places we've been, you would not ask," said Kylac.

"We have come close to death several times," Deka added. "We cannot protect you as well."

Stephen's scent fell at the same time his body sagged. "I knew you'd say that, but I had to ask. Well, I hope I'll see you again."

"We might stop by once things calm down," Deka said.

"Please do. I'll be more prepared for guests next time. Shit, it's one in the morning. Stay as long as you want. I gotta get to bed. Good luck finding survivors and helping people recover."

Stephen went to his room, and the house fell silent. Deka and Kylac switched to the Relian language.

"Should we answer him?" Kylac said.

"No. It will only make things worse. He can barely understand portal physics. How will he handle knowing what's wrong with the world?"

"It might be a comfort. He seems intelligent. Just isolated. We should tell him."

"I don't think he will understand even after we explain it."

Kylac's ears folded back.

"Stop that, Kylac. You know I'm right."

"I think he can learn."

"His species has to learn it on its own, if it can. We're only two Relians. We can change the world, but we can't change the people."

They rested on the couch and stared at the blank TV screen.

Hartha

The way closed behind them, and the raptor and the fox scented around. Hartha was a hot world, and the Harthans were all furless mammals that laid eggs and shed their skin every few years. Everyone joked they had evolved in every direction at once, and it happened to work for them. Stephen would have called them moles, but the resemblance was only superficial.

The Archeons here opened ways in the air above each volcano, gave them a spin, pulled the gasses out of the atmosphere, and vented them into space. It kept the planet from overheating, it kept the atmosphere clean, and it meant the mammals would not have to burrow anymore. They could live on the surface and not have to devote their entire lives to digging deeper and deeper to escape the dangerous volcanic fumes.

Deka and Kylac expected to find this world overtaken by volcanic clouds and the people walking on hot ash, but spheres on the hub led to other parts of this star-baked world, which meant the Archeon on this planet was alive and well. The Relians were relieved civilization had not been lost.

A hairless rodent about half the size of Kylac's torso ran up to them on two legs. She was built low to the ground, as her species had evolved means to burrow. Almost completely blind, she navigated by touch, vibrations, and scent. She didn't see Deka and Kylac arrive so much as she had felt their footsteps when they came through the portal and recognized these footsteps were the correct weight and shape to be Relian. When she came near, she dropped to all fours and walked the rest of the way.

"Deka? Kylac?" she said in her own language.

"Re'e'e'ehn," Kylac said. "Glad to meet you again."

"Are your Archeons all right?" Deka said. "Something is destroying planets. Archeons are falling unconscious. Some are dead."

"When the first disaster struck, our Archeons were in a coma for fifty days," she answered. "We had to start burrowing again to escape the gas building up. Then they awoke and reopened the ways. Just when the atmosphere was clean enough for us to be on the surface, the second disaster hit. We lost one of our Archeons then, but our other survived. That's when two Relians arrived."

Kylac's ears perked. "Relians?"

Deka's neck danced as he rubbed his claws. "Who?"

"Rive and Friend."

Deka's toe-claws twitched. "Are they still here?"

"No. They did not say where they were going, but another Harthan saw the way they opened when they left. They went to Meze."

"Meze," Deka echoed.

"I'm working on a way right now," Kylac said. "It'll be a couple days—Rive and Friend! Alive!" He turned back to the rodent. "Did they say anything about where they'd been since the disaster? What happened to them?"

"Come with me," she said.

She led them from the hub to one of the spheres and hopped into it. Kylac and Deka stepped through, and they emerged on the shore of a freshwater lake.

Back on Earth, the Relians had come across the word "snake" to describe creatures like this. It stuck in their minds, as it was the best way to describe both the reptiles on Hithe and the underwater creatures of Hartha.

Numerous snakelike creatures floated under the clear water, all as big around as Kylac's entire body. They saw the creatures on the shore, recognized the Relians, and swam close, never disturbing the water.

The Glig were an aquatic species of serpent not unlike the Ven on Hithe, but the Glig had no lungs and never left the water. The mammals on Hartha had no direct means of communication with the Glig for generations. They knew about each other, they knew each was intelligent, but communication seemed impossible.

Deka and Kylac slowly descended into the warm water, submerging themselves all the way up to the tips of their snouts. Re'e'e'ehn followed, also leaving only her nose above the water.

Deka and Kylac exchanged glances, remembering when they first came to this world as children. Deka had heard of aquatics who communicated with land dwellers by the electromagnetic sense, and Deka spent entire days in the water trying to learn their language, experiencing life as an aquatic. Kylac had to force him to emerge once in a while so he wouldn't starve, or fall asleep and drown.

The Glig communicated by projecting magnetic fields around their bodies. Sensing these fields took years of practice, and not all of the ideas could be translated. The Glig reproduced differently from the Harthans, so much of what they said still remained a mystery. Deka and Kylac closed their eyes and used their own sense of electromagnetic fields as a language.

Have not seen raptor or fox for a long time, said the one closest to them. The Relians now recognized the one closest to them as one of this world's Archeons. Her name was unpronounceable, so offworlders referred to her as Kree.

Replying was tricky. Kylac's muzzle was most similar to the Harthans, so he already knew he would be the one to speak for them. He dipped his muzzle under the water and spoke in the Harthan language.

"What did Rive and Friend do while they were here?" He straightened, raised his head above the water, took a breath, and then submerged again. "Did they say anything about what happened?"

The Harthans were not the only ones who had to learn how to adapt to another species. The Glig learned how to sense vibrations in the water, just as the Harthans had to learn how to sense the changes in the magnetic field around the serpents. This effort to perceive reality as another species did lead both to discover portal physics generations ago.

Friend did speak of other worlds. He spoke of the disaster. He spoke of death and fear across the universe.

"Did they speak of survivors?" Kylac said.

Survivors but them, they did not say. The raptor did not enter the water, and the fox was not well. The raptor looked strange. But they reopened the ways above the mountains. Cleared the air. Waited until I awoke. Then they left.

Kylac glanced at Deka and then spoke to the snakes again. "We are relieved they helped you. How long ago did they leave?"

Four days since.

"They could still be on Meze," Kylac said. He took a breath. "Did they say why they went to Meze?"

No. Friend did speak of finding a large planet. I wanted to go with them and help however I could, but the water is seasonal on Meze.

Kylac and Deka looked at each other.

"Thank you," Kylac said. "I am sorry about your other Archeon, but I am glad you survived."

I am elated you and Deka are still alive. I hope you catch up to Rive and Friend. You will have much to discuss.

Kylac swam back to shore, climbed out of the water, and shook off. Deka ran from the water as well, jumping from foot to foot.

"They were here! Kylac, they were here!" Deka held onto Kylac and hopped about.

Kylac was just about to remind him that so far they hadn't found any females, so both their species were doomed, but Deka's excitement was catching, and he held Deka and danced with him.

Then Deka took off running full speed, leaving Kylac behind. Kylac dropped to four legs, but even as a quadruped, he was not as fast as a raptor. Deka left him behind and ran straight through the portal back to the hub.

He stopped, turned in all directions, and remembered there were no portals to other worlds here. He stabbed the ground with his killing claws, snarling.

Kylac finally caught up to him, stood on his hind legs, and laid a hand on Deka's shoulder. "I'm working on a way."

Deka growled again. "They could be gone by the time we arrive!"

"We're on their trail. We'll catch up." He rubbed Deka's shoulder, neck, and face. "Survivors... Other Relians! Finally!" He grabbed Deka and shook him. "*And we're going to Meze!*"

Deka rubbed his claws together. "Guess Rive couldn't keep Friend away from it either."

Meze

The portal closed behind them, and Kylac instantly dropped to all fours, scenting the brown soil. Deka also scented the area.

"They were here!" Kylac said. "Raptor and fox scent! But... Strange. Only one raptor footprint. No scent for the other."

"How old?"

"Days. They were just here!"

"And they walked in this direction." Deka straightened and followed their scents.

Kylac rose and caught up to him. "I hope they're still here. Deka, you realize it's been over a year since we've found another Relian alive?"

"I know, and smelling their scents again..." Deka finished the sentence with a determined growl.

They walked, occasionally verifying they were still on their trail. They passed multiple spheres, all leading to different parts of Meze.

They were on a savannah, a grassland with sparse, angular trees. Other places on the planet were cold and snowy. Still other places on the planet were waterlogged swamps. The two sentient species on Meze did not live in those areas, though, preferring the dry scrub of this place.

An entire planet to live on, and the people had adapted to survive on only this tiny sliver of land. The portals to the different regions were open for explorers, education, and other resources. Water was scarce on the savannah, so they frequently brought water from the colder regions.

One of the trees came into view. Kylac's tail waved around and around, and he ran up to it. The low-hanging fruit was never very good, so Kylac leaped onto a branch, scrambled up the tree, and picked one of the higher fruits. He sniffed it. It smelled so good he came out of his sheath all the way.

Kylac took a bite. The fruit was sweet and fleshy. It smelled like sex and tasted like orgasm.

Both sentient species on this planet were herbivores, and they both ate the fruit of what they simply called the Tree. It had developed the ability to release pheromones that matched those of both species, thus enticing them to eat the fruit and spread the seeds across the savannah.

Kylac realized he was not alone here. Mammals with wings for arms clung to the branches, too. They behaved like birds but smelled like mammals and had reptilian faces. They were watching Kylac, fluttering their wings, laughing at him in their own unique way.

"Don't laugh!" Kylac said. "You do it, too. You're just better at hiding it."

The bat-like creatures clicked and squeaked at him, then flew away, leaving Kylac alone with the piece of fruit.

Deka gazed up at him from the ground. "Are you done?"

"This is only my first piece!"

"Bring it with you."

"But it smells so good up here!" Kylac was on full display for the whole savannah to see. He took another bite of the fruit, inhaled the air coming from the tree.

"Get down here, Kylac."

"Just one more."

Kylac took the last bite, tossed the core down, and picked another fruit.

"Don't make me come up there," Deka said.

Kylac crunched into the fruit and chewed.

Deka backed up twenty paces, bolted into a full run, jumped and landed on the trunk. His killing claws sank into it, and his hand-claws held him up. He looked so precarious hanging there. Kylac shifted and moved a little ways out on the limb. Deka let go of the trunk and hugged the branch. He then let his killing claws go, and he was on the branch, crawling to Kylac.

Kylac scooted over and searched for other branches in easy reach. "When did you learn to climb trees?"

"I learned from you." The raptor was approaching fast.

Letting go of his half-eaten fruit, Kylac grabbed an overhead branch and pulled himself one level above Deka, but the raptor reached up and snatched Kylac's ankle. Kylac whined, wagging his tail.

Deka growled. "No more sex fruit! We're here to find Rive and Friend!"

"But the trees smell so good," Kylac said, trying to break Deka's grip. The raptor had a strong grip. "If you were a mammal, you'd understand!"

"You may have all the fruit you want after we find them. There's a good chance Friend is up one of these trees and Rive can't get him down either."

Kylac was holding on with all his strength, but Deka was stronger, and Kylac's hands slipped off the branch. He fell onto Deka's branch. It bobbed up and down, Kylac rolled over, and Deka slipped, smacked his jaw on the branch and rolled off. They both landed on their backs in the dry grass, gasping.

Kylac looked at Deka and waved his tail. Deka looked back at Kylac, clicking his claws together.

Bat-like creatures landed all around them. They had watched the whole thing and were still flapping their wings without taking off, their way of laughing. Quadrupeds also gathered around them. They walked on four hoofed legs and had necks that reached the treetops. Deka wasn't used to being around a species with a longer neck than his.

Kylac was the first to roll to his feet and stand, still out of his sheath. The ambient scent from the trees affected all Relian canines in this way no matter where they were on the savannah. The natives thought it was funny.

"Rive and Friend," Kylac said. "Does anyone know where they are?"

Deka climbed to his feet as well. The bat-like and giraffe-like creatures stood around him. The flying mammals were the Serya, and the long-necked creatures were the Oln. They had long competed for the trees and often fought bloodless territory wars until each realized the other was intelligent. That's when they started learning how to communicate, how to share, how to cooperate. Now there were more trees than ever, and they spoke a unified language of high-pitched squeaks and low-pitched moans.

"They were here," someone said. The voice sounded Oln.

"Nobody saw where they went," said one of the bats.

"Aire is in the sixth region," someone else said.

"Thanks!" Kylac turned and ran back to the hub.

Deka caught up and quickly outran him. He dashed past several spheres, turned, and dove into one. Kylac followed moments later, emerging in the frozen region of the planet close to the poles. The only reason she would come here would be to bring a piece of glacier to the savannah. The rains would come to the savannah soon enough, but the portals freed everybody from enduring the hardship of long droughts, scarce water, and withering fruit.

Kylac caught Aire's scent and led the way. Deka followed, holding back so he wouldn't outrun the fox. There was no snow here, only ice, and lots of it. Deka was already miserable, but he gritted his teeth and forced his metabolism to speed up and generate heat. Kylac felt relief. The daytime star was weak at this latitude, and he was grateful to stop panting.

The Oln was in sight, standing on the glacier, very still against the frigid wind. Her legs were so thin they seemed incapable of holding up her body and neck, let alone stand in the wind.

"Aire!" Kylac called.

The Oln curled her neck down and around to look back at them. Her body turned to match her head, and she ambled toward them.

"I'm glad you survived!" Kylac shouted. "We're trying to find Rive and Friend! Did you meet them?"

"Kylac! Deka! I've heard so much about you two! Yes, Rive and Friend were here."

"I'm surprised they're not still here!" shouted Deka. "You can never get a fox away from those trees."

By now they had caught up to her. She wrapped her neck around their bodies in the usual greeting. Deka shivered but tried not to show it.

"Actually," Aire said, "Friend did not eat the fruit."

Deka curled his neck. "He didn't?"

"Not a single piece. Never went near the trees. Everyone was waiting for him to give in, but he seemed disinterested."

"That's strange. Where are they now? Did they say where they were going?"

"No. Curious they opened their offworld portal in seclusion after making sure everyone was away."

"Did anybody see the portal?" Kylac said.

"Not that I know, and I wasn't there. I'm sorry."

Deka growled. "Why did they come here if not for the fruit?"

"Rive said they wanted to make sure we were all right."

"Were you?" Deka asked.

"I was," said Aire. "The first disaster left me unconscious for days. The second disaster did not hurt me, but I closed all my portals offworld just in case. I am about to move some ice to the first region. You may wait for me there." She looked at Deka, ears flicking around. She was laughing. "Unless you like the weather."

Deka turned and bolted for the portal. Kylac wagged his tail and faced Aire again.

"I will be along shortly," said the tall quadruped. She walked away and stood in the same place she had been before.

Kylac turned around and walked with the wind to the sphere. Exiting region six and entering region one was quite jarring. The wind went from frigid to pleasant, the starlight went from weak to powerful, and the air went from cold and dry to hot and dry.

Deka lay on his back, warming his underside in the starlight, mouth agape in relief.

"You'll never impress Norh like that," Kylac said.

The raptor clicked his claws. "It's time I stopped trying!"

Many breaths later, a portal opened in the middle of the dry lake a few dozen paces away from them. The sphere was full of ice, and it grew to incredible proportions. Most Archeons never opened a way this large in their lifetimes, but Aire opened a few of them every dry season.

The portal reached its final proportion and then closed, leaving behind a sphere of solid ice. It immediately began melting, cool air falling off it. Deka rolled to his feet and stood beside Kylac. The melted ice began filling up the lake. Eventually it would overflow and fill the rivers. Daylight sparkled off the pure glacier water.

Serya landed in it and splashed around. Oln walked into it and drank, flicking their ears. Right before their eyes, the leaves on the Trees filled out and perked up, the branches stood taller, and the bark thickened. The grass around the once-dry lakebed straightened and became green again.

The trees emitted even more of their scent. Kylac breathed it in, and he came out of his sheath again. Oln and Serya laughed at his lack of self-control, but Kylac did not care. He stood admiring the view, watching the land change from dry underbrush to vivid grassland.

Aire walked up beside Deka and Kylac. Deka caught her scent first.

"Where would they have gone from here?"

"They left rather suddenly, without saying farewell," Aire said. "It was unusual."

"We know they went to Hartha and Meze," Kylac said. "Both of those were worlds they were fond of. So was Rel. So was Genzin... Deka, where else did they like to go?"

"They *were* fond of Genzin," Deka said. A moment later, his Archeon mind connected several variables. "Genzin is a large world, and a major hub for the contacted universe. So are Hartha, Rel, and Meze."

"And far away from its star," Kylac continued. "I can think of one other world—"

"I'm making a way to Crexa," Deka finished. "It fits the pattern. Rive liked the reptiles. Friend liked the hunting."

The fox wagged his tail. He would probably be out of his sheath until they left.

"There is something you should know about Rive," Aire said. "I did not recognize him when I smelled him. Then I realized he is not a raptor anymore."

Crexa

Crexa's main hub stretched around much of the planet. Before the disasters, it was so large it needed dozens of portals just to navigate it, similar to Rel's. As Deka and Kylac stepped through the portal, they saw a vast, empty hub from one horizon to the other.

The road was wide enough for a ten people to walk side by side. Portals used to line each side of the path, and it had been built solely for the purpose of keeping the ground from wearing down from the thousands of visitors who walked here every day, traveling from world to world, gaining new perspective on their lives, new knowledge about the universe, and the possibilities open to them. The planet reminded them so much of Rel. It was of a similar size, similar gravity, and similar atmosphere with a white star in the sky.

Now the hub was silent.

Pain welled up behind Deka's ears. He released the portal from his mind. The way closed, the pain went away, and Deka stood up straight again.

Kylac was already on all fours, scenting the area. "They were here. The scent goes this way."

Deka bent down and scented the stone himself. There were so many scents here, representing close to every species in the contacted universe. He had a difficult time detecting all of them, as he had to build up the scents in his head, but Kylac could do it with only a whiff. He followed the fox down the empty road.

The trees here were tall and thin. Small animals continually hopped about. Without all the people, they could venture everywhere on the path. Tiny furred animals no bigger than Kylac's hand, hoofed mammals taller than Deka but walking on legs as thin as his fingers, tiny canines with stingers on their tails, and tiny felines with wings that carried them away after a running start. Kylac dodged a number of them as he ran on Friend's scent trail.

"I can barely smell Rive," he called back. "Aire was right. Something is wrong with him. Only one footprint."

Deka was trotting just behind Kylac now. The animals poured off the road as they whizzed by.

"Where is everybody?" Deka said. "I don't smell anyone here."

Crexa was inhabited by three sentient species, one for each biome on the planet's surface: the mountains, the desert, and the water. Centuries ago, the two land species had constructed canals far inland for the water species to interact with everyone else.

Some of those canals reached the road, which arched over the water. Kylac looked into one, and nobody was swimming in it. Before the disasters, there would have been a few dozen portals in the water linking the water creatures to oceans and lakes on other planets, as well as other canals across Crexa. No portals were in the water now.

The scent veered off the road, and Kylac followed, dropping from stone roadway to dirt. The soil clung to scent much better than stone, and there were fewer scents off the road as well, so tracking became easier.

They followed a canal into a settlement of the desert reptiles. The canal ended in a lake, which formed the center of the community. The Relians ran into this settlement,

347

slowing to a walk. Then Kylac stopped. Deka stopped and stood beside the fox as he rose to his hind feet and scented around.

More than five thousand natives lived on this world, and easily ten times that number in travelers and visitors, but this settlement was empty. Kylac turned to Deka.

"Everyone's scent leads to the road. And I mean everyone. I can catch hundreds of individuals."

"Except Rive and Friend's. Is their scent still here?"

"It is... But then it disappears. Probably into a sphere."

Deka scented the air. "We'll go to each settlement and search them one by one."

"That will take days."

"The scent trail ends here. Rive and Friend led all those people to a portal. They might have visited every settlement."

"Why would they do that? Why would they lead the people to a portal?"

"They probably did what I did on Xce. Link each settlement together and lead everyone to a central way offworld."

"Why?"

"They might know what's causing these disasters and evacuated everyone."

"I'll start a way offworld for us, just in case."

"Pick a warm planet. I'm working on a way. We'll search the mountains first."

Deka sat down and thought, and Kylac sat next to him. The animals began to return, hopping and jumping around the Relians. Even the predators seemed oddly unconcerned.

"Predator and prey standing next to each other," Kylac said.

"And not hunting or running... It's about to happen. Rive and Friend knew it, too. That's the only reason they would lead everyone to the hub."

"Where would they send them? There are plenty of worlds that could accommodate all of them."

"We'll go to the settlements and try to pick up their scent again."

They waited for the way to become clear to Deka, and Kylac began thinking offworld thoughts. A large creature with brown fur, balancing on four thin legs, pranced around some trees. It walked among many of the animals it hunted, and these animals had no fear of their predator anymore.

Deka rubbed his claws. "I remember when we first visited this planet."

"Yes, we were apprentices, and you got it in your head to hunt one of those things."

Deka rubbed faster, clicking and clicking. "I heard about them so much I had to know what they were like to bring down."

"You led us through the way. Then we found ourselves on that road." Kylac looked back. "And oh the people! I never smelled so many people at once, even on Rel. So many spheres. It took us all day to find the right way to the desert biome."

"Then we had to move away from the people just to reach the animals. Walked for several days in the wilderness. Then I finally caught the scent. Didn't know if it was the right one or not, but it smelled big and hairy, so I followed it."

"You mean you got me to track it." Kylac lightly raked his claws down Deka's neck. "We followed it into the desert. Two days you made me sniff it out, and when I got tired you finally started tracking it yourself."

"Then we reached the end... And what did we find? A group of reptiles, and a carcass on the ground."

Kylac's tail was waving so hard he fell over on Deka. "We were so young we didn't know an old scent from a fresh one!"

"You should've known better," Deka said. He raised a hand to the back of Kylac's neck, scraped him down his back. "You're the one with the good nose, and you couldn't tell me it was an old trail?"

"I'd never tracked anything for that long before!"

Deka clutched the fox's neck, tapping it with his claws. "We were starved and dehydrated. The people helped us recover. They even let us eat some of the meat from that animal. After a hunt like that, it tasted awful."

"Worst meat I ever had. Great trip, Deka. Let's go to Crexa and hunt one of the biggest predators in the universe! Oh, wait, it's only tasty to a certain line of reptiles, which we aren't."

"At least we didn't have to freeze to learn that. And then I found out about the aquatics." He rubbed his claws. "So it wasn't a complete waste of time."

"You forgot all about the disappointing meal floating in the water for days."

"The fish made me part of their school. That was so special. Learning their language inside their environment... Thanks for reminding me to breathe."

They held each other, laughing. Before them, the beast milled about, prey all around it, and yet not hunting.

2

The way opened, and Deka stepped out of the portal. Kylac followed moments later and immediately started scenting the ground.

This settlement was in the mountains. The people who lived here were large and covered in layers of fat to protect them from the cold. The lake in the middle of the community, extending far into the cave, was frozen. Before, there would have been a spinning portal underneath constantly circulating warm water to it, so the aquatic species could communicate with the mountain creatures as well as the desert reptiles. Now there was nothing but snow everywhere.

"Scents lead out of the cave to this spot," Kylac said.

Deka tried not to shiver in the icy wind. He walked to where Kylac stood.

"The scents end here, and I only smell one of Rive's feet."

"Eleven more to go," Deka said.

He turned around and trotted for the portal. Kylac followed and ran through it as well, and it closed behind them.

All the caves were alike: lakes frozen, the caves abandoned, all scents leading to a single place.

Deka began opening ways to the desert settlements. The first one they visited happened to be the same one they'd discovered while hunting the beast so many years ago. It was nighttime, and everything was just as they remembered. They were too large to fit in any of the burrows, so all they could do was stick their snouts inside and take a whiff of the air.

They walked from opening to opening, inhaling. Nobody had been in these burrows in at least twenty days.

"Still nothing. And only Rive's scent," Kylac said.

"So where is Friend?"

Kylac had no answer. Nothing but the desert animals were around. Predator and prey standing side by side, and they did not seem to notice, all eerily peaceful.

"They evacuated these people," Kylac said. "I can feel what these animals feel. Something bad is about to happen."

"If Rive and Friend know what's going on, why didn't they tell anyone on Hartha or Meze?"

"They might still be here."

"They would've left with the last of them, Kylac."

"That's not what I smelled back there at the hub. Their scents were newer than the ones on the road. Rive could have made the ways between the settlements, and Friend opened the way offworld, but they did not leave."

"Why?"

"Maybe they're trying to stop the disaster."

"So where would they go?"

"If it were me, I would do it on the hub, in case anyone else came to this world so I could warn them to leave."

"But they're not on the road."

"Not where the way to Rel used to be. We need to open ways to the rest of the desert settlements. There may be a more recent scent at one of them."

"Which one? There are thirteen more places they could have gone."

"In what order do you think they would have visited them?"

Deka thought for a moment. The planet's twin moons glared down at them, one red from iron, the other green with copper.

"I was about to visit them in order around the planet. Rive might have done the same to be sure he visited all of them. I'm working on a way to the last colony now."

Kylac flicked his ears. His heart was racing. Deka could hear it.

"I'm nervous, too, Kylac."

"It's difficult to concentrate," said the fox. "I'm trying to keep the way offworld in mind."

Deka looked around at all the animals. They weren't doing anything. They weren't eating or drinking. They just stood in the sand, staring off into space, shaking and nervous. Deka shivered, even though the sand was still hot.

3

It was nighttime here, but the daytime star was just about to rise. The settlement farthest from Rel's portal location on the hub was as large as the others. Hundreds of reptiles lived here, hundreds of mountain creatures visited, usually at night, and many more aquatic people lived in the lake. Without a spinning portal to maintain it, the heat had dried up the water.

Even more animals milled about. They either stood still or hopped or crawled out of Deka and Kylac's way only when they were close enough to be stepped on. Kylac immediately sniffed the area.

"This scent is newer. It's Friend!"

Kylac walked around the whole settlement, sorting out the multitude of scents and identifying direction. He had to push animals out of his way at times. They seemed completely oblivious to him, as if trapped in their own minds. Some shivered. Others groomed their ears. A few groomed their enormous eyes with their tongues. All of these were gestures of nervous behavior.

Kylac rose. "They went this way."

Deka tore across the sand, and Kylac ran after him. A hundred paces away, Deka noticed footprints. Relian footprints. Rive and Friend had been here, moving in a straight line away from the last settlement—away from civilization —away from any portals that might open. Something felt wrong. The animals knew it as well as the Relians.

The wind blew across the sand. Deka and Kylac didn't have to follow the trail on the ground. Now it came to them from the air, and it was close. Deka ran faster, and Kylac pushed himself harder to keep up.

Deka saw them first. Two figures on the horizon.

"Rive!" Deka yelled.

Kylac jumped, waved his arms. "Friend!"

The two dark figures on the horizon turned their heads.

"Deka!" shouted Rive.

"Kylac!" The faint voice of Friend.

Hearing those voices again, it was as if the disaster never happened. The distance closed. Deka collided with Rive and embraced him, rubbing his neck against the other theropod's. Kylac and Friend collided in mid-stride, grabbed each other's fur, and scented one another.

Rive's scent was metallic. Deka felt cold metal against his scales. He jumped away in shock. Aire was right. Rive was not a raptor anymore. Her language did not have the words to express what she saw, but Relian did.

Rive's tan-colored flesh had been fused to metallic skin that wrapped around his neck and down the front of his torso. One of his legs was completely metal, sculpted and formed from what looked like a single piece to resemble a raptor's leg, even down to the killing claw on the inner toe. His lower jaw was metal, and the grey material reached around his face. Both of his eyes were real, and the top of his head was still real skin and bone.

"Rive...?" Deka said.

Rive rubbed his claws. The arm on the same side as the artificial leg was completely metal, but he could still laugh. He reached out and embraced Deka again. Deka embraced him back, the rest of his words caught in his throat.

"The disaster," Rive whispered. His voice was still real, but it echoed slightly, as though one of his vocal cords were metal and the other still flesh. "It ripped me apart."

Kylac, meanwhile, expected to be riding Friend by now, but the older fox had hopped out of the embrace and held his distance five paces away. Friend's scent seemed distant. He looked preoccupied and agitated.

Then Kylac noticed something.

"Friend, where is your tail?"

Friend seemed unable to stand up straight or make eye contact. "The way off Rel closed on it."

Kylac whimpered.

Deka chirped as he felt Rive's injuries.

Kylac noticed Rive and scenting him over, touching where the skin fused with the metal. Rive winced.

Kylac poked Rive's metallic leg with one of his claws. "Can you feel that?"

"Yes. I don't know how, but I can."

"This is..." Kylac was out of breath. He backed away and looked the other raptor up and down.

Deka was scenting at the stump where Friend's tail ended. It had been sheared off, leaving his tail a mere three vertebrae long.

"Who did this?" Kylac said, still staring at Rive.

"The disaster ripped Rive's body apart," Friend said. He sounded as if he hadn't slept in days. "We were both running to a portal. I saw him hurt, and I turned back, picked up what was left of him, and ran through the nearest way. The portal closed just as I was entering it. It cut off my tail. I was lucky it wasn't my head. It was days before I could open a way to Reth. Rive was long dead by then, but I had to try... The people on Reth were able to rebuild him out of metal. They restarted his brain as well."

"What is Reth?" said Kylac

"That's..." Deka stammered at the same time. "That's... It's... Grotesque."

Rive moved his arm around. There did not seem to be any joints or places for the metal to flex. "But I am alive."

"I couldn't let him die!" Friend gripped his skull and panted. "Reth is an uncontacted world, and the people are a lone species, but I had to take him there. They where the only ones who could help him."

"The disaster hurt us as well," Kylac said. "We can't open portals long-term anymore. Many of the Archeons across the universe are dead. The ones who are alive are afraid of reconnecting with other worlds. They're afraid of being hurt again."

"They have every reason to be afraid," Rive said.

"What are you doing here?" Deka said. "Did you evacuate these people?"

"I did," said Rive.

"Another disaster is coming, isn't it? How did you know? How can we stop it?"

Rive and Friend stood still and stared at them. The animals around them huddled together and shivered.

"Do you know what happened to Rel?" said Kylac. "And Genzin?"

Rive and Friend remained silent.

"I'm just a few moments from making a way to Meze," Kylac said. "We can talk about this there. Someplace less..." He glanced at the animals. "Ominous."

The older fox approached Kylac and gripped his shoulder. "Listen to me. Please. Did you consider any of our theories on the nature of time?"

Kylac's heart stopped. Deka did not breathe.

"Listen!" Friend screamed. He panted, caught his breath. "Do you remember what I was talking to the other Archeons about? That motion equals time? The only reason anything progresses is because it is in motion. Always going somewhere. Always moving forward. My theory stated that the universe itself is in motion, going someplace, and that is where time comes from—that's why time only moves in one direction—because that's the only direction the universe is moving."

"Friend..." Deka began.

The tailless fox let go of Kylac and wandered in front of them aimlessly, talking to the ground.

"I had been working on it for years. If the universe is traveling someplace while it expands, that means it has a location somewhere, within something, and the universe must leave impressions behind in this medium. I wondered how it would be possible to open a portal to one of these impressions—to make a way to the universe of the past—but how can you navigate something that is not spacetime? I thought about it for years, and then I had it. I had the answer! It was just an idea, and it was perfect! Then... a way opened, and it would not stop."

"Friend, you—" Kylac reached out to him. Rive grabbed him with his metal arm and held him back. His grip was incredibly strong.

"Let him finish," Rive said.

"The way was unlike anything I had ever opened before. I couldn't stop it from growing. It just kept expanding!"

"Time travel," Deka whispered. "You—!"

Rive kicked Deka in the snout with his metal leg. Deka's neck whipped around, and he stumbled backwards a few steps.

"Let him finish!"

"I was almost there," Friend continued. "I almost had the solution. It's just a matter of controlling it. I knew I was close to understanding. That's when it happened again on Reth. I didn't even mean for it to happen that time! The portal opened on its own! I was thinking about it, and another way outside of the universe opened up, and I couldn't stop it! Rive had been working on a way offworld, and he carried us to safety. The portal closed when I was far enough away from it. Ever since then... I can't stop thinking about it. I'm so close! I'm so close to discovering what was impossible! It's a problem Archeons have been pondering for generations—what is beyond the universe?—and I figured out how to go there!"

"So stop!" Kylac said. "Stop thinking about it!"

Friend was walking in circles beside his raptor. "Once I started, I couldn't stop! It's a song that sticks in your head and you can't get it out. It keeps happening! I'm trying to control it, but every time the entire planet is pulled through the way instead of me! Going to the largest worlds gives me more time to tame the way, but it's not enough. I have to think about it! It won't leave me alone! I have to control this—it's just going to keep happening. It's happening right now!"

The animals around them huddled into each other.

"The equations are falling into place. The variables are predictable—they're not variables at all. I can predict how they will change, and the math makes sense. The universe... It exists *somewhere*, and it's expanding into *someplace*. I want to see where it exists. I'm almost there."

Kylac stepped toward Friend again. Rive stood between him and the tailless fox.

"Friend, we can take you to Selta—we can find a way to deal with this."

"I won't risk Selta!" Friend screamed.

"We'll bring help to you," Deka said, trying to approach Friend. Rive eyed him. Deka halted, still a dozen paces from the tailless fox. "Friend, you can practice on uninhabited worlds. Why not go there?"

"Every habitable planet has life. Everyone who can help me I'll destroy once the equations begin to return. I lost three worlds that way. I won't lose any more. That's why I'm so glad Rive is alive. If not for him, we would have lost all the people on Crexa. It's happening... It's happening again! Don't speak to me. I need to control this."

Deka and Kylac got that feeling again, the feeling of wanting to huddle into themselves and disappear. Kylac's tail curled between his legs. Deka lowered his neck to just half a pace above the ground.

Crexa's star began to rise. Crexa was the farthest planet from its parent star in the contacted universe, but it still filled up a sizable part of the horizon. Friend was looking out at it. Suddenly the light from the star flickered and winked away. Something was pulling pieces of it down from the inside.

The light dimmed more and more. Pieces of the star fell away and extinguished. Something was coming to the surface. Something that was the opposite of light.

It rose out of the star, a sphere with nothing projected around its surface. It gave off no light, no energy, no reflection. According to the eyes, it did not exist. There was nothing to hear, see, taste, or smell. It wasn't black—it was nothing. It wasn't nothing—it was everything. It extended far beyond what the senses could perceive, and yet the mind knew it was there.

The antisphere had ripped the star apart from the inside, and the way was already the size of the former star. The light on this world went out. Only their night vision remained, and even that was insufficient because now there was no light, no x-rays, no ultraviolet. Their eyes had very little to sense.

The world around them vanished from sight. The only things in the sky were the nighttime stars and the growing antisphere. The flecks of light disappeared behind it until only the sphere remained. It overwhelmed their senses as it grew.

"Friend..." Deka said.

"I'm almost in control!"

It was difficult to wrap the mind around the scale of this portal. It was consuming a solar system, and it was still growing.

Deka lunged for Friend. Rive instantly pounced on Deka, flattened him to the sand, and held him down with his metallic leg and arm. Rive's growl echoed within his metallic parts.

"Friend, stop!" Kylac dashed to him.

Rive pushed off Deka, leaped and slammed into Kylac just before he reached Friend. He stood on Kylac with both feet, and Kylac reached up and raked his claws down both the metal leg and the real one. He drew blood from the flesh, but it did not seem to faze the raptor.

Friend grunted and panted as he stared at the sky. "Just a little longer."

The sphere consumed more and more of the sky. All the stars on that side of the horizon were blocked. The animals were petrified.

Deka tried to stand, but Rive propelled himself off Kylac and leaped onto Deka, grabbing him and dragging him across the sand. He dropped Deka next to Kylac and then stood guard between them and Friend.

The sphere was still growing. Friend was gazing up at it, the lone sentient creature in the entire solar system who did not give off a fear scent.

Deka and Kylac exchanged glances and charged Rive at the same time, both aiming for his flesh side. Rive stood firm. Kylac and Deka snarled and screeched. Rive did as well, though it still sounded metallic.

Then Rive charged them. He reached with his metal arm. Kylac rolled away, but Rive changed direction fast on his metal leg and impaled the fox on his claws.

Deka leaped on Rive's flesh side. Any other raptor would have tipped over, but Rive spun around and threw

Deka off. The dark blue raptor landed in the sand and rolled a few times before stopping.

Rive picked up the fox with one arm and threw him out to Deka. Kylac screamed the whole way until he landed next to his raptor. He was bleeding from his flank badly.

Rive stood in front of his fox, who was calmly gazing up at the approaching antisphere in the sky.

Deka screeched and charged Rive again. Rive crouched low, ready. Deka stopped just short of the raptor and squared off against him. Rive screeched at him, slashing his claws at the air between them.

Kylac made a wide circle around the fight, trying to approach Friend from the side. The older fox was completely absorbed in his calculations. Friend hadn't behaved like this since he was an apprentice. Kylac remembered those days. All four had become apprentices at the same time. They had helped each other improve, and they had pondered the nature of the universe together.

That was when the idea of time travel first occurred to Friend. From the very beginning Friend wanted to know if it was possible. Everyone told him it was not, and the more they did, the more Friend talked about the idea. It was his hobby, pondering the nature of the universe. It was natural for all Archeons to think about things like that.

Kylac had a good angle now. He glanced at Deka and Rive. They were still squaring off, some slash marks down Deka's face now, and a few new ones across Rive's real body.

Kylac dropped to all fours and bolted for Friend. He was just two strides away when something grabbed him from behind. Kylac went down to his stomach, an enormous weight pressing on his upper back, claws sinking into his flesh. Kylac screamed. Rive grabbed him, raised him into the air, and tossed him. He slammed into something else, rolled with it, and lay still in the sand, tangled in Deka.

They separated and climbed to their feet. Deka bled from multiple gashes across his face and body. His blue scales were streaked with red, barely visible now in the growing darkness.

They faced the metal and flesh raptor, who still stood between them and his fox. His claws were bloody. His metallic parts dripped blood—their blood, not his. Rive was not bleeding at all, and he did not seem hurt in the slightest. Deka screamed and began to charge again.

Kylac grabbed his tail and held him back. "Deka!"

He hesitated and looked above Friend. The atmosphere was on fire. The antisphere had intersected the planet, and it had become the sky now. The entire world was shaking. Cross-sections of ground rose from the horizon and fell into the antisphere. The sections went down to the planet's core. Magma from deep under the surface came up and disappeared into it.

Rive stood guard before his fox.

More rods hundreds of thousands of paces tall lifted from the planet. Pieces of animals were visible in them. Sections of underground water sources were in them. All flew straight up and vanished.

Friend snarled and screamed. "Stop! *Stop!* The calculations are perfect! Why isn't it stopping? Why isn't it working?"

That must have been Rive's cue. A portal—a normal one—opened just in front of Rive. Rive backed up and placed a hand on Friend's shoulder. The fox snarled, turned around, and ran into the offworld sphere.

Rive looked back at Deka and Kylac.

"I'm sorry. My fox needs me." He hesitated, then spoke again. "Friend prefers larger worlds, far away from their star. They last longer when something goes wrong. No more hub worlds."

Rive stepped through the sphere, and it closed.

The planet was pulling up. The antisphere had reached the horizon.

"Kylac..."

"What?"

"The portal!"

"Oh... Yes! The portal!"

Kylac had it. He knew he had it, but in all the chaos he'd lost it somewhere. Kylac looked down and thought.

"Kylac, hurry up."

The planet rumbled and roared as the antisphere approached. Column after column rose out of Crexa and disappeared into the core. The horizon was shrinking—it was only a few thousand paces away and coming fast. Deka wanted to run. Kylac wanted to run. All they could do was stand still and shiver, just like the animals.

The horizon was less than a thousand paces away now. The vast amount of magma in the sky cast an orange glow on the Relians.

Kylac dropped to his knees, closed his eyes, and tried to find the equations. They were there—he had not forgotten the variables—but he had to reach harder than ever to manifest them.

Deka watched the planet shrink. He watched the columns of planetary sediment, ocean, and magma rise straight up into the air and vanish somewhere else. He watched the animals picked apart by it.

He shivered.

Suddenly a way opened up a few paces ahead of him, and he saw the beautiful savannah of Meze. Deka pulled Kylac up and led him to the portal. The fox was bleeding from a nasty wound in his side. Deka was in pretty bad shape himself, but they were almost to safety.

The planet stopped rumbling. Deka halted. So did Kylac. They both turned back at the same time. The distant stars had returned. Crexa was quiet. The antisphere had vanished.

The horizon was only sixty paces away. Kylac and Deka separated and ran around the portal to the horizon and peered over the ledge. Below them, Crexa had been sliced away. The many layers of rock were visible, as well as the layers of magma. Far below them was the core, the magma leaking into space, cooling, going dark.

Some of the extracted columns now floated in space. A few of them collided and broke apart. Water dissolved with no pressure to hold the molecules together. The magma coagulated and fell into orbit.

The wind kicked up as the atmosphere leaked into space. The animals on the surface still huddled together. Some became swept up in the wind and were carried off the edge and into space.

The Relians turned and ran for the portal as the wind tried to push them off the edge as well. Animals flew around them. The Relians saw one of the beasts they had hunted all those years ago, all the massive bulk of it being pulled along the ground. They watched it slip into the sphere.

Kylac was the first through. The wind stopped as soon as he was out, and he knelt, bleeding. Deka came through a moment later and dropped to his side. The daytime starlight felt good on his scales.

The wind blew more animals through the portal. Kylac left it open. They needed to be relocated, too.

Earth

I

The sphere opened in Stephen's living room. The raptor and the fox stepped through and looked around. It was dark again, but they could see just fine. Kylac scented the air.

"He's not home."

They both sank a little. The whole reason they had decided to come here and not take refuge on their private planet around Proxima Centauri was to talk to Stephen, and of course he was not here.

Deka peeked inside the bedroom. Kylac walked to the kitchen. The clock read just past one, and it was dark, so that meant one at night. He remembered what Stephen had said and opened the refrigerator. It was nearly empty. Then he opened the other door on top.

"Deka!"

The raptor walked from the back of the house to the kitchen and looked in the door to the freezing compartment. Ten packages of ground beef lay stacked inside.

"Perfect!" Deka reached in. For the first time in his life, he wanted to eat without hunting. He removed the packages and set them on the counter. "We'll let them thaw."

Deka closed the freezer door and walked around the house. All the curtains were drawn, the heat was low, and the lights were off.

"He hasn't been in here days."

"We can wait."

Kylac plopped down on the couch, inhaled the dust, and gleefully sneezed. The remote control lay on the middle cushion. Kylac picked it up and clicked it, and the TV whined to life.

Deka walked around the couch and lay on the floor lengthwise against it, head upright beside Kylac's legs.

"It's still painful to watch."

"We may as well learn more about them."

They sat in the glow of the TV.

"...and only nineteen ninety-nine plus shipping and handling! Call now and you'll also receive..."

2

The trash can was full of empty ground beef rolls, and the sink was streaked with watery blood. Deka had found the thermostat, and over the last couple days the temperature in the house varied from fifty degrees Fahrenheit to eighty-five, depending on who had changed the setting last. It was freezing outside, with two feet of snow on the ground. Kylac wanted to go out and experience it. Deka was glad to be indoors in an artificially warm environment.

The VHS rack was half empty, with the missing tapes stacked on the floor by the wall.

Rambo
A Boy and His Dog
The Fox and the Hound
Beauty and the Beast
Star Wars
Planet of the Apes

Young Frankenstein
Spaceballs
Police Academy
Dracula
Star Trek: The Motion Picture
War of the Worlds

One of the boxes was empty as the tape played in the VCR. Kylac sat on the couch, but Deka stood in the middle of the room, yelling at the screen.

"Come on, come on! Get them! They're right there! Just get them!"

The theropods on screen had the humans surrounded, huddled together, helpless. One of the raptors was croaking and about to jump on them, but then a jaw came out of nowhere and chomped the thing, lifting it into the air.

"What?!" Deka screamed.

Kylac huffed and grumbled. "Where did that thing come from?"

The view panned up and showed the enormous T-Rex chewing on the raptor. It cast the thing aside and took on the rest of the pack.

"How did it get in there?" Deka gouged the carpet with his killing claws. "This isn't even close to real! The humans are helpless, but they still win!"

"Oh, what do you expect? It's their story. They always put in a way for themselves to survive."

"The dinosaurs can barely move, and all they do is kill things! No wonder Stephen told us not to go outside if this is how people think I act!"

Deka went to the VCR, ejected the tape, and slipped it back inside the box.

"You don't want to watch the rest?"

"No. That was awful." He looked at the box, huffed, and set it in the pile of watched tapes. "Next up... Is another title I can't read."

"Let's stop," Kylac said. "I've had enough. We've been watching these things for two days. My eyes won't recover for a year."

"One more."

Deka pulled a box down from the rack.

Back to the Future

He recognized the vehicle on the cover, but Stephen's did not have a door that opened upwards, so it still made no sense. He slipped the tape out, popped it in the machine, and lay back down in front of the couch.

3

Stephen unlocked the door and walked inside. He was surprised the light was already on. Then he smelled it—dog and reptile—and immediately shut and locked the door. The TV was on a blank screen. All his tapes had been stacked in three piles on the floor. His Back to the Future tape was out of its box and lying on the carpet. It had apparently been chucked across the room and made a dent in the wall just above where it rested.

Stephen walked to the couch. Kylac lay across all three cushions, asleep. Deka lay on the floor with his head and neck draped over the couch, curled up in Kylac's arms.

His hand reached down and touched Deka on the neck. The scales were firm and smooth, like a snake's, and the raptor was warm. This surprised Stephen. He expected Deka to be cold with hard skin like an alligator's. He gently shook the raptor.

Deka opened his eyes and raised his head. "Stephen!"

"I didn't think I'd ever see you again." Stephen looked up at the stack of tapes. "And you've been busy. How long have you been here?"

Kylac was awake now. "Three days."

"Go figure! I was down in Pennsylvania visiting my sister and nephew. Did you find the meat I left you?"

Stephen walked into the kitchen, shrugged off his coat, and looked down at the sink.

"Yup. That's all of it. I knew I shoulda bought more. Guys, listen, I'm sorry I let you go like that. There was so much I wanted to ask you. I can't believe I just went to bed. Yeah, I had work in the morning but... what did that matter when you were here? I should've said so much more, but now that you're back..."

He rounded the corner and stood in the living room. Deka and Kylac were standing side by side, staring at him from across the room.

"Is something wrong, guys? You don't look too good. Did something bad happen?"

The Relians looked like they had so much to say they did not know where to begin. Finally, Deka spoke.

"Would you like to know what's wrong with your planet?"

About the Author

James L. Steele has had the idea for the Archeon series in his head since the mid-1990s.

He has been published in various anthologies and magazines, including: *Solarcide, Allasso, Different Worlds, Different Skins: V.2, Tall Tales with Short Cocks V.2, Bourbon Penn, Gods with Fur, Claw the Way to Victory*, and *Fictionvale*.

His sci-fi novel *Huvek* is published through Argyll Productions.

He lives in Ohio, where he pursues his hobby of becoming a wine connoisseur while having between two and six existential crises per day.

Website: JamesLSteele.com

Blog: DaydreamingInText.blogspot.com

Twitter: @JLSteeleAuthor